FOR PEPPER AND CHRIST

# For Pepper and Christ
## a novel

KEKI N. DARUWALLA

PENGUIN BOOKS

PENGUIN BOOKS
Published by the Penguin Group
Penguin Books India Pvt. Ltd, 11 Community Centre, Panchsheel Park,
New Delhi 110 017, India
Penguin Group (USA) Inc., 375 Hudson Street, New York, New York
10014, USA
Penguin Group (Canada), 90 Eglinton Avenue East, Suite 700, Toronto,
Ontario, M4P 2Y3, Canada (a division of Pearson Penguin Canada Inc.)
Penguin Books Ltd, 80 Strand, London WC2R 0RL, England
Penguin Ireland, 25 St Stephen's Green, Dublin 2, Ireland (a division of
Penguin Books Ltd)
Penguin Group (Australia), 250 Camberwell Road, Camberwell, Victoria
3124, Australia (a division of Pearson Australia Group Pty Ltd)
Penguin Group (NZ), 67 Apollo Drive, Rosedale, North Shore 0632, New
Zealand (a division of Pearson New Zealand Ltd)
Penguin Group (South Africa) (Pty) Ltd, 24 Sturdee Avenue, Rosebank,
Johannesburg 2196, South Africa

Penguin Books Ltd, Registered Offices: 80 Strand, London WC2R 0RL,
England

First published by Penguin Books India 2009
Copyright © Keki N. Daruwalla 2009

10 9 8 7 6 5 4 3 2 1

This is a work of fiction. While it is fixed both historically and chronologically
and some of the characters are not wholly fictional, situations, incidents and
dialogues in this work are products of the author's imagination and are not to
be construed as real. They are not intended to depict actual events or to change
the entirely fictional nature of the work.

ISBN 9780143065814

Typeset in Sabon MT by Eleven Arts, New Delhi
Printed at Gopsons Papers Ltd, Noida

For
Anaheita and Rookzain

# prologue

Those were the good old days—time itself took ages to move its ass. For a century the Portuguese had been slowly scouring the seas, gathering data, opening up schools of navigation, collecting maps, sending spies along the Red Sea to find out how the Arabs carried on their spice trade with India. Their light caravels kept going down the West African coast—Cape Bojador, Cape Verde, slowly reaching the southernmost tip of the continent. The remarkable thing was that the world never knew, or cared, if it knew. To translate an Indian proverb, while all this was happening, not a louse wriggled across the scalps of other Europeans.

In the fifteenth century, Portugal was a poor country of just about a million, but it had ambitions—the poor need to have more ambitions than the rich. Why not? They wanted gold and slaves and spices; and they wanted to cut out Venice and Genoa who bought pepper, ginger and cinnamon from the Ottomans and the Mamluks at excessive prices and sold them to Europe at even more exorbitant rates. What a ducat could buy in Calicut, cost over sixty in Venice. What was so special about Venice and Genoa except that they had good shipyards and were perched next to the lands of Islam, just across the Mediterranean? They had to be outflanked. A route other than the one along the Red Sea had to be found. To sideline Venice, you had to be secretive—never mind if decades earlier the Doge of Venice, Francesco Foscari himself had given Marco Polo's memoirs (perhaps containing the *mappa mundi*?) to Prince Pedro of Portugal, even as the Doge hosted and escorted the prince through a whirlwind of balls and feasts.

How could tides keep a secret? How could a trade in slaves and gold be kept under wraps? Slave trade meant raids, pillage and abduction. Slaves were cheap, mind you; a horse fetched you between six to fourteen slaves those days. You voyage over half the world, decade after decade, and the world (which of course means only Europe, come on) knows nothing about it. If the darkies from Mombassa or Milind, Hormuz or Hind, learnt about it, how did it matter?

The spies had clearly told the King that there was no land obstacle between Africa and India. They had travelled to Africa after visiting Malabar. No wonder then that when an arrogant sailor approached the Portuguese to finance his exploratory trip to India, the court told this Christopher Something-or-the-Other to fuck off. The Portuguese already knew the way to India. When eventually, through Spanish help, the fellow made landfall at some godforsaken piece of earth, the fool thought he had made it to India.

Portuguese souls also had aspirations—they hungered for the glory of the true faith and for Prester John. You had to find his kingdom whether you went to Benin or Ethiopia—from slave habitats to saint-king lodgings. The pursuit of a legend can be pretty thankless, but it catches human imagination by the forelock. Notice how Galahad and Co. went after the Holy Grail. The Persians spent a lot of time in quest of the legendary King Jamshed's wine-bowl, called Jam-i-Jamshed. It was supposed to have mystic, if not oracular powers. Sundry Ayatollahs may still be looking for it, you never know. But back to the myth of Prester John which festered in the Portuguese psyche for centuries. There was that emerald table of his and a thousand true believers munching on mutton and fowl around it. There was that magical stone with the saint-king which restored sight to the blind. You aspired to revel in his glory. Veils had to be penetrated, the one around his face, for instance. According to rumour only one foot of Prester John had been revealed to the populace. The other foot had been curtained off. You could never tell which fidalgo would be the first to see through that blessed veil. Never mind the veil, even if one saw through the piece of cloth that curtained off his other foot, the viewer would be blessed.

If your soul hungers for the true faith, there's a flip side— your dealings with the infidel. There would be no true faith if there were no infidels. The Kafirs are as essential to Islam as the unbeliever is to the followers of Christ. Infidels are not a nuisance. How else would you pride yourself in the true faith, if there were no false gods?

Infidels also gave you an excuse to kick them hard on their backsides. What more could you ask of the Lord?

If the Portuguese confronted Islam, the Spaniards went for the Jews. (They had done with the Moors. King Ferdinand of Aragon and the great Isabella of Castile had married in 1469, joined their two kingdoms into what is now called Spain, and embarked on throwing out the non-Christians. Muslim Granada was at last conquered in 1492.) The Jews had vulnerable jugulars. It was the 1490s after all, and the extra-pious doomsdayers (piety and doom-dread normally go together) thought the world might well end in Anno Domini 1500, the end of the first half of the millennium. If that came to pass, how would Ferdinand and Isabella confront the Lord, having neither baptized the Jews, nor exiled them? Harrowing thought. So, over 200,000 Jews were thrown out of Spain, penniless. To be fair, they were given a choice, baptism or banishment. Promptly the disease spread to Portugal. In fact, the Spanish monarchs compelled the Portuguese to follow suit, which they did in 1497. Many of the Jews migrated to Asia——to the lands under Islam, and were received well.

A historical novel is neither history nor fiction. Or, perhaps it is both. This one is about life as lived in Cairo and Calicut and about events on the seas. There is an Abbottt and a pair of dervishes. And of course there is the sighting of the Virgin Mary and her silver doves floating over the steeple of the church in Shentena al Hagar. (The silver doves, incidentally, were again seen in 1998.)

We have three voices here, firstly that of Brother Figueiro, a member of Captain-Major Vasco da Gama's fleet on the 1497–98 voyage, as also the one in 1502. His vision is very clear—their task was the conquest of heathen souls. Pepper, ginger and other tawdry things came a distant second. The other voice is that of the young pilot, Taufiq, who hails from Oman but was sent to Cairo for his studies at al Azhar. He has lived in Gujarat as a boy, while accompanying his father on the latter's sailing trips. He has sailed under the guidance of the legendary Ibn Majid and is feeling his way around the world, whether during his voyage to Tyre and Sidon, or to Africa. He takes his time to negotiate the political and religious currents that are moving into the Indian Ocean.

Regrettably, there's also the voice of the obtrusive narrator, mostly preoccupied with Ehtesham the painter, and his troubles with the Muhtasib, the feared Inspector of weights and measures, who lords it over the traders in the souks of Cairo. The city's morality also comes under his severe gaze. Ibn Majid gets a look-in. Lastly, it is life under the Mamluks and the Zamorin that comes into view, along with the threads that twine and intertwine around those lives.

# THE COMING OF
# VASCO DA GAMA

# brother figueiro

Our ships dropped anchor at sunset, on the command of the Captain-Major. Blessed be the Lord for having put us in his charge, for a better man than Vasco da Gama could not have been found to lead us across this infinite stretch of sea. We were barely half a mile from the coast of Milind but the harbours of the east cannot be trusted. Nor can their men, if you ask me, but we will come to that later. And it is good to have a stretch of water between ship and shoreline, especially after nightfall, for one never knows where treachery lurks. Hence, throughout our voyage the Captain-Major placed his trust only in anchors, those spiked solids of gravity, and we can't say they did not serve us well.

Even from this distance we could hear the wind soughing through the palms, the sea dying on the shingle. We could certainly *hear* the town, the noise that seems to rise from a city before it goes to sleep. Having left Mombassa just two days ago, we could imagine how it was, houses of mud and wattle, crowded markets with people squatting on the road and selling everything from bird feathers and beads to maize and fowl and beef cuts; the mounds of coconut and the mountains of fruit. It was not difficult to visualize the haggling that went with all this buy and sell and barter. We could imagine the jokes and the laughter, especially of their women as they hunkered down on the dirt roads, their petticoats tucked above their knees.

We had heard that their women were dark and hence ugly, but Satan puts queer thoughts in one's mind when one actually sees them, their arms and torso bare but for a skimpy sash across the breasts. And they laugh with everybody, be it Moor or Indian. Conversation, as far as we are concerned of course, means only sign-talk and gesture, not forgetting laughter. But whenever I had talked to them in Mombassa (and the occasions were few and far between) I took care to first reach for my rosary. Say your beads even as you converse with them, that's the advice I would give to anyone interacting with dark women. And may the Lord keep you from temptation.

One picks up words on a voyage. Like gulls, they seem to hang around the coast wherever languages have come ashore and used the mooring rope, however briefly. Wherever commodities are sold and bought, words also become a part of the barter deal. Early in my journey I picked up the words *kharid-farokht*, buy-and-sell as one section of the Moors called it. Frankly, I had no knowledge till then that there were different sections among the Moors, that they did not come from the same dark sludge. There was the desert Moor and the Gulf Moor and the voyaging Moor. When this thought first hit me I made the sign of the cross.

Next morning the great 'onlooker saga' as I call it, started. In boat and barge, on plank and raft, paddling away furiously in sliver-thin crafts, the hordes circled around us. It had been the same in Mombassa. They just gaped and goggled at us, with a permanent grin stuck to their wide mouths. They could hardly believe their eyes. They had never seen white skin and hair with a blond or brown tint before. One pitied them—their contact with all that is civilized and cultured had been so minimal. Those forsaken by the Lord need sympathy. Is it their fault that they have never partaken of the sacrament, or that their children die unbaptized, in sum that they have been kept away from the true faith? What can one say of a people with no recorded history, no holy book or chronicles to go back to? But sometime or the other we have to face the question that if a people just live on coconut and fruit and speared fish, and hunker down on the road for gossip, with no commandments to abide by and no line of prophets to respect, why should anyone bother to write their history?

The events in Mombassa I will leave for another time. On the face of it, the people of Milind were not gaping at us less intently than their brethren in Mombassa. Yet they seemed friendlier, more open. Intuitively, or perhaps keeping in mind that it was Easter Sunday, April the fifteenth, the Captain-Major decided to release the hostages we had captured only a day earlier. But that again takes us back to Mombassa. There is no getting away from it, it seems. But before Mombassa one has to talk of the islands visited earlier and the flogging we gave to our Moorish pilots, and slide back in time further, to Mocambique.

Scurvy had already taken a toll of our men before we reached Monocobiquy, or Mozambique. Their hands and feet had bloated, the gums turning purple and swelling to an extent that they draped the teeth. All this had taken place at the Rio da Misericordia, river of mercy, as irony would have it. We anchored off Mozambique on Friday, March the second, the year of our Lord, 1498. Promptly Nicolau Coelho managed to ground the *Berrio*, the smallest vessel in our fleet, and shatter its helm, mistaking a channel for the Bay. This had further strengthened the well-known opinion of the Captain-Major that we needed local pilots. The people were friendly enough, though boastful. The Sultan himself visited the *Berrio*, and presented Nicolau Coelho with a jar of preserves made out of bruised dates with plenty of cloves and cumin. That evening over a repast of dates and figs, he was requested by the Captain-Major to give two pilots, and he readily agreed. Thirty miskals each were given them, in gold, mind you. Things went all right till they finally discovered that we were Christians and not Turks or Moors from the Levant. Then all hell broke loose, but in the manner of the Orient, where even hell wears a smile on its lips, with the assegai hidden behind the back. The assegai is itching for your back in case you are a white man. They wouldn't give us water and even threatened us to come and try. Vasco da Gama had our bombards placed in their poops and sallied forth. What could their arrows and sling-shots do to us? Soon our bombards drove them behind their palisades. Then we chased an almadia, or in common parlance, a boat which belonged to the Sharif, a drunken white Moor, if you please. We found it contained all sorts of goods from fine linen to baskets made of palm fronds, glazed jars containing butter, scented water in glass phials and even books of law! And we took four Negroes on board.

All seas have their own secrets, their hidden if not clandestine currents, and each island, each estuary has its shoals. Your ships may be thrice as good, and your instruments backed by the best that science can afford. Our captains may have learnt the art of navigation by the stars at our first observatory in Sagres, built by John the Navigator, may his soul rest in peace. Yet a local pilot managing a country craft that has no nails, its planks held together by coir ropes, with a single sail of palm matting hoisted on its rickety mast may outwit you. From the start the pilots, as and when we could get them, which was not very often, caused us problems. Of the two we had got at Mozambique, one had run away and we had to bind the other fellow to prevent his escape.

*keki n. daruwalla*

On April 1 we reached an island where we flogged our Moor pilot because he wanted us to believe that some islands we had come by were in fact the mainland. The flogging was administered because he had spun his yarn so well that we actually believed him! Such effrontery could not go unpunished and we named the island *Itha do Acoutado*, *'Island of the Flogged One'*. Some days later we made sail to the north west and on the eve of Palm Sunday, the seventh of April, we anchored at Mombassa.

Whether pilots or guides, they tried to mislead us, especially when it came to our enquiries regarding Christians. For instance, as we passed two islands encircled by shoals and the guides recognized them, they told us that we had just left behind an island inhabited by Christians called Quiloa, or Kilwa as they pronounced it. We wasted a whole day to somehow get to it—the urge to discover and be with our fellow followers of Christ was so intense—but the winds proved stronger than our desire and at length we gave up this fruitless scramble and made sail for Mombassa.

Such a near-miss was nothing uncommon during the voyage. The heathen guides—their souls dark as their skins—would stretch a gleaming arm and say 'Beyond this island or ahead of this lies the realm of the Christians. On that island half the people are Negroes and half Christians!' How many? Maannyy! More Christian than bird there. More Christian than grass! Varryy Maannyy. Pitter Jaan? ('No, no, Prester John, you fool', we'd correct him.) Pitter Jaan also there. My unkal seen him. ('You told us yesterday you didn't have an uncle!') My Grand Unkal seen him, brother of wife's grandmother! First they would say that 'Pitter Jaan' lived north. 'Shamal, shamal!' they'd shout, which in their foul tongue means north. After we had traversed a hundred leagues north, the heathens would start screaming 'Junoob, junoob', which in their abominable language means south. How could one ever rely on this spawn of Beelzebub?

From North West we changed course to N.N.W. and saw *Sao Raphael* run aground on a shoal, but when the tide rose she floated once again and how we cheered when she did! The next day we hit Mombassa, where, guide and pilot told us, half the population was Christian. There were many vessels in the harbour arrayed in flags. We put on all the finery we could on our ships as well, hoping that the next day (Sunday, April the seventh) we would be able to go on land and hear mass with our fellow Christians. We'd be received with great eclat, our pilot had told us, and our Christian brethren would insist on taking us home and share their repast with us . . .

They were actually waiting with knives and cutlasses. Not the Christians, for there were none. It was the Moors. In fact they didn't even wait for Sunday. At midnight itself a *zavra*or, Zabra or dhow or boat—they have six wretched words for the same thing—an open vessel sharp at the stern with a square sail, with a hundred men armed with cutlasses came to board our vessels, but were not permitted except for a few. The next day came a sheep from the king and basket upon basket of oranges, lemons and sugarcane. We didn't know what to make of it. The cutlasses at night, the sugar cane in the morning. The people who brought the gift were 'almost white' as our 'official' chronicler called them, and they professed to be Christians which they certainly were. In return Vasco da Gama sent them coral strings and beads. But what value can you put on an exchange of gifts if the heart is black and if the hidden knife nestles near the itching hand?

Two days later as one of our ships ran aground while entering port, the Moors with us jumped ship as also did the Moorish pilots. That night Lord Vasco interrogated two of the

*keki n. daruwalla*

Moors who had come with us from Mozambique and aided them in their answers by pouring boiling oil on them. It was the general feeling that boiling oil was an excellent aid to memory and the revelation of truth. They stated that we would be captured the moment we entered port. It seems the Moors wanted revenge for what we had done in Mozambique. Word travels fast along the sea lanes here. The kings of Mozambique and Mombassa had a sort of vassal-liege relationship, though which of the two rogues was overlord would be difficult for me to hazard. The Moorish pilots were smart and wily. Perhaps the hot oil made them more slippery. And though their hands were tied behind their backs they, each in his own good time, managed to jump into the night sea and escape. That night, armed men swam silently to our ships to cut the cables but were discovered. How could our Lord let these treacherous dogs succeed, seeing they were unbelievers?

It wouldn't be right to suggest that we were always guarding our flanks against treachery. It was a good voyage as voyages go, with its usual hazards and incidents—a mooring rope snapping somewhere, drinking water running so short at a place or two that fish had to be cooked in salt water and our daily water ration had to be reduced to a quartilho, or three-fourths of a pint. We ran into islands peopled by seals, the big ones roaring like lions, the smaller ones bleating like goats, as Alvaro Velho put it. We came across, what some of our friends, including Alvaro Velho, thought were featherless birds that they called Sotilcaires. But a sailor who had visited England—he had actually been gaoled there for thieving at one of their ports—said these were called penguins. And once in a while we ran into a storm but escaped lightly, running before a stern-wind with the foresail very much lowered.

It was nice observing the coastal people whenever we touched port, the way they lived, their huts of straw, their long bows and daggers sheathed in ivory, their calabashes in which they carried salt water and which they poured into pits to make salt. And with great generosity we gave apt names to the places we passed—Terra da Boa Gente (Land of Good People) or Rio de Cobre (Copper River) or Ilheo da Cruz (Cross Island) so that the land there could be sanctified.

It was not everywhere that we encountered hostility. There were people who welcomed us with their smiles and their flutes, people who sold us their best oxen. We once bought an ox for just three bracelets. It was excellent meat, as toothsome as in Lisbon, as Alvaro said to me. We were hoping to pick up some fresh meat from Milind as well. I was ruminating on such matters, watching the sea, the swell less than halfway, when I got the summons that the Captain-Major wanted me along with the captain of my ship, Paulo da Gama, Vasco's elder brother. Paulo was commanding the *Sao Raphael*; the Captain-Major sailed on *Sao Gabriel* while Nicolau Coelho commanded the *Berrio*, the smallest of the ships in the fleet. Goncalo Nunes was in charge of the store ship.

How could I, a mere priest, be of any interest to the Captain-Major? It wasn't Sunday, when one would be needed for saying Mass. I sat quietly in my boat with Paulo, who intrigued though he must have been at my presence, never wasted a look on me. When we boarded *S. Gabriel*, I just followed him as he walked determinedly to the quarter deck. We were seated in the Captain-Major's citadel or castle, and felt a bit cramped, the four of us—Alvaro, Fernao Martins, Goncalo Pirez and me, apart from the three ship captains.

We sat in silence till the Captain-Major opened up. 'We are here to take stock of the voyage as a whole, and not just Milind and what is likely to happen or not happen tomorrow. Everywhere we seem to meet open hostility or treachery. I prefer the former, but there isn't much to choose. The Negro and the white Moor hate us equally—that is the surprising thing.'

'We are emphasizing the wrong categories. It is not Negro and Moor who loathe us. It is the white Moor and the black Moor.' Paulo da Gama spoke softly. His brother nodded and went on as if he had not been interrupted.

'We are on a voyage to open up the seas. We want to trade! And they are out to kill! I don't understand! Do you, Brother Figueiro?'

'But obviously, my Lord, the Antichrist will try to kill. What would you have it do? Make peace with you?' Here I made the sign of the cross. The others followed. 'The Antichrist has to be defeated first within ourselves and then without.'

Sometimes one doesn't realize what one has said till others react. I noticed an uneasy silence fall upon the company. 'Explain yourself, Brother Figueiro,' said Vasco after a pause.

'What Brother Figueiro means is . . .' began Paulo, when his brother interrupted him. 'Never mind what you think he means. Let the priest speak for himself.'

Perhaps Paulo thought that since I was billeted on his ship, he was in some way responsible for me. At least that is what I think now as I sit down to write my journal. Of course, at that moment I was too involved with the theories churning in my mind ever since the voyage began on Saturday, 8 July, in the year of our Lord 1497.

'My Lord, I wish to say two things or maybe three. Provided my Lord has the patience.'

'Don't worry, Brother Joao Figueiro. We have at least half the night before us. But by the second watch I would like to turn in.'

'My Lords, to all appearances we seem to have come for trade. As long as that is just a part of the appearance, one has precious little to say. But when we get so involved with appearance that it becomes a part of reality, or rather supersedes it, we are following a headwind into dire trouble. My Lord, it does not behove me to remind someone of your eminence that it is barely a century and a half since the Moor was thrown out of Portugal. And it is the states of Leon and Castile who did it. Our people haven't forgotten that. But for the grace of God, we may have been slaves to the Moor today and the infidel muezzin would have been calling the flock to prayer on the cobbled streets of Lisbon!

'My understanding was that trade was a facade. The main intention was to circle Africa and strike at the infidel kingdoms. We should have come for war, to strike at the unbeliever from the south, as Henry the Navigator—may his soul rest in peace—had planned. It is not for me to remind my Lord of history. I am just a village priest! He wanted the sea route around Africa to be discovered, not to exchange knick knacks, but to strike at the heart of Mawmetry. Whatever he did or intended to do—life after all is shorter than history— was for the greater glory of Christendom. We seem to have forgotten all that. Our main obsession lies with trade and barter with the heathen. Glory be to Henry the Navigator who built our first observatory, our first naval arsenal, and our first, and till today, only school for navigation and map making. Glory be to . . .'

I was interrupted. 'Let me correct you Brother Figueiro. Seamen have greater reason to respect Henry than the clergy have. For, if he had not done what you so felicitously rattled off just now, we would not be the first among the world's seamen. The oceans would have had to wait for some other nation to explore them. But let me remind you that Prince Henry knew both Morocco and the Ottoman empire. Navigation was a means to get to the spices as well.'

Paulo broke in before I could reply. 'Even earlier than Henry the Navigator, our eyes were fixed on the seas. The era of voyages had not begun but already we were staring at the skyline and beyond. King Diniz may have belonged to the thirteenth century but it was he who invited a Genoese captain to Portugal and developed our mercantile and naval fleets. No one wanted merely Genoa and Venice to dominate the seas. It was not to serve the crusades that we built our naval armadas bit by bit.'

'My Lords, I may be forgetting my station, but this search for spices is a search for illusion. After all, why do we need spices so desperately?'

'Because our meat smells, Priest, smells! We can't get it down our throats. Not smoked meat and dried meat, hard as leather. If you slaughter in autumn and eat the same meat mid-winter, you have to put a handkerchief to your nostrils to enjoy the repast!'

'My Lord, these spices are not being sought for themselves but to bring about a change in appearances. Kill the odour, and give another flavour to meat. Can that be our sole aim in trying to circumnavigate the earth?'

'There is much in what you say, Priest, but no one single thing can be stressed today. Whether it is trade or discovering lands or people, charting new routes, or whipping the infidel, all are equally important. Neither sailors nor soldiers can fight on empty stomachs. If you want fleets and armadas, you need gold. And the only way to get at gold is through commerce. Unless of course you are thinking in terms of loot.'

'Heaven forefend!' I cried in genuine horror. 'But, my Lord, gold was always used in the service of the church. If Europe started making money, it was primarily to raise funds for fighting the crusades. Even the coin was named after the holy war. Cruzado, we called it, and we know after what it was named.'

'But how did the cruzado come about?' asked the Captain-Major. 'This century alone the price of gold went up a thousand times. Such was the shortage of gold. Yet we managed to bring things on an even keel. The slave trade helped us—and ivory, not forgetting gold dust. That is how the King minted the first gold coin in seventy-odd years and called it the cruzado. There is more to voyaging than crusades, Priest.'

This I could not stomach. If you denigrate the crusades, you are denigrating the church. 'My Lord, I hope we are not forgetting the Papal blessings we sought so ardently all these years. And whenever they were solicited, they were forthcoming. Must I remind my Lord that there were as many as three papal bulls in which the Popes Nicholas V and Calixtus III praised Prince Henry and put the seal of St Peter, as it were, on our exploits. They stated clearly that Portugal was doing nothing but carrying out the work of the mother church in conquering Moorish lands in Morocco and enslaving the people. May I remind you that the Papal Bulls did not praise Portugal for the slave trade because it brought in cheap labour, or rather labour at no cost. If the slave trade got its share of praise from the Holy See, it was because it brought converts into the Christian fold. If the flock increases, the Church cannot but approve.'

'Yet, I repeat, Brother Figueiro, there is more to voyaging than the Holy Church, or the crusades. One can't venture out into the seas with just the name of the Lord on one's lips. The Phoenicians never took the name of our Lord Jesus Christ and yet they were the best seamen of their times and sailed around Africa's western coast. The name of the Lord helps but you need navigational skills to go with it. Many of our skills came from the Jews and the Moors, and I don't think you would take too kindly to either of them. But enough of the past. What we need is a guide who can take us through rock and shoal to India, someone who knows these rain-bearing winds the Moors have named monsoon and tell us how to evade them. We don't care where he learnt his mathematics and what he calls his stars, as long as he knows his sky and his sea, of course.'

'And tomorrow? What do we plan for the day?' asked Paulo.

The Captain-Major knew what he wanted. You don't captain fleets if you don't know your own mind.

'The question is what happens if we get treated the way we were at Mombassa? How do we react? With bombard and matchlock? Or do we avoid a fracas and leave port in case the fellows are hostile? Have you noticed that King and subject are like-minded when it comes to hating us?'

I thought Vasco da Gama's little speech would elicit a hundred responses. How to deal with the Negro and the Moor called for at least a three-hour peroration. But an unaccountable silence descended on the company which no one seemed too keen to break. Finally, Paulo da Gama spoke up. 'When bombards are the only answer, so be it.'

So it was decided. If you must have water and guides, then you have to get them whether through gifts or the sword.

As we left Gama's ship, the *Sao Gabriel*, and rowed back to our ship, doubts surged within me. Was India really our destination? Did we need a pilot to this land? Or was the paradise kingdom of Prester John beckoning us? It was in Africa somewhere, locked in among jungles, the trees so tall and thick that the country was like a stockade against the visitor. No envoy was known to have been to this court. It was not just the kingdom that was palisaded against intrusion.

The king himself remained aloof and content, screened off from inquisitive human eyes. My mother's brother was at court in Lisbon the day Joao Afoso de Aviero returned from his African voyage with an envoy from Benin in tow. It was fifteen years ago to the day. The envoy stated that a twenty-moon march eastwards from Benin led one to a kingdom where a benevolent monarch called Ogane reigned over a happy people. He was renowned for virtue, charity and piety. He distributed crosses among his people, crosses of different shape and size and metal—copper, iron, zinc and silver. But such was the splendour that radiated from his presence that he placed himself behind a curtain when he met anyone, lest the fellow's eyes get scorched by his (Ogane's) radiance. Only his right foot protruded from under the curtain. That was the only part of his body people ever saw.

When the envoy from Benin had spoken, a thrill ran through the court. My uncle stated that as if by magic, the name of Prester John sprang to everyone's lips. Acclamation and applause followed. Blessed be the Lord, for the saint-king was around. A century old legend had caught up with us.

With this hope in mind, I tried to sleep, but to no avail. The mundane slowly crowded back. I felt the sea against the boat. The sensuality of a wave sloshing away at a moored boat! It was now the turn of the fine silt of doubt to slowly clutter my brain. What if all this effort were a waste? What if there was no sea to India? What if southern Africa was connected with Asia by a landmass? Ptolemy had said this as far back as the second century, and no one had proved him wrong, not for the last thirteen hundred years. Who could say that we knew better? Once we rounded the Cape, I started believing in our enterprise. Even the Holy Church had held that Jerusalem was the world's centre, and that the world consisted of the trinity of three interlocked continents, not these vast lands at the end of the seas, and then again the seas after the land.

Yet when sleep overtook me I dreamt not of vast expanses and endless space, not of Moor and Negro, not of fights, the boarding of ship and the flash of cutlass, but of waters blocked off by rock and reef, the sea turned into a lagoon with the dead and the eyeless watching us from a towering coast that seemed to encircle us.

Easter Sunday passed off without incident. We just lay at anchor watching the town of Milind. From the beach the townspeople gawked at us. Their looks simply reflected curiosity. We failed to see any hostility there. A rumour ran around the ships that the Moors we had taken from the boat had talked of four vessels in port which belonged to Christians from India. (The Moors called them Banyans.) O for a Christian pilot! Our worries would be at an end.

Earlier in the day I had prayed, confessed my sins to myself, (what else can you do when you are the only priest on the ship?) and just focused the mind on the Easter Week. Since Good Friday itself, my spirits had automatically been buoyed up. After all it was the Easter week which transformed the world, didn't it? The universe would be never the same again. I could have given a fine sermon on humility in the village church. The Saviour who could raise Lazarus from the dead went to his doom quietly except for that one anguished cry of 'Eli, Eli Sabakhtini!' How could he suffer, his disciples must have thought, in their false Messianism. He showed them how. Sometime or the other the world would have to learn that there could be victory over death. That death was not the dread finality that it was supposed to be. The rising of the Lord saw to that. Only, how does one explain to the heathen, the Negro from Africa, the Moor from whichever hell he came from, what this is all about? 'I am the resurrection and the life: he that believeth in me, though he were dead, yet shall he live.' How will the Moor understand this or the half-naked Indian?

The Lord saw to it that we got the pilot! Perhaps this is how miracles happen. We left one of the old Moors on the sandbank in front of the town. He was released on the Captain-Major's orders. We saw him being picked up by an almadia or ferry-boat. He had been well tutored. We wanted peace with the coastal people and their king. We wanted to trade with them. We had no ambitions here. (Though even if we had, how could we have confessed to them?) The Moor must have done what he was told, for by noon he had returned on a zavra—now that's a different kind of boat—with two emissaries of the king. One of them had a huge sword and a moustache as big. He was obviously one of the king's generals. The other wore a white robe to go with his white beard. He had a venerable air about him, the kind one would associate with an old friar or an Abbott. The King would wish to make peace with us, he said as he presented us with a sheep. The Captain-Major pretended to be pleased with the present and in turn handed over as gifts two strings of coral, three basins to wash your hands in, a hat, some bells and a balandrau worn by the Brothers of Mercy in Portugal. We also gave some striped cotton cloth called lambel.

Next day we entered port. This time the King sent six sheep and cumin and cloves, nutmeg and ginger and a whole lot of spices. That augured well. The next day the King came in a zavra and Vasco got into a boat and went to meet him. Two cushioned bronze chairs had been placed together to seat the King. A canopy of red satin shaded him from the sun. He himself wore a cloak of damask trimmed with green satin. A short sword in a silver scabbard was carried by a retainer in front of the King. And he was accompanied by people who played on intricately carved ivory trumpets which were blown from a side-hole. There were players on anafils as well. After all, what purpose royalty if it is not accompanied by music and damask robes and swords with a silver sheath?

The Milind king opened all trade with Portugal and we saw the two chatting away, the Captain-Major and the king, with Fernao Martins, a mere sailor, acting as interpreter.

However sweet the king was, he could not persuade Vasco da Gama to land and visit his palace. My king would be annoyed, was his excuse. But before the king left the boat, Vasco had released all the Moors we had captured before we entered the waters of Milind. The king told us that this gesture pleased him more than if he had been gifted a city. This man had nothing against the Christians. He didn't have a dagger hidden away in the folds of his cloak. He seemed simple and straight and wonder of wonders, turned out simple and straight! God bless his soul. Since we rounded the Cape in the terrible equatorial heat in November, this was the first friendly ruler we had met.

We anchored here for a few days, saw a sham fight among two horsemen, and met some Indians who claimed to be Christians, small-sized tawny men with long beards but hardly any clothing. They had braided their long hair. We took them to our ship and showed them our altar piece displaying Mother Mary at the foot of the cross, with our Lord in her arms and all the apostles gathered around them. The Indians to a man fell on the ground prostrating themselves with their arms extended, elbow, forehead, knee and toes all touching the floor. This pleased the Captain-

Major. And when he toured the coastal town on boats accompanied by most of us, the Indians fired off bombards and shouted 'Krishn, Krishn', which is how these outlandish people pronounce Christ, our Lord.

But Vasco da Gama never took goodwill on face value and two days later when a boat brought a confidential servant of the king, he was made a hostage and a pilot was demanded off the king. And a pilot was produced.

# CAIRO

# a preamble

*To move from Milind to Cairo, one would have to go through a good bit of the world. But we must leave Brother Figueiro and his chronicle, as also Vasco da Gama and his fleet in mid-ocean, as it were. The winds have dropped and the sails have sagged, and the sun is beating down on the lookout atop the mast. We have to burrow into the past of the pilot who brought the Portuguese ships from the eastern coast of Africa to Calicut. Time has to stand still while we go back to Taufiq and his friends, Ehtesham, and Murad and his mentor, the legendary Ibn Majid, the greatest sea-man of his times, what the West would have called a Renaissance man, poet, astronomer, navigator all rolled into one.*

*Even today, the fifteenth century Cairo is identifiable; the old city of brown-stoned mosques and vaulted ceilings; the city of the Sultan Hassan mosque and the Ibn Tulun mosque, known more for the geometry of the radials on its prayer yard (all paved with flagstones) than for the grandeur of its domes; Cairo, the meeting place of Muslim and Copt, Mamluk and Ottoman, slave and Amir, the khamsin and the Nile flood. The citadel of Salah al Din (whom Europe called Saladin, if not Soldan) had come up three centuries before the times we are talking of. Of course it was not crowned by the great*

Mohammad Ali mosque—its stepped half-domes and its tall minarets, an unforgettable sight today. The citadel, begun in 1175 with the object of encompassing both cities—al Qahira and Misr—within its huge walls, was half complete by 1193, the year of Salah al Din's death. (Salah al Din was a Kurd, incidentally, and came from Tikrit, now better known as the birthplace of Saddam Hussein.) Gangs of crusader prisoners had been at work here since construction had begun. To the west of the citadel lay al Gamaliya. Bab Zuwaylah, where convicts were executed for the general merriment of the public, as it were, was already a dreaded landmark, now just a stone-throw from the Museum of Islamic arts. Narrow souks radiated from streets then as they do now. Al Azhar sat there then, as it does now, surrounded by a coil of narrow streets, where you could slip on a piece of fat or an intestinal shred thrown on the street by a careless butcher. Mud plaster peeled off from the walls, some of which seemed flayed to the bone. Students from all over the Arab world came to study here. They didn't know a word of any European language then, exactly as they don't today. The Coptic town, guarded today by barricades and vehicles (lest some fanatic from the Ikwan or Gama al Islamya attack the Copts) was very much in place, except that the area today is known as Mari Gargis, in honour of St George. The crypt where the Holy Family was supposed to have taken refuge existed then, as it does now, except that a church has come up around it. The synagogue was there in the vicinity and in its shadow, the place where the ark of the babe Moses was supposed to have come and rested. So we move to Ehtesham and Taufiq and Murad, and the Muhtasib, the great and dreaded Inspector of Weights and Measures and the regulator of morals of the city.

# the summons from
# the muhtasib

❦

The dawn prayers were over; he knew it even as he sat up in bed. He had not heard the muezzin's call. Normally, even when he got up late, the cry was registered, however fleetingly, in the backyards of his brain; fleetingly, because sleep would overrun it like stream water over rounded stones. The ferocity or otherwise of the light coming through that torn flange at the bottom of the door would tell him the time—golden in the morning, white at noon, blinding under a summer noon. He had been telling himself that he had merely to nail in a thin sliver of wood there and the door would be perfect; it would do what a door was supposed to do—keep insects and dust out and muffle the noise in the street, the cry of the hawker, the braying of a donkey. But then it would keep the light out as well. Ehtesham would not have wanted that.

The smear on that bar of light that lay under his door leaf drew him to it. As he walked up to it he smelt the perfume and saw the shadow outside, almost simultaneously. He felt the silence there, smelt and touched it almost. Even if someone was courteous enough to wait for him to get up, surely he could have cleared his throat now and then, spat his tobacco cud out, made it known that someone—stranger, messenger, summons-carrier—was waiting, sitting on the stool outside. He didn't wait. Caution was something alien to him. He threw the door wide open to find a soldier and the perfumer from across the street.

That at least explained the scents he had inhaled. It also explained who had led the soldier to his door.

'Are you Ehtesham ul Haq?'

'Yes.'

'From Asyut?'

'I am from Asyut.'

'The Muhtasib wants to see you.'

'Why should the Muhtasib want to see me? I mean, a lowly man like me?'

'That you will have to ask the Muhtasib.'

He nodded again. Good policy, he thought; speak less, gesture more. A spasm of panic followed.

'How do I reach him? Where does he live ? Who'll let me in?'

'That is our job. I will take you there.'

'When?'

'After the noon prayers. Do you want me to pick you up from here or from the mosque?'

'From here.'

'Don't you ever pray?'

'That is none of your business.'

'It may be the Muhtasib's. He is the keeper of the city's morals, the upholder of virtue and the scourge of vice.'

The soldier's face was now set in a frown. His stare turned stony suddenly. He hardly seemed to be looking at Ehtesham, but at the space behind him. Ehtesham knew he shouldn't have said what he had. He had observed the perfumer, who stood behind the soldier, gesture to him, Ehtesham, frantically to keep calm, when that business about the namaaz had come up. But he had chosen to ignore him. At least the perfumer wishes me well, he thought.

'You pick me up from here, all the same.'

The soldier stared at him, nodded and went his way. He now noticed his headache. The night had lasted longer than Ehtesham would have wanted it to. The liquor was strong, made out of aniseed, and the morning had been none too good. He washed, rinsed his mouth and put on his best clothes before the soldier came for him. The Muhtasib's house was large, with a sprawling terrace overlooking the Nile. But he was ushered into a small room on the ground floor, thickly carpeted and containing numerous cushions and bolsters resting against the wall. He sat down resting his back against one wall, but the servant told him that he was occupying the Muhtasib's seat. As he was shifting, the Muhtasib came in, tall and robust. Dignity sat lightly on him in a sort of a careless, natural manner. Most people, he thought, cultivated a dignified air by wearing a mask of false solemnity, and of course by not opening their mouths. The less you have to say, the more dignified you become in people's eyes.

'I sit here so that I can face the qibleh.'

Ehtesham bowed. 'There is great merit in that,' he said with as much humility as he could affect.

'You are Ehtesham ul Haq? I see. You don't have to bow each time I ask you a question. You have come a long way from Asyut to al Qahira. How do you like our city?'

'Sir, I have lived here for two years now. Earlier too I was here at the al Azhar. It is a splendid city.'

'Yes, but you left. Or were you made to leave? People don't leave al Azhar the way you left.'

'I was young, Sir, and my father died. I had to be with mother.'

'You went voyaging also?'

'A short voyage, Sir. I went with my friend Taufiq.'

'You are still young. Why don't you go voyaging now? It would be a good idea.'

'Your Worship is not asking me to leave Cairo, is it? I have not committed any trespass, Sir.'

'You haven't, that is right. I merely thought that if you were fond of the sea once, you would be fond of it now.'

'As I said, I went with my friend who is a sailor and whose father has sailed down the Red Sea for forty years. It is my good fortune to wait on the Muhtasib. Perhaps the Muhtasib has something else to say to me.'

'Yes, I want to ask you something simple. How far is the mosque from where you stay?'

Ehtesham was worried now. He didn't like the drift of the conversation.

'I have not measured the distance, Sir.'

'But I have. It is exactly one hundred and fifty-five yards.' He paused a little. 'That is not strictly true. I mean there is no doubt about the distance, but *I did not measure it*. I had it measured.'

Ehtesham bowed low again and praised the Muhtasib for his thoroughness. He spoke respectfully, trying desperately to see that no trace of sarcasm entered his voice. That would be suicidal, when dealing with a man who had the final word on morality, for that gave him the power over life and death. Or merely death. Life of course one derived from the grace of Allah.

'Those who don't know the road to the mosque may not find their way to the truth, either.'

'The way to the truth does not necessarily lie through the mosque, Sir.'

'We seem to be entering into an argument.'

*keki n. daruwalla*

Ehtesham made the right deprecating noises. Far be it from him to argue with as great a man as . . . blah, blah, blah. It didn't matter how respectfully he spoke, or what honorifics he heaped upon him. He knew that they were fencing. And he knew that the Muhtasib knew

'What do you do for a living?'

'Surely the Muhtasib knows.'

'You paint.'

'If the Muhtasib knew, why must he ask this of his slave?'

The great man was surprised at the temerity implicit in the rebuke.

'Because reality changes a shade as it issues from different mouths. Am I sounding too complicated?'

He kept quiet. The Muhtasib waited.

'Where do you get the dyes from?'

'Sir, the dyes are not important. It is the urge that is significant, to turn line into image, to just draw a circle with a piece of burnt wood and see there a bald head or the sun framed against a grey sky. The joy of it comes from not just creating something but also seeing in your creation what you want to see. When you see a brown swatch stand for the desert you can't feel anything but happy. '

'Creation is not a word I would use were I talking of my activities. Only Allah creates. To attribute creation to any of your activities is almost blasphemy.' There was silence for a while. The great man continued. 'There is one thing you can't paint though—the wind. What you can't see you can't paint. Isn't that right, Ehtesham?'

'That is right, Sir, but you can see the marks of the wind on a sand dune, and what you can see you can paint. You show the dust drift into your eyes and you show the wind. And if you are painting the seas, a full sail shows you the wind. So does a tall wave. One thing turns into another. There is almost an element of magic about all this. '

'Magic is not a word I would use, if I were you. You have no idea how many times you have condemned yourself in this little speech. You know the punishment for magicians in the Qoran.'

Despite his worry, Ehtesham could not help laughing.

'But Your Worship, Your Eminence, it is not malign tricksters or distorters of reality that I am talking of. This is not the magic of the proud who want to deceive gullible people and proclaim themselves as Mehdis and messiahs and the like. This is a child's make-believe, blue for the sea, brown for sand. It is innocent . . . harmless.'

'Nothing is harmless in front of someone who can quote from The Book, remember that. I fear for you, young man. You have a lot to learn and a lot to be careful about. Isn't creation the job of Allah and his sole right? If you start painting the sea, you replicate the tides. Only Allah can create tides. You are setting yourself up as a rival, don't you see? That is how a mullah will see it.'

'Sir, but people are creating all the time. Doesn't a potter make his urns? Isn't he creating? Doesn't a farmer create his wheat, or a weaver his cloth? Are they committing a crime against Allah? I am doing no worse.'

'Son, don't make things difficult for yourself. And don't make things difficult for me.'

There was a ring of finality about that. The interview had ended.

As he walked back to his house, Ehtesham felt that he had bowed lower than he would have normally. He did not feel very happy about that. His throat felt dry and he was disconcerted to find that he was shaking, with anger or fear, he was not sure. That someone should keep watch over him to find out if he was praying or not! He couldn't believe it! Surely, in those congregations there would be people who were merely going through the motions; someone agitated enough not to even think of the Lord he was praying to; someone who had come into the mosque after a fight with his wife, or having been abused by his son. The spine bent in prostration, the lips mumbling the right verses by rote, the thoughts dark with revenge; or lust. Could there be lust after ablutions, after wuzu? His mind was awhirl with such thoughts and he sat down on the steps of a house just to gain control over his tremors.

He had no idea how long he sat there. It could have been a matter of minutes. How much time does a man take to collect his thoughts, or still his trembling arm? Rage is another subject of course. It can disappear like a pricked balloon or it may simmer behind the facade of a smiling mouth. But he was interrupted in his reverie by a black veil. The girl also seemed lost in thought as she rushed towards the door almost stepping over him. An involuntary 'Yah Allah!' broke from her mouth. He wanted to stand but couldn't—he hadn't eaten the whole day. The hangover and the empty stomach had taken their toll. Ehtesham tried to get up but faltered and she caught him by the arm to prevent him from falling. He apologized for being where he was. She comforted him, made him sit down once again and then knocked on the door, which was opened by a servant woman.

From within the house a voice called out, 'Is that you, daughter? There's someone sitting at the door for the last half hour. Give him a drink of water.' Meanwhile, the servant woman who had opened the door gasped, seeing a stranger seated there, and took her hand to her heart.

'Who are you and what is your business here? Aren't you ashamed to sit at the doorsteps of strangers? Is that the way of gentlemen?'

She would have gone on had the girl not returned with water and a copper plate carrying some dates. She silenced the servant woman with a withering look. He thanked her profusely and asked how the lady inside could have known about his presence there. No one had opened the door earlier; could someone have peeped from inside? She laughed.

'Mother senses these things.' She went in giggling and locked the door but the servant woman reopened the door and said in a surly voice that it was time for the evening prayers and decent people should be on their way to the mosque and not loiter around houses which had no males.

He left for his rooms—he still called them riwaq—for that is what such rooms were called in al Azhar. The girl, whose name he had forgotten to ask, remained with him, her smile, her voice, and her laughter. And behind all this that benevolent crone, who knew he was there sitting at the threshold without having seen him. Yet, when he hit the bed after a fairly frugal meal, all this had gone out of the window of his mind. Only the interview with the Mutahsib had stayed, the words exchanged and much that had remained unsaid. That was certainly the larger, colder bit, the vast wordless desert at night. The words were merely the few patches of scrub before you came to the desert.

Things couldn't get worse, he thought next morning, they could only look up. The full import of the meeting with the Muhtasib had not sunk in. It was the first time he had ever been that close to authority, face to face on the floor, a two feet design on the carpet separating the two. It would be a good story for his friends. Would they believe it? But where in the name of the accursed Iblis were they? Didn't they know his predicament? Did he ever have a day like yesterday? Here he was fifty miles from home, with not a whiff of news of his mother for the last month, stricken with a headache and a hangover, summoned by authority and no one to pat him on the back or put an arm around his shoulder! Where was Taufiq, that son of a . . .

Taufiq walked in. There was a wide grin on his face.

'You have a way of coming in at the darkest moments. I was thinking of you, throwing stones, hurling obscenities! You will ask, why? Well, I had a bad day.'

'You have a bad day and I get cursed! You should curse the sky. All good and all evil descends from the heavens.'

'Blasphemy, Taufiq. No evil can come from anything to do with Allah, and the sky is his home. I've just had a lecture on the subjects—on creation, magic, sacrilege, blasphemy.'

When Ehtesham told him who it was, the laughter suddenly died down. The Muhtasib in person! That had to be serious. Taufiq set out to fetch Murad. Murad had his contacts in the alleys. He was known in Khan al Khalili and if he walked through the souks, the roadside hawker and the shop owner alike would greet him. After all, there were advantages in belonging to Cairo itself. How could Ehtesham and Taufiq compete with him?

Murad and Taufiq took their sweet time, turning up hours later. Murad was broad of shoulder but because of his gentle disposition, a gentleness that got adequately mirrored in his face, he didn't give the impression of toughness, once you knew him even slightly. His face was squarish, softened though by a small mouth and a smile that always lit up his eyes. He was always smiling and always agreeing with people, to the extent that one wondered if he had any opinion of his own. Ehtesham learnt that Murad had gone scouring the souks to locate one Tahir ibn Illyas, a mystic known to him. People knew him as the Sheykh. The mystic was restless and wandered around, sitting now at a pastry shop in Batiniyya, or at the perfumer's or at a candle maker's in Husseiniyya, in fact wherever his disciples could entice him to. His disciples loved him and he of course loved everybody. Ilyas made no demands of any kind. There was no binding regimen, no particular turban or habit to sport, no specific majlis to attend, no stipulated doctrine to profess in order to be his follower. In fact, disciples here were not disciples—all were friends—or so Murad made out.

Ibn Ilyas smiled warmly as he sighted Murad moving in with his two friends. It was a longish room, the floor layered with rugs. As Murad bent a little to kiss his hand, the Sheykh spotted Ehtesham. 'You are in trouble,' he said, his arm extended and his forefinger pointing dramatically towards him. 'And the trouble is not recent.' He lapsed into silence. None of the dozen other people sitting there spoke. The silence was like a bowl of water brought in after a meal in which everyone dips his fingers. Ehtesham noticed the large frame of the Sheykh, his slightly rounded shoulders and his long legs stretched in front of him. Ibn Ilyas woke up from his reverie and poured his thoughts out in a torrent.

'The one above will look after you.' The forefinger was now pointed to the roof. 'The one above will look after you, as long as even He can. Finally, each man looks after himself—and each woman. Sometimes He sleeps! Sometimes He rests! He must be tired of our petty disputes. He used to send a messenger every now and then once, one who with a whip or with his own blood would cleanse things up for the rest of us. The blood of others never cleanses. It only adds to the squelch. Your own blood, shed willingly, that's another thing. But now, after the last messenger, peace be upon him, Allah's hands are also tied. He can't send another, can He? Another Mehdi would be crucified as an imposter or worse, as an impersonator, wouldn't he? How can one be another, tell me, when actually the two sperm drops that make you—that is the only person you can be! And while the drops only make your flesh and blood, the soul that Allah blows into each body is unique. You can only be you. I can only be I. Murad can only be Murad. That is the law of the Lord, though it is not written anywhere. That is also the law of the sperm. Don't wince. When you face the truth you shouldn't even blink. Respect the Lord and his laws. There are laws of the spirit, which he has blown into the spirit, and laws of the flesh, which he has blown into blood and bone. Don't violate them. Don't try and cross the desert without water and without your camel. Don't let the spirit be troubled by too many questions. More questions mean more doubts.'

Ehtesham didn't know what to make of this amazing speech. Ilyas's eyeballs had rolled up and down and sideways as phrase and gesture had accompanied each other. If one were deaf, one would have thought a mime was being enacted.

The Sheykh resumes. 'Doubts actually are not bad things to possess. They are good for health, the health of the spirit. But they have been outlawed from the scriptures. Why, I don't know. Or do I? The moment you say, "The Lord sayeth thus", you have not left any room for enquiry. Yet the night of doubt must follow the day of revelation. Doubt is but the echo of the sacred word.'

He laughs loudly, innocently. This time his eyeballs haven't rolled. He withdraws into a temporary silence and then suddenly bursts out of it.

'You are in trouble, Son, what is your trouble?'

Statement and question come tumbling out in one breath.

'Well, Sir, the Muhtasib summoned me.'

'Ah, authority! Authority, the curse of mankind. Cruelty and oppression are but other names for authority. We all want a world free of authority—as things were in the days of Aadam and Hawa—ha-ha.'

Silence again. None of the acolytes speak. Why shouldn't they, Ehtesham wonders? The Sheykh continues.

'But Allah was there and he was pretty strict those days, and the only two people he had to oversee were Aadam and Hawa. The crusaders, may they perish in hell till qayamat and after qayamat, say that they were thrown out, Aadam and Hawa, because they ate an apple? So even Allah can be pretty arbitrary. Now of course he has millions to watch over. So he can't be too bothered about who eats what.'

'Well, Sir, that is exactly what is happening. I am being accused of . . .' Ehtesham stops unable to go on.

'And what are you being accused of, my Son? Something bordering innocence, I am sure. How sinful innocence can be at times!'

He laughs. Murad breaks in and tells the mystic about Ehtesham's drawings. Ibn Illyas starts nodding vigorously.

'Replicating Allah's creation, are we? Hmm, that can be grim business and one may have to answer grimly for it. Yet, we create all the time. Man and woman are enjoined to create, are they not? So are animals, though they would "create" even if no holy book asked them to. A child makes a cat out of clay. Is that such a sin? Perhaps they who look for sin in every shrub, it may be their eyes and ears which sin.'

The Sheykh laughs again. It seems he can't utter a thing without laughing. What can I tell the man, thinks Ehtesham? Do I start from the beginning, that I come from Asyut where the beards are long and the mullah's fiat is sharper than a sword; where contact with the outer world is restricted to the two flanks of the desert—eastern and western, or to perhaps a pilgrim who has returned from the Haj or bedouins coming in on their donkeys from some western oasis like al Kharijah; where people would be hard put to understand Cairene, the corrupt language of the Cairo resident, bastardized with

*keki n. daruwalla*

foreign words from Malta, Cyprus and Venice, tainted with the sailor's oaths and the lascar's slang. Do I tell him about the green thread of our lives running between the dun-coloured desert; our mud-plastered houses where life and vegetation are hardly ten miles broad, as the Nile gets squeezed between the two deserts. Despite all this our lands, the lands of our family are not to be sneezed at, and they would suffice for me and my mother—millet fields and carob lined with date palms. (?)

'Wake up, my Son' says Ibn Illyas. 'Dreams are not something a young man must get lost in. Yet, if the young don't dream, who will? The old only dream of the past. The young have everything to dream about—beyond the Nile and the desert. They can dream of love, not that the old don't. The old dream of love with regret, the young with hope. The young will not know, until it is too late, that love can also be a desert. But we should be talking of you! If you paint, you can dream in colours. If you draw, you can dream in line and curve. Forget the long beards! Forget their foul fulminations. Paint, my son!'

After a pause Ibn Illyas adds 'To the innocent of heart, nothing is forbidden. To the hypocrite, the *munaffiq,* even prayers could be forbidden! Who can tell? So go about your work with an open mind and an open heart. Nothing will happen to you!'

The acolytes started asking questions—on jinns, on their dreams, and what they meant, on stepmothers and one's duty towards them and so on. Ehtesham got up and saluted the Sheykh deferentially. But even as he turned around to leave, the Sheykh called out, 'They will kill you all the same. At least they will try.'

Ehtesham reached home and hit the bed. When he got up he started thinking; what exactly had the man said? He had kept on rambling about going beyond the Nile and beyond the desert. What on earth did he mean? Did the Sheykh want him to get out? Were these just the ramblings of someone high on hashish? What did he mean by that parting shot about them getting him in the end? The entire hour or more with the Sheykh had been one of reassurance, till the last moment when he sounded that warning. He couldn't make sense of it.

He was midway through his reverie when Taufiq and Murad came in. And when he told them he would be going to the mosque they said nothing, but just shrugged their shoulders and joined him. As they moved towards the mosque he started sniffing audibly. When Murad gave him an odd look, he said, 'Something tells me we will meet the perfumer.' And even as he said this he saw the man, redolent with his scents. He quietly pointed him out to his friends.

'We saw him before we could smell him!' said Taufiq, as all three of them laughed. They collected themselves, put on a solemn expression the way one dons a mask, and entered the mosque.

# of muhtasib and sons

છૂ

The Muhtasib was happy that his son Idries had come to him and started a conversation on his own—very respectfully of course and adhering to all norms of etiquette. This never happened, at least with the nobility. No one ever went and plonked himself on his father's rug and started chatting him up. You could do that with your mother. With the patriarch you waited till spoken to. The Muhtasib was happy. The boldness of the boy spoke of confidence in his father. He was uneasy with what the boy said. You can know a man by what is troubling him. Petty anxieties don't reflect a great mind, he thought. At the same time if you started questioning the functioning of the universe itself and the motions of the planets, then there was something extremely immature about you. After their discussion he wasn't sure where to place his son. In the Muhtasib's scheme of things, those not reconciled to the world were either destined, God forbid, to make a quick exit or linger on the rack. When he had said this as kindly as he could, drawing away the sting, his son had asked what he meant by being 'reconciled to the world'. He was taken aback. Youngsters were asking too many questions these days. He would not have asked this question of . . .

'What I mean by the world is obviously not the dust or the Nile or the *Khamsin* blowing in your face. As you grow you realize which way the river flows, where the current comes from. You get a hang of thrones, caliphates and decrees. By reconciliation I mean recognizing office and the robes of office, and taboos enjoined on us. And always there is this little thing about recognizing the sword. I hope you have understood.'

The trouble was he hadn't. They never did, the young.

'What you are actually saying, Father, is that the world is about power, though you haven't said so.'

'I did not even mention the word,' he said, aghast.

'But decrees and the sword are all about power, Father.'

'There are decrees in the Holy Book too, my son.'

'Yes, but power matters, doesn't it? They killed Imam Husain, didn't they, and no one could do a thing about it except wailing annually for him. Power means giving and denying. It is an obscene word, if you come to think of it. If the throne is placed in the east, that is where these people will kneel, never mind where the qibleh is.'

'May Allah forgive you your blasphemies,' he said, mouth aquiver in agitation. 'Power does not mean only the sword. Young men do not seem to grasp this simple truth that easily. Young fools do not understand this at all. You see the levies, the horsemen, men with the scimitars, the *baltagis*. But the army is not just there for oppression. When the Mongols ravaged all the lands of Islam, who beat them back? The armies of Egypt! It was because of power that we controlled the Red Sea all these centuries and that the caliphate came to Egypt, and we beat the crusaders. We need to be strong today. Our freedom is threatened today. The Ottomans are coveting the silt of the Nile, the trade along the Red Sea. We must have our hand on the hilt of the sword to preserve our freedom.'

'What freedom are we talking of, Father? We are being ruled by slaves, aren't we, and Turkish slaves at that.'

'Don't say that! Don't ever say that again! Do you hear! If someone were only to hear such words our necks . . .' he let the sentence trail off unfinished. He lowered his voice almost to a whisper.

'What is wrong with the Mamluks, tell me? Slaves? Doesn't the Holy Book itself give rights to slaves? Has any other religion treated slaves better than Islam? Wasn't it under the Mamluks that we defeated the Sixth Crusade? Wasn't it the Mamluks who established the Abbasid caliphate in Cairo barely three years after the Mongols had abolished it in Baghdad? Have you any idea how the Mongols killed him in Baghdad—the Caliph, I mean? They smothered him in a carpet!'

He did not want to eulogize the Mamluks. It would have had the opposite effect on the young man. Was there any point in taking the young man down the dark alleys of history—Timur's victory in Syria in 1400 and the exodus into Egypt of scholars, and earlier, the refugees fleeing from Mongol devastation. They had found the Egypt of Mamluks a haven. What was this young generation ashamed of?

'Does your younger brother have similar views?'

He hadn't been thinking of his younger son, Zakariya, and yet the question had popped out so suddenly, that for a moment even he was surprised. Idries, he noted, chose to remain quiet and not answer. He clapped his hands and Zakariya peeped down the stairwell, and then came down. Would the younger son, with fuzz on his chin, understand? He wasn't sure. He explained to the boy what the discussion was all about. The influx over the centuries had enriched Egypt. They were refugees—whether from Timur's conquest of Syria a hundred or so years ago, or from Mongol incursions. Many of them were thinkers, writers, astronomers. Why just Muslims? Copt and the Yahudi lived in peace here. They were thriving. No one touched them. The Jews had their synagogues including the one at Geniza, and they all wrote in Arabic. What was wrong with the Mamluks? They ruled Egypt and Egypt was a decent place to live in! He talked about the granaries being full and the treasure chests along with it; all this despite the plague which took away thousands, including his own father, less than two decades back. What more could the Mamluks do, he wanted to know?

Zakariya was not impressed. The dark centuries of the crusades sat heavy on his soul. This friendship with the Yahudi and the Christian, what was it in honour of? Not for the good health of Islam, surely. Nor were we doing the infidel a service. Even if it meant war, we would be doing kafirs a favour by bringing them into the fold.

Who had put all these ideas in that young, silly head? Didn't the boy know infidels from the people of the Book? Who was he hobnobbing with? Some mad, hashish-crazed fakir spitting venom, with his saliva sprayed all over his long beard? The Muhtasib's men were following half the people in the city, from syphilitic pimps to footsore fakirs, but he hadn't ever cared to have his own son tracked and reported on. It was a pit of his own digging, he thought, shaking his head.

'You seem to be disagreeing with what I am saying, Father?' the boy enquired anxiously.

He was amazed at the calm that had descended on him. 'What makes you think so?' he asked.

The sons laughed. 'You were shaking your head vigorously, Father'.

'I was doing so at my own follies, Son, may Allah who is always forgiving, forgive me.'

Then Zakariya went off on a tangent.

'Even our language stands defiled! If the Prophet, peace be on him, had been born in these times, Allah would have been hard put to have spoken to him in the Arabic of today. We have Christian words and Yahudi words. Words from every heathen port have sailed into our language. This is what comes of living at peace with the Franks.'

He tried to reason with the young boy. Thanks to their trade right down to the southern-most tip of India, an Arab could make himself understood to most people. Down the Indian coast and even in the land of the Zanj, people knew a bit about the language. Language was commerce. You traded in words, instead of goods.

Zakariya was not convinced. The trouble with the Mamluks was that they had reduced everything to commerce. What was this long peace with the crusaders due to? Was it because we wanted trade with the Christians—with Venice and Cyprus? And already there was talk of the Christians going to India through that other route. What would happen to Arab trade with Hind? Why couldn't the crusades of old be answered by the jehad of today?

He was stunned. His son was talking like some mad fakir raving about Kafirs and doomsday and jehad. It was a special part of his duty to see that such people remained quiet and did not stir up trouble. He managed this with a few small bribes to some and strong-arm methods with others. Now his own son was talking like them, and Idries, the elder one was sticking stubbornly to his theories. For, he had been asking what difference there was in being ruled by Mamluks, who were Circassians, and by the Ottomans, who were Turks, only they were freemen.

The bickering came to an end with the servant knocking on the door and quietly announcing a visitor. It turned out to be the perfumer. Idries and Zakariya left the room. The preliminaries with the perfumer were short.

'What is the news, Perfumer?'

'The boy from Asyut went to the mosque today.'

'Did you come to tell me just that? I know that already.'

The perfumer tried to hide his surprise. The evening prayer had ended barely an hour ago. The Muhtasib saw through the mask.

'You have no right to feel surprised at anything I know. After that warning from me yesterday, do you think he could have stayed away from the mosque? Did he see you?'

'Who? Who saw me?' The perfumer was flummoxed, for the question from the Muhtasib had come suddenly.

'The young man from Asyut. Did he see you?'

He wasn't sure. You spot a man in a crowd. How do you know whether he has also spotted you? Unfair question, thought the perfumer. 'I don't know.'

'That's not good enough. Does the chief of the Mokhabarat know that you are here?'

'He doesn't.'

'He will have known by now, if he is any good at his job. Did you come directly here?'

'Yes.'

'No detours?'

'None.'

'Good. A detour gives away your hand. Never be overtly clandestine. Never be too clever. It would be bad if the Mokhabarat came to know that you were meeting me. It would be infinitely worse if they thought you were going round and round, looking over your shoulder, and leading your trackers a merry dance, while all the while homing to my place. Such actions speak of guilt. Guilt is a confession of a crime. We—I mean you and I—have nothing to feel guilty about. A boy comes from Asyut and we get a report that he moves around with strangers—people from the Khaleej. A boy from Asyut and he doesn't go to the mosque. We have a right to know why. We have a right to rectify matters. So we who oversee the morals of the city on behalf of the Sultan—we don't have to hide among the shadows.'

The perfumer, used more to the Muhtasib's silences and his reveries in which he would lose himself suddenly without as much as a ripple, like salt in water, was a bit surprised at this lengthy peroration. Something was bothering the great man, he thought, something deep down.

'Was there anyone with him?'

'With whom?'

The Muhtasib was getting impatient. 'With the young man from Asyut of course.'

'If there were, I did not see them,' answered the perfumer.

'Either your eyes are failing you, or you are getting careless. I believe both his friends were with him. That is what I have been told. Next time you are watching someone of our interest, see that your mind is where your eye is. If the eye is pointed north and the mind is grazing in the meadows in the south the results are not going to be happy, either for you or for me. Do you understand?'

The terrified perfumer nodded his head.

'If you are bowing towards the Qibleh in prayer and your mind is with that blind woman's daughter, two lanes to the east of your perfumery, then too the results could be poor. What is her name?'

By now the perfumer was petrified. There was nothing the man did not know! He stuttered incoherently, finally saying that he had no idea what the Muhtasib was getting at. The Inspector of Weights and Measures of the city of Cairo, merely smiled sardonically and debated with himself whether to let matters rest, or to turn the knife and drive the poor man to further paroxysms of discomfiture.

'I could never dream that you can risk lying to me. So I take it that your memory has failed you for an instant. Don't forget that lying is betrayal, and you surely know what betrayal means.'

Even after the perfumer left, the Muhtasib kept reflecting on betrayals. Betrayals just don't happen. They are plotted. It takes two to betray. Come to think of it, the one who is betrayed needs to feel guilty—look at the tree of guilt he has planted in the other's heart! It never occurred to the Muhtasib that he himself could have broken faith by having his own informer, stalked. (If one is in power one is untouched by any such feelings. Guilt is the heritage of the weak.)

# the house with the
# three steps

જી

He should have been thinking of the Muhtasib or his meeting with the Sheykh, reflected Ehtesham, as he got up the next morning. Instead, he was affected by something that seemed to lift his spirits. He was almost hard put to recall what had caused this feeling of lightness. During his dreams that seemed to flow across his forehead the whole night, he had been confronted by a white wall with a green square encrusted halfway into it. But it was that girl, he knew, who had uplifted his spirit. He didn't know her name, didn't remember it, never got to ask it. He saw the twist in it—the names of those who bring happiness, unknown; but the ones who belched out threats with a whip in one hand and the scripture in the other—they were known to all. The muezzin singled them out in his after-prayer discourse; heralds proclaimed them to the winds, drums throbbed with their names.

He decided to go to the house with the three steps once again. This time he went after a spartan meal of bread and sweetened milk and figs. What was important was that he wasn't hungry and weak this time. The wall was not white and dazzling as it was in dream-light, but yellow, with the lime wash peeling off. Of course the green square was there right in the middle of the wall, but it was a glass window with green paper pasted on it from the inside.

Glass was not common, he knew, but those who traded with the Franks managed to get hold of it. He hadn't even noticed the green bit the last time he was here. How could he have missed it, he asked himself. He passed the house once looking at the window and went down the street, branched off into a souk and returned, parking himself on the steps a little before the noonday prayers. And the same voice called out, 'Habiba, that man is sitting on the steps again. Give him some water, will you!' The servant woman opened the door, grumpy as always, and served him water. When he had gulped it down she asked him contemptuously if he had no other door-step to park his backside on. Didn't he know that only women lived in this house and it was bad form coming here again and again?

'Habiba! How can you talk like that?'

The voice came from the interior of the house. Would he ever get access there, he wondered. And he thought of those rooms as dark and cool, perhaps even mossy.

'That room where the old lady sleeps must be pretty dark, isn't it?'

The woman gasped at the effrontery. 'What has that got to do with you? What business is it of yours whether a room is dark or lighted?'

From the interior he could hear a loud giggle. 'And even if it is dark we won't be coming to you for light, O owner of lamps!'

It was obviously the girl who had spoken, though he couldn't fail to notice the uncanny resemblance to her mother's voice. He couldn't think of anything witty to say in return.

That was the trouble always, the right repartee came to mind a day later. He still didn't know her name and did not dare ask it. Instead he asked Habiba the old lady's name, and found her gasping once again and taking her hand to her heart. She told him gruffly that the names of respectable ladies were not elicited through their servants! Then you take me to her and I'll ask her myself, he suggested. He could hear the young lady inside laughing loudly once again.

'Well, please tell the ladies that my name is Ehtesham.'

It was time to go, he thought, and moved on, but not before the servant woman, Habiba had called out after him, 'All your questions were about the mistress of the house, but I know where your mind was, and your heart. I hope you have understood.'

Barely two days later he strolled along the street in the evening twilight, past the house with the *mashrrabiya* and the green window, keeping his eyes lowered and his head down lest anyone question his 'morals'. Where women are veiled, a look can damn your reputation. Reaching the end of the street, he turned right. He had hardly walked a hundred yards further when he saw a young boy on the balcony hollering for help. From his ragged dress he looked a servant boy. The people in the street were passing him by without taking notice. What is it you want? Ehtesham asked the boy. His master was very ill the boy answered and there was no one to look after him. Do you want a tabib, a doctor, to be brought in, Ehtesham asked. A woman came out on to the balcony, her face covered with the black hijab. She went in and another one came out and shouted, 'No, we want him moved. We need a horse carriage.' She hadn't recognized him in the dim twilight, but he apparently did. There was no mistaking her: she was the stocky and truculent Habiba. He brought a horse carriage and then went into the house.

This time Habiba couldn't help spotting him. Oh, it is you, she said despondently.

'Yes it is.'

'Many thanks, Ehtesham Bey.'

'Since when have you known my name?'

'You announced it to the whole street, remember, sitting on those steps.'

'But how come I become Bey suddenly?'

'When in need I would even call my donkey a Pasha.'

Once he was in the house, it was Zainab, for that was the girl's name, who came forward and told him what the trouble was. The boy who had shouted from the balcony was her uncle's servant. Her uncle lived alone and was very ill. Habiba and she wanted to shift him to their house. Could Ehtesham please help? He went into the sick man's room and saw the frail body and the vacant look in his eyes. After a few minutes the sick man came to and asked Ehtesham who he was. He asked Zainab for water and when told that they were about to take him to his blind sister's house, he agreed willingly, to Zainab's surprise. Ehtesham helped to carry the old man to the horse carriage, sat holding him, and took him to the house. It was again Ehtesham who carried him up the stairs. A house with three women, how does it get along with day-to-day living? Is there a *tabib* nearby, he asked. Could he go and summon him? They thought it was too late in the night already. Habiba would prepare fenugreek tea with some ginger and herbs and they would cover him with blankets. That would do. Allah would take care of the night. The morning, God willing, would bring in the tabib and good health.

He realized he hadn't been seen at the mosque lately. The Muhtasib, Lord Inspector of weights and measures, of the consistency of cream and purity of milk, and self-styled enforcer of morality would come to know. He remembered

Murad who had said once that the Muhtasib had a license to inspect a water carrier's *mashq* to see if it was clean, or look into your heart—by carving it out.

Next morning there was still no doctor at Zainab's. It fell to his lot to bring one. After the doctor had prescribed his herbs and left, Habiba took him to Zainab's mother so that he could be thanked properly. She could hardly see a yard in front of her, he noticed. He made the correct noises, asked her about her health, told her a bit about himself and his days at al Azhar. The old lady's eyes lit up. 'Al Azhar, then you must have heard of my brother.'

When he didn't respond, she said, 'Surely you must have heard of Abu Khalil!'

'Abu Khalil, the chronicler, the historian? Who hasn't heard of him. If I am not wrong, he had a wife who was from Asyut.'

'Yes, of course. Let him rest for a day or two. You must come again and meet him. He will be happy to see you.'

A week later he was back and this time the reception was different. Even Habiba was pleasant. When face to face with Zainab, he introduced himself as the owner of lamps who had wanted to sell light to her. The mother heard the banter and called out, 'If anyone needs light it is I. But only Allah can give that kind of light.'

'Allah doesn't sell anything, Mother, neither light nor darkness.'

He had stayed the day with Abu Khalil, who seemed to get cramps in his legs and was coughing all the time. He had coaxed him to walk a bit. When they first met the old man didn't talk much. But over a series of meetings, he opened up. Ehtesham told his friends later that hearing the old man talk was like listening to a national heritage. ('You are getting pompous, aren't you?' said Murad.) Over a century of events sat comfortably in his memory, as secure as in the Sultan's treasury; and he seemed to have his finger on the pulse of the world. Mamluk or Ottoman, Mongol or Seljuk—he seemed to know every important figure. To his horror, Ehtesham found that many of the names mentioned by Abu Khalil didn't quite register with him. Of what use were these studies in al Azhar where he had spent so many years?

He had stayed on for lunch served by Habiba and managed to exchange a few words with a veiled Zainab. As he walked out that evening, he felt exhilarated and for once he noticed the minarets silhouetted against the dusk and a flock of doves circling a mosque dome twice, their shadows scrimmaging over street and wall as they flew away.

When he went again a week later, Abu Khalil complained about the absence of his books for lack of space. Suddenly his sister said, 'I hear a drumbeat, must be six streets away. An announcement is on its way.' Is the old woman given to hallucinations, thought Ehtesham. Do her ears ring with sounds that are not sounds? Minutes later the staccato drumbeat was audible and so was the town crier.

'People of al Qahira, listen. The holy month of Ramadan is drawing near. Except for infants and those on their death beds or those critically ill, fasts are enjoined on all. By the Sultan's orders, from dawn to the evening hour of the cannon, let no one be seen devouring food or drinking water. Anyone caught will invite punishment from the Muhtasib, Inspector of Weights and Measures of al Qahira and Upper Egypt. This applies to the Dhimmi as well—the Yahudi and the Copt. Be warned, people of Qahira.'

An outburst of anger greeted the announcement. 'Who do they think we are, Kafirs?' asked Zainab's mother. 'I have never heard such a decree in my fifty years in the city. What Muslim will not keep a fast in Ramadan?' Servant and daughter also

*keki n. daruwalla*

chipped in. Who has given the Muhtasib the right to issue such a decree, asked Zainab. 'Didn't you hear, child, the Sultan himself,' answered the mother. Abu Khalil put the finishing touch to the debate.

'The name of the Sultan is the cloak, the hijab of the Muhtasib.'

Two days later, Ehtesham went with some fruit and found Abu Khalil in a nostalgic mood. When he mentioned his home in Asyut, the old man told him his wife came from the same place. He started reminiscing about her, how she kept house, what an early riser she was, a woman who in his memory had never missed a dawn prayer, no matter how ill she was, and she was often ill; and he remembered the fragrance of baked bread in their house early in the morning—the first thing he noticed when he rose from bed, for he was a late riser and invariably missed the dawn prayer. On dark nights other women would steal a few moments on the rooftop to savour the cool night air—not his wife. May Allah grant her peace.

Ehtesham talked of his childhood in Asyut, the boredom of a small town, whiling away the hours watching the night skies. He recalled how astrologers were in demand in Asyut especially when the season of Haj drew near. Travelling was dangerous business, what with robbers on the road, and the desert with its simooms, and of course jinns, both the Muslim jinns (may Allah keep us from them) and the infidel jinns (may Allah slaughter them). He talked about how mullahs would rail against astrology and dub it un-Islamic, but when it came to their own trip to Mecca, they would consult the same soothsayers on the sly. Abu Khalil derided astrology and laughed at the Indians who honoured their stars. He grew exercised over all this.

'We would never have had the abominable crusaders on our doorstep but for the extraordinary activity in the heavens. For them each shooting star indicated the divine will being scripted on the skies. They thought the crusades had blessings from above. Otherwise, do you think they would have embarked on such a mad venture—twenty European countries, most of them at war with each other, wanting to conquer Jerusalem thousands of miles away. Mad clerics and sham saints led them on, and those who read the stars reinforced their faith. It was our people who paid in blood.'

Crusades? How many people in Asyut, or for that matter in al Mansha or Abnub or al Mina or any of the habitations near Asyut, would have heard of the crusades, thought Ehtesham. So he questioned Abu Khalil.

'You are right, Son but ask the people of Aleppo and Tarsus, Antioch and Homs, Tripoli and Acre. They would know. The first man who led the first crusade rode on a donkey and looked like one. Most of their hermits are donkeys, sometimes high on hashish. They started by murdering Jews. The turn of the believers came later and we of course did not die without drawing an equal amount of blood. The Yahudi were slaughtered in the cities—they are good at offering their necks. Such was the bismillah of the accursed crusades.'

# recalling the crusades

&

Abu Khalil had to be visited again. There could be no doubt about that. Not merely because the shadow of Zainab was falling across Ehtesham's dreams. He was actually getting fond of the old man. If there was all that learning stored in his brain, surely someone must tap it. One had to know more. A Friday morning appearance, dressed in one's best for the noon prayer, his prayer cap perched securely on the head, would go down well, he thought. Habiba was not unpleasant any more. He was taken upstairs just when Zainab was coming down after serving the old man his rather frugal repast— milk and dates and flat bread. Her arm touched his, almost setting him on fire. He would have given anything to brush his body against hers. Even as he greeted her he was not sure if she had noticed the colour burning on his cheeks. But she had just smiled, hurriedly looked down and went past. And he would have to live with that feel of her arm against his arm.

As soon as he saw Ehtesham, Abu Khalil blessed him. How many young men have a thought for the old these days? Ehtesham didn't know whether he was talking to him or muttering to himself. After the initial pleasantries, Ehtesham veered the conversation his way. I don't think it is a fair question to ask of an old man, he said gently, but when you look back what was the greatest thrill you got out of life?

'What did I enjoy most? Dreaming of the crusades. I not only dreamt of them, I fought those who led them, may Satan always squat on their hindquarters.'

For a moment, Ehtesham was stunned. This mild-mannered man, with his skin lying in folds over his bones, could he ever have fought? Actual thrust and slash?

'The one thing I can't forget about the crusaders—the smell. They stank like desiccated fish.' He sank into silence. Surely, he was not going to leave it at that, thought Ehtesham. You can't touch upon something like the crusades and then lapse into reverie. Abu Khalil could. Over the next month he unwound, and with Ehtesham by his bedside, and sometimes Zainab, he rambled and reminisced over history and Egypt, the Levant, Mamluk and Mongol. Sitting below, sewing or stitching or winnowing the wheat, the women would have their ears glued to his words, for wars and history were hardly the subjects he would ever discuss with them.

'A crusade was a cosmos in itself—belief versus unbelief, good versus evil, Allah versus Iblis, depending on which side you were on. The crusades were a history in a permanent state of non-completion; a hopeless war to reconcile the irreconcilable—they were, after all, launched in the name of Issa whom they call Christ, may Allah's blessings rest on his head. But Christ preached love, the crusades preached murder.

'They took us for heathens, we took them for Kafirs. Of course both sides faced blood and perfidy, fire and famine. Only death was common. Hunger ransacked stomachs—pagan and Muslim alike. The marches were long and never-ending, longer for them—for, once they crossed the seas they just walked—horses died like fleas, and knights just had to foot it, carrying armour and victuals on their backs. Every so often they got diverted—to Aleppo or Antioch or along the seam of Armenian principalities—Ravanda and Tilbesar and Edessa—through scrub and wasteland with not a hearth-fire in sight. There was no telling who the besieger was and who the besieged. The matter was very involved. The crusaders would besiege Antik—they call it Antioch—and hunger besieged the crusaders. (Though with the river running along the city, whether you could actually besiege Antioch was a moot point. You could build forts across the river though, which the Christians did.) Hunger makes robbers of us all—of crusader and jehadi alike. So the besiegers went in all directions and they would have tried to fly on bird-back, were there birds large enough and were there food in the sky. They went everywhere—northwards to Cilicia, eastwards to Harim and Yenisehir and southwards to Latakia. The soldiery had to be paid! Knights became servants. They were actually doled out wages! The shame of it!'

Ehtesham laughed to see the old man giggle suddenly. Not that it made much sense to him. Nothing about European chivalry had ever filtered down to the likes of him. He wouldn't have known a knight from a blacksmith or a cardinal, and the Arabs had no idea that they themselves were Saracens!

Time and again his mind would wander off to the actual figure of the crusader and the panoply of iron in which he clothed himself. That remained a fixation. 'They were a curse upon our land. Two hundred, maybe three hundred years were wasted in this useless fighting. Their eyes brimmed with arrogance, their bellies with greed. I am not ashamed to say it: they ignited a kind of terror within us. That chain-mail armour, that long straight sword and iron helmet made them look unreal. We had never seen anything so peculiar before. We dreaded it—that iron-cloaked face, eyes peering at us through the visor. When they died I am sure their souls never got any peace. The soul, after all, passes through the eyes, the ears, the mouth, surely not through any other orifice (may Allah forgive me for even mentioning such a thing). If the face itself is covered, like a prison, how could the soul ever escape? Not through that castle of iron they wore on their heads and around their faces. Their ghosts remained here, I am sure, to haunt their mothers and their wives, and may Allah protect them. Yes, the weak are in His care and we should invoke His blessings on them, even if they are infidels. When it comes to women, the difference between infidel and the faithful needs to be narrowed.'

That drew a shrill protest from Habiba below. 'Why must the women of the Musalmans be herded with the others? Don't we pray and fast, don't we teach our boys to become better Muslims? If all that doesn't matter, instead of going for pilgrimages, why don't the men go to the land of the Farangs to get their women?'

'Habiba! You speak foolishly!' snapped the blind woman. Zainab joined in. 'They are all pink pink and red red, I am told. They've red hair and faces so red you can't distinguish their cheeks from their lips. Only their legs are dark because they keep them uncovered.'

'And they open them readily,' added Habiba.

'Habiba! Hold your stupid tongue!'

'Oho, I was only mentioning the uncovering of legs!'

'I know what you meant!' said Zainab's mother.

The old man chipped in. 'It would be good if the men were to go and get the women of the Franks. Then they would embrace Islam and increase the ranks of the faithful.'

'And what happens to Muslim women? Then they would have to cross the waters and get the Franks!'

This barb from Zainab was greeted with a gale of laughter from Habiba, but the mother was scandalized and beat her breasts.

'Take refuge in God. In no respectable house in the entire city would women be talking like this, shame on you both. And you who sit up there, smiling to yourself, why can't you shout at your niece and shut her up?'

Abu Khalil answered to loud giggles from Habiba and Zainab, 'You are addressing Allah, isn't it? So I don't have to answer, I presume.'

'I am addressing you! I mentioned your niece! Our families can't boast of a relationship with either Allah or his angels.' She muttered to herself that with old people, the brain proceeded to the grave earlier than the rest of the body.

'Anyone with the kind of beauty Zainab has should be considered Allah's niece. Ask our young friend Ehtesham, if you don't believe me.'

This was followed by a deathly silence from the three women. Such things were not to be expressed. They were never talked about unless a child blurted it out of sheer innocence or an old man because of senility. What exactly was this boy doing, she would have liked to know. How much was he earning? She had never even thought of all this.

In the room above, Abu Khalil had started off again. 'Your trouble is you want to know what the past was like, feel it with your hands, and savour the flavours that have gone. The past is like a hollow flute, but where is the breath to make it sing? You are overly ambitious, Ehtesham Bey. What were the crusades like, you asked? Depended on the seasons—heat or frost . . . and the place—sleeping on the sand dunes you'd find in the morning that the desert had kissed your lips and left some of its grit in your eyes . . . if you were near Sidon or

Jaffa, the sea breeze unburdened itself of its salt in crystals on your body. So it was either sand or salt, isn't the simplicity of it all wonderful?

'For them, everything was simple. We were the accursed devils and they had to "liberate" the Holy city Jerusalem, as if it was not holy for us. There was a time when it was our kibleh, till the Prophet told us to bow towards Mecca. When you come with this bent of mind, the Devil finds it easy to plant dreams. In the first crusade they were a beaten lot in front of Antioch. Then one of these infidels met Christ in his dreams. And he was told they would win. Another soldier saw a saint they call Andrew. The saint showed him where a lance was buried which had pierced Christ while he was carrying the cross. Next day they discovered a fake lance. The Devil had led them to think that God was with them. Their spirits revived and they captured the citadel of Antioch.

'The important thing is that the crusades were a world in themselves. There was Rome and there was Rum. And while originally Rum was worried about Rome, it soon got frightened of the Mamluks, as who would not? The Christians had two Caliphs. Two kings, two wives, two masters, always a problem. But now Rum sought the help of the other Caliph against the Mamluks. All trade with us was declared haraam by this Roman Caliph. No buying and selling with Islam, and certainly not with Misr. As if they were trading with Iblis! If the Isahi merchants from Venice and Genoa were to trade with us, they would be branded as murtad, apostates! The crusades almost became sea borne. Their ships were ready to block our ports.

'One never knew where these infidels would launch their jehad, for that is what the crusade means. Today it could be the Yahudi, tomorrow their own eastern church and the third day against the Muslims in Spain, Granada, to be precise.

Everywhere the poor gathered—England, Flanders, thirty thousand of them, holding their infernal crosses at night during eerie meetings. And their Roman Khalifa whom they call the Pope, who usually sold a seat in heaven for a good price, now made it free! All you had to do was to fight Islam, and you were assured a place in heaven, given a certificate on a piece of paper signed, sealed and embossed by the Caliph. We too buy a place in heaven, but with the blood of martyrs. They purchased it with silver! They sold heaven bit by bit, yard by yard. After all, heaven is not a cemetery where six feet of space would do. In heaven you are free and can surely move around. Allah be praised that Jannat is not small or the Khalifa of the Isahis would have sold the whole blessed place by now. Where would the faithful have gone when they received the call from Allah?

'The Lord, of course, does not forget his worshippers. He sent the plague to the Isahis. Every country in Europe got what they called the Black Death. Some cities invited a revisit.' It was here that Ehtesham interjected.

'Didn't Cairo also get the plague, Uncle Khalili?'

'That is right, my Son, the scourge did fall on a city or two. But Allah was with us and our Prophet—our shield and sword and shelter.'

# THE NARRATIVE
# OF TAUFIQ

*Taufiq the Voyager hasn't spoken so far. The spotlight has been on his friend, Ehtesham. Taufiq had sailed down the west coast of India with his father when he was a boy. Then he moved from Oman to Cairo for his studies.*

# and left with only a
# stubble of words...

~~~

There is no God but God. Allah is my protector, and as my
father told me, all good comes from Allah, and all evil
from Iblis. When I related this to my Maulvi who taught me
in Oman, he kept silent. This kind of silence also speaks in its
own way. Father had also said, as I was leaving for al Qahira,
'Keep away from lesser sins and the bigger transgressions will
not come your way.'

You can share your dreams with people, but not memory.
Both Ehtesham and Murad know what I wish to be, what I
hold nearest to my heart—the sea. They also have a vague
idea of what brought me here from Oman. They are aware
of my two voyages to the southern coast of Hindustan. If you
ask them, they'll say, 'Of course we know him! We know our
Taufiq inside out.' Yet what they know is a few signposts, some
markers. There are some things you don't speak of and they
remain in your blood or in the darkest moss-covered corners
of your dreams. Memory is one such, and childhood—both
have survived in your blood.

Murad and Ehtesham are younger than me, at least by
four or five years. They haven't been through what I have. I
remember layers of heat lying over me like a sheet. The house I

lived in was made of straw and mud, and we faced times when father and I were forced to fish because there was nothing else in the house to eat. We had a better house once and lived well. Mother died, then father's fine boat got wrecked—he had hired it out and a storm destroyed it. That was when we moved into straw and mud—there was no alternative. As I narrate this I am hung up on memory today. A day comes when memory just becomes stubble—of words, events, faces. It can't be the actual thing, can it? Between living and re-living in the mind lies a *khaleej*, a gulf. You cannot physically leap across it, for the past is after all the past.

Yet memory does the best it can. Father said, don't waste your time. History moves so slowly here, you'd think it was recovering from paralysis. It is as slow as salt deposits on a sea rock. Nothing happens. The click of a sand lizard is a big event. Nothing grows here but thorn. Go to Cairo where the sights are and the smells! You must be sick of the smells of salt and seaweed. Go and see the Nile and the citadel, the Khan el Khalili where there are more shops than men in our country. Go to your mother's cousin. He has a good house in Husseiniya.

It was surprising he could talk like that—history coming to a standstill and all that—for he was unlettered. You don't pick up alphabets in old age. He later acquired a small boat of his own on which he would carry cargo to nearby places. It was unfit for a voyage of any length. He also hired himself out to owners of bigger boats. He would put on a coarser garb then. I remember him in his rough home-spun clothes, which must have chafed his skin, and his rope sandals, which left their burns across his instep and around his ankles. He would take me on short voyages down the gulf, climb up a mast, unloosen his turban and wave to me, I, a mere boy looking up, thrilled and proud, shading my eyes from the sun. He carried his prayer rug in his boat and as he spread it and turned west, an expression, not so much of solemnity as of bliss, would flow down his face as he knelt facing the dusk. In ten years he has aged. Salt has got hold of his beard and lined the creases on his face. But though he gets darker by the day and his eyes crinkle against the sun, the smile is as wide as before.

Or so I suppose, for I haven't seen him now for the last so many years. He must be keeping count even though I am vague about the time I have been away from him. There are times when the unlettered know their numbers better than the ones who have studied at al Azhar. Even though his admonitions were few, I have, sadly, forgotten them, except one. Al Qahira will be a test, he said. From rope-sandals to riches, from the wilderness to the heart of civilization (he didn't put it that way), is always a trial. Survive there! There is no life beyond life. Survival itself is heaven—may Allah forgive me for saying so.

Sometimes I feel uneasy with memories about him—there was too much of truth in his speech, always a tough thing to bear. What is hard to bear is always heavy. Paradise must be light and rose-tinted—like falsehood. Allah have mercy on me. In one of his sad moments, Ehtesham warned me not to get too involved with memories, 'You won't be able to cut loose. The more you indulge memory the stonier it gets. There are some memories you can almost touch.' Ehtesham somehow thought that his message, such as it was, had not gone home—he could underestimate people. (And he could turn cruel, now and then.) 'It's a superstition with me. If you remember some people too much, they become only memories. You never see them again.' (I could have struck him for saying that, but I knew that he was thinking of his mother in Asyut, even as he said that. I, of course, didn't have a mother to think about.)

When mother died, father hired a Maulvi to come and teach me Arabic and the prayers. It had been a long-standing demand of my mother. The Maulvi was very particular about writing and had different copies of the Holy Book, where the calligraphist had let go, each letter unfurled like a banner in a stiff breeze. Though it was my father who paid him, the Maulvy gathered the other boys from our village and taught them as well. His village was far, and so he came only every alternate day, often riding a donkey. He insisted on good writing. If you made mistakes, if the letters were smudged or disfigured, he would ask you to open your left palm and the cane would descend on it with the thin hissing sound of a serpent before it strikes. If you were too afraid to open your palm, the stick would descend on the shoulder or elbow—but always the left one. He wouldn't hurt the right, so that your writing did not get impaired. 'The right hand commits the error and the left hand pays. That'll teach you the ways of the world,' he would say. 'That is what the world means by even-handedness. As for justice, it is reserved for the Day of Judgment. Don't expect any as long as you are alive.'

I have other memories about how poverty came to our door. The sea eroded some of our date palm groves. Others withered. Caretakers of our groves in other villages stopped paying us. Father didn't have the energy to fight the swindlers, once mother died. He himself became a sapless tree—at least for some time. But Father knew the Khaleej and the Red Sea very well—'the way one knows one's mother', he'd say. Pilgrim ships wanted him to steer them down the Red Sea. He went back to voyaging, taking me along with him. Then a Muslim from Gujarat asked him to steer his ship.

'What? I leave the pilgrims and the Hajis to fend for themselves; and take on a trading ship?'

The trader said, 'You ask around and find out how much I give in charity. Only then give your final answer.'

He was right. The man's charities were well known. Moreover, he was willing to pay father twice what he was getting from pilgrim ships. Father agreed. A spice ship, of course, meant going to Hindustan. Initially, we were trading (he look me along naturally) between Cochin and Gujarat. We would bring spices up to Gujarat and take back cotton. Later, it was voyaging from Calicut to Aden, sometimes to Hormuz. He and others on the ships taught me. I was a favourite because I worked willingly without payment. Father's pride came in the way of my accepting any money—we were not *that* poor. Rather *he* was not that poor that his son also had to earn a wage!

During one monsoon we got stuck in Gujarat. There was no way of getting out, the wind was so strong and the rain so ceaseless. I even picked up their language—boys don't take long in picking up words. Then I got a mother. Father married a woman from Khambat—she was Muslim and a widow. She looked after him well and never said a harsh word to me. In fact, she was afraid of me and feared my rejection more than anything else.

I had two good years in Gujarat, but then father started talking of Cairo once again. How long would I shift from port to port? Cairo was civilization. I must be lettered, literate. I was getting too mixed up between Arabic and Gujarati and a smattering of the Malabari language. I should be in a position to be a captain of a ship, a *nakhuda* as we called him. One fine day I was shipped off up the Red Sea, up the Nile, then by foot to Cairo. (Here people hinted that I may have been nudged out of the house because of the new mother. I don't believe a word of this.) Father had given me enough money to support myself, not only through the journey but for a few months in Cairo.

I remember him and the other mother. It is not face or expression that I remember as much as speech; memory, scythed by the years, left with only a stubble of words. Except that the voice also haunts—timbre and tone and pitch—all of which adds to nostalgia. Bones darken with time. Memory doesn't. (Ehtesham, you bastard, I too can philosophize!) Why do I switch to Ehtesham when speaking of Father? On another occasion—one of his pensive moods again—Ehtesham said to me, 'Time eases you into the grave. Memory eases you out of it.'

Uncle Uthman took me in. He started laughing even as he saw me, why I don't know. I can't imagine anyone in Cairo being so happy to see a nephew, and that too from the outer wilds of the Khaleej, someone he'd never seen before. Even my aunt looked happy in a restrained but totally unaffected sort of way. Uncle had no children and I was treated well. As I got used to the life here, and the rhythms of the city, my only regret was that Father couldn't share the good things my plate was being heaped with. It is funny. You share a lifetime on the borders of penury without a thought, and then all of a sudden, when the better things of life come your way, you are periodically affected by gusts of despair. You can't share even a tenth of all this with the people you love.

Uncle Uthman Asturlabi, to give him his full name, did what Father had done—hired a master for me to brush up my studies before I went into al Azhar. The Qoran is the word of Allah himself, he said. But there are things besides the Holy Book, and you better know something about them. And how many years later did we discuss astronomy? Astronomy? I don't recollect whether I knew what the thing meant. Perhaps I had a vague notion about it. Perhaps I asked him. Who knows? But I did laugh once when I heard that the subject dealt with a study of the stars. Didn't we know all about them, we who

lived by the sea and on it, fed on its bounty, we of the Khaleej?
We didn't have to learn all this from the people of the city.
Surely not! Those who live in the desert or on the sea coast
know more about stars than city-dwellers. What can you learn
about the planets where light and shadow both become oblong
and geometrical and where you can't see half the sky because
of the buildings? The other half you can't observe because of
smoke from kitchen fires.

Uncle Uthman laughed. 'You have noted my name, I hope.
It is al Asturlabi, maker of Astrolabes, an Astrolabist. My
father made Astrolabes. Apart from other things, he was
also a maker of sundials. It is only I who am a shopkeeper.
But still, I learnt a lot from my father, as you learnt from
yours.' Even before I had moved into a riwaq in al Azhar I
had been initiated into some of the mysteries of the skies.
But my uncle was a taciturn man, and it was only later when
I came in contact with the great Ibn Majid himself, that the
full import of all this sank into me. No better determinant
of the rising or setting of the sun and the stars, or the exact
position of a star or planet at a given time had been invented.
And it was from him I learnt that over four hundred years
ago, in 442 AH, the Andalusian astronomer al Zarzuela (or
did he say al Zurquali?)made a contraption, which, through
mechanical means, enabled one to determine the celestial
longitude of any planet.

Everything is new to the eye, to the senses, when wilderness
comes to civilization. After all, no reed flutes or tambourines
greet a country yokel when he comes to Cairo. For the first few
days even the streets appear similar. How does one distinguish
between the Bait al Mal alley and the Bait al Qadi? (Uncle?
told me to avoid walking near public baths for women, or to
look up at roof tops on hot sultry nights, for women would
come there unveiled to take in the cool air.) Uncle took me

around to the citadel and told me it was constructed by Salah al Din (he was very particular that I pronounce his name right, though I kept referring to him as Salahdin); that its huge walls encircled both the cities, Misr and al Qahira (I didn't know they were two cities—Misr I thought was the name of the country; it was, but it was also the name of the city); of course all this hit me like the cave of gems must have staggered Allahdin. How I must have gawked at Uncle when he told me that twelve years after they started building the walls, crusader prisoners were still working on brick and mortar here. Yet when I look back, it was not the sights—mausoleum and burj and mosque that affected me so much. The people were more fascinating—the crowds in Khan al-Khalili, the call to prayer soaring up from different minarets within moments of each other, the varied garments of Syrian and Libyan, Yahudi and Copt, each with a distinct turban and beard and visage. I wouldn't move if a troop of Mamluk horsemen clattered by. Even more compelling were the scenes that typified life here, as it rolled by—the potter walking beside his donkey laden with clay urns, the fellahein singing away at work, the bicker of gravel beneath a cartwheel, the Nile, vein-blue in the morning haze.

# the sea demands . . .

Beyond all this—Ehtesham and the blind woman's daughter, al Maheeni, the Muhtasib, the perfumer who is tracking us, my uncle Uthman Asturlabi, the two dervishes, the dreams at night that roam dangerously near my crotch, the thoughts about women—beyond all this is the sea: shell-encrusted sand, the roar of the high tide, the backwash, the undertow scrambling to pull back the lace, which the tide has left on the beach. It is the salt air I wish to feel on my cheek. I can't feel it here. Even a child knows that there is a vast chasm between voyaging on the sea and up the Nile. I have travelled up river and down the Nile, but so what? The sea is like nothing else on the planet. The boat snuggling up the deep, gulls squatting on the low breeze, the salt in the air, the sight of another boat—all this has a different feel about it. And what when the sea boils over, water foaming over the stern, the skyline inclined and tilted, as the sea bucks and rears, and the boat dips and then keels over, at one with the turmoil beneath?

The sea demands passion. I think now I understand what Father meant when he said that you become a seafarer only when you are one with the timbre of the boat. Two years at al Azhar and my uncle Asturlabi called me and said my father wanted me back for some months. I thought it was bad news at first—the kind a son always fears to hear about his parents. No, my Uncle said, I think he wants to take you on an enterprise. I was barely eighteen then. But things had been arranged by Uncle. I got money and a guide (already paid for), became a part of a caravan, till I reached the mouth of the Gulf and then sailed down to Oman.

After a gap of seven years, Father was looking none the worse. His hair was as grizzled as ever , though the beard was greyer. I just gazed at him, at a loss for words. His delight at seeing me was apparent and after a hearty meal he told me that we would be on ship for the best part of a year. We were going to Africa (we called it 'Zanj') and from there to Cochin, sailing up the coast past Calicut and Cranganore and coastal Gujarat to Hormuz and then further up the Red Sea. It was a good ship, the *Nakhuda,* the owner was known to my father and the payment was good. You will never get a chance like this again, he told me. What happens to my education, I asked. There is enough time to learn, he answered. I took you as a child to Hindustan—that was ten years back. You need to see it again—and Africa is another world awaiting you. See the world. After I am gone, who is going to show it to you?

I am not about to relate the tale of my travels, though this is a time to look back. The entire ship was manned by Omanis, with a sprinkling of other Arabs. Years after this voyage, when I went under the captainship of Ibn Majid himself, to Sidon and Tyre, I first learnt of the Arab suspicion of the sea, the same Arabs who were to later bring the square lateen sail to the Mediterranean and enrich navigation, as later we did with the astrolabe. The Governor of Syria had asked permission from the second Caliph, the great Umar, if he could attack Cyprus by sea. The island was so damn near the Syrian coast, he said, that you could hear the Cypriot dogs bark, and their roosters crow. He couldn't have exaggerated further to get the nod from the desert-bound Umar. Umar was very wary of the deep and consulted someone who knew the sea. Umar's adviser in this regard got the blues, and to get over them he started philosophizing—ships are but tiny dots on the vast ocean, that kind of stuff. All that a ship can encounter here is the blue of the heavens and the blue of the sea. The sea's calm is heart-breaking for the sailor and the sea's stormy mood is even worse, it brings death too close—or things of this sort. He added for good measure that a man on the ocean is like an insect on a sliver of wood. Umar wrote to the Governor to drop the idea as he couldn't trust his soldiers 'in the accursed bosom of the sea'. So dogs kept barking and the hens cackled on in Cyprus undisturbed by Mu'awiyah, the Syrian Governor and his lust for conquest.

My father was a bit surprised that I didn't know fairly elementary things about a ship, for instance the categories of the crew. I knew that the captain of the ship was called Rubban or Mu'allim, the man who knew his stars and his astrolabe, and had a good knowledge of the winds. And through experience he knew the shallows where a ship would get stuck. There was the Tandel, the chief of the khalasis or sailors. The Nakhoda-khashab supplied firewood and helped in unloading the cargo; the Bhandari was in charge of the stores; the Panjari was the look-out from his perch on top of the mast, a post that my father held in his youth. It was his job to sight land and pirates or an approaching dark cloud and warn the Mu'allim. There was even a man whose special task was to throw out the water in case of a leak. I was treated as an ordinary sailor or Kharweh, who furled the sails—diver when need be, leak-stopper, and one who freed the anchor when it got stuck.

Next to the fear of storms and shallows, the fear of pirates was all pervasive. The Indian pirates were the worst. Their ships were lighter and faster than sailing ships. There were occasions when they had as many as forty oars, often rowed by strong Abyssinian slaves. They even had fire-throwers or naffatun, as we called them.

We encountered them only once. The sea was choppy that evening and the wind strong. The look-out on the mast, the Panjari spotted them. Two similar boats far apart, with a phalanx of rowers, he shouted. The waves were high and obstructed our view. The helmsman started shouting back, asking for directions. A call to arms was given by the Rubban and spears were handed over to each of us. We brandished them and shouted, and the slanting light glinted off our blades and must have been visible to them. However, they were gaining on us only marginally and the Rubban told us not to be too bothered. They would soon tire, and moreover, with approaching nightfall, they'd give up. But we kept a look out at night, none of us slept, and we weren't allowed to talk. The question which bothered me for some days was, what if we didn't have a strong tail wind?

With the horizon clear at dawn, we gave thanks to Allah on bended knees. We made up for our silence during the night. For the next few days the veterans among us plagued us with stories about pirates, how they slashed and robbed and threw you in the sea. At our first port on the coast of Gujarat, we were congratulated for slipping through their tentacles so easily. 'Allah has been kind to you, Allah has been kind,' they said.

CAIRO

# the perfumer and his dream

ॐ

That a dream could disrupt one's life was not something the perfumer, Saleem al Attar, could adjust to. Perhaps he had not thought of it this way, namely that his life could be turned on its head by as ephemeral and insubstantial a thing as a dream. Reflection was not his strong suit. The dream appeared, as dreams always do, an image moving across the eyes and merging into another. Yet it had pursued him, slowly taking on a haunting character of its own. He had seen this woman naked—arms, shoulders, neck and the beautiful oval face. The eye had refused to register anything below, as if a moral filter had come in between. He had put his arms around her saying I want to . . . after that the words were missing. Her words were clear: 'The more the better.' He had woken up, his hand on his crotch.

The face in the dream stalked him—the face and the naked shoulders. He cursed himself later. If he had only woken up a little later, her whole body would have been unsheathed, for ever his to recall. As things now stood, that which had not been revealed, how could it be recalled? If this half-dream could grip him thus, what would it have been like if the entire thing had been allowed to unwind from the dark cellars from where dreams emanate. The obsession gripped him—that face had to be real. He would encounter it in some shadowy street, while walking around the citadel, or in that candlestick souk, named thus not because they made candles there but because it was so dark even during the day that shop owners had to burn candles at noon.

The belief took an unshakeable hold on him. Some day he would catch a glimpse of that face, that mouth which had said 'the more the better'. Love, kisses, embraces, whatever it was, she had desired more of it. He wanted the dream to recur. What is more, he wanted the dream to turn flesh. He paid scant attention to customers now, stared at women, his eyes drilling a hole into their veils. While crossing streets he stumbled into people, got almost overrun by a horse carriage. Often when he bumped into pedestrians and then shambled off shamefacedly, people would stare at his retreating figure, thinking he was drunk or mad. He started ill treating his alarmed wife. She thought someone was practising black magic on her husband. Who knew? He kept away from her at night and on the rare occasions when he did come to her, he performed with such fury that she didn't know what had got into him. He was restless in his sleep and muttered to himself, traits he hadn't exhibited earlier.

She tried stratagems to ward off the evil eye. Nothing worked. Her friends started enquiring about her husband. Why do you ask, she would question them, in return. He was in perfect good health, by God's grace. Business was good. People had not turned away as yet from perfumes. But her friends wouldn't meet her eye and turned away slightly embarrassed, even as they tried to allay her anxieties. Of course he was in fine spirits. They were just making casual enquiries. Was it a crime to ask about his health?

People were now talking of the way he was staring at

*keki n. daruwalla*

women—'as if his hands were itching to rip off the veil'! Ya Allah! the women listening to this gossip would exclaim, carrying their hands to their hearts. 'God keep us from the evil eye, whosoever it may belong to.' There were gibes too. 'The stench from his heart will overpower the aroma of his perfumes.' 'I think he is fed up of his wife. Before the year is out there will be a second marriage in that house.'

He needed to confide in someone, but he didn't have friends close enough. This kind of a story you could only relate in jest, probably during a drinking bout. But he didn't drink. He envied those who did. Those wretches barely out of al Azhar, those dregs from Oman and Asyut quaffed down large draughts every second day and here he was nearing forty without having tasted anything forbidden, not opium, not wine. Thank heaven for those escapades with whores or I'd have nothing to show when it came to enjoying the good life, he thought. Then he got his first summons from the Muhtasib. He had quaked. What could have brought this on his head? The soldier who took him there was dismissed by a wave of the Muhtasib's hand. So was the servant who had brought in the narguile. Taking a long puff, his back resting against the boulders piled around the wall, the great man ignored him for a few minutes.

'How do you make perfumes?'

'The way everyone does.'

'Tell me.'

This is not what he has called me for, thought al Attar. The Muhtasib perhaps wants to get this out of the way. He didn't know where to start and while he was dithering the great man added 'al Kindi talks of a hundred and seven ways of making perfume. Which is your way?'

'About al Kindi I know very little though I come from a family that has been in this rosewater business for two centuries. My grandfather visited Damascus, the greatest centre of perfumes, as your honour obviously knows. He visited Jur and Sabur in Persia, also well known for their perfumeries. I will explain what we do.'

He started from the beginning—the steam oven for the distillation of rose petals; the hearth or kur, bellows or minfakh and crucible or butaqah, the box in which rose petals were spread, layer on layer. He went on detailing the entire process—till finally one gathered the distillate in phials, the qarurah, or flasks, the qananni. The Muhtasib, he noticed, had lost interest, and but for the narguile might have fallen asleep.

'For a perfumer you are an enigma. That's what people say. Your heart stinks like a dead rat floating in a drain. It is they who say it. I've added nothing of my own. I am merely informing you about your reputation.'

It was not the most auspicious start to a conversation. Attar cowered, cringed and acted indignant by turns, but the Muhtasib knew what he wanted. 'Women don't feel safe with you. They say your looks seem to undress them.'

'Can women be undressed so easily? If that were so, half the women in the city would be roaming around naked.' He was surprised at his own audacity.

'Are perfume sellers going to address the Muhtasib of Cairo thus?' He clapped his hands and two men came in, daggers tucked under their girdles. They waited for a sign from the Muhtasib but the great man kept an impassive expression on his face, concentrating on his narguile, as it were. With a slight shake of his head he indicated the door to his servants. They went out obediently. 'The women of Husseyniya are saying that a genie has got into you. You know the punishment I could visit on you?'

'Don't mention it, Muhtasib, I am your servant.'

'Have you ever watched, from a hilltop, people moving about below?'

'There are no mountains in the valley of the Nile, Your Honour.'

'It is a good sight, Perfumer. The people below look tiny. A cross, that is what I had in mind for you. When you are crucified and nailed atop a gate or something equally tall, so that the people can see you (but not smell you—for your flesh will putrefy), you will have a lot of time on your nailed hands. You'll be able to observe urchin and pedestrian gazing up in awe at the heights you have obtained.'

'Whatever the Muhtasib commands, I am ready to do.'

That was more like it. But he was still not happy. This al Attar was too frank, and the wretch had seen through his game, namely that he was after something. That people of the ilk of the perfumer should be able to see right to the heart of the web he was always spinning, did not reassure him. It would be in the fitness of things to dismiss the fellow from his presence for the day. Keep the bastard in suspense for a while.

'You may go today. I will send for you some other time.'

But the perfumer was now on his knees. 'No, no my Lord, enough of this—whatever you want, say it now. I won't be able to stand another meeting.' But that is precisely the point. I want meetings frequently, said the Muhtasib. Al-Attar had started fearing that he would be asked to put a dagger through someone. What could one say about the demands of the great? But slowly, the great spider started moving onto the outer reaches of his gossamer web. How would he sniff out a polytheist with that perfumer's nose of his, he was asked. Polytheist? exclaimed the poor man aghast. Yes, and apostates, added the great man.

'Polytheists? Apostates? I hardly know what they mean, Muhtasib. Surely you have mistaken me for someone else.'

'No, al Attar—I think I should call you al Itr. That suits you better. It is my job, as the upholder of the city's morals to keep an eye on polytheists and thieves and homosexuals.'

'And what about pimps and prostitutes, my Lord?'

'Don't be cheeky, Perfumer. You could pay for this with your life. I am far too lenient with you. The whole trouble is, people take advantage of my kindness.'

He was not being pompous, thought the perfumer. The fellow had smiled sardonically when he had mentioned his kindnesses. People who knew themselves so well could not be trifled with, he thought. The Muhtasib now moved slowly to the inner core of his concentrics. How was it possible for one man to uphold the morals of an entire city? Who would keep the heretics in check and those long-bearded, long-robed Sufis who danced on the streets and drugged themselves with opium? God knew one had trouble enough keeping shop owners in line and seeing that they didn't profiteer or indulge in usury or use the wrong weights. Now and then you chopped off a usurious hand and the bazaar got the message. But intellectuals, polytheists (one led to the other), they were not easy to handle. And foreigners—it was so easy to lose sight of them, someone from the Khaleej or even Asyut—that hellhole from which all fanatics came. One couldn't be too careful. If you wanted to pin down a man, a churner of the trouble pot, one needed to know who he was, where he was most of the time, whom he met, whom he ate with, sang and danced and bedded with. How could one administer otherwise? One wasn't going to get all this data in a dream after all. One got such information from good, loyal citizens, like al Attar, may Allah preserve people. And that is how, when al Attar, in the first flush of nervous excitement, mentioned those non-praying unbelievers from Oman and Asyut, he found that the Muhtasib already knew about them.

But the dream did not let go. People who saw him so unsettled thought he should seek the blessings of a saint. They spoke to their wives, who spoke to al Attar's wife. Saints, he asked with contempt when she brought the subject up rather timorously, where are the saints? They are all in heaven, woman! And why in God's name should I run to a saint? What have these friends of yours been telling you? Do you feel there is something wrong with me?

Heaven forbid, she answered. But who can deny the existence of saints in the city? After all, the shrine of al Hussein is here. People talk with great respect of Tahir ibn Illyas; and there is Ali Hasan 'Zulm' who is all the while to be found near the shrine.

The fellow would be doling out talismans and amulets to keep off the evil eye, for a price of course. If that face he had seen in the dream had something to do with magic or the evil eye, he would rather have the evil eye. Ibn Illyas? Where had he heard the name? Didn't the Muhtasib mention him? He remembered the other one also, Ali Hasan. The man had scourged himself or got himself scourged and bore some marks of the lashing on his back. The richer classes kept away from him, in part because of his violent temper, but he had a big following among the demi monde.

Yes, on second thoughts he could do with some advice. He had tried prayers and they hadn't helped. He had put faith in his daily visits to the mosque, but his mind wandered even as he knelt. What he couldn't stand was the mind haring off to the dream, especially during prayers. That was sin. At times the woman in the dream acquired a look as haunted and out of focus as his own. As if by accident he stumbled into the dervish one evening. Tahir and his followers were returning from one of their congregations. He followed them. Because of the rain the followers started dispersing. The perfumer followed him till the door and when the dervish turned around and saw a stranger's face, he asked him what brought him there, and took him into his lodgings.

Tahir, who lived alone, got his own narguile ready and offered his guest a smoke, which the perfumer declined. When Tahir finally asked him his problem, the perfumer found that it is one thing to barge into someone's house and quite another to explain why he was there. He was troubled by a dream, he said, but try as Tahir did, he couldn't get him to divulge more.

When Tahir started on his rather rambling monologue, he sounded a bit incoherent to the perfumer. 'A dream is like a genie—it inhabits you, lives with you. It can disappear suddenly the way nestlings fly away once they grow up. A night can't be without dreams just as a cemetery can't be without a corpse. Formerly we had *kahin*s, interpreters of dreams. All dreams are funny things. I have heard it said that Mamar bin Muhammad al Jauhari offered Ibn Tulun a partnership in his flax trade. Then Tulun dreamt of sucking marrow from bones. His kahin told him that bones were leftovers, thrown generally to dogs. The trade in flax did not promise much. So Ibn Tulun decided to withdraw from the partnership and whatever money he had put in the venture, he gave in charity to the poor.'

'A dream shakes a man up because you are alone with your dream. The dream knows what it has revealed and what it is hiding. You know only half, or even less, and don't forget that the two of you are alone with each other in the middle of the night. Moreover, while you are thinking about it, it is already disappearing from your memory. The sad part is that fearful dreams are remembered while happier ones sink through memory like water through a sieve. Don't get distraught, Son. You are a perfumer who extracts essences. If you had to

*keki n. daruwalla*

extract the essence of a dream and put it into a sentence, as you put perfume in a vial, what would you say?'

He paused for an answer and when none came he said rather theatrically—'To sleep here and wake up there.' He took a long puff on his narguile and resumed. 'One should not worry about dreams. The humours have a lot to do with it, as the Holy Book itself tells us. If black bile prevails over everything else in your body, you will see horrors and defilements. If phlegm has the upper hand you will see whiteness and waters—most of it turbulent. If yellow bile dominates, you will get visions of fire, blood and hands, smeared with yellow. And if blood is strong and dominating, you will see wine and lutes and pipes. Lutes can appear otherwise also. Man dreams of a tunbur or a lute being played in a mosque and immediately knows he has sinned. He prays, fasts, averts his eyes from women passing by; and he stops going to concubines. If he could help it he would even stop drinking, but that as you would know, is never possible. The angel, Siddiqun, sends such dreams so that people can go back to the straight path. Though a time comes in the life of a realised Sufi when he transcends the straight as well as the crooked paths. But this will confuse you. You have not told me what bothers you. Is it a voice you have heard which disturbs you? Or is it some act you have performed in a dream which troubles you? Dreams come with different veils on different faces. You could find yourself naked near a shrine. Or see the face of a holy man simultaneously with your own naked figure in a mirror. But such visions do not necessarily speak of abominations. They can mean different things. Satan can also plant some dreams to lead you astray. If you want help, one must know why you are so upset. Since you won't tell and it is getting late, we should meet another day.'

# TAUFIQ

# the whiplash mystic

༄

The voyage to Hindustan is in the past. Now, in this packed room, we are facing Ali Hasan who is in full flight, talking of dog feet and mutilated visages. 'Have any of you, in a dream, been grabbed by men with disfigured faces and dogs' feet?' No one answered. People seemed too befuddled. Ali Hasan chose to respond himself. 'I can tell you the answer. No. You haven't dreamt anything like it. Can you tell me why?' The fellow was getting really theatrical. No one answered. 'Because,' continued Ali Hasan, 'if any of you had dreamt that, you wouldn't be here. You would have been dead!'

All three of us were supposed to meet at Ali Hasan's, but Murad was late. Ehtesham and I were on time and had been shown in. Ehtesham had not been feeling comfortable. Neither Tahir ibn Illyas nor the historian Abu Khalil had been able to satisfy him. The warnings of the Muhtasib still hung over him like a cloud. Tahir, while encouraging him in his art, had almost predicted that the effort would come to no good. Abu Khalili, while encouraging him, had been unable to tell him what to do. The old man was like an angel who had lost his way in a den where sorcerers were sharpening their spells and robbers their knives. Murad had suggested we go to Ali Hasan 'Zulm'. He was known for having himself scourged once.

Murad was insistent that we go at least two hours before the evening prayer so that we could get a long sitting with him alone. Later his 'majlis' would get too crowded. He himself turned up late, by which time the fairly large-sized room was packed with bazaaris, haberdashers, hashish smokers and the like. Ehtesham and I had gone with a gift—a stick with a silver knob. We were shown into his room and were instantly confronted with a whirlwind of aromas—rose and jasmine and other sweet scents, which my rather indelicate nose could not identify. A casket of ebony wood stood open in front of 'Zulm', the whiplash mystic. And with him in a corner stood the Perfumer, the one who had made it his life's business to find out how often we offered prayers.

Ali Hasan Zulm did not take to our presence kindly at first, till we advanced and deposited our gift with a lowly bow. He liked people kissing his hands but we refrained. Slowly his acolytes started filing in behind us. As they bowed and sat down, Ali Hasan started talking.

'As I was telling this man'—he was addressing all of us now, rather than just the perfumer—'dreams are as false as women. Which means more dreams are false than true. So don't pay too much heed to them. When you are asleep, that is the time the Devil is on the prowl. There are dreams of the flesh which need ablutions immediately afterwards. To sleep in that clammy wetness is a sin.

'Dreams can be warnings from Satan, as he tries to strike terror in your hearts. Equally false are such dreams where you see yourself today, but looking twenty years younger. What kind of a mirror is this, which has erased twenty years of your life? What mirror is this, which has taken you back into the past? But if instead of women, animals appear in dreams and start speaking, they speak the truth. An animal, unlike a woman, is incapable of a lie. The dead, too, cannot

*keki n. daruwalla*

dissemble. Similarly, where you actually live has a lot to do with your dreams. If you live in the desert and dream of hot winds, things are going to worsen for you. If you dream of snow in winter in Alburz, you are again in trouble. If you dream of snow in the valley, it is good. It could mean that the rivers will water your fields.

'There are instances where the signature of death is visible in a dream, as clear as if death had put its seal on a document. If you walk southwards, surrounded by dead people, it signals death. If you are tied up by a black woman dressed in red, who drags you south, then too it is a sign of coming death.

'I have related these dreams so that we know when the angel of death hovers over you. A friend of mine here has had a bad dream, which I haven't been able to extract from him as yet. The Unanis, whom the wretched Franks call Ionians, were good at deciphering dreams. They were good at defying death too. The trouble with the Unanis was they knew too much. Allah, in his wisdom, wants everyone to be kept within the confines laid down according to His will. The Greeks, as you know, had pagan gods and goddesses. As if divinity also could be sub-divided into sexes! A divinity with breasts and milk in the breasts! Allah have mercy on us. I have sympathy for the Unanis. That, wise as they were, they will roast in hell, is not a happy thought. But they had goddesses of war and love and must have had one for disease as well. The Indians have a goddess for pox! Can you imagine—a fissure god, a fistula god! The Unanis couldn't care what Allah's will was. They hadn't even heard of the one and only Lord, because what I am going to tell you happened hundreds of years before the Prophet (peace be unto him) was born.

'The knowledge of the Unanis became so knowledgeable— I mean so profound—that they started unravelling the mysteries of the universe. Now only Allah in his wisdom has the right to reveal these mysteries—for instance, why night is night and day is day. But the Unanis even got to know when death would knock at their door. Anticipating a visit from the angel of death, one of them made preparations to forestall the inevitable. When the angel of death arrived at his door, this scholar had made nine other human beings exactly like himself. All look-alikes! Same face, same hair, same clothes. They stood in a line as if it was a reception committee! And the angel of death, invisible sword in hand, fire streaming from his eyes, was foxed. Which one does he take with him? Can he go to Allah later and say I made a mistake! He can't. This is not some Muhtasib confronting the Sultan and telling him, 'Sorry King, I have made an error.' Nothing can be allowed to go wrong in Allah's scheme of things. Which one out of the ten does he take with him? Which one does he send to hell? For, it was hell that he had to go to, anyone conceited enough to replicate himself.

'The angel of death walked past the ten and back like the Sultan does when he inspects his swordsmen before battle. The moment of death, pre-ordained and written in the great book of destiny, was passing by. If the moment passed, the arrogant Unani could become immortal! After all, in the book of destiny, you can't have two death-moments written against a person. The entire cosmic scheme of things, immaculately prepared by Allah no less, would wobble. Doomsday would have to be postponed! The accursed Unani would have been the first to cheat death!

'The fire went out of the angel's eyes and they became soft. The permanent frown that squatted on the angel's mouth was banished and replaced with a smile. The arrogance of certitude departed. His shoulders drooped. "I accept defeat," he announced. The angel of death said, addressing all the ten, "I cannot but admire what you have done, these nine other

*keki n. daruwalla*

beings you have so dexterously created. In our chronicle above we have no account of them, and so I cannot take them away. Your creations are perfect. I have witnessed perfection at a human's hand today."

'The main culprit, the magical Unani, creator of the other nine, tried hard to remain impassive. Still he could not help a serpent-of-a-smile slide out towards the corners of his mouth. Only one out of the ten had displayed this imperceptible smile—a smile of pride and satisfaction, of arrogance in his own prowess, which had been certified by the angelic orders themselves! The angel's eyes lit up like two hidden rubies suddenly uncovered. And at once the angel of death sucked the breath out of him and bottled it, grabbed his soul, put it into his knapsack and hurled it to hell.'

Listeners gaped at each other, struck with the wonder of it all. No one had the gumption to ask him what happened to the other nine . . .

But Ehtesham has changed. As for Taufiq, he has left his narrative dangling in mid-air. Some chronicles remain unfinished like history itself, or like the present, which like a river, never seems to stop flowing. Time, the obstreperous narrator, takes over. Ehtesham has devoted his energies to beautifying manuscripts, including the Holy Qoran. He is earning good money and the Muhtasib is off his back for the moment. The perfumer is getting into trouble. Tahir ibn Ilyas has become untraceable.

Murad has suggested that they meet Tahir again. Why must we meet him, asks Ehtesham, there's nothing to be got from him. 'One never goes to Sufis to get something out of them,' says Murad. Ehtesham counters, 'Then why go there at all, to see their scruffy faces? Some of them don't wash their armpits, you know.' Murad says, 'Their love of Allah could rub off on you.'

'And the aroma from their armpits,' says his friend. All the same they go in search of him and Tahir's acolytes tell them he is missing since the last new moon. They don't know where he has gone. Their explanations are of no help. 'Who knows about Sufis? Their moods are like whirlwinds and their destinations lie in their dreams.' Very helpful.

The Muhtasib has also been on Tahir's track. That someone should vanish without his knowledge is not something he can easily stomach. The informers tell him no one would murder Sufis; another says they could die of starvation or an overdose of hashish. A third says he could have fallen in a well. The consensus is he must have gone on a pilgrimage—Karbela or Najaf. The Perfumer gets out of it neatly. 'I am supposed to track presences, not absences.' When pressed further by the dumb-struck Muhtasib, he answers, 'Tahir was not my responsibility. He was neither a polytheist nor an apostate!'

# the perfumer's proposal

❧

The perfumer had not had any luck. He considered the trip to Ali Hasan 'Zulm' a disaster. The man had talked on and on and had ended his ill-omened peroration with death. What had all this to do with his dream? What was the point in going to these dervishes? What could they tell you? Who was interested in the angel of death or the angel of dreams, al Siddiqun, or whatever the fellow's name was? Why did he go to him at all? He couldn't have told him his dream, surely, and he didn't want that dream exorcised, if indeed dreams could be exorcised. He wanted it to be turned into reality. He wished to see that face once more—or rather, the woman naked till the shoulders, and surely naked below it if only he had the courage to look that vision in the face, or rather in the torso and below.

He hadn't liked the crowd, hashish smokers and people on the fringe. Some of them had worn dirty clothes. They stank. He at least smelled good. Trust a perfumer to smell good. Once home, he had cursed all the dervishes of the world and slapped his wife, for advising him to curry favour with 'saints', before a fitful sleep overcame him.

Business next day was desultory. Women wandered in, sniffed at the bottles and went their way without buying. As the afternoon wore on two women came in. He was not surprised at the difference in their attire and the quality and texture of their hijabs. Obviously one of them was a domestic or a sort of a housekeeper whom women from better families took along with them. The women of nobility never stirred out except to attend weddings or circumcisions or things like that. The young mistress stood at a distance while the maid pottered around the caskets, lifting the heavy stoppers of the bottles, which were placed at the counter, and carried them to her mistress. She lifted her veil to sniff at a stopper and al Attar saw how she puckered her nose in distaste at the scent. She pointed at a particular bottle but the maid couldn't get it right and brought the wrong one. 'Habiba, I want the one near the jar!' When Habiba brought the bottle, her mistress sniffed at it and then finding it good, inhaled deeply in a sort of rapture, lifting her veil and splashing a little on her face.

'I'll buy this one,' she said turning to the perfumer. Seeing the astonishment on his face, she thought it was because she had lifted her veil for an instant. But the perfumer stood transfixed, for that oval face, those dark eyes with the curved eyebrows and the long lashes belonged to the woman in the dream. Except that this one wore clothes and a hijab to boot.

~

In the perfumer's shop there is a stuffed civet cat snarling at you from the counter. A stuffed wolf waits for attention on the floor, very much in the shadows to the rear. Business before Ramadan is surprisingly brisk this year. What have aromas to do with fasting? He isn't bothered with such things as long as his vials sell—thick, squat bottles with more glass than distillate in them

He has followed Habiba once and knows where she lives. He has loitered around the place but never managed to spot

Zainab. The good thing about Habiba is that she keeps her face unveiled when she goes to the market. It is a bit tough to bicker and haggle and bully with your face covered and the words turning indistinct as they squeeze past the netting. She is surprised one day at being accosted by him in the market but he makes it seem he has met her by chance. The next time he addresses her as sister and gives her one of his squat perfume bottles, the concentrate so strong that half the street can inhale the aroma. One evening he lands up at the house with a wooden casket containing a hundred small bottles. Habiba is amazed at the effrontery but can do little, for he knows her name by now and if he calls it out loud, what will Zainab and her mother think? She forgets to bolt the gate as she goes in timorously to report that a perfumer has come to the door selling his wares. Perfumer? Why here? Why is he at our door of all places? Does he know you, Habiba? Zainab wants to sample the perfumes but is afraid of her mother, who has become cross all of a sudden. It is unusual, this surliness. Ask him if he wants to be cursed by an old woman? she says in a shrill voice. You'll bless me, Mother, once you allow your daughter to inhale these perfumes, al Attar calls out. The old lady whispers to Habiba, how does he know of Zainab?

'We've been to his shop sometime back, Mother.'

The perfumer has squatted on the grass now and has spread a sheet on which he is arranging his bottles methodically. The gate is still unbolted and urchins from the street step in and stand around the casket gingerly, sniff the bottles tentatively and giggle. The old lady has had enough of it by now. She screams at him to get out of the house or she'll call the Muhtasib's men. But Attar is unmoved. 'I have not come just to sell perfumes, Mother.'

'What else have you come for then? Ya Allah, this visit from an unknown scoundrel, and the holy month of Ramadan so near!'

'I have come to ask for your daughter's hand.'

This is too much even for Habiba. A torrent of abuse flows from her. People gather outside the house, the incident slowly turning into a scandal, even as the neighbours push the perfumer out. The call for the evening prayers saves him from getting belaboured.

The beating takes place the next day when Ehtesham goes to the shop and thrashes him, and hurls the stuffed civet cat at his bottles. He announces to the crowd that has gathered that the perfumer is a mukhbir, an informer.

~

Meanwhile, Ramadan arrives with a cannon burst and the town-crier announcing the Muhtasib's message to the Cairenes. 'By the Sultan's orders and in the words of his servant, the Muhtasib, let it be known men and women of al Qahira that the moon of the holy month of Ramadan has been sighted. Rely on prayer and fasting and you will find that Allah is all-forgiving. Anyone seen eating or drinking in the streets during the day will no doubt kindle Allah's anger, but with that will also invite whips from the Muhtasib's men. This edict will apply to the faithful and also to Copt and Yahudi. If they have to eat, let their doors be shut so that no one sees them. Be warned, men of al Qahira!'

This hasn't happened before, says Zainab, an order to keep fasts. As if any true Muslim would not keep one! Habiba adds her two bit. 'Next he may ask us to do our ablutions before prayers!'

But mother and daughter frown at her. She is not in favour since the incident of the perfumer. How come he knew her? How come she let him in, the mother had kept asking.

Summer comes to al Qahira like Allah's qahar or scourge. And Ramadan came in the heat of summer when the city itself takes on the colour of the desert and the cracked-skin look of drought. One evening, Zainab had just served Abu Khalil his evening meal with which the fast is broken—dates and milk, bread and meat—and as she was coming down the narrow stairs, Ehtesham ul Haq took her hands in his and kissed them passionately. Zainab merely gasped, whether in terror or delirious pleasure he had no means of knowing. But she had made no frantic effort to withdraw her hands or hasten down the stairs, and that gave him hope.

*keki n. daruwalla*

# mother and asyut

&

Hypocrisy did not come easy to Ehtesham. He was pious in his own way—kept all the fasts of Ramadan, and as long he had been in Asyut prayed regularly, at least at dawn and dusk. If ever he chanced to think about it, he was terrified of divine retribution. The semitic religions had turned God into such a punishing Headmaster that it was a problem coming to terms with him. Sin, damnation and the Day of Judgement with its yawning fire-pits—all this became a part of the calculus of the soul.

He hadn't met his mother in two years now. He didn't want to think of Zainab the whole day long, while ostensibly fasting. You did not just stay away from food and water. You were supposed to keep away from lust and lechery, and yes, gluttony. You couldn't fast during the day and hog at night. A wet dream could be an abomination, a calamity during Ramadan. He quietly went off to Asyut—took him over a week by camel-cart, stayed with his mother there, saw the tears well up in her eyes, found that the lines ran deeper across her face since he had last seen her, noticed how particularly well-dug was that one wrinkle that ran from her cheekbone down to the corner of her mouth—more crevice than wrinkle. Otherwise she looked small and spry as ever.

The house looked dustier, the street in front of her house dirtier than the streets in Cairo. Yet it was different. This was home. If a dervish danced here or a madman whirled around supplicating Allah for some favour or the other, or calling upon Him to destroy evil, you would know the man, or at least the street he belonged to, the mosque he went to. Everyone seemed nearer to everyone here, though he sensed the distance between himself and the others. That's what moving out of town does. Ehtesham fasted and prayed at the mosque, the same one where his father had taken him as a child for his first public prayer. (He remembered how nervous he had been—kept looking around and the moment he saw the others kneeling he had followed suit.) He took the goats to pasture, as he had done as a child, always on the bank of the Nile or around his mother's lands—two acres thick with date palm. And he talked to her about a blind woman, her brother Abu Khalil and her servant Habiba.

Of course his mother knew Abu Khalil. Wasn't his wife from Asyut? Her lands lay adjacent to your father's fields, she told him. I had to sell those fields since I couldn't look after them. She died young, his wife, and Abu Khalil never married again. Not that he hadn't fallen for someone. It was his wife's widowed sister herself, very comely looking. But then he decided to send her to Asyut along with his son, who was not all there. This fever had got hold of his son, Khalil, and travelled to his brain and left him a bit wonky. He died a few years back.

But Asyut was Asyut. People still treated him like a fifteen-year-old boy. Someone or the other was sure to waylay him and ram some advice down his throat. His school teacher talked to him at length on the fickleness of fortune. There was that religious scholar, he narrated, who gave a call to the faithful from a minaret in the evening. Next morning he was hanged for having killed a woman who was carrying his seed. The Maulvi met him and smiled almost involuntarily before he became self-conscious and his expression turned severe. What are you doing in Cairo? Are you earning enough money? Are you earning anything at all or still sponging on your mother? If you are making a living there, are you sending anything back home? Do you have a job? Why don't you take your mother with you? Must she alone look after your father's date palms? Are you through with al Azhar or have you left half-way as many of these wastrels are doing these days? In our days if we did a thing like that our backsides would have been caned till the skin went north and the buttocks went south. The cleric had given him a cold look and walked on, apparently uninterested in his protestations.

Alone with his mother, he would find himself tongue-tied, not knowing what to say to her. Had al Azhar done this to him? Talking of his earlier studies or even of al Qahira itself was like talking to her about some other planet. Just a few years back he had been able to gossip with her the whole day. He had been so enthusiastic then, had described to her the sights of Cairo, the citadel known throughout as the Burj, its height, its giant halls, its vaulted arches, its chandeliers. Now after the first few days when he had talked of his friends and where he lived, there was precious little to say. What had dried up in him? He was sinking into sleep, or was it stupor, one afternoon, and almost wearily he let drop a word or two about Abu Khalil and his blind sister and their servant, the robust Habiba, and what a scholar this Abu Khalil was, his voice sinking into a sort of a drone as he found no response from his mother. He wasn't even sure whether he had mentioned this ever to her before or was bringing it up for the first time.

On another day, he talked of the Mamluk troops and the way they paraded their horses and how handsome they looked in their uniforms. She asked about the Sultan, may Allah keep him in good health. What would I know of the Sultan, Mother? What are you asking? The Sultan doesn't walk the streets! I know that, Son, but people must be talking about him.

'One doesn't talk about the Sultan in the public bath. One doesn't even listen to such talk, Mother. The Mukhabarat are everywhere. You would be reported. This is al Qahira, not a village like Asyut.'

'Asyut is not a village, Son. It is the biggest town in these parts as you ought to know. People from all over come to our city with their wares, pots and their pans, their textiles, their beads. And we have as many religious scholars as in al Qahira. All I wanted to know was about the well-being of the Sultan, may Allah keep him from his enemies.'

'All of us need Allah's help, Mother.'

'Yes, but he more than others. He also needs our prayers, for he has to look after the whole kingdom.'

'As far as Cairo is concerned, it is the Muhtasib who looks after it, Mother.'

'Don't say such things, Son. The Muhtasib is only a servant and can be thrown out like a fly which has drowned in milk.'

'Why are you so concerned about the Sultan, Mother? He's a Sultan of the Mamluk, he's not our Sultan.'

She put her entire palm on his mouth, her look fearful. But he wasn't deterred. 'The Mamluk don't even let us ride on horseback. I'd be killed in Cairo if I rode there.'

'Well, you ride as much as you like while you're in Asyut. But a pony, Son. Not a horse. Don't forget our status. The lowly must always crouch low.'

He was not as lowly as his mother thought him to be, he told her. He had a friend who had Asturlabi as an uncle.

He owned a great shop and knew big seamen. May Allah bless him, she said. Have you ever been to the mosque where Husain's head is buried? Some people say it is in al Qahira, and some say it is in Damascus. Have you ever prayed there, my son?

'Now Mother, what brought that into your head. Don't you see it is a bad omen?'

'The Imam's head can't be a bad omen, my son, even though severed. It is blessed. Always remember that.'

'That's not the thing, Mother. It's a bad omen, don't you see? I talk about my friend and his uncle and you talk about the Imam's severed head.'

'It slipped through, my son. One can't keep a check on one's thoughts. As you grow older it is your thoughts which speak. The words only follow like the Sultan's cup bearer. If Hussain's name has been spoken it is a good omen for the man, not a bad one. You don't seem to understand.'

They both did not seem to understand each other, he reflected. Then it was time to return and his mother let drop a remark, almost as casually as he had. That blind lady with such an uncanny power of knowing who is at her door (Did I tell you all that, Mother? Yes you did), she who has that very scholarly brother, does she have a daughter as well? Yes, didn't I tell you that, Mother? No, you did not. But he saw her smiling, and as he left, he noticed that though she wasn't crying, her cheek was as wet as a dog's nose.

# blazons and the tree of pearls

*The Mamluks came to power when Egypt had the terrible misfortune to have been actually ruled by a woman—the Queen of the dead Sultan, al-Salih. How could Egypt tolerate this insult? Queens who rule, don't last in Egypt, as the great Hatshepsut, she of the magnificent Hathor temple, found to her cost. Her nephew , who would become the great Warrior-King Thutmose, killed her and then set himself the mammoth task of erasing her from all the frescoes portraying her in her own temples. He broke her canopic jars, destroyed her cartouches, lest she bounce back in afterlife to the throne of upper and Lower Egypt, to the symbols of the lotus and the papyrus which adorned the crown. The most frenzied concerns of the Egyptian nobility centred on afterlife for itself and denial of it to one's enemies. (Erasing, not just the present, but also the future, was Thutmose's contribution to the philosophy of self preservation.). But we must start from the beginning—chronology sits heavy on the eastern mind.*

*Unknown to his own people (and perhaps to himself) the last Sultan of the Ayyubid dynasty died in November 1249. His wife, Shajar al-Dar, hid the fact from the world at large, in true oriental fashion. Meanwhile the Egyptian army, oblivious of their Sultan's death three months back,* took on the Crusaders at the famous battle of Al Mansura, in February of the year 1250. The banners fluttered, drums rolled and trumpets sounded in the Sultan's name. The poor crusaders never knew they had been routed by a dead king! But we must go further back in time—beginnings keep receding in the Orient.

The queen Shajar al-Dar, which means Tree of Pearls, was originally a part of the Caliph al-Mustasim's harem. The Caliph lived in Baghdad, which had yet to taste the fury of the scions of Genghiz Khan (as the Europeans call him, though we Indians know better and call him by his right name, Changez). The Caliph presented her to Najm al-Din al-Salih, the Sultan of Egypt, who married her. She ruled for several months after her husband's death till her son, the hated Turan Shah, returned from Syria where he was a governor of one of the principalities and ascended the throne. Even loved monarchs were murdered in a fairly routine manner and at short intervals those days. A hated upstart was not about to test the patience of court chroniclers. Turan Shah was murdered within two months. The Mamluks elected the Tree of Pearls as their monarch. This is where the Caliph in Baghdad (he hadn't been slaughtered till then by the Mongol hordes) came into the picture. He was loath to put his seal on the investiture to the monarchy on a woman, however beautiful and resourceful, who had once graced his harem. So they made Shajar al-Dar marry the commander of the Mamluk army, a man called Aybak. She abdicated after reigning for just eighty days following her son's death and her husband ascended the throne. After seven years or less (in 1257) Aybak made the fatal mistake of wanting to marry someone else—the princess of Mossul.

The Tree of Pearls did what angry queens around the Aegean are good at (remember Clytemnestra?). She inveigled her husband Aybak into her bed chamber, did with him what is done in bed chambers, took him to the bath where he could clean himself and there had him murdered, joining in the daggering herself. Within three days her luck ran out—Nemesis is quicker on the draw in Egypt than in Greece. Aybak's first wife (what was her name? Sapling of Sapphires? Daughter of Diamonds?) could not have been harbouring any great love for the usurper of her conjugal bed. The concubines of Aybak were also in a vengeful mood. Under instigation from the first wife, the female slaves and concubines got hold of the queen, battered her to death with their clogs and threw her body down the palace walls. The throne passed to Aybak's fifteen-year-old son. Thus was formed the Mamluk state which lasted from 1250 to 1517 AD. The Arab chronicler was perhaps more florid than truthful, when he declared that the Mamluk state was a fruit that had dropped from the branches of the Tree of Pearls.

The Mamluks were a slave oligarchy that laid down its own rules of governance and succession to power. They were not Arab—they came from the Euro-Asian steppe, mostly Kipechac Turks and Circassians and had Turkish names. They were 'white' slaves, enfranchised, from beyond the lands of Islam. It was during the Mamluk period that the great monuments had come up, that the arts flourished, calligraphy flowered, both physically and metaphorically, for manuscripts were adorned with rich floral designs. And the blazons that the important Mamluks used were magnificent, starting with the emblem of the lion used by Baybars, the toughest Mamluk sultan. Door and pulpit, lectern and bookstand were adorned with blazons. Banners, boats, tents, buildings carried them. Of course if you fell from grace, or were executed—a fairly likely possibility those days—your blazons were erased much in the same manner as Thutmose had erased the cartouche and the frescoes of Hatshepsut.

# asturlabi

৵

Taufiq gets a small note from his uncle one morning. Could he come to the house after the prayers at dusk? When he goes there he finds he has company, a tall man with a bearing that speaks of an aristocratic lineage and an aquiline nose that must have taken two hundred years of good breeding to fashion. The greeting at his uncle's is especially warm. He is hugged at the doorstep and taken in and introduced to the stranger whose name he fails to catch. (Did they mention his name at all?) His aunt Bilqees comes out and serves sherbet from a curved, long-necked flask. Taufiq thinks that if his uncle had a daughter, he would have suspected a matrimonial trap of sorts, so effusive has been his reception.

'You are going on a voyage, Son. To Zanj, Africa. It's all been arranged.'

It sinks in slowly; to be actually on ship now, not as his father's son, but in his own right! But not India. He has to hide that flicker of disappointment from registering itself on his face. His uncle must have arranged this for him. It would smack of ingratitude to let him see through this thinnest of chinks in his armour.

'A voyage is a big thing, Son, and though you have been on such trips with your father, this time you would be on your own. By Allah's will, this is a greater day than any in your life, for you meet a great seafarer and a great man.' He points to the man, tall and black-robed, seated on a divan with a drink, which Taufiq initially thinks is sherbet.

Taufiq makes his salaams, but when he wants to know the gentleman's name, the others don't hear him. He is too inhibited to speak loudly. Asturlabi asks the stranger a question. Of his many callings, which would he like to be known by?

'A map-maker.'

Taufiq cannot restrain himself.

'A map-maker! Really, Sir, I never thought I would meet one here. I thought all along that it is the Farangs who make maps. Forgive me if I am wrong.'

A cloud passes over the stranger's face. 'Franks are good at maps, it is true. Maps are for people who aren't there. We Arabs have been all over the round disc of this earth. We rely more on the stars and our reading of the meridian.'

The visitor topples back the drink and seems to lose his way. 'Where was I, what was I saying?' he asks Asturlabi.

'What you were saying but never said, was that Islam never lacked for maps. Ibn Haukal authored the *Book of Ways and Provinces*. It had more maps than written pages. Al Idrisi drew a map for the whole world for some Christian king or other.'

'A king of Sicily it was.' Taufiq is impressed. The man seems to know everything. How come, he asks? You just talked of being *there*. You must be a sailor. It is then that Asturlabi reveals who his guest is.

'This is a great day in your life, my son. You have just met the greatest sailor and reader of the stars in the world. You are in the presence of Ibn Majid.'

Ibn Majid himself! Taufiq perhaps has not ever heard of the Phoenicians and certainly never of the Argonauts. But here is a sailor, who at least in these parts is better known than any of these myths that keep wallowing around the Golden Fleece. He is the great scourer of the seas, the great reader of the stars. Taufiq finds it difficult to express himself. He talks of the honour done to him in meeting Ibn Majid.

'I never thought, Sir, that I would be lucky enough to meet so great a man. I have met you often in your books though. And it is not just sailing one is talking about. You, Sir, are the greatest astronomer and mathematician we have. They say that even when the pole star is not visible, you know where it is. To find an invisible star through the altitude of visible stars—to us this sounds like magic, Sir.'

Asturlabi intervenes, unhappy with the flattery. 'When he is in his cups, he sees more stars than all of us put together!'

Not one to be easily embarrassed by praise, Majid nevertheless wishes to deflect the conversation from him.

'Are you excited about going to Zanj? It is not the healthiest of places. No one dies a natural death in Africa, you know?'

'You are either poisoned or shot by an arrow, unless of course you are done in by an assegai,' Asturlabi pitches in. His wife looks at him in horror.

'He is right,' continues Majid. 'They get suspicious if a person dies because Allah wills it so, and his last moment has come. Haven't you read al Beruni?'

'Didn't they teach you that at al Azhar?' his uncle asks. Before he can reply, Ibn Majid quotes the historian:

'The Zanj is so barbarous that they have no notion of natural death. For them, each death is suspicious if a man has not been killed by a weapon.'

A little later they put him at ease as his aunt Bilquees serves varieties of meat and bread. Things have changed since the times of al Beruni. 'But this Ibn Batuta fellow has left too many problems for our young friend,' says Ibn Majid, laughing.

'You mean al Beruni.'

'I also mean Ibn Battuta. People didn't know whether to believe him or not, initially. He found not much good in Africa. One place he passed through—I think it was called Taghaza—he found that all the houses, and even the mosque, were made from blocks of salt. He found no roads or tracks in the desert, though I hope he was not foolish enough to expect them there. But then why write about it? At one court which he attended he found ambassadors waiting to thank the king. The king had yet to step into the chamber. But the people around were feeling very uneasy. What do these wretches want to thank the king for, he asked one of the courtiers. (The damned ambassadors were covered in blood!) The courtier told him that the previous evening the King had presented each of them with a woman slave. After that the courtier clammed up. 'Well, so what, if the King gifted them a slave?' asked Battuta. 'A slave each,' corrected the courtier. 'All right, a slave each. But why are people here so uneasy and tense?' By now the courtier had had enough. 'Haven't you got eyes? The blood you see on their robes belongs to the slaves. The ambassadors ate them up!'

The shock of the story wears off slowly. Bilquees makes protesting noises from behind the wall. Asturlabi tells Taufiq not to believe Ibn Majid. Things slowly drift back to where they were before the African ambassadors intervened. The evening goes by in a sort of a haze. He soon realizes that both gentlemen are drinking wine brought from Syria. They talk about maps . . . how it is through maps that oceans know where they slosh and mutter to themselves and winds get to know their own names as they whine over the seas. Would the monsoons know they were monsoons, were there no maps? Moot question. It is through maps that deserts know where they stand, or rather, shift. And it is through them that dreams come to know where they blow, if indeed they blow. If dreams didn't blow on the seas there wouldn't be any voyages, Son. Which of the two said that? He doesn't remember. But he recalls distinctly, later, that it was Ibn Majid who had added that a map must foreshadow trade, conquest, dream. It should look like a letter from fate, he had said. Not just lines. I am not discussing a map of Ali Baba's cave here. I am talking of carrying the flag of a country to some far corner of God's earth. That is a big venture, the kind of thing one undertakes with humility.

The great man turns to Taufiq who notices that as he goes on speaking, his voice gets softer and the eyes more and more unfocussed till it seems he is speaking to himself.

'I noticed that your reaction to Zanj was not as ebullient as it could have been. It is not Hind of course. India is different—its insect-peppered nights, its dusks glazed with the smell of flowering shrubs, the champa and the jasmine, the gnat-buzz and the hum of moths, its shallow, saucer-shaped lakes which they call jheels, their edges serrated with the croak of the bullfrog. But the Zanj is also an experience—the men dressed in feathers, the dances, drums throbbing through the night. And landfall is a sight for the angels. If you reach the coast or an island just as it is getting dark, you see the palm trees strung out like our calligraphy—the beach looking like some luminous chronicle opened in a crypt darkened with candle soot.

But Africa comes later. First we go to Sidon and Tyre. The voyage to Zanj will follow if Allah wills . . .' His voice turns softer by the minute and Taufiq has to strain his ears to get at the words. He finds himself edged out of the conversation as it drifts into memories and an exchange of notes between the old friends. Nostalgia takes centre stage. Names of friends crop up like spirits summoned by magicians with a snap of a finger or by rubbing some special ring on an occult stone. Mutual friends are recalled and rubbished or caressed with a word that speaks of decades of love. Taufiq senses the vivid presence here of years gone by; notices their ache and love for the past for which there is no appropriate word in any language.

Ibn Majid speaks softly. 'Remember Ibrahim, Iftikhar Ibrahim? Great fellow. You followed what he drew on parchment and when you reached the place you felt you had already been there last year, so vivid were his pointers. Though the way he dotted his maps with figures—that almost cost him his life.' They both laughed and almost inadvertently Taufiq asks how a map can endanger the cartographer's own life. Voyagers, yes . . . a bad map can possibly lead you into danger. Things are explained: Ibrahim signposted his maps—with elephants to mark a port where ivory was available; with a tiger to denote a forest. And he marked his own Aden with a butcher, and the butcher had the Sultan's own face! The king certainly had more blood on his hands than any practitioner of *zibbah*, that three-stroke ritual with the knife on the wind pipe, which turns meat into halal. Poor Ibrahim had to flee port and stay away till the Aden Sultan kicked the bucket.

'Now he's old, poor Ibrahim. There are not as many lanes in the sea as there are wrinkles on his cheeks. Map-makers age earlier than their maps. I've always felt that map-makers travel far, not always by boat, but also by the boat of the mind.'

It is his wife Bilquees, sitting in the adjoining room, who now butts in. 'May Allah forgive me, but I think you have had too much to drink.'

'Those who drink, they need to ask forgiveness, not you, wife. What I am trying to say is that in a map you don't see just headland or forest, but tied up in that piece of parchment is a vision. Am I sounding silly?'

*keki n. daruwalla*

'You are not. Aren't we saying the same thing?'
Ibn Majid breaks into verse:

Why must we speak on different planes?
Blessed with the self-same beloved?
Sa'adi and Qais both spoke of love
Eternal, what if both are dead?
(Scholars studied all their words—
Their passion more or less unread.)
The winepress and the vat have burst!
The liquor has gone to the head!

'The fault, my dear, is the wine's or Satan's. Thank heaven
for Satan, or the entire burden of our sins would have been
on our shoulders. Map lines are just lines of ink. They come
alive only in the hands of a voyager, a scarf of foam trailing
his boat. There is nothing to equal this delight—to find on the
ground what is written on parchment—promontory, shoulder
of rock, or a lighthouse. Then a map becomes a prophecy.'
After a pause he turns to Taufiq. 'There is some difference.
Maps deal with place, prophecies with time.'

Ibn Majid conjures up another common friend from the
past. Sa'ad Sabur is his name, a seaman of sorts. 'But he
fancies himself a great, far-footing voyager. When I last met
him he told me "When I am at sea I feel exiled from land.
And when I am on land I feel exiled from the sea. How does
one bear this double burden? How do you bear it?" he asked
me. I wanted to say something obscene, but nothing came to
mind. May Satan sodomize him!'

A cry of horror is heard from the adjoining room where
Bilquees is sitting.

At dinner the two men put Taufiq at ease once again by

telling him the ship is not going to Africa. When dinner is over Asturlabi turns to Taufiq. 'You know what to do?'

'Yes, Sir, get ready for the ship.'

'You have till Friday. And you know who your captain is?'

'No, Sir.'

Asturlabi buries his head in his hands. 'He is standing in front of you. You sail with Ibn Majid.'

*keki n. daruwalla*

# of abu khalil and
## mount etna

ॐ

Before setting off for Tyre and Sidon, Ehtesham brings Taufiq to Abu Khalil and the old man blesses him and the voyage. 'My friend is feeling nervous,' says Ehtesham.

'Why so? Haven't you sailed before?'

'I have, but only as a boy, on voyages to Calicut and Cochin. Al Azhar intervened—for five full years. But then I took my apprenticeship at the docks here, as well as at Alexandria. This is the first time I'll be sailing and getting paid for it. That's a nice feeling, though.'

'All the more reason you should feel good. What is there to be nervous about? Once you know the winds, the currents and the stars—you have nothing to fear.'

'One should know one's boat as well!'

'True, just as a painter should know his brush and a soldier his sword. That means knowing oneself and one's limitations. These days you young fellows feel you can catch the wind and reach the end of the world. Tell me, why are you nervous?'

'Who says I am? But we are going to crusader country—to Sidon and Acre and Sour. I have never met Farangs before.'

'What is so special about Farangs? Incidentally, they call themselves Franks, and Sour is known to them as Tyre. The

Franks worked as slaves here in the Citadel during al Salahdin's time, hundreds of them. Do you think they are a superior breed?'

'No, no, Sir. How can infidels be superior to us in worth? The thought never crossed my mind, I swear.'

'I think it did, but never mind. Incidentally, the worth of a person may not have much to do with whether he is a believer or not. The Franks, believe it or not, consider us infidels.'

It turns out to be a long afternoon. Abu Khalil is in form. Everything is grist to his mill, from cruelty and kings to slaves and eunuchs, not to speak of harems. (In Christian Constantinople, he tells them, children were made eunuchs by crushing their testicles in hot baths!) 'Don't look at me like that! I didn't do it,' he says with a twinkle in his eye. (Habiba tells the old lady that 'filthy talk' is going on upstairs and Abu Khalil seems to have gone soft in the head. Who asked you to listen? Men talk like that! replies the lady, almost imperiously.) Somewhere during the discussion Ehtesham intervenes, suggesting that the Farangs had a greater say in ruling themselves.

'What use? What use? The rabble is infinitely worse. What happened when the cities became "free" in Spain? By free I mean when they shook off the yoke of king and priest. When they got their so called liberty, they erected gallows in their market squares! Freedom for them meant hanging their criminals themselves! I am sure if the people in Khan al Khalili were to be given their "freedom", they would do something similar. Power should remain with sultans and the nobility.'

Abu Khalil can't be kept from the Franks and the crusades for too long.

'Never forget Allah was always with us. When Frederick of Sicily (a good king, mind you) prepared for a crusade and gathered forty thousand people at Brindisi, Allah sent a plague on them. One doesn't know if more people died or more of them deserted. Yet Rome urged him on to lead the crusade, threatened him with excommunication and finally did excommunicate him! (The Caliph of Rome has the power to declare a Christian an unbeliever.) If plague hits your army, can you go and fight? As irony would have it, he came to Palestine after he was excommunicated. And in Jerusalem he crowned himself king, as no Christian would touch him. He did that in the Church of the Holy Sepulchre, as they call it. The clergy declared the shrine desecrated, and forbade religious services in Acre and Jerusalem. Some of their demented knights went further. They learnt that he would go to Jordan to visit the site of Christ's baptism. They promptly sent a message to the Muslim commander, al Kamil, informing him about Frederick's plans so that he could be captured. But the gallant Kamil had already signed a truce with the Sicilian King. He refused to act and instead sent that so called secret letter to Frederick. Such was our chivalry.

'It didn't save Frederick from humiliation, though. When he went to Acre the Christian population threw filth on him. That's how these fools treated their best king. He was a little soft in the head no doubt, walked with a train of chained lions and leopards and what have you. He knew nine languages. Spoke Arabic better than an Arab, wrote good poetry. That accursed Dante, may he and his progeny rot in eternal hell for having criticized our Holy Prophet (peace be upon him), thought Frederick a fine poet. This Dante himself wrote good poetry, though I wouldn't put him in the same street as Imr ul Qais. But we are talking of Frederick. He preferred Muslim learning to his own Christian thought. Though he led a reluctant crusade, he also preferred us to his Christian fighters. The Muslims he captured he brought to Rome, and turned them into a militia. He made these Muslims fight against Papal troops. They killed him with a lie! The worst lie is to put words in someone's unsuspecting mouth. Spread a rumour that the fellow said this or that, and the person is doomed, be he king or caliph.'

The two young acolytes naturally ask what exactly they put in this weird king's mouth.

'Forget it! The lie they attributed to him was that he named three Prophets—Moses, Jesus and Muhammad—and called them conjurors who had gained mastery over the world. When he died people said that Satan came in person to carry away his soul to hell through the sulphur and the smoke of Mount Etna. If a thousand devils were to carry every European soul who deserved hell through that volcano, there would be a traffic jam in Mount Etna!'

# to sidon and tyre

૭૦

Taufiq is off on his first major voyage. The Captain is Ibn
Majid, the destination Sidon. But the ship will halt at
Tyre, or Sour as the Arabs call it, and unload some of its cargo
there. There is pre-embarkation excitement, slave and fellahin
weighed down by the load, the sacks of grain curving around
their backs; owners seeing to it that all their merchandise
has been loaded; fresh water splashing out of pitchers as it is
brought in. The ship looks like a busy road, or a house where
a wedding is about to take place, with goods piling up and
people going out and coming in, excitement splashed all over
their faces.

This is not a voyage to the Zanj, the African coast, in search
of cargoes exotic—ivory and horn, slaves and ambergris. The
ship is even carrying passengers, for traffic with Sidon and Tyre
has always been heavy. Taufiq has been forewarned that Ibn
Majid would always be on the lookout for a good listener and
could sometimes bore you to death. He'll pile on details of the
great navigators of the past—starting with Noah, no less, they
have warned him. But Taufiq finds him more businesslike, at
least on the first day. He explains the winds first—the North
wind or *Shamal* did not necessarily come straight from the
north, but from slightly to the west of it. What is navigation
but the science of directions? And if you are looking for

merit, it is this science that will come in handy when one is called upon to answer on the Day of Judgement, for this is the science which will tell you where the Qibleh lies. It is not an easy science. Next to the service of temperamental kings, it is the most difficult. He talks of the west wind, the Dabur, and its tantrums; and yet it does not come exactly from the direction of the setting sun, but from south-west, from the direction of the setting of Canopus.

At night, looking at the stars, Ibn Majid lets himself go, points out the Ursa Major. Look at it upside down—it is Noah's boat! At such moments Taufiq keeps his eyes down and says nothing. He cannot afford to offend the great man; but however impassive the face, Ibn Majid sees in it the flicker of doubt. Even today, he tells Taufiq, the sailors of Zanj and Qumr which the Franks call Madagascar, call the fifth and the sixth stars of the Ursa Major, al Hirab, that is, the keel of the ship. It is of course the keel of the boat of Noah. Feigning agreement is sometimes difficult, and Ibn Majid is left with the feeling that these youngsters are hard to convince and that doubt has been ingrained into them a bit too thoroughly.

Conversations continue the next day and again he prods Taufiq with Noah. The ark went seven times around the site of the holy Kaaba. There was no Kaaba then of course, just red sand. But he sees the red sand in Taufiq's eyes; he sees the red sand on Taufiq's face. The red sand is everywhere! True enough, Taufiq asks, 'But how would you know that the ark went around the place, when there were no markers there and when the matter is so ancient?'

Tyre was on the Lord's hit list and vengeance was not slow in coming. Taufiq learns all this by and by through Majid and a Druze inn keeper at Tyre. He is amazed at the city and its walls, each with a high, imposing gate of its own. Who could imagine that this was the city so often reduced to rubble?

Taufiq does not even know of its earlier destructions. It is only on his last day in Tyre as he sits down to his noon meal alone with the Druze inn keeper, Saad, that he learns a thing or two about the city. (Ibn Majid, who has been chaperoning his ward all along, has been too busy with matters dealing with navigation to bother educating him about the city.) Why does a city need that many walls, he asks. The inn keeper reminds him of the Lord's prophecy against Tyre: 'I am against you, Oh Tyre, and I will bring many nations against you, like the sea casting up its waves.' But now it is Sour, and Christian prophecies don't hold good in Arab kingdoms! Saad's face puckers up as he laughs.

One must begin at the beginning. The very first day Ibn Majid takes Taufiq to the inn of Saad, the Druze, situated just a few yards from the quay, for lunch. Saad can't contain his joy at seeing the great navigator. Even his old mother remembers him, and Majid is taken to her to be greeted by the pleated veil of her smile. There is such joy in the wrinkles and striations on her face that Majid cannot but help being moved. The inn has a rugged stone floor and is crowded with people. But Saad takes him up a curved staircase to the second floor where a better class of people seems to occupy the tables. The floor here is wooden. Tables and chairs are laid out in one part of the room, while the other half is covered with rugs and heaped with cushions where Orientals can squat with comfort on the floor. From the window Taufiq can see the becalmed Mediterranean sloshing away against the quay. A flask of wine is brought out, and such is the fuss Saad makes over them that they become the cynosure of all eyes. Taufiq notices it.

'Those two Farangs are eyeing us and possibly talking about us.' Taufiq is in for a gentle reprimand from his mentor.

'You must stop using the word Farang, or Franks as they call themselves, indiscriminately. Those two you've pointed out seem to be from Portugal. It is a small sliver of a country, once under Islam. But its sailors have done well on the seas. Their progress has been steady for almost a century. Since 1419 by their calendar, when they recorded the landfall on the Madeira Islands, they seem to have been destined for a conquest over the waters. According to rumours they are going around Africa now.'

Ibn Majid may not have known the details of various landfalls. But he sensed that they had crossed those psychological and historical barriers: going around the 'Green Sea of Darkness', for instance.

As they finish their meal the two Portuguese, one a member of the nobility and another a priest in a black smock, approach them, seeking permission if they can join them. They make some general enquiries about the Arabs. Is it true they sew the planks of their ships together and hardly use a nail? Majid nods. Yes they caulk them up later with tar to safeguard against a leak. They can't imagine how, in this day and age, they can use such ships. You should see our Portuguese ships, they tell the Arab. They make enquiries about the Lateen sail that the Arabs use. How does it work? Slowly they veer the conversation around to the Indian Ocean and ask him if he has ever sailed to India? Majid nods and laughs. But they are not interested in his voyages from the Red Sea. Has he gone there from Africa? He has done that run so often he can't remember—he doesn't keep a scorecard. Now we hear you people are getting a fleet ready. We wish you luck.

The Portuguese fire more questions about the west coast of India and what lies beyond, both south and east of the country. Then comes the one question that has been troubling Iberian voyagers for the best part of a century, 'Sir, where exactly is the Green Sea of Darkness? We have heard so much about it. How does one traverse it, or is it a wall of water which none can pierce?' Majid notices the undertone of sarcasm here—they themselves don't seem to believe what they are asking.

'The Green Sea of Darkness, as you call it, exists only in your minds. This is a ghost story about a ghost sea that doesn't exist.'

Majid's straight answers surprise the Portuguese.'You are very forthright, Sir. It is not a quality we've found in some of your other countrymen.'

'You underestimate us—most Europeans do. We both harbour our prejudices about each other. We should blame the crusades for that. They have left a scar on both our people.'

The priest, who has not been so vocal till now, asks about the people in the country, their religion, whom they worship and things of that nature. Here Majid is guarded. 'A seaman is concerned with his boat and the winds. He'll worship whoever steers him to the right shore. Ask a seaman about currents and stars, not gods.'

Through the voyage and his stay at Tyre and later at Sidon, Taufiq finds himself rubbing shoulders with Jews and Copts, Venetians and Florentines. He discovers that the projected Portuguese voyage has caused a ferment in mercantile circles everywhere from the Rialto to Constantinople. And on the docks of Alexandria, people hardly know of it! You must do something about this, the Venetians tell Ibn Majid and him. Tell your Sultan that this voyage will end your spice caravans from the Red Sea. Your monopoly over the spice trade ends the day Portuguese sails sight Indian ports. These Portuguese have factories where they produce slaves—do you Arabs know of this? They call them Feitorias, trading posts for slaves—they set up the first one as far back as forty years ago. What will these people trade in? The only things that have a good market in Lisbon are parrots and monkeys. But they have wormed their way into the arse of the church. You can't imagine the encyclicals and Papal Bulls that have been issued in their favour. You understand what a Papal Bull is, don't you? They don't. Neither Majid nor Taufiq would have known a Papal Bull from an Egyptian cow.

'It is a final pronouncement from the Christian Caliph,' the Venetians explain. 'Once his seal is put on an order, it almost becomes the word of the Lord. Do you Arabs understand this?'

It would take the Jew Izaac, in Sidon, to explain to the two the intricacies of Christian politics. The Italians are all united when it comes to Portugal. They carry tales to the Pope and importune him. Holy Father! The Portuguese are enslaving people already converted to Christianity! Isn't that a crime against the Saviour himself? They are indulging in slave raiding. Holy Father, if they ever find the kingdom of Prester John (Heaven forbid) they could enslave the saint-king himself, or at least his people. But the Holy Father is too impressed by Lisbon to stir a finger.

The first meeting with Izaac at Sidon is accidental. Taufiq goes into an eating-house alone and finds there is hardly a table vacant. A bearded man invites him. 'My name is Isaac and you can please have a seat at my table.' After a few exchanges, Isaac says, 'Your accent tells me you are from Egypt. You must have come with Ibn Majid's boat.'

'Yes! You know him!'

'Who doesn't?'

'Your name, Sir, is Ishaaq, did you say?'

'It is the same thing, but I am Izaac, a Yahudi. Are you taken aback?' Taufiq is confused. He almost blushes as he stammers a denial.

'I have met Copts in the company of my friend Murad. But I haven't met a Yahudi before.'

'Never? But there are so many of us in Cairo, and surprisingly they are not being badly treated, let me tell you.'

Why should that surprise him, thinks Taufiq. The elderly Jew reads his thoughts but says nothing.

'Where are your people most numerous?'

'We are not numerous anywhere. When your temple is smashed, you disperse. But you also want to know why I said that we are not badly off at Cairo.'

'Why should it surprise you if you are well treated?'

'My son, I never said we were well treated. I used the words "not badly". For over a thousand years, from the Romans downwards, people have walked over us and tried to bury our heads in the dust. There's nothing much we have done about it. If the suffering is in excess of the sin (and we all sin), some of us believe that we will be compensated in heaven.'

'We all believe in heaven, don't we?'

'Yes, only we thought of it earlier than you.'

'Are you people happier in Christian lands?'

'Please note that we have been ruled by everyone, Christians, Persians, Islam. During the Christian era our taxes were twenty times higher than those of others. If a king died, the agreement that he would defend us against murder and plunder died with the king. We have been subjected to such exactions that mothers have had to sell their children in slavery. Is it any wonder that when the crusaders came we fought shoulder to shoulder with Islam? When the city fell we were herded into a synagogue and burnt alive by the crusaders. And don't forget that al Salahdin welcomed three hundred rabbis who fled England and the countries of the Franks. But our story is rather long for a casual meeting over bread and meat. You will hear about us from others.'

During the week that he stays at Sidon, Taufiq comes across Venetians, Florentines, Genoese. They are traders and seamen, men who have beaten back pirates and slithered on decks as storm waves engulfed them. It is a revelation to Taufiq that each of them comes with a sort of a national view of his own—the Venetian swaggering away as if he was walking on San Marco Square, for he thought he owned the globe; the Florentine withdrawn and tentative because the Florence fleet had been eliminated, about five years earlier by the Pisans, and the merchants had to invest in other countries.

The Florentines had money and they could fill the void caused in Portugal by the expulsion of Jews just a couple of years earlier. They could finance shipping and exploration. Why, they could even provide the cargoes. Merchants were already lining up, like the Florentine Girolamo Sernigi and the Genoese Antonio Salvago, to throw in their lot with the Portuguese.

The Florentines are scouting around. They have many questions for the Arabs. If Europe finds its way to India through the seas, how would they look at it? Taufiq answers brashly that it would hit Arab trade all along the Khaleej and along the Red Sea. It would hit the Arabs who had settled on the Indian coast and married Indian women. Ibn Majid chides him. The world belongs to all Allah's creatures. The Portuguese are welcome to find their way to India, and so are the Spaniards who had already discovered new worlds. The sea belonged to every one and so did commerce. The Genoese consider the Arabs dimwits. They don't conceal their contempt for the Portuguese. You are not going to do a thing to them, are you? You'll let them scour the oceans, will you, and just scratch your anus while they take away your trade? We are telling you, your prosperity will vanish. Your camels and cameleers will starve on the caravan routes and die. Instead of pepper you will have dust in your markets. What is Portugal, if we may ask? There are people in Genoa who have never heard of the country.

But the Venetians stand to lose the most. Already the preparation of the Vasco fleet is causing disquiet here. Already feelers are being sent to the Egyptian Sultan to try and make the Indian Ocean a hazardous place for Portuguese ships should they ever reach Indian shores. But the swagger never leaves a citizen of the queen of the cities. Who are the Portuguese, their looks seem to ask. This little kingdom covered for six hundred years under the mantle of Islam now venturing to discover the East! They found the Canary Islands and should be content. That's how Henry the Navigator must have got his title. And they laugh. They even want the price of pepper lowered and are passing the word around so that it can reach the Mamluk Sultan. If the Sultan won't heed their request, who knows some Venetian black sheep could finance a venture (Portuguese or Dutch or Spanish, who cares) to the lands of the pepper vine.

All this is buzzing around Taufiq's young head. In a fortnight he knows more about the world than he had picked up in a lifetime. In Cairo no one could have talked so openly, so loosely, so brazenly, he feels. Not with the Muhtasib Al Maheeni in his seat, not with people like Ali Hasan Zulm prowling in the souks.

# a season of blood

ಖಿ

Wind, dun-coloured from the desert. Sometimes you can see it, the thin shroud of dust wrapping itself around nothing in particular. At times it rises like a devil-worshipping dervish standing on one leg and whirling around. The heat is a solid blur. Azans get a little shriller, tempers a little frayed. Sherbet vendors make a killing.

These are the dark days, Ehtesham squarely under the Muhtasib's shadow, Taufiq before his voyage to Sidon and Tyre, when no ship would take him. Is the sword hanging over Ehtesham? The question has the friends worried. When they visit Ali Hasan 'Zulm' it turns out to be an exercise in humiliation. The surprising thing is that even people who have smarted under insults, return. The same face you saw being rubbed in the dust only the day before, will be there again, eager-eyed, when you go there next. The victim won't even be shame-faced. The higher born you are, the sharper the rebuke. Taufiq and Ehtesham find themselves, following, almost blindly, a crowd into the hall. The evening has hung heavy and they have slipped in, merely to listen to some weird story, like the one they last heard about the angel of death and the Greek impostor who replicated himself ten times over.

Even as they enter that rather packed room, Taufiq asks

quietly 'Why are we here?' Ehtesham's only answer is a dirty look. He is still looking for some succour from this dervish. He can't believe it. If the Muhtasib bans painting, who but the Sultan himself, can withdraw the fiat? Except that no fiat has been passed; merely an admonition. Can these dervishes be an effective counter to the opinion of the Muhtasib?

Ali Hasan spots the two and his eyes light up. 'You are the one who talked about painting?' He looks hard at Taufiq and seems a bit confused as to which of the two had broached the subject. Ehtesham admits it was him.

'You got the answer, I hope.' Both friends feign innocence. 'There was no answer.' The Dervish laughs.

'My answers are for those who have the brains to understand. I don't waste my time on fools. Didn't you hear me on the angel of death and that Unani fraud who had created another nine men in his own wretched likeness? And how the angel of death won, as he has to, always. Didn't you recognize what replication is? There couldn't be a bigger crime against God. If you create, you challenge the creator, the counterfeiter challenging the Sultan's mint. And people want to paint! Tomorrow they will want to make idols—the Christians call them statues. By giving evil a good name, things don't change. An idol remains an idol. Some Agha or Bey, stupid as all such Beys are, may be tempted to order his statue. From this to making idol is but a short step. Only Allah has the right to create. He can create ten fools like you and we would still bow the head in reverence, though why He should do such a thing would baffle me. But we cannot be baffled by what Allah does. For, in that case we could even question why he created someone like you in the first instance.'

Much sniggering from the crowd, some suppressed laughter. It is not that people don't know how to react to Ali

Hasan 'Zulm'. They are not sure how he will react. If he had laughed, people would have guffawed. Taufiq cannot stand it. 'Let us go,' he says rather loudly, 'there is no point staying here and getting insulted by people who don't measure up to you.' Sharp intake of breath; collective gasp. No one talks to Ali Hasan like that. No one even talks about him that way, not even behind his back, for word gets carried to him from alley, souk and drain in Cairo; his disciples are many.

Ali Hasan's falcon eye falls on him now. 'Boy, come here,' he says mildly, as if talking to a loved child. Taufiq moves up unhesitatingly. Ali Hasan, sitting on his divan gestures to him to bend, as if he is going to whisper something in his ear. As he stoops, he caresses Taufiq's cheek. Then he asks an acolyte to bring him a bowl of water so that he can wash his hands. When a basin is brought, he washes with great deliberation, pouring water right up to the elbows.

'Wuzu we perform before prayers. We also need ablutions after touching the likes of him. Observe his face, beardless and smooth, like a catamite's. A Muslim without a beard, is he Muslim, I ask you.' People are too stunned to react. The two friends are not cowed down and shout back. Again the crowd is slow to respond and before the acolytes can get into the act, Taufiq and Ehtesham make a quick getaway.

As days go by, more people throng around Ali. He seems to hold them all—barber, cobbler and kebab vendor—in mesmeric thrall. And then what he has been looking for—a cause—falls into his lap. A traveller has come from the north, and somehow travellers do not bring good news, not in Zulm's reckoning. The man's name is Haamid and he brings back wondrous tales from Shentena al Hagar. Flashes of red light have been seen near a Coptic church there. On a new-moon night, mind you. Immediately thereafter a pair of silver-white doves flew over the steeple of the church of Virgin Mary. The reaction is mixed. One of the acolytes is thrilled. After all, the Virgin Mary is the mother of a prophet, he says, and isn't it written:

> On the day when Allah will
> Gather the Messengers together . . .
> Then will Allah say:
> 'O Jesus the son of Mary!
> Recount my favour
> To thee and to thy mother.
> Behold I strengthened thee
> With the Holy Spirit' . . .

The others wait for Ali to react and he is already sullen, hearing the news. Those who know him are aware that when he is angry his right eye starts twitching. Well, the damned thing seems caught in a spasm so strong that along with the eyelid, the beard is also jerked into motion.

'How can white or silver doves suddenly descend on the steeple? Where did they come from? Did some jinn produce them, propelling them with a jet of smoke from his nostrils? What is so special about a church steeple that cannot be found in our mosques? Why don't we have lights blazing over al Huseyn's shrine or silver or golden doves perching on our minars? I shiver at the edge of disbelief, I know. But that is better than slithering into apostasy or idol worship or dove-worship. Why should I be afraid? In fact, I don't believe any of it! And if you are true Muslims, you will not believe it either.'

An acolyte puts in his half a dirhem worth. 'Someone takes a puff from an opium pipe and sees doves or cranes or ibis flying, and there is no dearth of fools who will believe it. If some wretch, utterly knocked out by his pipe, had seen a mare flying, even that would turn into a miracle.'

'No. This is not some drunk or an opium addict dreaming up silver doves over a church at night. This is planned and well thought out; a conspiracy by the *shirk*, the polytheists, to lead people away from the true faith. If you tell the simple fellahin that you saw night-lights and night doves over a church, he will believe it! Then what happens to his faith when he reads his namaz, when he bows towards the Kaaba?

O ye who believe!
If ye obey the Unbelievers,
They will drive you back
On your heels, and ye
Will turn back
To your own loss.
Turn back from what? From faith. But never fear. For
Soon shall we cast terror?
Into the hearts of the Unbelievers . . .

'No friends, it is not opium or wine, which did this. Apostates, idol-worshippers, conspirators have got together. Some evil mind is at the core of it all. I will have to go there to see things for myself. Who will come with me?'

A good fifty arms are raised. Two days later they set out for Shentena al Hagar. It takes the camel caravan the best part of a foot-weary week to reach Shentena. They find that events here have moved rapidly. There has been an inexorable progression in the series of miracles. The flashes of red light seen over the church have doubled. Now they are seen, not in isolation by a cloistered few, but by all and sundry—by Sunni and Shiite and Copt and, if there were any, Druze or Mormon around—and there weren't—they would have seen them too. In the shadow of the red lights, before they have blinked and disappeared, come the silver doves, red-lit, flashing past. Then

*keki n. daruwalla*

comes the miracle, for surely all this is leading to something overwhelming. And as the doves sort of disappear from view, the Virgin Mary herself alights on the steeple.

Donkey carts and camel carts have been trundling into the casbah from all quarters. Not just Copts but Muslim peasants goggle-eyed, Sufi and dervish dancing away, the sceptic Sunni and the appalled Shiite, watching their own faith take a knock—they all thronged to the village, most of them uncertain how to look the Copt in the eye. But not the Sufi, not the real dervish. He can't be tied to a scriptural tether. The muezzin and the mullah are unhappy. They watch the goings on through slits, the white of the eyes visible, and the eyeball lowering itself like a sinking sun—a phalanx of sullen faces, all with the same expression of thin-lipped disapproval, looking for all the world like severed heads nailed to a plaque.

The Christians are having a great time. Their women are busy preparing dough for the ovens in anticipation of relatives and friends who will be flocking to the place. Bread and pastry in the ovens, sherbet in flasks. Entire families are coming in, women, dressed in their finery, singing away.

The sullen phalanx of faces, the silence of desert nights frozen on them, watches the goings on at this miracle carnival, for carnival it is. Seeing the crowds at the village, hawkers have thronged here with dates and melons and candy, and slivers of meat around a drum. Vendors are shouting away, singing the praises of Miriam, peace be unto her. Watching this, the bearded brigade gets surlier. It is when they hear of the approach of Ali Hasan Zulm that their spirits lift. He is within a few miles of the village, just a league perhaps! Suddenly they are galvanized into action—the hawkers are attacked and their handcarts overturned, with the melons rolling on the road. The candy sellers find their wares on the ground, now coated with dust and flies. Some of them still desist from running away, half angry and half afraid. One melon seller refuses to budge. 'We are selling melons. We are not committing a crime.' A zealot takes out a large knife and strikes at the handcart. The blow slices a melon exactly into two half moons. The melon vendor bolts. An urchin darts out from nowhere and runs away with the sliced melon. A man is piddling away against a wall. When the rioting starts he tries to pull up his trousers and run, his trouser cords still untied. He makes a mess of it, can't pull the thing cleanly over his knees as he runs, his pestle swaying and dribbling with urine like a hose still dispensing water though the tap has been turned off. He stumbles and falls and the chasing zealots pull off his trousers and move away, laughing. An urchin gets a stick on his behind. 'You want to watch silver doves! We'll give you silver doves.' A beggar playing on his rabab is chased. His plangent notes suddenly stop whining as the muthawallis catch up with him and give him the stick.

Next morning the Copts wake up to find Ali Hasan taking a round of the casbah. Many have not heard of him. Those who have are, of course, not happy with what they have heard—his flaming certitudes, his flaming fiats—everything is fiery about the fellow, including his ginger-coloured beard. Meanwhile, word has gone around that after last evening's rioting the governor of the area has asked for Mamluks from Cairo to restore order. Mamluks riding out of Cairo! Even they would take three days and many dead horses to reach here. What happens till then? An unreal air hangs around the place. Some people think they heard the muezzin's call during the night. Not 'think', the others chip in, they heard it! And it was blared forth from the church! There was a cavernous ring to the call that could only have emanated from the church, for they were familiar with its deadened, muffled acoustics.

Then Ali Hasan pulls off a coup of sorts. He spouts tolerance. He quotes the Holy Book. The froth of fanaticism is suddenly wiped away from his lips. Throw away your knives, he says, or keep them in your kitchen. Knives are good only for slitting throats of rams and goats. Surely not of men! Or women! People nod. They would nod if Ali Hasan asked them to de-gut someone; such is his authority. You don't have a choice. It is not just his words that sort of emboss themselves on the crowd's will. It is also his looks. He can look at them, his head slightly lowered, with just the whites of his eyes. When his expression changes, the eyeballs rise like a pair of black suns inching up at dawn from carob fields flanking the Nile. There is a stillness about him today, a deliberate stillness and calm. When he wants, his voice can swell like high tide and his gestures can be strident, his hairy arms moving around like a windmill. But today it is ebb.

Word gets around. The bearded brigade actually becomes apologetic. Daggers are sheathed. Muslim and Christian smile at each other for the first time since the lights danced on the steeple and the silver doves flashed past. Peace has descended here. On the day of Ali Hasan's departure, the Christians honour him with a robe. Dates are presented to him in a large silver tray. He picks up a date and goes about offering dates to the people around him. When the dates vanish, he keeps the tray. Slogans are shouted in his honour, vociferously by the Muslims, a little nervously by the Copts. They may be nervous about him, almost by instinct, but a public display of gratitude is called for. He leaves Shentena al Hagar with an almost visible aura, as if he had plucked the halo from off the church steeple and crowned himself.

When the Mamluks arrive, all is orderly at Shentena. Yes, the Copts tell them, things were a bit awry till Ali Hasan came. After that, all is fine, no windows smashed, no shutters broken. Not a stone has been hurled at a Christian since. The Mamluks return and word spreads in Cairo about the wonders wrought by Ali Hasan. The Sultan himself gets to hear about it.

~

Power has to be visible. Those who wield power from the backyards are destined to remain in the backyards. Power flows from the top, of course. To exude power you should be seen with powerful people. No wonder the Muhtasib's sons are unhappy. The Sultan has not summoned their father for ages now. They are worried and they pester al Maheeni, promulgator of edicts and caveats, each stricter than the other. He hasn't been seen with the Sultan since he went to greet him on Eid, the day rams are slaughtered in memory of Abraham's almost-sacrifice—his son's windpipe that was never cut, the head that was never severed. What will the nobility think of him? What will the Mamluks think? They'll soon start sniggering when he makes an entry. Can't he go to the Sultan on the pretext that he has some important news to give him? Something important must happen first, he tells his children.

And then it happens, for the Sultan summons him.

This has come after such a length of time that for once he finds it difficult to master his emotions as he hurriedly puts on his robe. He stands quaking before the Sultan, hoping he will not notice his lack of composure. The Muhtasib with his X-ray vision, he who could see through to the yellow swathe of fat beneath your skin, he himself palpitating like a fish which has just been hooked and wrenched out of water!

The Sultan wants Cairo peaceful. He does not want Shentena al Hagar or Shaitan al Hagar or whatever the name of the bloody place is, to be repeated in Cairo. Have you understood, Muhtasib? Not a dry leaf should crackle, not a hen should cackle. Or your bones will be made to rattle until your body turns ramshackle. (The Sultan has a flair for rhyme.) Have you any ideas, asks the great man. The Vizier is also present. He launches into a far roving dissertation on the Franks, Mongols and the Ottomans—this trinity of threats to our state, as he terms it—and the importance of keeping Christian and Muslim together, and . . . The Sultan cuts him short. He has had enough.

'Have you any ideas? If you have, I hope you will be short winded, unlike our illustrious Vizier.'

Al Maheeni sees his chance and talks about that rundown Coptic Church in Cairo, which contains a cell where the Virgin Mary was supposed to have lived during her stay in Egypt. The Sultan is alarmed. He doesn't even know that the Virgin Mary had ever stayed in Egypt. Moses, yes. Mary, no. But he is, for once, contradicted. The Muhtasib plays his courage card. Kings are so swarmed over by smarmy sycophants that they admire someone who they think is bold. That is how one can wield some semblance of influence on the king. Al Maheeni continues with his statement as if the Sultan had never interrupted him. A vault under the church, which contains an oven-like aperture, is believed to be the place where the infant Jesus rested. People have been visiting the place in dribs and drabs, not just from the Sultan's own country but from far-off cities like Aleppo and Sidon. They carry off relics and talismans from here. The thing would need careful handling now.

Well, handle it carefully, says the Sultan. First, see that a Muslim is not hurt. Then see that the Christians are safe. And make use of that fellow, Ali Hasan Gloom. Zulm, Sultan, Zulm. That's his name, says the Vizier. (He hasn't got a word in for quite some time.) The Sultan is unhappy. He doesn't care for people who can't appreciate his sly humour. The fellow sounds gloomy to me, he says. We shall persist in calling him Gloom. Any 'zulm' that has to be done will be done by us or our Mamluks and not by this dervish in rags. (Incidentally, he is dressing much better, my informers tell me.) But the Mamluks say that he did a very good job in that place up north. People who can bring about peace are useful. See that he is in the thick of things. If only I had more Ali Hasans, there would be peace in the land and people would live like brothers!

The Muhtasib lowers his head in submission—he doesn't want the Sultan to look into his eyes, which have widened with disbelief. What would the Sultan think if he were to tell him that he had put his informers, including the perfumer, after the dervish? After taking leave, the Muhtasib goes straight to the church. He is too late.

Already there are small crowds of Christians outside. Already people are saying that if the Virgin Mary could visit that outback up north called Shentena or something, could Cairo be far behind? And if she were to alight here, it would not be the synagogue next door or a mosque. She would like to grace the place where she had lived. He finds from his agents that maulvis are already fulminating in secret conclaves, though none has dared to raise the issue after the Friday prayers in the mosques. Clusters of fanatics hang around ominously. The Sultan had said to him, 'Thank God these troubles occur far away from Cairo.' He hopes the Sultan has not spoken too soon.

Goons have been seen increasingly around the church and suddenly rowdyism breaks out. We'll burn the church, say the fanatics, and that vault beneath it. Some of the church goers are beaten up and the relics torn away, sometimes along with the sleeves of their kaftans. It can be painful, the tear and rip of these talismans—all those slivers of wood beams, which the Christian pilgrims, wore around their necks or their arms. This, despite the fact that one of the leaders has maintained that the Christians must be encouraged to scrape off more shavings and slivers from the beams so that the wretched beams get weakened and come crashing down one day.

The Muhtasib has a cursory meeting with Ali Hasan. He promises to keep his men in line, harangues the Muhtasib on compassion—Allah as Rehman and Rahim, as compassion incarnate. The Muhtasib sits through an hour of this, his eyes closed in boredom, but the expression on his face so respectful that the dervish thinks he is being listened to in rapt attention. Not once does al Maheeni fidget in impatience, though he is overworked and anxious, wants to meet his agents, go around the city with a small body of armed men—it always creates an impression. A good administrator never lets someone know that he hasn't got all the time in the world to listen to him.

The Muhtasib doesn't want to use force. That would give the game away. The entire city would come to know of the trouble. What would the Sultan say? A temporary disappearance of some of the troublemakers is the answer. He gets his agents to quietly spirit away the leaders. A little thrashing has never done any harm to religious fervour. People get worried when they don't see their street leader for a few days. They don't know where to turn. A troop of horsemen posted around the church does the rest. Cairo is back to normal.

But trouble has a knack of oscillating, jumping from one place to the other and back. Shentena al Hagar is on fire once again. Every fanatic in the area is visited by the same dream one night. Ali Hasan 'Zulm' erupts in each dream, exhorting every single person to teach a lesson to the apostates and the polytheists. His voice is at its shrillest. His face, 'which they had seen pasted with tranquility', as a man relates later, now bristles with anger. Pillage! Burn! Stone! his voice says, his lips frothing with spittle.

This sudden plural strength of his, an approach both conciliatory and cruel, soft Sufi speech going hand in hand with this malevolent urging to arson and destruction give him two dimensions, make him angel and demon in one. It gives him a hypnotic switch-on, switch-off authority over people.

The attack on the church does not commence with stones hurled at the controversial steeple on which visions alight and vanish. Instead, that curved bit of stained glass above the curved doorway, that lung of light in the smothering browns all around, is the first to feel the red heat of the assault, is the first to crack and splinter as a shower of stones assail it. The steeple comes next, with stones bouncing off its steep flanks. There are stray attacks on Copts, and ruffians get into their houses and beat the inmates up. 'Now show us your miracles!' they shout, 'show us your silver doves and the Virgin Miriam.'

That night there are no red lights over the church, no silver doves and no Virgin Mary, white-robed and blue-veiled, over the steeple.

When even miracles abandon you, fear takes over—fear and outrage like twin blasts of a double-barrelled blunderbuss, always supposing that some freak blunderbuss would have two barrels. It didn't. So what? Outrage is a temporary feeling and does the vanishing trick. As stones rain against the walls and small crowds hammer at doors, sometimes breaking in, fear prevails and musks the air. Sweat breaks out as if from a water tap as fat deliquesces under the twin assault of heat and fear.

# ehtesham meets the abbott

❧

The warnings have been too many for Ehtesham. He knows he has to earn a living. There is unfortunately no one he can sponge on. He has realized that human figures are not all that he can paint. There are manuscripts waiting to be ornamented, pages from the Holy Book to be illuminated, glass to be enamelled and gilded, lamps to be painted and metal containers waiting for patina and inlay work. He could become one of the *arbab al qalam*, men of the pen, as opposed to—*arbab al suyuf*, men of the sword, a clutch of offices reserved for Mamluks only, though Beduins, Egyptians, Palestinians and Syrians could enlist with the lower ranked auxiliary troops.

Actually, metal work and ceramics provide ample scope for his talents. And of course there are blazons. Every amir boasts of a specific blazon. Heraldry is not limited to the Templars and the Hospitaliers. Blazons were not limited to banners. They were placed on the amir's house, his tents, his train, garments, his weapons and armour. Only in case of disgrace would the blazon be erased. The sultans had their own majestic blazons. Some of them wanted to be identified with their previous stations. Aybak, the first sultan to sport a blazon, used a round table as his symbol. He was the Imperial Taster to the former Sultan. The heraldic emblem was invariably enclosed in a shield. Baybars, the great Mamluk Sultan, had a lion as his symbol. Animal motifs were common, and horse and duck and fish were used liberally for ornamentation.

Ehtesham buckles down to earning a living. He works on brass lamps and takes them to important mosques. They hang from a lofty circular disc in the mosque yard. The disc itself stands on a twenty-foot-high tripod. The calligraphy on his lamps is immaculate, the verse chosen from the Holy Book just right. Yes, the keeper of the mosque buys it and asks for more. Slowly his reputation spreads. Glass lamps are brought to him, flat-bottomed bowls, which will hang similarly from ceilings or walls. They don't ask for calligraphy alone, but ornamentation, a fruit bearing branch, a grape-vine, flowers. The nobility send him glass panels. What do you want me to do with these, he asks the servant. Paint anything you like on them is the answer. He says no to wood. Working on wood with a knife is too cumbersome. Chandeliers are brought, some delicate and some massive in all kinds of colours—purple to a bilious green. These don't need any ornamentation, he tells the amir's representative. But the amir is a big shot. He could one day be the commander-in-chief, the amir-kabir, or the president of the council of amirs, amir-majlis, or the minister of the Sultan's palace, the ustadar. So the chandelier would be painted lamp by lamp, a floral or a geometric motif on each and the amir would be pleased as punch.

He slowly starts ornamenting walls and floors of villas and palaces. His compositions depict astral bodies finely balanced with a centrifugal star flare. He does this kind of work in coloured stone. Today, perhaps, they would pass off as murals. Maulvis urge him to copy the Qoran. His name would, in that case, be numbered with the great calligraphers of yore—with Muhammad Ibn al Walid who copied thirty volumes of the book for Baybars in 1304; or with that of Ibrahim ibn Muhammad al Khabbaz. But he declines politely. Copying the holy book and ornamenting it would be a lifetime's work. You should look for better men, he tells his interlocutors in all humility. Moreover, he doesn't have the patience to learn all the cursive scripts—thuluth, naskhi, maskh fada—nor is he versed in the kufiq script.

Most of all he is thrilled to work on blazons. It brings in good money. But more than that it gives him elbow room for originality—dividing the shield into two or three sections, working on different symbols in each section and yet seeing to it that the entire thing stands out as a composite whole.

Then, one day, Murad comes over and asks Ehtesham if he has ever met the Abbott? The Abbott? What for? Well, he is an interesting person, and what is more he has heard of you.

'And I have not heard of the Abbott!'

Ehtesham bursts out laughing. On their way Murad has to explain what the Abbott is. The artist has no idea. He is not even sure what a monastery is. Khanquah, he asks? Murad explains as best as he can. How do you know so much about the Christians, asks Ehtesham. I'll tell you another time, he answers.

That moment would take a long time coming.

They have to go past the Coptic town to reach the monastery. No one can go past that area in Cairo without being impressed—the neatly cobbled lanes, the church of St Sergius, church and synagogue almost cheek by jowl, the women, beautiful as all Egyptian women are, but uninhibited, moving about without veils and the black robes that go with them, and the streets inhabited by laughter. When he asks about the church, Murad tells him about Abou Sarga, as it is known, named after two martyrs Sergius and Bachus from the al Rasfah village nearby. Both were executed by the Roman Emperor Maximian. He tells him about the legend, how the Holy Family had taken shelter here in a crypt, though Murad can't tell him whether the crypt existed before the church was built.

When they enter the monastery, Ehtesham is a bit awestruck. The well-kept lawn around a fountain, the row of trees leading up to the two domed, white-stoned building comes as a surprise to him. The Abbott is imposing, broad-limbed and tall, with a benign, bearded, well-fleshed face. His smock hides his protruding belly. He welcomes Murad with a smile and greets Ehtesham formally. Pleasantries are exchanged.

'How long have you been in Cairo?'

'The best part of six years now. And you, Sir Abbott?'

'Oh I have been here for about twenty five years now. We get chained, bonded you know.'

He didn't know. The Abbott explains. Each time a new head of the monastery comes in, the Order has to pay 20,000 to the Sultan's treasury. That's the understanding. By staying on for long periods we avoid these back-breaking imposts. Our Order wants to send someone from Europe. But what about the 20,000 pieces of silver? That deters them. But in twenty years one becomes a Caierene. I would like to die here. But life and death are in God's hands. He selects the time, he selects the place.'

Murad intervenes. 'Apart from you, the others in the monastery belong here, don't they?'

'Yes, of course, they are all Egyptians, Copts. But we are different, aren't we? When I say "we", I mean my flock of course.'

'Why should we be different, we who have lived in the same land these thousands of years?' asks Ehtesham.

*keki n. daruwalla*

'You are right, my son. But we've been different and not been different. Pardon me if you think my arguments are littered with paradoxes. It was the Copts who revolted against high taxes in the delta in the first century of Muslim rule. Then the Coptic language was replaced by Arabic. Still the Copts picked it up earlier than Muslim Egyptians. They fought shoulder to shoulder against the crusaders and they couldn't drive a wedge between us. There are contradictions and paradoxes galore here. Because we (and by "we" I mean the Copts, I consider myself a Copt now) have had a hard time. We have to be more Egyptian than the Muslim Egyptian. People tell me with dismay that an Arab can't ride a horse in Cairo today after the Mamluks took over. Copts didn't ride even earlier. Copts had to get down from a donkey if a Muslim happened to pass by. If a Copt dies, the state takes away all that he possessed, declaring the dead man a bankrupt. Nothing goes to his heirs. Yet we were never lepers. We didn't have to carry a bell around our necks. There were periods when the two communities lived like brothers. There were also times when conversions to Islam stopped. This was because taxes on non-Muslims got reduced to a trickle. When the Nile did not rise, the Sultan, the Caliph, the Copt Pope and the Rabbi, along with their followers, all went to the Nile and prayed, each from his own scripture and in his own tongue. Each carried his Holy Book and the Nile always rose a few days after the prayers. But enough of this. I thought we should be talking of you.'

Ehtesham feels embarrassed. 'What is there to talk about me, Sir Abbott?'

'A good deal, if I may say so. From what I have heard, your youth is being plundered, Son.'

'I don't understand.'

'Well, I hear you are a fine artist.'

The Abbott claps and a servant comes in with sherbet and sweets coated with linseed. 'Bring the lamps also,' the Abbott tells him.

When the glass lamps are brought in, the Abbott holds them up and asks, 'I believe this is your calligraphy?' Ehtesham examines it and nods.

'This is lovely calligraphy—as good as any I have seen. But isn't calligraphy itself restrictive? You have vast talents, I am told, but are unable to use them. That can be very disappointing, isn't it?'

'One has to adjust. Circumstances won't.'

'But if the circumstances are unjust, one must try and bend them to one's will.'

'But I couldn't. When I was painting, all sorts of people got after me, from venerable teachers in al Azhar to men like Ali Hasan. Word also reached the Muhtasib himself. That, as you know, can be dangerous for a boy from Asyut.'

The Abbott shakes his head gravely. 'The Muhtasib can baptize a new morality when he chooses. Though he also works under various pressures. But as you must have guessed by now, this is not some aimless discussion to which I have invited you. I would not have asked you over if I had no specific proposal in mind. We are repairing our church at Shentena al Hagar. It is built of old stone. You are free to paint on the walls.'

A stunned silence follows. Ehtesham notes that even Murad looks as shocked as he himself.

'You are asking me to paint on church walls? Do I get you right?'

'Yes, both at Shentena and at Cairo. But the motifs will have to be religious. You can't paint a peasant in a carob field, for instance, or a fellahein plying his boat up the Nile. The cross, Chist on the cross—what we call 'Ecce Homo'—the birth of

Jesus, the manger, the adoring Magi, these are the kinds of paintings one expects in a church. Jesus walking with the cross on what has now come to be known as 'Via Dolorossa', is another popular subject with painters. You could choose any scene from his life—Jesus throwing out the money changers from the temple, Jesus healing lepers, raising Lazarus from the dead. You don't have to be restricted to the life of Lord Jesus. There are saints galore. Reading the Bible would be of help. It would give you a hundred ideas.'

The three fall quiet suddenly, but the effect of the discussion on Ehtesham is that of a mallet striking a brass gong. After a long silence he shakes his head in bewilderment. 'I hope you realize that by painting these scenes I would be committing apostasy, at least of a kind. *Shirk* is a bad word around here, Sir Abbott.'

'I realize what is going through your mind, Son. But this is one chance you have of exploring your talent. And Issa is your prophet as well. Don't let these thoughts of faith and apostasy bother you unduly. Bigger minds than yours or mine have been unable to wrestle with them. If God has given you a talent and a love for colour, don't waste all of it on making these floral designs on glass and chandelier globes. Paint.'

Murad speaks for Ehtesham. 'In this city there will be no dearth of daggers thirsting for Ehtesham's blood.'

'I understand that,' says the Abbott rising from his chair to indicate that the meeting is over. 'But my advice is, reap your harvest before others reap you as harvest.'

On this enigmatic note, the meeting ended.

# of calligraphy and printing

Insults and bodily harm don't go unavenged in al Qahira. The Perfumer has not forgotten his drubbing, and one day he and his cronies waylay Ehtesham and pay him back, blow for blow. Murad has to nurse him and Habiba comes calling one day to enquire .

Word gets to Asyut and his mother arrives. She surveys the surroundings and the first thing she says is, 'Change this wretched room. It is neither fit for my son nor for his bride.' The bride bit leaves his friends nonplussed. She digs into her bag, brings out a large handful of silver coins and without counting them, hands them over to Murad, asking him to hire a decent house for her son. Then she turns to her son and says, 'I thought you were in a worse state. You Caireines can certainly exaggerate.' She makes him get up from his bed and walk and doesn't fuss over his bruises. Ehtesham can't get over his surprise. This is not the mother he knew, cautious and tight-fisted and always anxiety-ridden.

Within days she gets in touch with people from Asyut who live in Cairo, and accompanied by some of them she proceeds to Zainab's house, carrying a silver tray full of sweets and rosewater and silver coins. Of course Zainab and her mother know what she is coming for. With great dignity she asks for

Zainab's hand for her son from her mother and Abu Khalil. And the wedding is settled.

Nothing like a marriage to bring out both your strengths and inadequacies. Ehtesham doesn't have to be told that there is more to a marriage than love. There is more to love than the hand touching the naked small of the back, feeling the muscle packed on either side of the spine; the blood-beat on a cold night against the palm of your hand; and the heartbeat as you caress her breast; more to it than the rustle of her clothes as you hug her fiercely. There is more to love than the scoop and the swell of the love act itself as she rises with the tide, both reaching a sort of a crest before the eventual slide.

There are a hundred things she doesn't know, he reflects. She has no idea of his meeting with the Muhtasib, the warning about painting, the fact that he would for ever be in the fellow's sights. She doesn't know that the perfumer was, and probably still is, the Muhtasib's informer. The great man may not have been too happy at his agent getting roughed up by him. Who knows, perhaps the goons who beat him up were the Muhtasib's men? That was both unnerving and reassuring. Unnerving because the official had taken a personal interest in the matter and thought it fit to intervene. Reassuring, in the sense that a thrashing satisfied the Muhtasib. Normally, it should have meant the end of him. Most probably, he thought, the Muhtasib was not involved in his affair.

Zainab, on the other hand, has been very frank. He had been discussed as a prospective groom a good year back. The relatives had been aghast. How venerable is the family? What does the father do? Which part of Cairo do they come from? Each answer brought a gasp from the old aunts. They didn't know much about the family. His father is dead. He lives in a riwaq. And he comes from Asyut. Asyut! Are you in your senses, Khalida, they asked the blind lady. You are going to marry this pearl of a daughter to someone in Asyut! But the old lady answered that Abu Khalil was impressed with the boy and that he had his heart in the right place. Right place? No one has his heart in his stomach or his buttocks. Abu Khalil is now old enough to be senile. When Khalida reprimanded the speaker, she excused herself by saying, 'I never said he was senile. I only said he was old enough to be senile.' The barrage of questions rattled on. Does he have a shop? Is the family well off? The answers were negative and the old aunts whispered among themselves that Khalida was now blind to the daughter's future as well. They had shaken their heads vigorously and that had been the end of the matter.

Then the 'scandal' of the perfumer occurred and things changed.

Zainab, of course, had no inkling of Ehtesham's meeting with the Abbott. He wouldn't dream of telling her that. She would be aghast, coming as she did from a fairly devout family. He wondered if she had noticed that his work had faltered a little after the meeting. The hand turns slower, the fingers a bit stiff, once interest drops even a wee bit. Some questions trouble him. Writing a few Arabic words on glass or carving them on metal with a flourish, is that all he is good for? Would his entire life just amount to that, calligraphy? And geometric designs? Carpet weavers were doing as much, he thinks. Sometimes, he admits to himself and even to Zainab, the weavers are better. He stands rooted at the roadside sometimes looking at the wares of rug vendors and admiring their designs. He often chats them up. Do you weave these carpets yourself? Of course, or how would we fill our belly? Since when have you been working? Since as long as I can remember. Who thought of the pattern? That last question always brings a disappointing answer. No, says the boy, he didn't think it up, these designs are handed down from generation to generation. Does his father make the designs? The vendor laughs. No, these designs are heirlooms, older than fathers and grandfathers. Yet they often seem more innovative, more pleasing to the eye than his efforts.

For the first few months after the wedding Zainab has only seen him working on calligraphy on metal and glass. Inlay work takes a long time and sometimes his fingers blister. He goes to mosque and mausoleum to work there itself. It saves him transporting lamp and globe, especially the delicate glass ones. He also works at the house, which fills with glass lamps and metal lamps, and Zainab has to walk gingerly after dark because the lamps are scattered all over the floor. The turnover used to be quick. It seems to have slowed down a little. He brings paper to the house and starts drawing—street scenes at first, minaret and dome and a shop or two nearby, a handcart-pusher, a rug vendor displaying his pile of carpets. She asks him if there is any money in all this and he just shrugs. Everything can't be valued in terms of money, your face for instance. He starts painting her, makes her pose. But all these efforts are futile. When I finish the painting your face will be veiled, he says and laughs. Why waste my time then? Why don't you paint some woman walking the street? But he makes her wear the black robe and pose. He first paints the board black so that the burqa is hardly visible. Yet as the painting progresses, the folds and the creases of the black robe come through. Only the face glows white. The hands are slightly darker, as if some shadow has fallen on them. Initially Zainab is disappointed till, in slightly strong light she can see the folds, roll on roll, of her robe, and the glow on the face surfaces, stroke by stroke of the caressing brush.

Things don't end here, obviously. He paints a Mamluk warrior in his suit of armour, an amir on horseback, a farmer in the delta ploughing his field, a Bedouin kneeling in prayer with dusk and desert as backdrop. Drawings follow. There are many variations on boys trundling handcarts and greengrocers with their donkey carts. Abu Khalil is drawn wrinkle by wrinkle, a wistful smile peering above the beard curled and white.

Do you like any of this stuff, he suddenly asks her one day, rather impulsively. She laughs, not at the question, but the shy, hesitant way he asked. She is aware of the effort it cost him to speak thus.

'Of course I like them. Who wouldn't? I haven't seen anything like this.'

He knows that's true. She couldn't have.

'Which do you like the best?'

'That's difficult. But why are you tense? You should become restful after a painting, after you've got it out of your system, isn't it?'

He has no answer. He wasn't even aware that he appeared tense. Trust a woman to unravel your feelings, thread by thread, he thinks.

But now she notices a slight aimlessness about him. He seems to have slowed down. He still goes out in the mornings but she isn't sure where he is heading. When he returns he doesn't talk about what happened at the mausoleum or the mosque, what the muezzin said to him or he said to the muezzin. He has been seen wandering around in the Coptic district. What could he be doing there?

*keki n. daruwalla*

# CALICUT

# the zamorin

The Zamorin's palace was not ostentatious, as palaces go. It didn't have the scale and grandeur of Mughal buildings, for instance. (It is another thing that the Mughals had still to arrive in India. They were either conquering Kabul or fleeing from the bloody place and had not yet dreamt of the land called Hind. Not as yet.) You could call it a large house, or at a pinch, a very large one, with two halls facing in the direction of the sea. It was open and airy, and the breeze from the ocean could scythe through the halls to a series of smaller rooms opening up on the inner courtyard, around which the Queen and the women had their rooms. The house had two fountains, one in front where the Zamorin sometimes reclined, and one in the inner courtyard. There was nothing ornate about the doors. The floor was of red mosaic, smooth as glass, over which everyone walked, rather glided, barefoot, including the Zamorin and his queen. A wooden palisade encircled the house. Many of the planks were of sandalwood, so that the air was heavy with its fragrance.

The Zamorin was in a contemplative mood as he sat near the fountain, downwind, so that the breeze coming through the spray could cool his sweating body on this summer evening. He never wanted the fountains. It was his part-Arab confidante, Rahman Sarwar, who had insisted. One of his ministers, Chirukandan was present at the meeting and had intervened. Why does the Zamorin need a fountain? He rules the sea. What can the fountain give him which the sea can't? But Rahman had insisted. A fountain was not just water spouting away from a few holes. It held within its spray an entire culture. No wonder the Muslim paradise abounded in fountains, and, of course, houris. There could be no paradise without the two of them.

The Zamorin had no reason to be dissatisfied with things. True, he was losing some revenue because of his largesse, if that is what one-could call the benign imposts levied on ships calling at his port. The duties on goods sold by a foreign ship came to one-fortieth of the value of the sale. If no goods were sold, they paid nothing. On the other hand if ships were driven into the Calicut harbour by strong winds, they had nothing to fear. At other ports if the same thing happened, the people robbed the ship under the plea that the sea had driven it onto the coast, and hence the ship belonged to them. That is what the Arab historian Abdur Razzaq had written fifty odd years ago in 1442.

The Zamorin may or may not have been aware of Abdur Razzaq or Nicolo Conti, the Italian who had come two years earlier than Razzaq. Indians don't sleep well with history. He definitely did not know that the Roman Empire, according to Pliny's estimates, paid a hundred million sesterces to India, China and Arabia for 'luxuries' imported by way of trade. India did send ivory, muslin and silk, but the bulk of the money came from the sale of spices from south India; spices that were equated with gold and silver by the Romans . The name given to spices by Sanskrit writers was 'yavana-priya' (dear to the Yavanas—Ionians/Greeks/Romans—Indians were never bothered to distinguish between them—they were all bloody foreigners, outside the pale of caste). He could also not have known that when Rome was besieged by the Goths in the fifth century AD, the Goth king Alaric asked for 3000 pounds of black pepper as part of the deal to spare Rome from ravage. The Zamorin, incidentally, did not even know that he was Zamorin! He knew himself as the Samudriya Raja, Lord of the Sea. But the Europeans found both Samudrya and Samudri a tongue-wrencher and so he became the Zamorin.

The Zamorin was a practical fellow and modest as kings go. He was no great believer in his jaw-breaking titles— Kunnalakonatiri and Salibdhiswaran. They both meant the same thing (pomp and tautology have always gone together)— 'King of the lands between the mountains and the waves'. His kingdom did not even extend to the Vindhya Mountains. He would have liked people to believe that he had shut the door to the north and all invasions from that direction. But he knew he had very little to do with that. The Lodis and the Rajputs were all the time attacking each other or planning to attack. They were blissfully unaware of the Dakhin (the south), or Deccan, as the Brits were to mispronounce the word later. And while in the north all this frenetic activity was taking place, punctuated with 'suttas' from the opium pipe and a fair amount of concubinage for the nobles and *randi baazi* for the riff-raff (you must have different terms for the notables and the rabble even when it comes to fucking), Calicut was flourishing through international commerce.

He was savouring this rare moment of solitude. It wouldn't last much more than an hour, he knew. Still, it was such a relief to be without his seven senior ministers breathing down his neck. The Mangat Achchan, the senior-most was conservative but he could not remember the man ever giving wrong advice. There were rumours about the other very senior minister, Chirukandan Nair, that were doing the rounds with the women. For women, rumours are facts, he reflected. It was said that he had walked out on his mistress! Abandoning wives for other beds was a common enough male pastime. But the mistress! That raised eyebrows. Was it because the once beautiful Kanni was turning heavy in the hip? The Zamorin's aunt had laughed at the suggestion. 'The heavier you are the better for the man. Otherwise, you make too much sound, no? A frail woman buckles and flexes all the time. Men delight in cushions.' She had winked and laughed wickedly.

All rulers have their worries—so had the Zamorin. The *Kutiravattathu* Nair (the General in charge of the cavalry— and the Zamorin had a fine cavalry, what with all the fine horses supplied by the Arabs) had reported that one of the District Governors, a *Naduvazhi* by the name of Kellu Kutty, was perpetrating atrocities on the people. The governors of Nadus (districts) were hereditary. The new incumbent paid a succession fee (*purushantaram*) to the Zamorin and sent presents on festivals like Onam, or the King's coronation. According to the Cavalry General, Kellu Kutty, in league with tax collectors, was extorting money. Even their names were similar, thought the Zamorin, for the Cavalry General was called Kellappan. But you'd need ten men to keep them from each other's throats. The District Governor had blamed the Cavalry General for unruly behavior and exactions. What did one do in such cases? Whom to believe? Inaction was the easiest way out, but inaction led to laxity. Oh well, we will see to it the next day with his ministers standing behind him and the clerks handling leaves already signed by him and bearing his seal. Once he gave an indication, they wrote it down and the leaf became fiat, diktat, warrant, an order to execute a person—the works. Tomorrow then!

Rahman Sarwar was announced. He came fully robed, unlike the Brahmins and the Nairs, who came half naked covering themselves only from the waist down. His bow was not obsequious. After a few preliminary pleasantries and salutations, Rahman got down to business. He started by saying that it was none of his business, but the next day the Zamorin, as the king, would decide on the allegations and counter allegations between the Cavalry General and the District Governor. The Zamorin held up his palms, indicating that the other should stop speaking.

'The moment you started by saying that it was none of your business, I knew you were about to put your foot into something really troublesome. We are discussing justice, aren't we, a judgement I have yet to deliver?'

Rahman was unfazed. Yes Highness, he said, we are discussing justice. He was aware that the Zamorin was the living fount of all justice, and in fact the only judge in the land. All-important judgements were given in his name, and normally after consultation with him. But one was dealing with the cavalry, Highness. Yes, their men could be guilty of exactions. The Naduvazhi and his men, however, were infinitely worse. More important, the morale of the cavalry had to be kept up. 'What about the foot soldiers?' asked the king with a wry smile. There was no answer. And what if whatever the Naduvazhi said, was true? Then the complaint should have come initially from him, replied Rahman. This fellow seemed to have an answer for most things, thought the Zamorin.

'What you want to say, Rahman, is that the cavalry should not feel let down. The morale of the horses is important for the state. Back them, for the cavalry will fight. Except that I can't see any enemy on the horizon.'

'Highness, enemies don't announce themselves by beat of drum.'

'Yes Rahman. Is that all?' The interview was over. The Arab bowed deferentially and walked out.

~

Even as this meeting was over, his minister, who everyone knew was the main tale carrier, had come in. The fellow was a bit ridiculous and often brought poor information. But he could never brook any delay in meeting the king. His information must have priority! He was a bit long winded, a necessary trait in a tale tattler if the news at hand isn't vital. But the Zamorin had no time for him today. Don't flail around, come to the point, he told him. The long and short of it was that a monk from Lanka had come across and met Kelu Kutty. The fellow wanted to trade in sapphires. Sapphires? The minister noted how the Zamorin's eyebrows had curled up. Blue? Yes blue, Highness, but the Lankans have white and yellow sapphires too. White? Those must be poor quality diamonds, or glass maybe. Sorry to correct you Highness, but they do have white sapphires. The monk was showing them around and some of our merchants fell over each other when they saw them, ignorant fools.

Well then I too am an ignorant fool, said the Zamorin. I have heard of the yellow stone though.

Yellow stone, Highness? The fellow has yellow sapphires as big as cat's eyes. And they flare at night like cat's eyes near a fire.

Big cat or small cat?

Big cat, Highness.

And what is he after, this monk from Lanka.

He wants a ship, Highness, and sailors and swordsmen.

Whom do they want to attack, these Lankans?

I've to find that out.

Well, find out and let me know.

It had been a tiring day, and as he went to bed that evening, the Zamorin's mind was clouded. Yet somewhere in his consciousness the dregs had settled down—the struggle between Kellu Kutty and Kelappan, that salacious titbit about his minister Chirukandan, and that monk from Lanka who wanted to buy a ship with his sapphires. If you bought a war ship, you also bought war. What kind of a connection could he have with that Kelu Kutty? And why Kelu of all . . .

~

Chirukandan had started balding a little now. He was solidly built and his manner was masterful. He was after all an important minister, in charge of customs, the main source of revenue for Calicut. When big ships came in, he would himself go on board along with a Chetti, a broker. An invoice would be made of the cargo. Then a day would be fixed for valuing the goods. Chirukandan's deputy would now go to the ship. When the valuation was arrived at, to the satisfaction of the parties, Chiru's representative, the broker and the ship owner or Captain would all hold hands and the deputy would shout, 'The value of the cargo is fixed. Now nothing can alter it.' When the valuation figures were placed before Chirukandan the next day, he would go over them minutely. The Chetti and the deputy knew they would be in big trouble if the minister suspected that they had undervalued the cargo. He was not above manhandling them personally. Nothing should cause loss to the state, for once the goods were sold, one-fortieth went to the state.

While the Zamorin had been busy with his meetings, Chirukandan had taken his boat and sailed off to Ponnani some miles north. It was dark when he arrived at the headman's house, but this time the reception wasn't the same. On the last occasion , the headman proffering a garland and his wife carrying the lamp-lit aarthi, had welcomed him. Well, one can't have ceremony each time you want to sleep with the headman's daughter, he thought. It wasn't right, he knew. But what could he do? He couldn't sleep last night. The whole day he was thinking of her, her brown irises the size of a small copper coin, a damdi, and the ringlets in her hair. And he had kept looking down at his mundu, afraid that his desire might show. Thank heavens his langoti was really tight, or what a scandal it would have been. The Minister for Customs—the most lucrative post in the kingdom, doing his duties in painful and permanent rigidity. He could hardly sleep that night, as he tossed around on his bed, till his wife told him sarcastically that he might as well spend the night with his mistress. That way at least she could sleep undisturbed. Even she didn't know, he thought, that he wasn't thinking of his mistress. It was this young daughter of the headman who was the flame of his loins, and who stoked those fires in his dreams.

She stood up as he was ushered into her room, came burning into his arms as he enveloped her. He passed his hands down the black fountain of her hair, trying ineffectively to straighten her seductive ringlets. His fingers got lost in her hair. He held her close, staring for a minute into her eyes before he kissed them. She felt him turn uncontrollable as he kissed her all over, circling her neck, her lips, her forehead with his lips. She straightened her arms suddenly and held him back.

'Are you always going to come like this?'

'Like what?'

'Like this, after dark?'

'You don't understand. I have commitments, I have a position to protect, can't you see? What if word of all this reaches the Samudri Raja?'

'What if word of all this reaches your wife?'

She is overreaching herself, this daughter of a mere headman, but in clandestine darkness you have to tolerate some insults, he thought. Still, how dare she talk of his wife, reach up to her, the mother of his children! None of the other

*keki n. daruwalla*

women he had slept with had dared to do *that*. A day would come when he would have to fix her. But at the moment he had other things on his mind, and they were all to do with fixing.

'My life would be ruined if this gets known. Do you know what it means to stand close to the Samudri Raja every day and take down his orders, to be able to suggest things to him, to give him advice, god forgive me for this insolence. Your hair stands up, just to be near the man.'

'And what does it feel like being near me?'

He mumbled a hundred things now, his words getting mixed with his kisses and his saliva, as he overwhelmed her, took off her blouse and flung her on the bed. She responded as only someone new to passion could. It was only when, caught in the flurry and the fidgeting with his waist cloth, he blew on the lamp wick and snuffed it out that she asked why he was snuffing out the light in the room. He didn't care to answer. She wasn't even sure he had heard her.

When they were done he tied his loincloth—he had not taken off his mundu, just parted it at the front. She straightened her hair and her blouse—must maintain a veneer of respectability before her parents. Then she asked, 'Will you always come like this, like a thief in the dark?'

He slapped her hard. But even as he did so, he was muttering a hundred apologies and frantically kissing the weal his palm had left on her cheek.

~

Over the next two days, the monk from Lanka had two long meetings with the Minister of Customs, Chirukandan. But Chiru was not sure what the fellow wanted. Simple commerce he understood, you buy and sell and fill your coffers. Fine.

War he understood. You have an enemy and wish to demolish him, or failing that, subvert and sabotage his plans. Religious aggrandizement was alien to him, but still he could visualize it as a concept. After all the Lodis were ruling over Delhi, though like most people in Calicut or Cochin he had never been north of the Narmada. But what this Buddhist monk with the saffron robe and the shorn head from Lanka was aiming at was an amalgam of all three. Or so it seemed to him. He talked of buying land for monasteries. He also talked of a safe passage for pilgrims going to Sarnath and Bodh Gaya and Lumbini. The fellow had no idea. The Zamorin couldn't have promised free passage up to even the Cavery.

He was beating about the bush, this monk. The fellow had something else on his mind. His figure was impressive—he was tall and well built, and though his belly protruded, one could observe the muscles on his arms. His face was full-fleshed. His body, his demeanour, everything about him exuded strength. The large frame, the tonsured head, the saffron robe worn almost regally, everything about him was daunting. Yet his conversation seemed to make no headway.

Chirukandan was blunt. 'Bhikshu, with respect, why are you wasting your time and mine? What do you really want? Surely not a safe passage which we can't provide, or ships that we can't sell. You have come for something else.'

'What could I be looking for? Why are you suspicious?'

'Suspicion should come naturally to a man in my position, Monk. If I believed everyone, I would be swindled. By lunch I wouldn't have a mundu round my waist. I respect your robe though, and of course you.'

'Is there any harm if we exchange views? Don't you think we should sit together and talk. Every boat coming from the Zanj is full of stories of pink coloured people, who have anchored there and are looking for pilots to carry them east. What does the east mean ? Our shores of course.'

'Is that all? We too have heard of the pink people as you call them. Sailors are full of such stories—of half-fish and half-men and sea animals bigger than a ship. I thought you would have something more by way of information to give us.'

But the monk had sapphires for sure, and the yellow ones were dazzling. Chiru wasn't interested to start with. Stones dazzle you for an instant, but it is women who drool over them. He had other things to think about.

Dodging one woman was bad enough. Dodging wasn't the right word, he knew. What he meant was the whole round of subterfuge and lies and not being able to look someone in the eye. And of course face the ultimate humiliation of being found out. Sometimes his wife would almost anticipate his lies. But all that was in the past. Now she had resigned herself to his escapades. What was worse, now he was dealing with two disbelieving women. His mistress of six years, the well-padded Kanni, she whose hips he had widened over the years with his thrusts, or so he believed, she too had to be cajoled and lied to, and appeased with presents. Yellow sapphires would be right, he thought.

Yes, he would like to buy some of those yellow sapphires, he told him. The monk was well versed in the ways of men and ministers. His smile was so benign one would think one was in the presence of a saint. Shaved head, assertive belly and the yellow robe guaranteed solace of sorts and respect, if not veneration. A string was passed on, nothing big or startling. The money proffered was refused. It was the monk who bowed as he left, though the minister went barefoot to the gate to see him off.

~

Kelu Kutty, the District Governor, knew he had to do something. One couldn't just sit back and mull over things, hoping there would be a way out. This Kelappan and his cavalrymen had to be put in their place—the stables preferably. They couldn't be allowed to do what they bloody well pleased and tramp all over the peasantry. Well, tramping over the peasantry was not very unique, he thought. His own men did much the same. Collecting taxes was no party—how the peasants tried to hide their paddy harvests. They'd tuck it up their orifices if they could, he thought. But Kelappan's bastards were tramping over officialdom—over Kelu Kutty and his men. God knew he contented himself with silver. This whole year he hadn't touched a gold coin, not even the kind handed in by Arab traders. What greater honesty did the Zamorin expect from his officers? It is another thing that no one had offered him a yellow coin either. But that was neither here nor there. And to think of it that that Customs Minister would get all that *nazrana* from the Arab dhows, but wouldn't accept any. That was the rumour—could be self-generated. He felt a little mean, harbouring such a thought.

He hadn't done anything to extort money from the Arabs either. This Kelappan of course was in cahoots with the Muslims, be they Mappilas or Arabs, he was convinced. Was that the reason none of them had offered him gold? And why did we need a bloody cavalry anyway! Were they going to charge against the waves? Were we at war with the King of Lanka? The images of Swarandwip came to his mind. He hadn't been there ever. Sailors and pirates went there—and tidal waves. And all that Swarandwip meant to Kelu Kutty was thick forests, orphaned elephants (he had heard some stories to the effect) and the ten heads of Ravana.

That was till he met the monk from Lanka, and heard of sapphires. Sapphires? Was Lanka rich in sapphires? Didn't you know? asked the monk. Kelu was good at ferreting out things from people. While all that talk of monasteries and Lumbini and Gaya glanced off his radar screen, he latched on to the information that the monk had stopped at Cochin before his arrival in Calicut. Cochin was always a rival port and a rival kingdom, and the Lankan had traded with Cochin earlier. That was a nice bit to extract from him, along with some sapphires.

A messenger came and whispered something in Kelu Kutty's ear. The monk saw consternation creep upon the administrator's face. Gathering the folds of his mundu, Kelu Kutty got up to indicate that the meeting was over. 'If you ever find yourself in trouble, remember the men of Swarandwip are behind you,' said the monk before leaving.

It was a bad story as stories go. The cavalrymen had raided his district and caught a fellow trading in women. Trafficking in women was older than the Ramayana and the Kama Sutra. You could get a woman from Nepal or from the hills in the northwest in a remote corner in the south. But this fellow was getting them here and sending them as far north as Taxila, perhaps across the Khyber. Or perhaps through dhows to the Gulf. He had bought this woman's daughter—her name was Lakshmi, the mother's not the daughter's. The messenger was in such a hurry to tell his tale that he now and then tied himself up in knots. Well, when the trader came to take her away, the mother threw a fit. Histrionics became her. She asked (all the while wailing and tearing her hair and beating her breasts), 'Are you taking my daughter to make a dancing girl of her, you pimp?' All this, after she had taken his money a week earlier.

The flesh trader had had enough of all this by now. 'No,' he answered sarcastically, 'I am taking her to a monastery to make a nun out of her.' People resented the remark and there was a fracas. The flesh trader's henchmen were armed with staves. A skirmish occurred and the cavalrymen were called in to control matters. They caught this Manohar Lal—that was the pimp's name, and he was from the north and they beat him up and jailed him. It was rumoured he would be presented before the Zamorin.

They'd make a mountain of it, he knew. This was all in his knowledge and he had turned a blind eye, they would say. 'A free rope to pimps, Highness, a free rope.' Another would chip in: 'You think he didn't know, Highness? A grain of sand can't move, a leaf can't stir without Naduvazhi coming to know! And here is this bastard exporting the entire womanhood of Calicut for prostitution in the north, and Your Honour in your kindness, thinks Kelu Kutty didn't know of all this? The flesh trader and he were buddies! The fellow had bribed Kelu. See what dishonour he has brought on Malabar! She would have become a devdasi at some sordid temple.' A dancing girl at a brothel more likely, would snort another. He could imagine all this and the smirk on the lips of Kelappan. Kelu Kutty knew his goose was cooked.

~

Chirukandan instinctively felt that a personal meeting with Kanni, his mistress of six years, the one whose wide hips had given him such pleasure, was not on, not just as yet. She might not give him the time of day this time. Best to send a gift first. *Nazarana*—he loved the word. It rang like a coin. One must hand it to these Muslims for coining such fine words. They also minted fine coin, perfectly rounded, not serrated and rough edged as the ones from Cochin or Calicut. Ministers should not be at the receiving end of nazranas always. That string of sapphires had to travel to her. He marked his boatman out for the job. A bag of rice, a bag of coconuts, a silver thali with an old raffia-covered coconut placed on it, and the sapphires in a velvet pouch. An honest boatman was worth as much as a boat, he reflected.

How did she receive them, he asked the boatman on his return, the next morning. She stood there without saying much. Did she look at the contents of the pouch? Not at first. But then I requested her—told her it was a gift from Your Honour. She opened the pouch then. Did she smile? She did not, Your Honour.

The boatman had barely gone out of the room when he scuttled in again, his hands folded. Yes? Honour, she didn't accept the things at first. Wanted me to take everything back, coconuts, rice, everything. Then the mother shouted from her bed.

'Did she? And what did she say?'

'You have got to accept these. Your Swami has sent them! And Your Honour, she said to her mother, I have no Swami now, I am Swamini, my own lord and mistress.'

He hadn't told his master that her hair was dishevelled and her eyes red with weeping and there was a grimace on her mouth that would have frightened a cat in a dark alley.

~

Chiru had no idea that the Lankan monk had met Kelu Kutty. He liked Kelu, because Kelu Kutty did not get on with Kelappan, the Cavalry General, who was so close to the people from the Red Sea. Was it because of the horses, which they brought, he had often wondered? Why need we get mixed up with them, these people who looked to the west and prayed to the One and Only, hated more than one god, and certainly hated the goddesses. They didn't want anyone else muscling in on the trade, as if our pepper and our spices belonged to their fathers! They wouldn't let the boats from the east come in, or from Lanka, or even China. Had they taken a contract, a *karar*? No other flag was seen on a mast, or at least not enough of them. The entire coast was peppered with their dhows, and all the ports spiked with mosque-minarets, and they were marrying our women and settling down. If his father was alive he wouldn't be able to recognize the place, butcher shops everywhere and the azan floating across the sunset.

Since the monk wanted an audience with the Zamorin, it could be arranged. Actually when the monk came in, in the company of half a dozen merchants of Calicut, he discovered there was no need for prior appointments. You just barged in, sat in an anteroom, if such it could be called, and were ushered in as soon as the Zamorin was free. It was not like the formality one encountered at the court of the King of Kandy. He also noted that there was no special gravitas on the monarch's countenance. In fact he noticed a sort of a bovine impassivity. Yet he was surprised at the Zamorin's initial remark.

'You look more like a Mudhalali than a monk.'

Mudhalali was the term for a rich trader in Lanka. The monk answered as best as he could. The Zamorin was obviously referring to his rather prosperous belly. But he was just a poor monk, rich only in some of the scriptures he had memorized.

The Zamorin's second remark was even more odd. 'Are the waterholes in your country running dry?'

The monk didn't know what to make of it. Does he think that Lanka is all jungle, pocked with waterholes, where we home in along with deer and wild pig for a lick of water? Would the next question be about our salt licks, he wondered.

*keki n. daruwalla*

Nevertheless he bowed and said the rains had been rather plentiful in the winter. The Zamorin then asked the monk if he had come to trade or to preach and set up viharas. It was just an exploratory visit, he replied. For commerce mostly.

Commerce would be difficult, the Zamorin said. We have the same things to trade in—spices, pepper, cardamom, cinnamon. And coconuts of course. You have what we have. How do we trade? We buy your pepper, you buy our pepper? Ridiculous, no? But come all the same. If Cochin can welcome you, so can Calicut. (He wiped his lips with the back of his hand, almost as soon as he mentioned Cochin, the monk noticed. So he knew about his stay in Cochin. But how much did he know?) The Zamorin was not finished as yet. Are you going to set up viharas, monasteries? he asked as a parting shot. Will more of your Bhikshus stream in from Lanka? The monk tried to assuage the King's fears, but he came away unsure whether he had succeeded. He wasn't even sure what the Zamorin's misgivings were.

~

When Kelu Kutty was put up before the Zamorin, he knew, like everyone else, that it would be a disaster. He didn't need a palmist to tell him that his fate line had ended suddenly, and that Rahu was circling over him. But it was bedlam in the corridor which he had to traverse before entering the Zamorin's presence. There was a mass of people there, just waiting to watch his humiliation, people craning their necks to see this man, this powerful lord of a district who would now be shown the door, the man who allowed women to be sold to the north and the west, for all you know, to the Punjabis and the Arabs, the fellow who indulged in the export of women rather than cinnamon bark and pepper and cardamom. People were already jeering, and gesticulating as if they were witnessing a dogfight. Some were cursing him. It looked as if by common consent he was transformed into a criminal overnight. And as Kelappan, the cavalry general in his uniform (though barefooted, for you couldn't go into the Zamorin's presence wearing shoes, could you?) walked behind him, there was a muted cheer, and people rushed forward to see the saviour, the man who had the grit and the integrity to catch this swine of a woman exporter.

In the Zamorin's presence, even as Kelu Kutty folded his hands, a sea of arms forced him down on his knees and even as he babbled some words in his defence to the effect that he had no idea that some bastard was running this kind of a trade, the Zamorin made a gesture with his left hand, which said 'take him away' and he was pushed out even more unceremoniously than he had been pushed in, and that mass of people in the corridor swarmed around him, so that he could hardly breathe, as he was kicked and shoved and thrown out.

~

Kanni had smouldered in the fires of envy for the past few months. First Chirukandan's visits had turned more and more infrequent. That had aroused suspicions. When fires die in a man's loins, mistresses need to take note, her mother had told her, and one of her jobs was to keep the fires burning. But how was she to stoke his fires if the man didn't come to her? Then, through rumour, the long black ringlets of a rival's braids got entwined around her. Who was she? She had no idea, to start with. But the grapevine said she was sinuous and smooth-skinned and younger. That didn't bode well for Kanni.

When he had first come to her, she had pretended to feel sorry for his wife. She could dissemble convincingly, though

*keki n. daruwalla*

Chirukandan had felt uneasy when she mentioned this. Leave Lakshmi out of this, he had told her. 'Out of what?' she had asked, feigning innocence, eyelashes fluttering. He had pointed to the bed. She had not taken kindly to that gesture. To her friends, she was known for her wit and her music. She hoped that with time he would be able see her for what she was, a woman with talents beyond the hurly burly of the bed. He tried to, but never really did. When she started singing, after their lovemaking, she noticed his impatience to get back to work.

Secretly, she had gloated over his wife's discomfiture. 'Lakshmi may be the mistress of his house but I am the mistress of his heart,' she had told a friend. And the friend had answered, with a sly smile smeared on her bitchy face, 'You mean mistress of his loins.'

Her mother had said that the heart is all very fine, but she must become the mistress of his wealth as well. Chirukandan could talk loosely at times, especially if the toddy was cool. In a reminiscent mood, he had told her once how desperate Lakshmi was becoming. One night, out of sheer exasperation, she came to him stark naked. That is the way of lower women, he had told her. Go and wear your clothes. Kanni had put on a real performance then, pretended to be very upset, had got up, flopped into a corner and cried. Of course she had gloated later and laughed. Now it was another's turn. That chit of a girl with long braids would be laughing her guts out. Would he be telling her stories of how she, Kanni, had wept like a sea storm each time they had met lately, but so infrequently; or how she had stamped on the floor when his parting gift had been sent to her, the sacks of coconut and rice. (He wouldn't have mentioned the jewels to this newfound love of his loins—or *she* could have turned jealous.) The daughter of a mere headman and she had encircled him in her thighs, the little whore!

But he couldn't get away with this, could he? Dump her and just walk away. Already her friends had started mentioning slyly that Chiru had not been seen lately. Was he unwell? The bitches knew perfectly well that he was in good health, although rumours of the girl with the black ringlets had not reached them as yet. Once that happened, life would be unbearable for her. She'd have to run away. Where were those forest hermits and their ashrams surrounded by deer that one read of in old stories, people like that sage Kanwa or that bastard Durvasa who had cursed Shakunthala, just because she hadn't 'received' him properly, poured water on his feet and put his wooden clogs respectfully away? Fortunately, Rishis didn't expect a maalish or god knows what scandals would have smeared our legends. But she didn't want her mind to run away with those wandering rishis. She would try and control her thoughts, but when the mind itself becomes a *bairagin*, what could she do? The mind roved from footloose anchorites to wandering gypsies with their mules and donkeys and their soot-covered tents and their dirty children with the most resplendent faces. And of course there were the tribes that lived near a lake barely five days' march from Calicut. There were hills around the lake, hills purple-dark, the tribes black and purple. She knew only one among those tribals, a fellow called Rayiru, and her thoughts started settling there like a swarm of flies around spilled jaggery.

~

Rayiru was one-eyed and wild, wanderer of the wilds, hunter of wild animals, adept at spearing fish and bringing down a stag or a doe with an arrow—he didn't put too fine a point on gender. There was no dearth of game here because this was virgin forest, swarming with greenery. On a summer

*keki n. daruwalla*

afternoon, there are more palm fronds than breezes here, the locals would say. It was virgin forest where the living and the dead stayed together, where lichen would still be flowering rust-red on a dead tree, where no one cared to pick up the fallen tines of a stag's antlers, and the bones of the leopard's last meal would remain undisturbed; where a dead tree would rot and still not fall because thorn and shrubbery had wound itself tight around its knees; where a banyan tree died but its prop roots thrived and kept it afloat, as it were.

Rayiru was one-eyed and he had such a pronounced stammer, he would leave most of his sentences midway, 'like a snake leaving an old skin', a fellow tribal said when he was put up for trial. But he babbled non-stop in his sleep, loud and clear and without the hint of a stammer. His friends called him ant-eater, why exactly, no one could tell. He crafted his arrows with care. He would trade deerskins and sometimes even fish for metal with which he would shape his long distinctive arrowheads. He had the eye of a hunter and he could spot a fish two metres deep in murky water and spear it. He would walk with his 'catch' to the market, three miles away, always taking his spear along, sometimes with a fish still stuck to the blade. Fishmongers would cheer the moment they spotted him. He was always the target of jokes and catcalls, and they would crack dirty jokes with him and he would blush. 'Do you have a home, Rayiru?'

'My home? Jungle.'

'Rayiru, I know a girl from a village here. Make a home in her thighs. Why is your face turning red, eh? You don't like thighs? You want girls without thighs? Listen to this,' and he would holler to the others.

But Rayiru's face turned blue the day the soldiers pounced upon him and tied his arms up and dragged him all the way to Calicut to the Zamorin's court. A one-eyed man had been clearly seen in a raid on a hamlet. Huts had been burnt, rice bins looted and the women beaten up. There were no men available for a beating, for they had run away. They often do. It's the women who get left behind. It took them a week to reach Calicut, what with Rayiru all tied up and hardly able to walk fast. The soldiers had taken no chances, for they had heard of his legendary speed and of his prowess as a hunter and of his conversations with demons in his sleep.

All this was said by witnesses and more as the judge, Chirukandan, had nodded his head. Talking to Rayiru had been useless. His speech was even more incoherent than it normally was. He couldn't understand any of this, being carted, all bound up like a sack, to Calicut, the charge, the court. 'How do you know he is the man you are looking for? How do you know he is the same one-eyed fellow who pillaged that hamlet?' asked Chiru.

'There is no other one-eyed scoundrel within ten miles, my Lord.'

'That is not sufficient.'

'A goat was found at the scene with an arrow stuck in its side. The arrow-head was long. He carves out his own long arrowheads. He is both mad and cruel, everyone knows. He knows bird speech Your Honour, and calls the birds, and when they come to him he shoots them. The forest demons are in him and a part of him, Lord. He is better off in jail.'

'Hey, you pariah,' asked Chirukandan, 'how long are your arrow heads?'

'Longer than your penis.'

He had said it very clearly. There was no bump in the speech, no hiccup.

'*What* did you say, you dog?'

His speech became slurred now, not a word distinct.

'The bastard is dissembling! Five years and twenty lashes.'

*keki n. daruwalla*

He was released in six—the jailer forgot for a year. He wouldn't go back to the lake and his hut. With what face would he meet the forest spirits? It was then that Kanni's mother had taken him to work in their grove of toddy palm trees and areca nut. He would squirrel up and throw the fruit down, as few could. He was wild as ever when he was in the grove, climbing trees, emitting birdcalls, whistling away to the winds and the four directions and the birds of the air. But when he came to lay the fruit on the floor of the verandah (he wouldn't have dreamt of venturing any further, pariah that he was), he would bend and crouch, submissive as a lamb, submissive and servile as a pariah was expected to be.

Then, one day, he saw the great man, Chirukandan entering the house and the fear of god quivered in his limbs, and the fear of lightning entered his primitive soul. Yet, his eye flashed as he recoiled and scurried back to his grass hut in the grove. It had taken an hour for the agitation in his limbs to die down. The caretaker of the grove, who came from a higher caste, had informed Kanni of the pariah's reaction. Slowly, over the months, they had been able to ferret out the story and put the pieces together from his broken incoherent speech and the loose strands of his half-uttered sentences. Kanni's mother had eventually asked if he had actually taken part in the raid on the hamlet concerned. Rayiru shook his head so violently that Kanni thought he would sprain his neck, and each drastic turn of the swivelling head was accompanied by a grunt that seemed to arise from the pit of his stomach. And his eyes had suddenly flared with hatred.

'Don't ever be seen when the great lord comes,' Kanni's mother had told him, wagging her finger. 'You are not to be seen by him. Become a ghost when he enters, turn into mist, cloud or one of your own forest spirits. Chirukandan doesn't forget a face.' The crunch line had come from the caretaker though: 'Rayiru should keep away from the great man's eye. But Thiru Chirukandan may also do well to keep away from the Ezhava.' In Kanni's estate Rayiru was a shadow, and shadows are difficult to shake off. He was the one who took the coconuts and the toddy to the market and he would wander into the house and could encounter the great man unwittingly. It was best to get rid of him. So he was asked to go.

Now, with the coming of the woman with the black ringlets, Kanni decided to call Rayiru back. There was no danger now of a sudden encounter between the two.

~

Once Rayiru came back, he found things changed. The mother had been stricken with paralysis and could hardly stir from the bed without help. Kanni was always weeping and talking to herself. He would come in crouching with his sack of coconuts before going to the market. Earlier her mother would make him spill all the fruit on the verandah floor and even count the lot. Now he noted nothing but apathy in the daughter. He was bewildered to find her talking to herself. His ears would twitch, the lid on his bad eye would start fluttering as he heard her moaning.

She made sure that he was within earshot when she started her high-pitched laments. Hyperbole was her strong suit. 'Take me Yama Raj, take me from this earth, lift me into the clouds, throw me in Narak if you like—anything but this earth, anything is better than this cursed life . . . to be abandoned by the man you love . . . to be betrayed by the man who I have taken for my lord and husband and master in the eye of God, to be ditched so disgracefully . . . give me death Yama . . . but

*keki n. daruwalla*

then what happens to mother? Take her away Yama, and then me—put us on the same funeral pyre.'

Rayiru would bang his head on the verandah floor and in his halting half-grunt, half-intelligible speech ask her what the matter was. 'O Rayiru, you may be a pariah but you are a better man than him. I am talking of Chiru, Thiru Chirukandan, the one who sent you to jail and ordered those lashes, those cruel, cruel lashes. He has left me, abandoned me! My curses on his head.'

As for the tears rolling down her cheeks and her face puckered in pain, she didn't have to pretend. The pain was genuine enough. Once, when Rayiru went in with his sack of coconuts and laid his cleaver on the floor, the cleaver with which he slashed the fruit from the tree, she asked him, why is this lying idle here? Through grunts and groans and a dribble of words that came out in spasms he told her that the cleaver had just cut a sackful of coconuts and had not blunted. And she said, aren't there better things to slash now than coconuts? A throat maybe? And she caught her own neck and drew her finger across it. His eye bulged in horror and he banged his forehead on the floor to indicate that the idea was unthinkably abhorrent. Kill her! He worshipped her, but took care never to show it, never to let the emotion appear in the guttering candle of his one good eye.

'Well, some other throat then, some belly full of shit?'
His eye had gleamed.

~

Lakshmi was wondering if her husband had noticed that she hadn't spoken to him for two days, not a single word. If he had, he didn't show it—possibly the man's attempt to put her in her place. Whether you speak or don't, makes no difference, woman, that's what he seemed to say. At least he could have done her the courtesy of asking her why she was annoyed. She wasn't. It was just disgust.

'So now they are saying you have gone after some other woman—some girl young enough to be your daughter!'

'Who has been telling you all this?' Chirukandan asked his wife. 'Don't listen to people. They *will* make up stories—they have nothing else to do, the dogs!'

'It is women who told me this!'

'They have nothing better to do, the bitches! If you are a minister, people will make stories about you, and the dirtier, the more they will be believed. That is the way the world is, you can't do anything about it. Ten years later they'll say I am in love with someone young enough to be my granddaughter. Will you believe them? I expected better sense from you.'

'Don't tell me all this. I am no fool. The whole town is talking about it. And as ships go out, your fame will reach other ports. Think of your self-respect.' She flounced out of the room, her bare feet slapping against the floor. Within minutes she came back, a thin sliver of a smile pasted on her lips. 'I wonder what that woman must be thinking.' Kanni's name had never been uttered in the house.

~

Chirukandan's boatman moored his boat in a shady cove at Ponnani and awaited his master's return. They were a little late and the evening twilight was about to fade. As Chirukandan shambled across the track, a figure sprang from the shadows. His face was wild and the minister couldn't make much of his foam-flecked speech.

'What do you want? Get out of my way, Pariah.'

He stank; he looked and smelt like a pariah, his mundu all tucked up and his red loin cloth showing, his dark legs planted wide apart as if braced to repel an attack. And the dome of his one eye flared though the minister hardly had the time to notice so minor a detail, facing a likely assailant who seemed rigid and cramped with tension. Nevertheless, he was not easily frightened. 'Give way! Don't touch me, Pariah!'

The Pariah didn't touch him, but that long, heavy coconut-severing cleaver did, ripping across the ministerial belly. Then a thrust through the heart and it was done.

~

The boatman waited an hour, then two hours. He hadn't taken so long ever, he concluded, and went haring off to the headman's house. He saw the worried looks of the inmates—in fact they were standing at the window, peering out, as if waiting for someone. 'Where is your master?' they asked. That was precisely what the boatman wanted to know. They jointly went out looking for him, armed with lamp and mashaal. They went down the track he usually took and found him, lifeless, all huddled up, his hands still holding on to his entrails that gleamed like a coil of snakes in the light of the mashaals.

The next day, when the soldiers arrived, they took away the headman, his wife and daughter—the moral being that you can't play around with a minister's crotch and get away with it, in the event of his murder. People gathered and protested vociferously in high-pitched voices—they pleaded, threatened, some even brandished staves, but the soldiers eventually took them away on the boat. 'We will just question them and set them free,' they kept reassuring the villagers. No one believed them. The Zamorin was given the news that his minister, Chirukandan, had been murdered somewhere up the coast around Ponnani near the house of a headman who had a beautiful daughter.

Half the headman's village arrived the next day, pleading for his life. They were the ones who were worried, Highness, they were the ones who went looking for him. If the guest comes late , or doesn't arrive, who gets worried? The host of course, Highness! And if as they say that he was in love with their daughter (we are not saying that, Highness), why should they harm him? He must have given them gifts (*we* are not saying he gave gifts, how would *we* know, Highness?), but if he has given them gifts, why should they kill him? If they had killed him, why would they go looking for his body by lamplight, let anyone explain, Highness?

Others joined in. A murderer runs away from the victim's body, Highness, everyone knows that. He doesn't go sniffing to find it out. The Zamorin, his face impassive as ever, said, 'He doesn't have to sniff. He knows where it is.' The law could be harsh, he knew, and the headman could well be the fall guy. He felt sorry for the family, but no one could make out what he was thinking. It was something he had learnt early in life. Scraps of feeling shouldn't flicker in the eyes. The face should remain patched up always.

Just before dawn, Rayiru padded up to the kitchen verandah. This time he wasn't burdened with a sack of coconuts. When Kanni came out, her eyes still sticky with sleep, he crouched and folded his hands. Without a word he took out from his bag his cleaver caked with dried blood which had lost it redness and was almost black in colour. She remained calm (the shivers were to get to her later).

'Throw it away in some well far from here. Very far. Not in the sea, for the sea has a habit of digging up its dead and

*keki n. daruwalla*

throwing them on the beach. Search out a well that is at least one day's march from Calicut.'

She went in and brought the pouch containing the sapphires Chirukandan had given her. 'Keep these. Give them to your beloved, if you have one (she couldn't imagine anyone being romantically entangled with him, not with one-eyed Rayiru). Now go from here and don't come back. Ever! It is dangerous.'

~

The Zamorin realised that his main bulwark against the Moors had been done in, for it was Chirukandan who always said to him, 'Know the difference between a Moor and a Malabari. Don't let the Moors run Calicut, keep them at a distance.' Now he was gone. That Kelu Kuti, he too wasn't in love with the Moors, and he had been thrown out. Selling our women in concubinage, hey Prabhu! He was fond of Chirukandan, that brusque no-nonsense man, honest to the core in money matters, who never bothered to flatter him and never gave wrong advice. He went to the house and condoled with the wife. The next day he went to Ponnani. Obviously a wrong had been done to the Headman. His daughter's relations with Chiru were now common knowledge and on top of that he was almost roped in on a murder charge. While he was assuring the villagers that justice would be done, and the headman released, a messenger came bearing the tidings that some pink coloured people, covered head to foot in alien costumes, had landed at Kappaat. Their leader said that he came as an ambassador of a King of Fartaqal.

# figueiro
## crossing the green sea
## of darkness

Perspectives can change abruptly; so can counsel. Till now the Moors repeatedly told us that the dreaded Green Sea of Darkness lay ahead of us. During the nine days we spent at Milind, and on meeting the Great Arab navigator and his protégé, who went by the name of Taufiq, we learnt that the Sea of Darkness was behind us, that we had left its waters the day we rounded the Cape of Good Hope. We were shocked that it was the ocean on the west coast of Africa which they termed the Dark Sea! The Arab navigator even laughed at us! Gama told us not to believe either version fully, but he looked relieved.

Perhaps things had been exaggerated, we thought. Perhaps the Green Sea of Darkness was in reality a sea of lies! I was told the other day, by my lord Paulo da Gama, that I tend to repeat myself. I had bowed my head in agreement. I do so in my chronicle as well. I am writing now on our last day in Milind where we had anchored for as many nine days.

On a voyage like this, through hazardous seas, along hostile Moorish coasts, it is well to be on your guard. The Captain-Major understood this, if anyone did. His philosophy could be summed up easily—get hold of smaller vessels, take hostages, anchor away from the coast and keep your bombards ready. He seemed to have learnt all this during the voyage itself. The sea can be a good teacher, if you are willing to learn, he often said. It was at Mombassa, where we laid anchor on Saturday 7 April, that our dream had turned sour and where we lost the little faith we had in the sincerity of the Moors on this coast. Mombassa looked grand initially—ship after ship arrayed in flags as if some emperor was visiting the harbour on inspection. We too had strung up our flags on the masts and our ships looked more gorgeous than the others. On Palm Sunday, 8 April, the King sent us gifts—sheep, oranges, lemons, sugar cane and his signet ring as a pledge that we were safe in his sea and would be allowed to trade. The Captain-Major also sent two emissaries so that a seal could be put on these assurances.

These two emissaries had to enter through four doors to get an audience of the King and at each door stood a fierce man with a naked torcado in his hand. Our men visibly quailed. The King of Mombassa asked his people to show our two men around the town. There they found many men in irons on the streets. (We later guessed that these must have been Christians.) What sort of a kingdom was this? And Holy Mother, they met a man who showed them a sketch of the Holy Ghost! Our men didn't know what to make of all this. Neither did we. The Holy Ghost himself wouldn't have known where he stood with the Moors. To confuse matters further the two men returned with gifts of cloves and pepper and Trigo tremez, that is, corn that ripens in three months. The message was that these were the articles we could trade in and take with us when we left Mombassa.

It was fortunate that next day the Captain-Major's own ship could not budge and hit the vessel that followed astern.

Or we would have entered the harbour and fallen easy prey to the malevolent Moors. It was at that moment that the two pilots we had brought from Mozambique jumped into the sea and escaped. We waited for nightfall. In fact this turned out to be the night of boiling oil, as we were to call it later, for Vasco da Gama, now thoroughly suspicious, and rightfully so, had boiling oil poured on two of the Moors we had on board from Mozambique. It was they who told us that the moment we entered port we would have been attacked and captured. This was also the night when we were stealthily attacked. Some of the culprits swam underwater in order to board our ships, but were repulsed.

It was later at Milind that we heard of other old stories of Moorish treachery, even with African natives. A tempest had driven one Ismail's ship to that part of the African coast where the people were believed to be cannibals. But they were treated fairly, not eaten up, and were allowed to trade in the city of Sufalah, where they had been taken. After some months they were allowed to return and the King of these parts himself came to see them off along with seven attendants and even boarded their ship. This Ismail from Oman thought to himself that the King would fetch at least thirty dinars in Oman as a slave and the attendants would also fetch a good price. The clothes they were wearing would be worth another twenty to thirty dinars. So he asked the sailors to raise sail and when the King and his men tried desperately to escape they were prevented and thrown into a throng of two hundred other slaves and sold in Oman. Can one think of anything more treacherous? This King became a Muslim, returned to his kingdom after some years, ordered a mass circumcision of his subjects and converted all his subjects to Islam! Strange are the ways of the Devil. Stranger are the ways of God.

On 13 April, at dawn, we had given chase to two barcas about three leagues to the leeward. Even though the two boats were on the open sea, one of them escaped towards the coast. The other we caught up with by vesper time. As we drew alongside, the people in the boat jumped overboard, even the ones who didn't know drowning, pardon me—swimming. There was one woman among them too, whom we rescued, as we rescued all the others. There was gold in the ship and silver and a large quantity of maize. When we finally abandoned the vessel, we took the gold and silver but left much of the maize in the vessel. We had the gold and silver, as also seventeen hostages on board. That was enough. As good Christians we were not supposed to display avarice.

A little after the capture of the boat, we anchored off the coast of Milind. The Moors we had captured told us that there were four 'Christian' vessels from India in port. 'Vessels manned by Christians?' we asked. They nodded. (All along the coast we were being told 'this Christian vessel', 'this Christian church', 'this Christian village'. Always our expectations had been belied. I had thought to myself after such contacts that if these were Christians, we'd be better off dealing with heathens.)

'From which port do they come?' we asked. From Cranganore, we were told, and if we wanted their help, the Moors would arrange it, as long as they were freed. The Indians would procure for us even wood and water and whatever we needed. What better could we ask for? It was Easter Sunday, April the fifteenth and the Captain-Major decided it was going to be lucky for us. So we cast anchor in four fathoms and a half, barely half a mile from the town.

Of the seventeen hostages, one Moor was very eminent, we learnt. Even if we hadn't been told, it was evident from the way he spoke and carried himself, that he was from the nobility. His wife was on board too, the one who had jumped into the sea. Next morning the Captain-Major had the Moor deposited on the beach, after telling him about our desire to have some Indian Christian pilots to steer us to the Indies. We waited patiently. We threw salted meat to the gulls and they came in droves and flew around us. Gulls came, people didn't. They gazed at us sombrely from the sandbank. We had learnt that once you capture a ship and have sixteen hostages on board, the natives don't trouble you.

When the Moor returned in a boat he had one of the King's cavaliers in tow. (The Moorish word for a cavalier is Sharif.) The Moor had convinced the king that we wanted friendship with him. (If the same message had come to him from the Kings of Mombassa or Quelue—some of the natives called it Kilwa—or Mozambique, he may not have taken them at their word. They hated each other, we were told.)

The Captain-Major knew what he was doing. He sent the King a handsome present—a *balandrau* which used to be worn by the Brothers of Mercy, two strings of coral, three wash basins, a hat, bells, and two pieces of striped cotton which we call *lambel,* a kind of cloth which the Moors had not ever chanced upon. On 17 April, it was the King's turn to send us gifts, and he didn't fail us—half a dozen mouth-watering sheep, cumin and clove, nutmeg and pepper all stuffed into coir sacks. The message was that he would come himself and would the Captain deign to meet him on a boat? Wouldn't he!

The next day the King of Milind arrived in a stately zavra, its square sail coloured red. The Captain got into one of his boats and the two met. It was the King who stepped into the Captain-Major's boat, where they exchanged friendly words. The Captain-Major was as wary as ever and when

*keki n. daruwalla*

the King invited him to his palace, declined, saying our King had not permitted him to set foot on land. Vasco made a desperate appeal for a pilot. We are up against the Green Sea of Darkness, he said. Yet we have come with great hopes. Can we somehow get an Indian pilot? An Indian pilot, the King snorted. I'll give you the greatest navigator that the Arabs have ever produced.

After that two days passed without any news of the pilot. Was this King also going to cheat us? We were in a quandary. Moreover, we had come in contact with four vessels belonging to Christians from India. Some of the Christians came on board our ship *Sao Raphael*, with Paulo da Gama's permission. The Captain-Major was himself present there and asked them to be shown the altarpiece displaying Virgin Mary at the foot of the cross with Lord Jesus in her arms and the apostles surrounding them. These Christians, long-haired and brown-skinned, immediately fell down and prostrated themselves in front of the altarpiece. They didn't give us good news. Don't go on shore, they warned and don't trust their 'fanfares', there is not much goodwill in their hearts. I had almost forgotten to say that on 19 April as the Captain-Major and Nicolau Coelho rowed along the waterfront they were treated to fireworks. (Incidentally, the Captain-Major had taken care to place bombards in the poops as a precaution.) The King was carried in a palanquin on shore and asked da Gama to come ashore, but he desisted.

On the following Sunday, 22 April, the King's Zavra brought one of his officers and da Gama had him seized and sent word to the King that he would not be released unless we got the pilot.

The next day, the King came again, dressed in a damask robe with a fringe of green satin. He was seated on two cushioned bronze chairs under a canopy of crimson satin. An attendant carried his sword in a silver scabbard. Two musicians blew on huge man-sized ivory trumpets and others played on an instrument the natives here called *anafils*. He brought Ahmed Ibn Majid, the great navigator and astronomer and a young Arab who had sailed these seas since he was a boy. The King left the Arab navigator and his protégé to discuss things with us. The King of Milind then went around our ships in his beautifully decorated boat. By the Captain-Major's orders, our ships gave him a fitting salute, firing off our bombards and our men cheered.

The Arab navigator Ibn Majid first asked the Captain-Major what our mission was, and when told that it was to discover the Indian coast, he laughed loudly. 'Have the Indians discovered you?' the Arab asked in return and laughed some more. The Captain-Major fumbled for words. The navigator then said that Arabs have been sailing to these parts for a thousand years.

'Well, you stole a march over us. You Arabs are a thousand years ahead,' said the Captain-Major. Ibn Majid sank into silence for a while.

'This is not necessarily true. Most of us are people of the desert. Many of us are suspicious of the sea. So was our great Caliph, Omar. The Governor of Syria, Muawiya bin Abi Sufian wanted to invade Cyprus. He had a fleet ready. But Omar had received a letter from the conqueror of Egypt, Amru bin al-'As. Amru was as frightened of the sea as a child is of the night. Amru had written: "The ocean is boundless, a vast expanse on which huge ships look like tiny dots; nothing but the skies above and the waters below; when placid, the sailor's heart is shattered; when stormy, his whole being reels; trust it little; fear it much. Man at sea is but a worm on a bit of wood, now engulfed, and now scared to death." That opinion of Amru sealed the fate of the expedition to Cyprus. Omar did not sanction the invasion. 'Yet our coastal people have sailed to India all these centuries. Not just us, even Jewish merchants went sailing as far as China, touching the Indian west coast all along. Traders went to Antioch, went by land to the Euphrates and then down the river to Basra and the sea. Our traders (meaning Arab traders) went down sometimes through Bahr al Farsi which you people call the Persian Gulf. But mostly our trading boats went through Bahr al Qulzum, which you call the Red Sea, and after Aden went east to the Malabar coast. Traversing the Red Sea was never easy, for there are coral reefs here and the sea itself flanks the desert. If your ship gets wrecked, whom can you call upon for succour in the desert?

A long lecture followed on Arab navigation. The conversation was much more dramatic than I make it out to be. For, after this lecture he told Vasco da Gama that he was late, very late for the voyage to India, which he called al Hind. You will be lucky if you can avoid the season of storms, al Mossum, which you call the Monsoons. (The fellow had at least two different names for everything under the sun, our interpreter, Fernao Martins told me.) Aren't you afraid? And Lord Vasco said, 'I am only afraid of God and His wrath, but I haven't done anything to invite it.'

This pleased the Arab, but he persisted in asking, 'You fear the unknown?' to which the Captain-Major gave an ambiguous answer—'There is always some uncertainty about the unknown.' Ibn Majid nodded and then turned expansive. 'Open your doors to the unknown and it shall be known.' The fellow was sounding almost Biblical, said the interpreter incredulously. Majid added, 'You people have been hugging the African coast too long and have suffered. You will face contrary currents and headwinds. Move out into the sea.' Now it was the Captain's turn to laugh. 'In our voyage we have avoided certain points on the western coast of Africa by a thousand miles!' The Arab nodded and took it well, I must say.

When the Captain boasted how our ships had gone around the southern tip of Africa, Ibn Majid said Indian junks have been doing that for eighty years. When Vasco da Gama didn't believe him, Ibn Majid told him to look up the famous map drawn up at Murano near Venice in 1459. (The Arab wouldn't know that he was referring to Fra Mauro's famous map.) The map, according to Majid showed an Indian junk crossing the cape in 1420 from west to east!

The interpreter noted that the navigator's protégé never opened his mouth once. One of the Captain-Major's companions asked about what to expect in India. 'What will we find there, apart from spices?'

'Fiery skies at dusk and the scent of night flowers thicker than sea spray. You will find everything—the odour of dreams, the song of lust, meditation on the mountains. In fact, the mountains themselves seem to meditate there. Depends on what you want to find. The lotus will open its petals to you provided that is what you want.'

A sour note crept into the conversation when he said needlessly, 'Everyone robs India. Be frugal in your thefts.' Lord Vasco positively bridled at this. He drew himself up to his full height. 'We come as ambassadors of a great King and a great country. We are neither traders nor thieves.'

He set some of our doubts at rest. The interpreter, on his own, asked if it was true that the stormy waves in this sea had no foam! Ibn Majid smiled and said they do have foam, but when the sailor is caught in a storm, and the wave is twice as high as the mast of your ship, he is in no condition to notice such fine details. Others asked, 'Where is this place called "Waaq Waaq" we heard so much about before we set out?'

*keki n. daruwalla*

Don't worry, your ships have passed it. It is that huge island which we call Qanbalu and you call Madagascar. There is another Waaq Waaq in the east as well, east of the al Hind coast and Sarandib, but I don't want to confuse you.'

When Ibn Majid bid the Captain-Major adieu, he left the young pilot behind. His name was Taufiq. The first remarkable thing about the man was that he didn't gape and gawk at us. His look seemed almost disinterested. In fact, some of us at the *Sao Raphael* took his quiet confidence for brazen effrontery. The shoulders hunched, the torso stooping ever so slightly as if caught in a cramp, and the eyes wide with ill-concealed disbelief—these were the reactions we had come to expect from Moor and heathen when they set eyes on us for the first time. This man stood erect, loose of limb, handsome in his own way as dark people are. Unlike other Moors, he didn't have a beard. By Moorish standards he was fair and he would have quickened the pulse of a Saracen maiden, I am sure.

That night, for some strange reason, I was called again to the flagship, *Sao Gabriel*, when the Captain-Major interviewed him. Why did Vasco da Gama want me there? To confirm whether he was indeed a Christian, as the King of Milind had told us? But the pilot never made any secret of his religious calling. He was out and out a Moor.

'Do you know the sea?'

It was an unfair question put by the Captain-Major. How can one answer something like that. Would he turn brash and say, 'I know it as well as birds know the sky' or something of that nature. Or would he speak modestly? I was intrigued.

'As well as one can know it.'

He got out of that moderately well. When asked to explain, he was matter-of-fact. He had sailed these seas with his father times out of number when he was a boy. Then he was sent off to Cairo to study. Later he had sailed under the shadow of his mentor, Ibn Majid. Shadow? Lord Vasco did not like the word. Was he being forced into this? The pilot did not understand Gama's anxiety. The Captain-Major spoke to the interpreter. 'What shadow is he talking about? He is not under someone's spell, is he?' The interpreter smiled and spoke to the pilot in Arabic, and they both laughed. The pilot replied, 'Shadow is a good word for us. It saves us from being burnt by the sun. In Hindustan we call it *saya*.'

The Captain-Major had obviously taken Ibn Majid's advice to heart. 'Don't tarry too long here, or the high winds and the high waves of the monsoons will catch up with you. They are stalking you like killer sharks.' So we raised sail on Tuesday, 24 April, for the great port city called Qualecut, where the coast runs north to south. There is a huge bay there, people had told us, a bay that had six hundred islands in its belly and many large cities of Moors and Christians, including one called Quambay. Within this vast bay was the Red Sea, which within itself enclosed the great house of the Moors, called the 'Kabah'.

To be fair, some of us were almost unhappy to leave Milind, because that was the one place where we had been received fairly and where some of our scurvy-stricken people recovered. We had seen a night-fair here and a mock joust between two horsemen in our honour. Would we have got the pilot if the Captain-Major had not had the officer of the King seized? That was a hot debating point with us as we set sail for India.

As we set out, one of our Fidalgos involuntarily burst out, 'Now we are in the hands of our Lord,' and another added, 'and of Poseidon'. Normally I would have chewed him up, for mentioning the pagan God but for once I refrained, having heard so much of this vast sea, and lived in dread of it for so long. The African coast remained in our sight for some days. The heat haze and the humidity prevented us from seeing the sky clearly at night. Five days after we set out we managed to see the North Star on 29 April. Then at last, for two nights we saw the Great Bear roam the skies. Nights are a time to ponder. Did we actually meet any Christians? This century-old search for a Christian kingdom in some elusive centre of the unknown, wasn't it futile—a national, or rather, a racial illusion? And yet hadn't we been less than frank about our own faith? What are we afraid of? These thieving people who inhabited these coasts—and their torçados? If we were afraid of cutlasses, what would happen to us if some evil day we were to come face to face with the Devil himself? If the Devil were ever to be physically present, he would obviously not be found in a Christian land where children were baptized and the Mass was sung. But the Devil becomes a possibility in a land of magic and mirages.

~

*Magic is what overtakes us. First a long blue trance where we lose count as day merges into hallucination and night into drugged dream. We can't ignore the monotony of the horizon—we are trapped within this circular skyline, as everyone is at sea. Then the thud of landing and land—land of princes as also of conjurors and bear-baiters and the thinnest smoke you've ever seen floating up from incense sticks stuck at the feet of Our Lady. We are the dust in the dust-devil, hurled in the land of magic, for no one has ever seen an example of more grotesque iconography, with the mother of Christ sprouting six arms and a long blood-stained rapier of a tongue. We walk through the wet floors of churches where people enter barefoot. This is a land of horizontal prostrations (not that vertical prostration can ever be a physical possibility); land of curious, inquisitive jeering throngs, of streets lined with cinnamon bark set out to dry. We turn to dwarves. Some of us turn to birds transported to some exotic aviary. We enter, wearing doublet and hose, a country where waist-cloths flutter in the wind like flags, displaying hairy shins and hairless inner thighs, and where Crotch scratching is considered a social grace. And it is a country where you swoon if you walk behind a lady because of the thick fragrance of flowers strung in her hair, white flowers that gleam in her thick black lustrous hair, white flowers that manage to gleam even on a dark night.*

~

It was during this stretch of the journey that people started coming to me with their dreams. I remember the odd ones. A sailor dreamt of a Turkish chest lined with arabesque designs but with a pair of live eyes at the centre, eyes that looked at you from left to right, or was it west to east. Someone dreamt of a red robe floating in the air without a body. I once dreamt of a mass in a mosque, got up in fright and made the sign of the cross. A *degradado* dreamt of a shoal of fierce fish swallowing up a band of *corsairs* or pirates. People dreamt of ice—they would, wouldn't they—it was so beastly hot and humid. One person dreamt of a bird with a slit tongue. I dreamt of a cloud of birds. The next day we sighted land, a thin line at first, turning slowly to sinew.

Actually, we sighted mountains, at least eight leagues off. It was Friday, 18 May. Month-long ( or to be exact, for twenty-five days) the wind had been favourable and we must have made more than six hundred leagues since we left Milind on

24 April. We gave thanks to Christ our Lord for having brought us here safely. We went down on our knees and prayed. We were still away from the shoreline and the pilot couldn't make out where we were. The mountain loomed above us and the pilot started steering southwest and kept his distance from the coast. The Captain-Major kept his curiosity on leash, and did not ask the pilot to tell us where we were. The others were more impatient and one of them even abused him in Portuguese. Though we knew he didn't understand our language, his eyes widened and flared for an instant. A sailor can never be moored to one language. He picks up words as an oriental prince picks up women for his harem.

That night we found ourselves in the midst of a storm and were pelted with rain and beaten by a high wind. But we were well anchored and no damage was caused to our ships. The Captain-Major recalled the words of Ibn Majid who had warned us of the high winds and the high waves stalking us like sharks. Thank God we hadn't delayed our voyage. It proved to some of us that even a Moor could speak truthfully. Obviously, because of the rain, Taufiq the pilot couldn't still tell us decisively where exactly we were. By next morning (Sunday, 20 May) the storm had abated and we were in front of another mountain. The pilot spotted the place and called the mountain 'Kadalur'.

'We are above Calicut. This is the country you wanted to come to.'

These were the most momentous words we had heard since we left the River Tagus on 8 July 1497. It is mean to cavil at small things, but the pilot had made a slight error, thinking we were at Calicut, when we were actually at Capua. (Later we learnt the place was called Kappaad.) By now it was regulation drill to anchor away from the coast. Four boats, or what we call almadias, approached us and made enquiries. Where did we sail from, under which nation's flag did we ply, what was our religion, what did we want? The questions were friendly, though. So was the attitude of the men. It was difficult to understand each other but they pointed to Calicut often and pronounced the name clearly.

The next day the same boats came again, and according to our well-established practice, the Captain-Major sent a former convict, a degradado, Joao Nunez, to go to Calicut. (He had done that at Milind and Mombassa as well, and we had no dearth of these degradados, for Vasco had brought quite a few of these on the voyage. They are useful, and if you lose them the country doesn't lose much, as Paolo da Gama told me.)

Joao Nunez brought cheer to us when he came back. In the market two wide-eyed (and delighted) Moors from Tunis confronted him. They called him names, as these people often do when they meet old friends. 'May the Devil take thee!' (They of course said something much worse, but that was not how Nunez could have broken it to the Captain-Major.) 'What brought you hither?' And there was much embracing and almost incredulous laughter from their side.

'Did they recognize you?' asked Vasco da Gama, suspicious that the Tunisians may have been involved in crime, piracy perhaps, and thus had got to know Nunez. But our ex-criminal made it quite clear that they recognized him as a Portuguese from his attire. Nunez was not above showing off (no degradado is). He said we have come in search of a continent. When the Tunisians couldn't comprehend this, he told them we were looking for spices and fellow Christians.

They asked, 'Why does not the King of Castile, the French King or the Signoria of Venice send their ships hither?'

Full marks to our friend Nunez that he replied, 'Because our King of Portugal won't let them!' The two Moors took him to their lodgings and gave him a repast of wheaten bread and honey.

Nunez had come back with one of the Moors and when he was taken to the Captain-Major, he burst out in Spanish, 'Buena ventura, Buena ventura—a lucky venture, a lucky venture! Plenty rubies! Plenty emeralds! You owe great thanks to God for having brought you to a country with such riches!'

For some of us this was too much to take in one day. After a voyage lasting almost a year, to meet a man who could converse with us, and knew the names of the countries of Europe. The world was not that large and never-ending. Nor was any region a locked casket. The second surprise was that we were meeting such friendly Moors! May the Lord bless even Moors.

We came to know that the King, or Zamorin as he is called here, was not in Calicut, but in Ponnani, some miles away. Our interpreter Fernao Martins and one Moncaide were dispatched to the King to inform him that an ambassador had arrived with letters from the King of Portugal. The two were well received, taken to the King where they were presented with fine cloth and silk and told that the King would be happy to receive the Captain-Major. In fact, he immediately set out from Ponnani with a large entourage for Calicut.

Meanwhile, a local pilot was assigned to us and we were asked to anchor near Capua because the anchorage at Calicut was not too safe, cluttered as it was with reefs. In addition, it had a stony bottom. This was very true and the anchorage at Capua was much safer. Even though the atmosphere was very friendly, the Captain-Major saw to it once again that we didn't anchor too near the coast, despite the insistence of the local pilot. By nightfall a message arrived from the King that we should move to Calicut. He had sent a *Wali*, which we later learnt was equivalent to our *alcaide,* a Governor, one who usually strode out with a retinue of two hundred armed men. (Our pilot Taufiq told us that he was actually the *Catual*, but too many titles confuse me.) This time he didn't have two hundred (how do they muster so many people?) but there seemed to be many men of distinction with him. By the time the Wali arrived, it was late and the Captain-Major, while thanking the King as also the Wali, declined to move, promising to come the next day.

The great day dawned, Monday, 28 May, and the Captain set out with his retinue—not two hundred as followed the bridal train of the Wali or *Catual* but with twelve of us. Inclusive of himself we were thirteen and I kept wondering at the rather odd number he had chosen. He took with him Diogo Dias, Joao de Sa, Goncalo Pirez, Alvaro Velho, Alvaro de Braga, Joao de Setubal, Joao de Palha, five others and myself. He also asked Taufiq, our Moorish pilot to accompany us—he knew the language and the people and could be of help. He did not take the other two captains, Paulo da Gama and Coelho, leaving them in charge of the ships. It seemed that when he was outside Portugal he trusted no one, for he instructed his two captains to sail immediately for Portugal should something happen to him and his twelve companions.

We were attired in our best finery, and carried flags and trumpets with us. Nothing like heraldry and pomp to impress the Orientals! The Captain also had bombards placed in the boats, for once not for any war-like purpose but for salutes and celebration. The reception was Oriental. What else could one expect? The Governor was there along with a retinue of men, many of them armed with unsheathed swords. (We never got to see any scabbards.) For once the Captain-Major didn't let his suspicion show—it would have gone down badly. They had a brightly coloured andor, palanquin, carried by six men, ready for him at the wharf. The Governor was also carried in an andor. The Captain got in and we set out in a small

*keki n. daruwalla*

procession, halting first at Capua. (Here the Moorish pilot, Taufiq, got annoyed with me and said the place is Kappad, Kappad, Kappad—he repeated it three times so that I and the others got it right. Some of us were actually calling the place Capocate.) The Captain-Major was taken to the house of a noble, or what we would call *um homem honnrado*. We were served rice with a lot of butter and some excellent fish cooked with a touch of spice. It was delectable. But the Captain-Major kept away from food.

Crowds had been gathering around us, grinning in a friendly way. Even women, with children forked on their hips, came to have a look at us, and our outlandish dress, which, to be frank, made us very uncomfortable in the heat. We embarked on two boats lashed together, on the Korapuzha river this time, till we came to a sort of a dry dock where many other ships were on the strand. All through our up-river journey the banks were crowded with a multitude of people such as one never got to see in Lisbon.

'The crowd is very friendly,' Joao de Setubal mentioned to the Captain. And the answer he got was, 'After all, it is a Christian country.' Right enough, as we disembarked and the Captain-Major was again put in the palanquin, they took us to a large church, hewn out of stone, its floor tiled and wet. The devotees inside were all barefoot. In deference to the practice here we took off our shoes and entered the main portal after passing a huge bronze pillar as high as the mast of *Sao Gabriel*. The figure of a bird was carved on the pillar. Was that a rooster, we asked each other in whispers, but no one was sure. In the middle of the church rose a *corucheo* or spire, and ahead of it a chapel with a shining bronze door. Within this chapel was the sanctuary. No one but the priests can enter the sanctuary, we were told, and within it an image of Nossa Senhora, Our Lady, was kept. The priests were naked to the waist and wore threads wound around shoulder and neck. We were given ash, which Christians here rub on their foreheads. 'Maria, Maria' shouted the priests at which the local Christians prostrated themselves while we knelt. Still, the other images in the church left us with considerable disquiet and Joao de Sa mentioned to Vasco da Gama, 'If these be devils, I worship the true God.' The Captain-Major smiled but kept silent.

It was the other images on the walls, which disturbed me more. They were certainly not of apostles. One of them had incisors protruding out and was decked with four or five arms. My disquiet was such that I wanted to give vent to my doubt, but was afraid of speaking out of turn. We were concentrating on the big event—the meeting with the King and no one wanted to say or do a thing that would come in the way. We now progressed through the town, but the crowd was so thick that it became impossible to move an inch. Seeing this, the Wali put us up in a house and sent word to the King who now sent the brother of the Governor, a big Lord in his own right to escort us. Drumbeaters, and people blowing anafils accompanied him. They fired matchlocks in the air so that the crowd was kept at bay. Still the crush was so terrible as we got into the palace that we couldn't move and in fact felt stifled. So thick was the crush of people that some of us hardly noticed the great gate that led to a vast courtyard, or the four doors of the palace we had to pass through to reach the king. Jostled by a Mongol horde of shoulder-blades, swivelling and swaying with a battalion of hips, prodded by an armada of elbows, we took recourse to the only thing we could think of—blows. We lashed at those nearest to us. Some of us even took out our knives, pricking and gashing the thickening clot of people around us, and at last reached the Zamorin's antechamber. There the High Priest of the Indians, a small old man, but very noble looking, embraced the Captain-Major and ushered us all into the presence of the bejewelled King. It needs be mentioned that by now it was dusk and we had been travelling the whole day.

The King was reclining on a couch draped in green velvet, the drape almost spilling on to the floor. On it was a mattress covered by the finest white cloth I had seen. Overhead was a gilded canopy. There were cushions covered in brocade around him and he held a huge golden cup in his left hand. It could have held eight pints of wine in the least. Perhaps this is a symbol of royalty, I thought. Instead of orb and sceptre the Indian Kings hold a golden cup. To his right stood a basin of gold so huge I could scarcely have encircled it in my arms had I tried. The basin contained many heart-shaped leaves and herbs and grated nut. The king himself was in white clothes. Golden rings and large rubies were stitched onto his clothes with silken threads. On his left arm he wore a large golden bracelet encrusted with jewels. He wore no crown, that was not the custom here.

The Captain folded his hands and raised them in salutation, as they do in this country, and then closed his fists. The King saluted likewise and smiled and asked him to come near, gesturing with his right hand (Indians don't use the left ceremonially) but the Captain kept his distance, in accordance with the advice of Taufiq and the others. Only the carrier of herbs was privileged to approach the King. The King invited us to be seated on a stone bench and ordered that water to wash our hands should be brought and fruit served. I at least felt self-conscious, for, as we ate, the King smiled at us while the courtiers almost laughed, placing their hands in front of their mouths, as demanded by etiquette in this country.

It was then that the King suddenly spat into the golden cup he held in his hand and all my notions of the cup went to ground. This was a spittoon, and of gold at that—must be a very rich country. All I had heard of Oriental potentates was coming true.

For some moments the King gazed at our attire (and presumably our fair skin) with ill-concealed wonder and even amusement. Then he turned serious and asked the Captain-Major to speak up. The Captain replied that he had a message from the King of Portugal whose ambassador he was, which he could only convey to him in private. So the King asked him to be conducted to a room and joined him. The Captain had to be accompanied by Fernao Martins, the interpreter, and the King did not take exception to this.

Fernao Martins told us later that the King again reclined on a gold-embroidered couch and this time the Captain opened up, but always keeping his hand in front of his mouth in accordance with the manners of this court. (Could it be, we wondered later, if it was the fear of spittle flying into the King's face, that made them frame their odd rules of etiquette?) The Captain-Major waxed eloquent on our country. It was the most powerful country in Europe, he said (though he didn't explain what Europe was). For over half a century his country had sent out fleets, nay argosies, to make contact with India, for his King Dom Manuel knew that India was a Christian country and that there were Christian kings like Manuel himself here. These Portuguese ships travelled for a year or two and returned when they ran out of provisions without finding India. Dom Manuel had ordered him to command this fleet and not to return to Portugal without making contact with India. If he returned unsuccessful, his head would be cut off. (We had no idea till then how dramatic our Captain could be and how he could exaggerate!) He also talked about two letters from his King, which he would deliver the next day. The King of Portugal wanted friendship with the King

*keki n. daruwalla*

of Calicut, and would like to call him his brother. Vasco da Gama also asked the King to favour him with emissaries, for how would his King believe him if he went to Portugal without some citizens of this country.

The Zamorin welcomed our Lord Dom Manuel's message, considered him a friend and brother and promised to send ambassadors to Portugal. By now it was raining hard. Torrents of water dropped from the sky and we wondered how we'd get back. The King told the Captain that he had small chance of reaching Kappad that evening and so would he like to stay at the house of a Moor or a Christian? Neither, said our Captain, could he have a lodging by himself? By now four hours of the night had passed. The Captain was again put in a palanquin while we all managed as best as we could, drenched with rain. Progress was slow, and the Captain was tired and said so to the King's factor, a Moor noble, who took him to his own house. We were placed in the veranda, while the Captain rested in a well-carpeted room. Huge metal lamps with four wicks flared in the room and the veranda. It took some time to prepare a meal but we were well fed before we retired for the night.

It had been one great day. Actually all these ten days since 18 May when first we had sighted land, had been historic. We had done what no one had done earlier. Our three ships were the bridge where Asia and Europe met for the first time across the seas. I don't know if anyone of us that night, was thinking in those terms. We were tired and some of us were snoring away while I pondered over what had happened. I had been thinking of Alexander for the past ten days. But his visit had been one of blood and conquest, the elephant brigades of the heathen Hindu king against the long *sarissa* of the pagan Greek. This was different—a voyage culminating in the meeting of two worlds. The discovery of the Antilles six years ago by that reject from the Portuguese court—what was it compared to this trans-oceanic discovery of the Indies? As for argonauts like Jason, they were ordinary boatmen, the kind you see on these Moorish dhows, compared to Vasco da Gama.

Not to be forgotten was also the fact that we had proved that all land on this earth nestled in the bosom of the sea. The oceans were all around us.

But it was of the things of the spirit that I was thinking, of our Kings who fifty years ago had petitioned the Pope and sought his blessings in our endeavours. I thought of the three Papal Bulls issued from 1452 to 1456. Now that I think of it, keeping in view that we had a Moorish pilot (though we discovered rather late that he was not a Christian) and the Moors have been so nice to us in Calicut, the first Bull, *Dum diversas* of 18 June 1452 was slightly harsh. For, the Pope gave full rights to the King of Portugal to attack and conquer Saracens, heathens and other unbelievers 'inimical to Christ', to confiscate their goods, grab their territories; to perpetually enslave them, and to transfer their lands and properties to the Portuguese King.

The second Bull, the *Romanus Pontifex* of 8 January 1455, was an encomium to our kings, praised the apostolic zeal of Prince Henry, described him as a true soldier of Christ, praised his intention of circumnavigating Africa thus making contact with the people of the Indies 'who, it is said, honour the name of Christ'. Allied to these inhabitants we could prosecute the struggle against the Saracens, who were to be compelled to enter the fold of the Church. We were empowered to convert even those pagans who were untainted by Muslim influence. It approved our bringing Negro slaves from Africa and getting them baptized. Pope Nicholas V had given a monopoly of navigation, trade and fishing, lest other powers come into the region and reap what we, the Portuguese, had sown.

The confirmatory Bull *Inter caetera* of 13 March 1456, Pope Calixtus 111 by gave to the Order of Christ, of which Prince Henry was the Administrator, the 'ecclesiastical and all ordinary jurisdiction, lordship and power, in ecclesiastical matters only . . . of all regions conquered by Portugal now or in the future from Capes Bojador and Nun, by way of Guinea and beyond, southwards to the Indes.'

Post Script: I was left with one great regret, however. There was no news of Prester John. Would we ever come in touch with his kingdom? It looks like a dream. Will we sit at his table, a table where every evening thirty thousand people dine, a table where twelve archbishops sit to his right and twenty bishops to his left? According to rumour, the table is made of one large emerald! (Couldn't be one emerald. The table must be dotted with emeralds, surely.)

~

The next day was the day of gifts. It didn't turn out right—I mean the gifts didn't and we faced much ill-disguised scorn. We got ready twelve pieces of Lambel, six hats, four scarlet hoods, four strings of coral, four wash-basins, two casks of oil and two of honey. The Wali and the Factor, the Moor at whose house we stayed, inspected the gifts and laughed. The poorest merchant from Mecca, from Cochin or Cranganore gave more, they said. The Chinese gave brocades, silks and gold. Merchants from the Taprobane gave sapphires, yellow and blue. How would these gifts compare? they asked. Give gold, they said, but the Captain had brought no gold and grew very sad. These were not his King's gifts, he said, they were his private gifts. The Wali told him that they would not forward his presents. Our euphoria of the previous day took a dive.

# taufiq
## allah brought me to calicut

~~~

A llah saw me to Calicut. All four ships survived. He
saw to it that no storm lashed us, even though the sea
was uneasy with rumours of disquiet. Wind and rain and
mountainous wave let us be till we reached Calicut and their
Admiral, whose name is Gama, met the King, the Samudri
Raja. It was a sign from Allah that he had spared us, or
why should it rain the first day we are on land? He withheld
the clouds till we were ashore. My mentor, my Admiral,
Shihab al Din Ahmad Ibn Majid al Najdi, told them they
were late. But then they couldn't have stayed on the Milad al
Zanj forever. Not after what they had done at Mozambique
and Mombassa.

His angels didn't grudge the fact that I was pilot and
helmsman in one. He and his stars guided our sails, even
though the North Star was not visible for five bad nights. Allah
saw me through all this. And the holy month of Ramadan,
which began one day before we left Milind, had a lot to
do with it. By the Christian calendar, I was to learn later,
Ramadan started on 23 April 1498. It was the year of the Hijr
903. Things were difficult for me. All that salt in the air, the
blazing sun and fasting don't go together. Thirst often seemed

to corrode my throat and my tongue. At dusk I would just eat wheaten bread. I wouldn't touch their salted meat, for it was not halal. In any case it tasted bad. No wonder I had become much thinner by the time the voyage ended.

My admiral, and the admiral of all Arab nations, Ibn Majid had told me, 'These people are not above throwing boiling oil on you! They have done it with another pilot. Will you go with them? The King of Milind has given his word, and he belongs to our faith.' I replied that if it was his will, and the will of Allah, I would surely go. (Actually I was afraid, but before one's mentor one must put up a bold front. Courage is a mask.)

And he replied, 'I will refrain from cursing them, for you will be on board. May your voyage be victorious.'

There are no victories in voyages. If the sea doesn't want it, he will not let you pass. I couldn't say that to my mentor though. Moreover, his anger and curses seemed put on. The things that came naturally to him were navigation and poetry and a thirst for wine. He didn't hate the people from al Fartaqal. He didn't hate any of Allah's creatures. When angry, he could curse, but without malice. 'Take them,' he said, 'they have been straining for years, but every time the sea defeats them. Perhaps it was Allah's will to delay matters. But if you keep knocking at a door, Allah in his mercy will open it some day. It may well be your destiny to lead them to that door.'

No one ruminated on what would happen once the door was thrown open.

The one thing that happened was the issue of the gifts. Yesterday the whole country had come out to see them—their white skins, their dress, the way they behaved. The King himself received them—travelling fifteen miles back to Calicut to do so. A day later they were in the dumps. But I will come to that later.

I learnt more in this month-long voyage than I would have in ten years on the sea. They are very good sailors. Their maps are correct to the last league. They had mapped the entire west coast of Africa, port by port, harbour by harbour. Yet their knowledge of al Hind was laughable. They divided Hind into three parts—so Fernao Martins, their Arabic interpreter, told me. 'Not just we, but all Europeans,' he said, 'speak of the Indies, but no one knows where they are!' (He was drunk that day and had offered me wine which I refused, because of Ramadan.) After we reach Calicut I will drink, I told him. They talked of a Near India, which meant areas to the north. They talked of a Farther India, which meant the south—Malabar and Coromandel. And they talked of a Middle India, which meant Abyssinia! I tried to argue with them sometimes, but you can't argue with a nation, a culture. A twenty-seven-year-old pilot of a ship can't shake national beliefs.

They kept thinking I was Christian! I would laugh at them. 'Look at my name! Does it sound Christian to you?' It made no difference. They were prepared to believe the word of the King of Milind. It took me a week to convince them I was a Muslim. And they kept asking about Christian kingdoms here. I didn't know what to reply. They had never heard of Hindus. Anyone who was not a Muslim was a Christian.

They had better instruments than we had. Their concentration was like an arrow's flight. They wanted to reach the Indian coast and nothing else. Nothing else? I may have overreached myself. They wanted everyone to become a follower of Issa. They wanted to find a kingdom where some great Christian King or Sheikh lived whom they called 'John'. And they wanted spices.

The voyage must be left behind. What is done is done. Yesterday they seemed to be in some place nearest to heaven.

Today, as I said earlier, they were in the dumps. The Wali at whose house they had stayed, came to me and said, 'You have been with these Farangs for a month. Couldn't you put some sense in their heads?'

I was a bit slow to understand. What had they done? I asked. Go and look at their gifts for the King, he said. They are displayed in the courtyard. I had a look at them and couldn't believe my eyes. I turned to their priest Figueiro and Fernao Martins, who was standing with him. Is this what you give to the Samudri Raja? I asked. I feel compelled to say here that throughout the voyage I had problems with these people from al Fartaqal in regard to pronunciation. Each time I called them Fartaqalis, they would say, no, Purtugalis. I acquiesced. What else can one do? But they couldn't pronounce any word of ours. When I talked of the Samudri Raja, they called him Zamorin and sometimes Samorim or even Camolin. When I told them we had reached Kappaad, they called it Capua. When I said the Kotwal had come to take them to the King, they called him Catual. Their tongues are like pieces of shale, they don't bend to inflections, to softer sounds, to sibilance.

Muslim and other merchants had now gathered around the courtyard and were laughing at the gifts—pieces of ordinary cloth, some coral (they were not gifting cowries, thank God) and some wash-basins! The basins caused the biggest laugh. The king had golden basins—they had seen one of them only a day earlier. A Muslim merchant asked me, 'They came all the way to give this! Yet they made a one year journey successfully—did Allah help them or some god of their own?'

The day passed without any news from the King. The next day, Wednesday, two Muslim Amirs came and took the Admiral to the Samudri Raja. I followed on the tail end out of curiosity. The men around the palace were armed this time. The area bristled with sword and spear, as if the Mamluks in Cairo were on parade. The Admiral, Lord of the Purtugali fleet, was made to wait four hours before the King met him. Only two people will go with you into the King's chamber, he was told. He took his Arabic interpreter Fernao Martins and another Purtugali with him.

Obviously the Samudri Raja had been told all about the gifts. The King did not waste much time on pleasantries this time. 'You say you come from a very rich kingdom, yet you brought nothing. You said you have letters to deliver and there are no letters. You call yourself an ambassador, but an ambassador should be as good as his word. My court would like to know who you are and why exactly you have come.'

The Admiral gave a long speech in his defence. A Muslim who was present told me later that he spoke like a woman of ill-repute trying to prove she was virgin. Later he said that Gama's speech resembled a serpentine crawl—he was a man of many metaphors, this Muslim. But Fernao Martins later declared to us all that the Captain (that is what the Purtugalis call him) gave a famous oration. I have come to discover, he said, and hence I brought no gifts. When I return to Portugal and come back you will see what my King sends to you. (I must add here that these Farangs were obsessed with the idea of 'discovery'. Throughout the voyage from Milind they had used this one phrase 'a descobrir', 'a descobrir'. Ibn Majid had laughed when he had heard the words, but I always maintained respectful silence, remembering the libation of boiling oil they had poured on their previous pilot. I used to joke with the other voyagers. 'That was the water from Zam Zam that you poured on the fellow.' But it was difficult to make them understand the joke.)

After talking of discoveries and continents and Christian

*keki n. daruwalla*

kingdoms, Gama took out the letter. Before the battle over the letter ensued (and it was a long battle) the King spoke. (I often sympathized with the Purtugalis. They had no knowledge of how we thought, how our minds worked. They had never heard of *nazr,* the ceremonial offer to the overlord, which was often only touched by the bigger man and then given to the poor—not always, but now and then. It was often the quality of the *nazrana,* that showed the value your subject or subordinate placed on you. And probably the Admiral did not know that no one was ever permitted to meet the Samudri without first proffering a gift.) Fernao Martins informed us later that the King mentioned casually, in fact so casually that the statement must have been pre-meditated, that he had heard that Gama had brought a golden image of Santa Maria. Gama replied promptly that it was not made of gold, and even if it was he would not have parted with it, for it had brought him safely from Portugal and would guide him back safely to his own country. He spoke bluntly like a camel driver or a muleteer. I know how a merchant from Jeddah would have responded to the same hint. 'Oh King of Kings,' he would have supplicated, 'permit me to keep this icon which is not made of gold. It is too insignificant to give to a King. A saint gave it to me. Saints are not rich, only their blessings are. It has brought me safely across the seas and will take me and my companions back safely, if Allah wills it. Let my men see their children once again!' and the matter would have ended there.

The King's quiver had not emptied as yet. What have you come looking for, men or stones? he asked, for if you have come looking for men you would have brought something. Why have you come empty-handed? Gama stuck to his *descobrir* stuff. 'I will come next time and bring my King's gifts.'

Then started the *dastan,* the *afsana,* the story of the male Scherezade and the letter, which the Admiral drew out with a flourish, the way an Ottoman cavalier draws a sword. He said that he wouldn't want a Muslim to read it out and translate it, for he would mistranslate it, hint at offence where no offence was meant to His Majesty. If he does that we will have him flogged, said the King. Majesty, he will not change the words, but these cunning Moors will tamper with the tone and the temper of the letter. And tone is more important than the words, the undercurrent more important than the wave, as you know so well. Hence, he would like an Arabic-knowing Christian to read the letter out.

The King said this was well. A short fellow called Khurram was brought. But then the Admiral drew another letter (not with a flourish this time). He said he had two letters, one written in the Purtugali language, which no one would understand and the other in the language of the Moors. The King was now worried that Gama may pull out a third or a fourth letter (who knew?) and hurriedly ordered the 'Christian' to read. The long and short of it was that the short 'Christian' was unable to read the letter and so four well-read Muslims, all of them learned and returned from Mecca, were asked to read. This was done and the King was well pleased.

What do you have in your country, he asked. Why, corn, cloth, iron, bronze, said Gama. He had brought samples with him. He could show them. But the King was happy once the letter had been read out. Go back to your ships, he said. Have them securely anchored, bring your merchandise to the market and buy and sell as you please . . .

I must intervene here to relate something that happened to me. Since we had come to Calicut I was under no restrictions from the Admiral. I could stay on land or at the ship. I was given the impression that I would be more useful to the Admiral if I stayed on land. I would get to know what the 'Moorish merchants' were up to. He thought that there was a conspiracy behind the low value the traders were placing on Portuguese goods. The Moors didn't want them there and so were driving them out of the market. A Gujarati trader had taken me home and he put me up for a few days, despite my protestations that I could have hired a place to stay in. He was happy and surprised to find that I could speak his language and that I had lived in Gujarat for a few years. It was here that a man who said that he was sent by the Wali, the Governor, approached me. I did not believe him. Governors don't deal with the likes of Taufiq, I told him. But he insisted and took me to the Wali's house. I was ushered into his chamber where a Muslim merchant of apparently good standing was also present. Both treated me as an equal. After the dates and the sherbet and some pleasantries, the Wali asked directly about the Purtugalis. You are the best person to tell us, he said, who exactly these people are. What have they come for? How did they pick on you to guide them here? Is it true they will stop our trade with Jeddah?

I saw no harm in telling them what I knew. But that didn't satisfy them. I even told them that I had met sailors from this country during my voyage to Sidon and Tyre. I had also met Venetians there, and I told them how perturbed they were at the prospect of the Purtugalis reaching the west coast of India. But they obviously wanted more. The merchant asked me if they hated the Moors, as he called himself. Did they hate the Mappilas more than the ones from the Red Sea? What arms were they carrying? asked the Wali. I felt sad at all this. We Arabs have a proverb which says that sad are only those who understand. By now even a fool could have made out the drift of the conversation. I told them there was no way I could help them. I was with the Purtugalis, my mentor Ibn Majid had handed me to them and with them I'd remain. There was no further information with me that I would like to part with. That ended matters.

These people of Calicut are very friendly and this time it was one Shakoor I fell in with. I discovered that there was no such thing as formality here. Perhaps they didn't know the word. People just gather the folds of their waistcloth, which they call *mundu*, in their left hand, kick off their sandals and enter another's house with a broad grin. The host grins and so does the guest. As I was walking down a street, a Muslim started walking along with me and struck up a conversation. He told me his name was Shakoor. He showed me boats of different kinds and took me to warehouses which stored goods from our Arab countries. People opened their doors to him with the ubiquitous grin pasted on their faces. Now and then someone would nod as a mark of respect. Otherwise they are very informal people. They dress alike and you can't make out the servant from the master. After giving me a tour of the market, he took me to an eatery where they served rice and meat redolent with spices. He owned more than one house and one of them adjoined his dwelling. That is where he made me stay. I asked him about the rent but he waved the issue aside with loud laughter. He showed me his areca nut groves and seemed especially proud that he owned wells of his own. After a day or so he took me to his own house, a fine place girdled with fruit trees and coconut palm. These people have no idea about fountains of course, or the place would really have been excellent. I remember a large green chandelier which accommodated a dozen candles. Another had a dozen oil wicks.

Shakoor was what they call a *Mudhalali*, a wealthy person. He owned a fleet of boats, which traded with Basra and Hormuz. One boat was reserved for pilgrims during the Haj season. But he didn't look prosperous; was thin, had a beard that grew out of his chin like a bush starved of water—and he wore a *mundu* like everyone else. The day he took me to his house his daughter Samina was lighting the oil wicks in a chandelier. As I entered, the candle with which she was lighting the wicks, got snuffed out. I knew the Indians would consider this an omen—they are so superstitious. I would be unwelcome henceforth, I thought. (Not that we were less superstitious. My father had once told me that if, as you enter a house, a crow caws or a lizard clicks, or worse, swallows a moth, it foreshadows bad luck.) But Samina was not put off at all, lighted the candle again and the chandelier's oil wicks and gave me a welcoming smile that seemed shy and frank at the same time, and full of mischief. She brought me sherbet and betel nut. I declined to take the latter, saying quite truthfully that I didn't know how to eat it. She laughed and brought me a tray with several sockets containing cardamom, cloves, raisins and grated coconut. Later I was served coconut water.

Sitting with father and daughter, I found myself unable to speak. In Egypt one doesn't come across women in this fashion. Finding me tongue-tied, she could barely suppress her laughter. Shakoor said to her, 'He has come with the Firangis and will be leaving early.' She answered, 'People should arrive early and go late.' There was a composure about her that was very striking. I tried to avoid looking at her, lest I be considered too brazen.

Things were slowly turning awry between the Purtugali people and the Samudri Raja. Not just the Raja, but also the court. If only the gifts had been all right. It is not greed on the part of the court. They have enough. But they put a value on people from the gifts they gave. These people boasted so much, and all they gave were wash-basins and four strings of coral (fishermen gave coral!)—what were the Malabaris to make of it? The Admiral Gama had fallen in their esteem, and now they were not sure if he would even pay the customs duties.

People added chilies to bad curry. Bad cooks in Malabar do that. Dark hints were thrown—they could be pirates, who knew? They had bombards, weapons, and they may have come to survey things. Survey, the King would ask, what do you mean? Surveying for conquest, of course, Your Majesty, or plunder. Sitting at anchorage or port, I could imagine all this. Moreover, they had talked so much about Christian that and Christian this, that the Muslims in the city were turning sullen. The Admiral, in his turn, was very suspicious of the devilish tricks the Moors could play. Gama also had a temper. A bad temper is fine in your own country with men of your own faith. Here no one of your race has ever set foot and you storm like the monsoon sea! A horse is brought without a saddle and you shout at everyone and refuse to mount. You are a big noble. At least I know that. But then you must present gifts worthy of a noble. A Gujarati merchant, wealthy like all Gujarati merchants, provided a *palki*, which the Purtugali people call *andor*, palanquin. The bearers of the palanquin ran so fast that the other Purtugali people were left behind and lost their way. Gama also lost his way and temper, by the time he reached Pantalayini. Then he asked for boats. The Wali accompanying him said, bring your ships nearer. This, I knew, would arouse the Admiral's suspicions. Nowhere did he ever allow his ships to come near the coast.

Gama kept asking for a boat and the Wali said it was dusk so 'rest here and we will get you boats tomorrow.' He argued. So they took him along the beach, the Wali marching ahead and the Purtugali party following him, tired and depressed, looking like dead fish being dragged in a net. Was this the way to treat a fellow Christian, asked Gama. Every request was followed by a threat, 'I will go to the King again!' The Wali got tired. 'I will give you thirty boats, if you want them.' This was a trap, the Admiral thought. He was difficult to understand. If you denied him, you were plotting with the Moors and keeping the Christian King in the dark. If you conceded what he wanted, it was a trap. He sent off three men to the ships to tell his brother to hide. But they couldn't find the ship's boats and got lost themselves.

Next day there were a hundred armed men around them and the Purtugalis were detained. The Malabaris had swords, spears and *bisarmas*—battleaxes with sharp edges on both sides. I saw bows and arrows as well. It all started with the Admiral again asking for boats. The Malabaris asked for the ships to be brought near. The Admiral refused. In that case we will not let you board the ships, they said.

'The King Camolin has ordered us to go to the ships,' the Captain says. 'If you don't let me embark, I will go back to the King who is a Christian like myself.'

In answer, they closed the doors, and more armed men entered to guard them. It looked bad. 'If we are not allowed to go to the ships we will die of hunger.'

'Die of hunger,' they said.

One of the three lost men came back secretly, saying Nicolau Coelho, the other Admiral was waiting with boats. He was sent back, equally secretly to Coelho, asking him to return to the ships and see that they were safe. Coelho did as he was told, chased by Malabari boats, which could not catch up with them. More guards were placed around the rest house and a multitude gathered around it to see the fun.

A bad day and a worse night passed, but next day, as their Padre said, the Malabaris 'returned with better faces'. Ask for your goods to be sent ashore, and we will let you go, they said. The Admiral wrote to his brother to send a few things. The goods were sent and Gama and his men were allowed to go to the ships.

The Admiral complained to the King who now sent eight

Hindu merchants to inspect the merchandise and assured Gama that he would punish those who had troubled Gama. He ordered them merchants to keep away. But the merchants sneered at the goods. Not a single item could be sold. Relations with them got worse and each time a Purtugali landed, they shouted, 'Purtugal, Purtugal' and spat noisily. (People here spit expressively, being well practised in this art through eating that loathsome betel nut.)

Gama again requested the King, who allowed him to take his merchandise to Calicut, and even supplied free labour. The people of Pantalayini seemed enemies to the Farangs. But Calicut welcomed them and they managed to sell many of their goods—chains, metal articles, coats, cloth, shirts. Mapilahs misreported the sale of chains to the King. 'Why do you think they brought chains? To enslave us, symbolic, no?' The Samudri Raja was not easily taken in. The roughest rock is smoothened by a river. He reminded the Admiral that he owed the King six hundred ashrafis as customs duties. The Fartaqali calls an ashrafi a 'xerafin'. One of their many convicts on the ship whom they referred to as 'degradados', took great trouble to inform me that in England (where he had been imprisoned), the Calicut xerafin would have fetched 7 shillings, 5 pence.

Slowly, Gama allowed his men to come singly and trade in the town. They bought spices and precious stones, which they found cheap. They found that their goods also fetched a lower price than in their country. The people in the streets were friendly and took them home, gave them food and made them sleep there at night.

During all this time things were happening with me as well. A local Muslim offered me his daughter in marriage, but I said no. Why, he asked? I work on ships and who knows when my ship goes down. At least see her, he said.

*keki n. daruwalla*

Who? My daughter, who else? But I got out of that one. I was also looking for a ship to pilot now, a ship going up the Red Sea preferably, past the Holy of Holies, the Kabah. I told Nicolau Coelho the same. Wait, the Captain-Major has something in mind for you, he said. Within a few days of our landing I noticed a well-built, slightly fat monk with a shaved head following me. He picked up conversation with me whenever he could and introduced himself as a Buddhist Fakir, but when I reached in my pocket to give him some money, he smiled and shook his head. He belonged to an order of monks who were well provided for, he said. I counted three chance meetings. I can lay down a rule that there can be only one 'chance' meeting. The second one is intentional. At length I asked him, 'You are a holy man. What do you want from me?' He answered me bluntly. 'You know the Admiral. Take me to him.'

I explained I had no influence on this rather foul-tempered man. 'Worse the temper, better for me,' he said. He is very busy, and has taken on the whole city, I said. 'Not just the city, but the whole Moorish race from here to Mecca', he replied laughing. I started liking the man. All the more reason I didn't want him to meet the Admiral. 'He is not above throwing boiling oil on visitors,' I said. He was prepared to face anything. 'He will take you for a Christian,' I warned, but finally agreed to take him to the ship. He said he had another favour to ask. 'I want to be taken to him without people knowing about it.' That would be difficult. But he had his plans ready. He had already talked to Fernao Martins and Diogo Dias, the man whom the Admiral now wanted to leave behind as his Factor.

I couldn't get to Dias. He was all the time going to the King with the Admiral's tiring messages. The Purtugali fleet had still not paid the Customs dues. I introduced the Monk to the interpreter. The next day Fernao Martins said 'Bring the monk today immediately after nightfall. I will be there. The Captain-Major will meet him.'

A boat had been arranged from the ship and I took the Monk at nightfall. The Monk was pleasant and in a talkative mood. 'You fired many warning shots at me that day,' he said ironically.

'But there was one bombard which I hadn't fired,' I warned. 'The Admiral doesn't hesitate in taking hostages.'

He was taken aback, but made light of it. 'I will be a strain on his provisions. He will run short of rice.' He patted his belly, which looked like a foresail with the wind behind it. 'You are the only one I know in this fleet. I hope they allow you to sit there and interpret them to me.' I shrugged my shoulders. Just before we reached the *Sao Gabriel*, he asked, 'Why did you say he will mistake me for a Christian?'

'Anyone who is not a Muslim is a Christian!' The Monk laughed. 'He has anchored here two months now, and still doesn't know Christian from Hindu?' I shook my head. Fernao Martins was at the rails, peering down, lamp in hand. They lowered a rope ladder for him. I shouted in Arabic that the Monk was too fat to climb a rope ladder and would need help. The Monk laughed again. He obviously understood Arabic. He grasped the ladder and climbed up, almost as quickly as I did a few minutes later.

# figueiro
## of monks, hostages
## and corsairs

The Monk from Taprobane looked impressive. He could have passed off for one of those fat friars, the butt of jokes in Europe once. But this man had a dignified air about him. Because of his height the roundness of his waist looked less pronounced. The Admiral wanted the pilot Taufiq to sit in at the meeting, but the Monk was not in favour. 'I don't want any Moors here,' he said. We kept Taufiq out of this.

(Taufiq didn't know that he was to return with us to Portugal. He wanted to get back to Cairo soon. But the Captain-Major wanted him on one of the ships on our return. The few who knew of the Captain's plans were surprised, for we had very experienced pilots—Pero d' Alenquer, who piloted *S. Gabriel*, the flagship, had voyaged with Bartolomeau Dias when the Cape of Good Hope was discovered; Joao de Coimbre, who piloted *S. Raphael*; and Pero Escolar who guided the *Berrio* were experienced and salt-bitten men who knew their boats and the sea.)

When the Captain-Major appeared, the Monk stood up and folded his hands, which he carried to his forehead. The

Captain bowed. He had deliberately come in later so that the monk would pay him the respect due to him. The Captain was brusque.

'Explain the purpose of your visit.'

The Monk took his time. He was not the type to be hustled. He explained he was a Buddhist monk from Lanka, known as Serendib to sailors from afar, also known as Taprobana or Taprobane. He talked about his religion and about his huge island—one of the largest islands in the world he called it. He talked about forests and ivory in his country, and precious stones—emeralds and sapphires. 'But it is not of my country that I came to talk here. It is Cochin.' He paused rather dramatically—Orientals do. Then he continued that Cochin also had a big King. Though he owed some fealty to the King of Calicut, he was great in his own right. The Zamorin denied him the right to coin his own money or even to roof his palace with tiles! Cochin was as rich in spices as was Calicut, and had a larger harbour. There is a good Christian population there, all of them from St Thomas's church. The King of Cochin was well disposed towards the Portuguese though he had never set eyes on them.

'You are from another country. How do you speak for Cochin?'

' Admiral, I have commercial ties with Cochin. So I go there often, sometimes for three months at a stretch.'

He hinted that there was not much love lost between the Kings of Calicut and Cochin. Of great interest to the Captain was the news that Cochin didn't have that many Moors. The dour-faced Captain smiled for the first time when he heard this. He had been particularly riled that the Moors had told their Christian King, the Zamorin, that the Portuguese were thieves and pirates. Lord Gama gave vent to his feelings about the Moors in general. Why couldn't a

Christian King understand the Captain and his motives? The Monk spoke up. 'The influence of the Moors here can't be easily imagined. They got one of the Malabari kings to convert to Islam and move for good to Mecca, leaving throne and harem behind. The very name Malabar is of Moorish coinage, or at least half of it. It stems from the Dravidian *mala* (hill) to which the Moors added the Arabic *bar* (country).'

The Monk went on. 'The Moors, as you call them, are not a nation. They differ in race, colour and language, even belief. Arabs and the Persians have traded on these coasts for a thousand years. They would be stranded at ports for months, because of the monsoons primarily. So they married on the coasts. They had a wife here and probably a wife somewhere in Arab lands. The children were obviously raised as Muslims and the coastal belts became Moorish. Here in Malabar they are called Mappilas. But you will find them in Gujarat, Coromandel, Kalinga. Hindus avoid the seas—they believe you get defiled if you cross the waters. Navigation and trade are in Moorish hands. Apart from spices, they trade in horses with the kingdom of Vijaynagar, and as far as the Mallacas and Indonesia— countries as rich in spices as we are. If you want spices, you need to come here in force. Bring your ships filled with soldiers, and stay on. Don't come and buy and set your sails back to your country. You are not visiting some fish or spice market. Swarandip and Cochin could combine with you. To control the seas you have to conquer and hold ports in the mouth of the Red Sea and the Gulf—Aden, Hormuz, which I believe you call Imogros.'

The Captain-Major was not going to be trapped into any commitment. 'Why are you saying all this to me?'

'Isn't it obvious? If Hindu kingdoms won't do it, then Christians must step in.'

'Don't take me for a fool. We have come to trade goods with another Christian country, not to trade blows.'

The thrust and parry continued, but the Monk seemed content to have dropped an idea. He would let the Captain Major mull over it.

~

Our troubles with the Moors continued. It was they who were poisoning the King's ears. 'You don't want their cloth or coral! You want gold and silver. They don't have it. So why entertain them?' The rogues added that we would put their entire trade with the Red Sea in jeopardy. (That was something we'd have been very happy to do.) We found that from Cambay to Imogros, no one was eager to trade with us.

On Monday, 13 August, the Captain decided to leave a Factor here, and deputed Diogo Dias for the job. Diogo was a purser with *Sao Gabriel* and the brother of the great explorer and voyager Bartolomeau Dias. The Captain sent a present through Dias—amber and corals, and wrote to the King of his intention to leave a factor behind, while the ships would be leaving for Portugal in a day or two. Surprisingly, he also urged the King to send a present to our King—and he asked for a *bahar* of cinnamon and a bahar of cloves and other spices. His factor could pay for them. Now a bahar is of considerable weight, 250 seers in Indian weight. The King made Diogo wait four days before he gave him an audience and a surly one at that. He did not want to even look at the present and said so. And he asked for 600 xerafins as the port duty. Dias, and our men with him, were detained at the house where our merchandise was kept.

Worse, the town crier went around town forbidding any boat to come to the ships. Fortunately, Dias got a Negro to carry a letter to us. This man contacted fishermen and on the payment of three fanoês, the fishermen brought the letter to us. We were really saddened. No boat came to us the next day. On the August 15 a boat came with some peddlers in precious stones. We did them no harm. The tension mounted. On 19 August the stalemate ended on a refreshing note, the way a gust of breeze brings life to sagging sails in mid-sea calm. A big boat came to our ships with twenty-five men aboard, among whom six were nobles. They came to parley. The Captain-Major's mouth watered when he saw them. He was not one to look a gift horse in the mouth. He had them detained, eighteen of them along with all the six nobles. He sent a letter to the King's factor, saying that these men would be released, if the King let off Diogo Dias and the men with him.

We waited four days, and since no response came, and the Captain was firmly of the opinion that they had killed Diogo Dias, we made sail for Portugal. We faced a headwind and so anchored four leagues to the leeward of Calicut. On August 26, as we were waiting for a wind, a boat came saying that we should release the men and that Dias was at that moment with the King. But the Captain-Major believed they had killed Dias. He threatened to fire his bombards at them and in addition cut off the heads of all the eighteen, including the six nobles with him. Send Dias back, or his corpse—(the last bit he added under his breath). Harsh measures always score with Orientals, Christian or Moor. If there is one language they understand it is that of the bombard. (The knife will also do—if it's at the throat.) The King called Dias. This time the royal mood was not as black as earlier. He feigned innocence, asking coyly why the Captain had detained eighteen men. He laid the blame for any misunderstanding on others and gave a letter for our King and sent Dias back.

The Captain freed the six nobles and others, except for six others from the lower orders, whom we carried back to Portugal. Without them how would we have proved that we had discovered the Indies? One of the six had lost an eye. Ever considerate and kind that he was, he had him dropped on 10 September. He also sent a letter to the Zamorin, apologizing for taking five people away, but swearing that they would be returned within a year.

The dessert was yet to come. At the Anjedive islands off Goa, there was a skirmish with corsairs, who were driven off. Later, when the Captain was on land at one of these islands, a forty-year-old man came up, dressed splendidly—he had a belt and sword, and spoke fluent Venetian. He hugged the Captain and others. He was a Christian from the west, he said, and served a Moor, the Governor of Goa. He got to hear about these Franks in Calicut and became desperate to see them. He asked for some cheese to be taken back with him and the Captain had the cheese delivered to him. To his ill-luck, the Captain's brother, Paulo da Gama made enquiries about him from other local Christians and they said he was an *armador*, a pirate, and was involved with the ones who had skirmished with us a day back. He had men in boats out of sight, who would pounce on us. We thrashed him so badly that he couldn't even speak and his further communications to us were through sign and gesture. In brief, he conveyed that armed men were hiding in the creeks to attack us. He had come to see for himself who we were and how we were armed. Such men have to be questioned with blows and thus he was questioned three times. The Captain-Major took him along in his ship and forgave him. Later, we found out he was a Jew, and he was baptized as Gaspar da Gama.

It must be said that the islanders were very nice. They brought us green branches of cinnamon with leaves on them. After twelve days at these islands, after filling up water and dining on fresh fowl and pumpkin every day, we sailed homewards—not knowing that we were sailing into sickness and scurvy and death. We had decided to return to India to regain health, till the Lord in his mercy sent us a headwind and we sailed for Lisbon.

# the lost coconut cleaver

Even before the Portuguese had left, certain people complained to the Zamorin that they were taking away pepper saplings. He replied, let them take the saplings, but how will they carry our *tiruvathira,* the special climate that ensures seven days of rain followed by seven days of sunshine so essential for the growth of the pepper plant? The Portuguese came and went and I don't want to hear more of it. Yes, said the Nairs and the Brahmins around him, but can we forget that they never paid the duties, and kidnapped five of our men, even when their Factor was returned? There was ill-will in some quarters although the people who had traded with them in Calicut were happy with them. Personally, he harboured misgivings. There had been hostility all around. He wasn't happy with that. These white visitors had dealt with him on their terms. If captains of every Chinese junk or Yameni batil or a Red Sea dhow were to deal with Calicut on their terms, the Zamorin would become a global vassal, a servant of the entire littoral. Moreover, these people had left with ill-will. He had made a show of being pleasantly surprised with Vasco da Gama's letter of apology from the Anjedive islands. He had even read the letter out to the families of the five people abducted by Gama, but it had not done much to console them.

These white nations were many. That much he knew. Travellers from their countries had been seen here, once in a decade or two, their appearance as rare as an eclipse. This hadn't been a good beginning. For, they would come again, he knew. The timing was none too good. That he should have got the news of their arrival when he was looking into the death of Chirukandan, was an unhappy coincidence. He would consult astrologers about what their visit boded.

Perhaps if Chirukandan had been alive, there would have been a counter to the Moors. He was not happy at their threat. 'If you take new friends for old, we will quit Calicut in a body.' They also added that the country would be ruined once they left. He had kept a studied silence. Very easy to say all that, he thought, but where would they go? And even if the Moors went back, what about the Mappilas, some of them new converts to Islam and most others offspring of Arab or Persian fathers and Malabar women? They wore mundus and went about shirtless like Hindus and you couldn't make them out but for their small white circular caps. They spoke Malayalam like everyone else and knew of no other home than Malabar.

All he wanted was peace: no piracy on the seas, especially near his own coast. He prayed for good order on land, meaning thereby that law breakers should be punished and the purity of caste upheld. No person of a low caste should defile by touch the purity of a Brahmin or a Nair. There should be no impediment to the flow of revenue in his coffers from varied imposts and taxes—*Chumkam*, or tolls and duties; *Amkam,* a fee for allowing a trial by battle; *Ezha*, proceeds from confiscated estates; *Kozha*, forced contribution for emergencies; fees levied on conferring titles, royalty on elephants caught in the forest and so on. Enemy ships (or their wrecks) which drifted ashore were the king's property. Any cow with five udders had to be handed over to the king, as also cattle having a white spot near the eye. The tail and the striped hide of a tiger and the leg of a deer killed in hunting were also the king's.

His mind was not on revenues, though. That Chirukandan affair had to be settled. No one could slash his minister all across the belly and get away with it. The investigators had told him that the Headman was not at fault. He called them and gave a final warning. Within a week he wanted a head. A short wooden stake (*mazhu*) through the heart—that was the punishment for murder—normally only after a confession had been extorted through torture. If the murderer was a Moor, he was executed by a sword-thrust. Trial by ordeal was fairly common if there wasn't enough evidence. The accused had to plunge his first two fingers in boiling oil. Then the hand would be wrapped in leaves and cloth and opened after three days. If the burns showed and the hand was disfigured, he was executed. If the fingers were not burnt, the accuser was executed or banished. In the case of a Moor the ordeal differed—no fingers in boiling oil for him. He had to lick the edge of a red-hot axe with his tongue. If the tongue got scalded, it was the sword for him.

Women were never executed. And they weren't tortured. That was the trouble here, for though the minister's wife, Lakshmi, was shouting from the rooftop that it was Kanni, the mistress, who had got it done, there was no proof. A mere boatman saying that he had brought gifts to her and she had scorned them and shouted was not good enough. What if she was weeping and her hair was dishevelled and her mother forced her to accept the gifts? The trouble was you couldn't twist her arm or beat her on the soles of her feet. As if that was not enough, one had to be polite! It was the mistress of a minister one was talking to, a rich person in her own right with palm groves and boats which traded with the Arabs. All that had delayed matters. (All that had also left the widow, Lakshmi seething. Not torturing an accused can sometimes become a torture for the complainant.) Once the royal ultimatum was given things moved apace. Kanni was grilled but to no profit. She loved her man. She too had become a widow, she said.

The manager of the palm-cum-toddy grove was tortured. Yes, he said there was a fellow called Rayiru who worked here, a paraya, who squirreled up tree tops and whose speech, if such it could be called, was understood perhaps only by birds. Yes, he must have been a good hunter, but he didn't kill anything here. He was frightened of Chirukandan. He hadn't been seen the day after the murder. That settled it. A hundred soldiers were unleashed on his trail. The jungles were combed, hutments of tribals raided—cove and creek and forest were a-crawl with pursuers. His name figured on kettledrums. You can't escape the state. Rayiru knew it and he wasn't going to put the woman he worshipped in jeopardy. He disembowelled himself and then thrust his knife through the heart to put an end to matters.

They never found the coconut cleaver, though.

# of lamego and the spies

While all these fights over spices and gifts, Moor and Christian, were in progress, life in Cairo went at its usual pace. There was no news of Taufiq. No one had any idea where he was. Was he in Africa or India, Zanj or Hind? It worried his friends. Murad saw very little of Ehtesham and one day met him over coffee in Khan al Khalili.

Coffee had been making inroads into Cairo since the first coffee house had been opened in Constantinople in 1475. In the past year, however, there had been a sudden spurt of interest in Qawah. Thick Turkish coffee, more dregs than liquid, served in small bowls, had become fashionable. Even women had started drinking it. According to rumour, the Ottomans were thinking of promulgating a law whereby if a man couldn't provide his wife with her quota of coffee, she could sue for divorce. The two friends talked about Taufiq first and shook their heads at the utter lack of news about the man. When Murad enquired about Ehtesham himself, he answered enigmatically, 'Dawns are nervous, dusk is nervous, but the day goes by wonderfully. I am exhilarated.'

Murad told him he was making a fool of himself. But Ehtesham stuck to his guns. 'I may sound foolish but this is exactly what I mean. I am nervous at dawn because I slip out to the church. Zainab doesn't know where I am going. In the beginning I lied—I was going to this mosque or that bazaar. But one gets found out. You need different materials for working on lamps and glass and for painting stone walls or wood. She is no fool. Lying seemed to demean her as well as me. At the same time I want to keep from her details about where exactly I go. Dusk is also a nervous time for me, for I am returning from painting in the church. The Muhtasib's men could spot me, or Ali Hasan's. There is this feeling of guilt I wear, like a cloak in winter, as I return. Zainab just opens the door and I walk in without looking at her. Within minutes life becomes normal.'

Ehtesham continued thoughtfully, 'I find the stone walls uneven and prefer to paint on wood. They hang the pieces on the wall. So far I have painted the child and the three *Gabr* who visited the child at his birth. At the moment I am quite nervous, for I am painting the man who, they say, was brought back from the dead by Jesus.'

'That is heresy!' Murad's eyes lit up with horror.

'You didn't let me finish. It is heresy all right but I become equally liable to the charge of apostasy. No human being can bring the dead to life. I hope Allah will forgive me for my sins.'

~

Ehtesham was sitting with the Abbott one morning and expressing his fears about the whereabouts of his friend Taufiq. The Abbott told him that he was expecting a man who kept a score of the ships on the seas, and of the sea itself. He knew all about voyaging and trade. He had carried on trade in Alexandria and Cairo and would visit his home in Portugal from time to time. He even set up a shop as a shoemaker in Alexandria. And he spoke Arabic fluently and knew many languages. But at present it was suspected he was a royal emissary from Lisbon! Ehtesham's interest grew in the man. When he came in, the Abbott introduced him as Jose de Lamego or Joseph of Lamego. The Abbott smiled and told Lamego of Ehtesham's fears about a friend who was out on the seas. Lamego laughed.

'There is a Persian quote—*sea-voyaging has many advantages, but security is not one of them*. Saadi is supposed to have said it and I wish I knew Persian enough to quote him in his language. It has taken us months to learn it, but the Portuguese have reached India.'

'And not through the Red Sea, of course,' said the Abbott.

'Yes, not through the Red Sea. They say an Arab pilot helped the leader, Vasco da Gama. It was he who overcame the "Green Sea of Darkness", the one which confronted all the men from Europe.'

Ehtesham suggested it must have been the great Ibn Majid himself who could have led the Portuguese to India. No one else was able enough. Lamego answered, 'I hope I am not boasting but we Portuguese are no mean seamen. We are easily the best in Europe and for a hundred years we have been exploring the seas and scouring the African seaboard. We have a saying: "To sail is precise, life is not."'

Lamego held forth. There would be a change in fortunes within some years. The caravans to Alexandria would stop because there wouldn't be much to carry. The pepper trade would slowly turn its sails toward Portugal. Ports along the Red Sea will be lined with beggars. Venetians wouldn't be seen in Alexandria now. They had better take to plying boats or invest in pearl fishery, or just catch fish. What is wrong with fish, I say? They could grow olives! They could blow glass!

Indian women love bangles and they could trade with them. Can you see it coming, a million bangles in the boat hold?

'You are enjoying this, aren't you?'

'Well,' answered Lamego, 'we have another saying— "pepper in the eyes of others is refreshment"!'

This was pepper in *our* eyes, thought Ehtesham. When Lamego left, he told the Abbott, 'How happy he looked! Portugal and its King may get rich but Lamego remains here, doesn't he? How will it benefit him?'

'These are complex questions, my friend, happiness, wealth, country, King; and what benefits whom.' The Abbott was speaking mildly and didn't sound ponderous at all. 'There's a further twist in the matter, for Lamego is a Jew and his people are having a hard time of it in Portugal recently. A year ago they were all chucked out of the country—yellow badge, beard and baggage. But not all baggage, mind you, for gold and silver and jewellery had to be left behind. That belongs to the state. You can take your pots and pans and your hide with you, and even the hair on your hide. Now isn't that enough! So then how does one feel about the country? You live in Portugal for hundreds of years, are suckled by its language and then thrown out. Yet you love your country.'

~

It was a brown dawn in Alexandria, for the wind from the desert had brought a bit of the desert with it. A man stood at the Governor's door, with what he considered was important news, important enough to bother the Governor. Two traders from Morocco living in a particular inn were very ill. Am I a *tabib*, a doctor? Find one and take him there, and see if he can do the Moroccans any good, snarled the Governor. Even by Egyptian standards, he was a bad governor.

Later, he thought he had been too brusque. One never knew how such matters turned out. Suppose the wretches were related to someone high up in Morocco? Or one of them could be married into an Amir's family in Cairo? So the Governor went to the inn after the evening prayers, and found the two Moroccans in a state of semi-delirium. He talked to the innkeeper and others to find out if they were well connected. They shook their heads. Seemed ordinary traders, the staff said. Is there any merchandise with them, the Governor of Alexandria asked. Just jars of honey, the innkeeper said. He took a look at the two. By morning they'll be dead, pronounced the Governor. Their property stands confiscated to the state, which means the Sultan.

Life and death, as Muslims put it so pithily, are in the hands of God. Delirium and fever took leave of the traders. The traders left their beds. The nervous innkeeper and his servants put on their false smiles and rushed towards them exclaiming, 'Allah be praised! Allah be praised!' The traders were weak and responded coldly to the rib-shattering hugs of the inn staff. They looked around for their effects, their jars of honey numerous enough to fill the hold of a ship, and found all gone. Has there been a robbery here? Who took away our things? There has been no robbery, said the innkeeper. It is the Governor of Alexandria who in his wisdom confiscated your property.

'Confiscated! He even took away our clothes, did he?'

The innkeeper nodded vigorously—he had an elastic neck.

'He was kind enough to leave us our skin though. Do we have to thank him for not confiscating our skins?'

The innkeeper said nothing. Innkeepers are good at sealing their lips when they have to.

'Confiscated! On what grounds?'

'The Governor thought you were dead, or about to die—it's the same thing . . .'

'It is bloody NOT! So now he can pronounce me dead when I am alive and alive when I am dead! I'll fix him! I am related to the King of Morocco—married his niece. I'll complain to him and the Sultan in Cairo. Hanging is too good for him, I'll have the Governor crucified. Ask him which gate he wishes to be impaled on. Does he want his arms lashed to a wall or should nails be driven through his palms? The choice is his—all is not lost for the bugger. Please console him.'

The jars of honey came back as they were. Bluster often works.

The two of them were neither Moroccans nor Muslims. They were Christian spies from Portugal! The year was 1487. The name of the passionate one who had threatened the Governor, was Covilhao. He is written of and pronounced in different ways. He is Pero da Covilhao, and Joao Pero da Covilhao. And he was Juan Pedro de Covilham in Castile where he served the Duke of Medina Sidonia, in Seville, early in his career. Since he was born in the town of Covilham in the mountains bordering Spain, he knew Spanish very well. Covilhao made his mark when he accompanied King Aphonso V to France. Covilhao was sent back to France on his first spying mission. He was a natural linguist and learnt Arabic, much of which he picked up in Fez, where King John II sent him as ambassador. His task was to cajole the Sultan of Morocco to return the bones of the benighted Prince Fernando the Martyr, who had died in a dungeon there. He had been captured almost fifty years ago in 1437. 'Return us Ceuta and we will give you your brother back,' the Moroccans had told the Portuguese king then. But would the king listen? The conquest and sack of Ceuta in 1415 had been a triumph for Portugal. The King had declared jubilantly, 'I have dyed my hands in infidel blood.' The Moors had been slaughtered, their goods looted and the Pope had been pleased to declare the adventure a holy crusade. The Portuguese had never seen such houses, muslins from India with silver embroidery and silks from Cathay. Some Portuguese even wrote that their own houses looked like pigsties in comparison. Moreover, it was at Ceuta that the Portuguese heard of 'the rivers of gold' in Africa.

To get to the spiceries, the court wanted details—navigation first. Was there a route from Africa? Other details had to be ferreted out. How did the Arabs trade with Malabar, the terms of the spice trade, where was the best pepper grown, and ginger and cinnamon—what were the dangers that ships would face? What arms should we carry when we go in there? What expense would all this involve? A mission was needed for reconnaissance, exploration. So whom did the king select but Covilhao, an Arabic-knowing cavalier who has been through Morocco, Castile and France without faltering. He was given a companion—Afonso de Paiva.

Secret missions need secret briefings. The last meeting was at the residence of a noble, Pero de Alcacova. The people around the table were the future king himself—Manuel Duke of Beja and two cosmographers, 'master doctors' who knew about continents and the oceans which washed them. Both the cosmographers were Jews, Moses and Roderigo. The briefing was lengthy, as one can imagine. The existence of Sofala was known—what if no white skin had visited it. There was nothing seemingly on the globe that they didn't want from the pair—trade and navigation on the Red Sea, the western seaboard of India and of course Africa and how to go around it. Find out who rules where, Muslim, Christian or heathen, who will tolerate the Europeans, and those who would war with them. More important, find the kingdom of Prester John, the Saint King with his vast wealth and his army of knights on whose table thirty thousand people dine every evening.

~

There were many other meetings with Jose de Lamego, for he dropped in now and then and the Abbott was glad to see him. Often, Ehtesham would be there but there were so many things Lamego could not talk about in his presence. Lamego had mixed feelings about his land now. The troubles for his family had started midway through the reign of John II, the 'O *Principe Perfeito*' or the 'Perfect Prince' as the Portuguese sarcastically called him, because he would have been Machiavelli's ideal prince. The troubles for rich Jews began when pauper nobles and kings borrowed money from them. John borrowed a lot for his sea ventures and Lamego's father got roped in. John II was ruthless and he had showed this streak in no uncertain terms. While he was heir apparent, his father, the King, went off to a monastery leaving the kingdom to John. The nobility hated him. During the first few years he just sat and waited. Some years later his father died and he ascended the throne. Let them make the first move was his motto. He sat like a man with a gun waiting for thieves to enter his house. They did. His spies intercepted letters from Fernando, the Duke of Breganza to Queen Isabella of Castile inviting Spanish intervention. Come and rid us of this tight-assed bastard, the letter must have said, of course all of it couched in very formal lingo and adorned with aristocratic flourishes. That was it. He had the fellow executed in Evora, and confiscated his lands. Some years later he summoned his own brother-in-law (and cousin), Dom Diogo, the Duke of Viseau, suspecting him of conspiring against the King, and thrust his sword through him. The nobility now started behaving. Nothing like a severed head and one sword thrust through the heart, to bring the aristocracy around. Before killing his brother-in-law, in fact along with the execution of the Duke of Breganza, he had the Bishop of Evora imprisoned and poisoned. It is here that one of Lamego's acquaintances came into the picture, Joao Pero da Covilhao in Portugal. He loved adventure. Covilhao got to know that the Bishop was poisoned. People who get to know such cavernous secrets of the dungeon, either end up dead, or they become close to the perpetrator. In this case it brought him closer to the King. An Arabic-knowing cavalier, who had been through Morocco and Spain without a falter, why, he was best suited to explore the Red Sea trade!

They set out from Lisbon on 7 May 1487, sailing to Barcelona and then Naples. They had set out with letters of credit from the Florentine bank of Marchionni. You didn't travel with too much money on you those days—robbers, highwaymen, pirates, they could smell a ducat or a cruzado, a florin or a frank on you from a mile. He had cashed his letters of credit in Naples. They went to Rhodes where they put on the disguise of Muslims. Of all things, they bought honey, filled huge jars with it and reached Cairo. Their disguise stood them in good stead in Cairo and they set out first for Alexandria, and then for al Tor in Sinai, and then Suaqin, that island port, to which, according to legend, Suleiman Ibn Daud or Solomon, son of David would banish his demons. The demons had obviously done a lot of good to the place, for it became a thriving port. It derived its name from suq, and was an ancient mooring place. Jeddah had taken over most of the trade, but a lot of African pilgrims boarded ship here for Mecca. The Portuguese spies stayed here and then pushed off to Aden, from where they went their separate ways. Paiva went to Gujarat where according to some people he died. Others contended that he returned to Cairo and died there. But it was Covilhao who blazed a trail across the entire west coast of India and then went down East Africa. Everywhere he posed as a Muslim. He first went to Calicut, and got to know the spice trade. He then sailed north right up to Goa, which was the centre of horse trade with the Arabs. Cochin, Cannanore, Cranganore—he visited all the ports on the Malabar coast, stayed there for months, noted how the trade was carried out and then returned to Aden. He then reconnoitered the east African coast down till Sofala, from where gold mined in the African hinterland, was shipped. When he came up the Red Sea again he got down at Jeddah and went to Mecca. He would have been beheaded had he been caught, but his Arabic was so good and his disguise so perfect that the 'pilgrimage' passed off without an incident.

In late 1490 Pero Covilhao returned to Cairo. Waiting for him were two emissaries from John II, the Portuguese king, both Jews, Rabbi Abraham de Beja and Jose de Lamego. It is they who told him of Afonso's death. There was a story to this too. The news that Afonso Paiva had died in Gujarat came just a week before Afonso himself landed at Alexandria. Rabbi Abraham's fingers quickened their pace on the rosary, the moment he saw him. Was this a trick of the Devil? But Afonso calmed the two and told them he indeed had got sick in Gujarat and people thought he was on his death bed. However he couldn't stave off death too long, caught a bug in the stomach at Cairo and passed away.

Lamego carried back his report to the King, while Rabbi Abraham and Covilhao went to Hormuz and Aden. Three years later he returned, met Lamego, who had by now set up shop both in Cairo and Alexandria, and went off in search of Prester John to Ethiopia.

Just a year back the Jews had been driven out of Portugal.

That was five years after Ferdinand and Isabella announced their decision 'to banish all Jews of both sexes for ever from the precincts of our realm'; and Christopher Columbus wrote in his diary that 'In the same month in which their Majesties issued the edict that all Jews should be driven out of the kingdom and its territories, in the same month they gave me the order to undertake with sufficient men my expedition of discovery to the Indies.' Portugal felt compelled to follow suit and drove the Jews out. Lamego was now devoting all his energies to settle the banished Jews in Ottoman Turkey, some even quietly in Alexandria. He knew the west coast of India and the synagogue in Cochin and was actively thinking of smuggling some of his brethren there.

# of covilhao and the
# exorcist

&

L amego had confided in only one man, the Abbott. Now even Lamego was a bit confused. 'I have misplaced my memories—at least some of them,' he said, trying to laugh it away. But he remembered some details of the dispatches of Covilhao and also the conversations he had with the adventurer. One particular evening he remembered distinctly. Pero de Covilhao, a little high on wine, was first depressed and quiet but later in the evening, expansive.

'I was very worried at the outset,' Covilhao had told Lamego, 'but I never let Aphonso know of my diffidence, never. The tasks we were saddled with were absolutely enormous. An army of explorers, an armada of ships, a legion of spies was what the King needed. Who were we, Aphonso and I, to get to the bottom of all this. Find out if Africa can be reached from the Red Sea. Find out about the spice trade. Find out Prester John. Find, find, find.'

Covilhao couldn't pen his dispatches during his journey. He had scribbled in code his observations on a map. Once in Cairo, he started writing furiously and unloaded his reports on Lamego.

Initially, Covilhao had been surprised to see black kings reigning in various parts of Africa. What did you expect, asked Lamego? Black people will be ruled by black kings, who else? Don't send this dispatch to Lisbon. But Covilhao would not budge. Whatever I write, you carry back, he said. Lamego was appalled to read a dispatch where the adventurer talked of moving about in Mecca and Madina and actually visiting the Kaaba, kissing the black stone, and later throwing stones at the Devil.

'You could have died for this,' he said, horrified. 'They would have decapitated you!'

Covilhao just shrugged his shoulders. 'No one suspected me.'

What the man had achieved just in navigational terms was astounding—Lisbon—Barcelona—Naples—Rhodes—Alexandria—Cairo—Sinai—Suakin—Aden. By then it was August 1488, a year and a half since they had set out on 7 May 1487. Afonso de Paiva goes off to Somalia, Covilhao gets into an Arab dhow and proceeds to Socotra, Cannanore and then on to Calicut. By then it is 1489. He explores the spice coast up to Goa, then moves to Hormuz and the African coast—Milind, Mombasa, Kilwa, right up to Sofala. Then he returns via Aden to Cairo in the winter of 1490. There are no dispatches. All he has is a map that he was ordered to keep very close to his chest. No one should get to know of it. It contained the sea routes and all that Portugal had discovered of the world for over a century of effort.

He met with strange adventures. Once when he got up from sleep, he found a ring of people around him staring in alarm. He was on a boat to Sofala, and land was in sight. His co-passengers asked, 'Are you all right?' Nothing wrong with me, he answered. They were not convinced. There was much shaking of heads.

*keki n. daruwalla*

'Have you an enemy who is after you?' asked an Arab trader. He shook his head. 'Why do you ask?'

'You have fallen foul of Satan, or an evil spirit. It is a bad sign for you and a bad sign for us, your companions.'

'I don't understand.' For once he seemed nonplussed.

'You were speaking in your sleep!'

'I have heard people babble and cry in their dreams. So what?'

'You were speaking in another language. That is not good.' The head-shaking started all over again. The faces around him were grim. Good God, he thought, how do I get out of this now? Would all his linguistic skills and disguises be of any avail? If he was exposed as a Portuguese or a Frank, it was the rope for him, or a blade across his throat, he knew.

'My friend, you have been possessed! The spirit of some Firang has got hold of you! You were speaking in his abominable tongue. You must have harmed one of them, may his soul rot. And he has reached out from hell!' Another told him, 'You need to go on a pilgrimage—Mecca, Madina or some place here, where a saint has been buried.'

'But before that we will get you to an exorcist. Land has been sighted and we will find someone to rid you of this spirit.'

Much as he tried to convince his fellow passengers that all was well and no fiend, spirit or Jinn had got hold of his soul or his privates, the other do-gooders wouldn't listen. Once they landed, his companions got busy. An hour before dusk, an exorcist had been produced by the Maulvi. He wore a billowing yellow shirt and a green wrap-around that trailed beneath his crude sandals. He came with a big *Habshi*, as Africans were called all along the African and Indian coasts. The exorcist, a stocky fellow with a wispy beard, was already mumbling a silent prayer. The *Habshi* had a big stick. What's that for, asked our friend Covilhao. Don't worry, said the exorcist. 'Don't you know it has been written in the scriptures? "If the one seized by fits is struck a blow sufficient to kill a camel, he does not feel it." So just close your eyes and no harm will come to you.'

'No harm will come to me. I am not seized by any Jinn or Devil. I am fine!'

The exorcist didn't understand. 'That is what I am saying, no harm will come to you! We will get the jinn out with our prayers to Allah.'

Prayers were fine, he said, as long as you can keep the stick out of the way. The fellow passengers intervened. 'No Jinn had inhabited our friend. It was a Frank, a bloody Firang, most probably from the grave.'

Here the exorcist, himself a Maulvi of sorts, snubbed the others. The dead can't possess souls, he shouted, chin and beard quivering in indignation. The Prophet himself said so, peace be on him. Then he asked Covilhao his date of birth, consulted his own Zodiac chart, called upon Allah and started his incantation. He tied an amulet around Covilhao's arm. Something in Arabic was written on it in a very convoluted style. The *Habshi* tied him up meanwhile but no blows followed. The exorcist didn't have the kind of voice that would frighten a kid, leave alone a Jinn. He beseeched Allah and the genii Qayupush and Rahush, and the angels Israfil and Amwakil. And he burnt black aloes and sprinkled rosewater on our spy. The *Habshi* meanwhile gave him some solid blows. When the ritual ended he found he had to pay a good round sum to the exorcist and his black assistant. Covilhao didn't speak in his dreams again.

The conversation at the inn, that evening was all about Jinns and exorcism. Jinns often possessed people in order to physically know the world, said one, while the others nodded, relieved that the exorcist was not there to chew them up. He kept on at it and said even the dead reached out to the living, but only those among the dead whose lives had been cut short. An old man remembered an exorcist who had come from Arabia: a holy man, he would fast before undertaking a fight with the spirits and he would burn wood-aloes and other perfumes in his room, before he set out for the struggle. He was always unhappy, because the exorcist's preparation should take weeks, he would say, and he hardly got any time. Even the diet of the exorcist had to be carefully selective. In case the victim was possessed of violent attributes, the healer had to refrain from meat and fish, eggs and musk. The stories went on till late in the night and Covilhao, when he went to bed, thanked the Lord that he had got away with a few blows, a small price to pay for jabbering so dangerously.

# taufiq
## the voyage back

~~~

The return voyage was not the kind I would wish even for my enemies. The winds dropped, the fleet stalled and scurvy was upon us. I had not seen symptoms of this sickness before—limbs bloating, the gums swelling so much that they drooped like a shroud over the teeth, and though the teeth didn't drop—Allah keep me from lies—the men did. Figueiro and one other Padre, would touch their own forehead and navel with the forefinger and then touch both shoulders. It was much later that I understood what it meant. They kissed their crosses and said prayers over the dead as they hit the sea. Overboard they went with a splash, and we would lean over the railings to see if the fish had got to them. Sometimes we observed a flurry of activity exactly where the corpse had been thrown. It's not a good feeling to know that someone you were talking to a few hours earlier, someone for whom you had sent up a prayer only last night was now dinner for the fish. I prayed five times a day, never mind what these people thought. I could hear sniggers as I placed my forehead on the wooden deck. I felt embarrassed putting on my cap and going through with the ablutions. Now I started praying fearlessly.

Allah, I prayed, do what you will with these Christians, but spare me. I have done no great wrong in my life. But even as I prayed it occurred to me that if they went one by one into the sea and Brother Figueiro kept kissing his cross, only he and I would be left on the ship. How would we survive? I prayed for all that particular night—Kafir, Christian, believer. Next day the wind rose.

Months had passed and we were told that the Admiral was thinking of turning back to India, when suddenly the wind filled our sails. In three days less than three months we were at the African coast once again. When I had piloted them to Calicut, the same distance had taken us twenty-five days. We avoided Mozambique. It had not been very friendly during the previous voyage, other sailors told me. Moreover, scurvy was said to be playing havoc there. A thunderstorm tore the ties of *Sao Raphael*. When an elephant is wounded, hyenas start prowling around. Some pirates in eight boats sped to the ship to get the loot but we drove them off by firing some bombards at them.

At Milind, I asked if I could get down and find my way back to Oman and Cairo. But the Admiral's brother, Paulo da Gama wouldn't hear of it. He himself was weakening and I hoped that the disease would spare him. When sickness and death attack the lowly, you don't feel frightened that much. It is when the great fall, Amir and Effendi, that you really sense the power and anger of Allah.

The Admiral could not meet the King of Milind this time. He asked for an ivory tusk, which he could present to his King in Portugal, and it was sent the next day. This was the one friendly port these Purtugali people had touched. Surprisingly I had started feeling and thinking like them. I too was happy to be here. The weather had changed but we had very few men left to man four ships. The *Sao Raphael*, which was already in a bad way, had to be abandoned and burnt. We watched in eerie silence as the fire crackled and the wind blew its splinters of fiery wood into the sea and the whole thing turned into a black hulk. It was after we had burnt the ship that I got a feeling that my gums were swelling. I was petrified. Others were healing now, for as we approached the southernmost tip of Africa, the Cape of Good Hope as they call it, the winds had turned really cold and disease and death were behind us. Had the Day of Judgement broken on me? Was I punished for consorting with the unbelievers? I reasoned that if lightning were to fall on the unbeliever, and if I am chained to him (same expedition, same boat), lightning would fall on me as well. I steeled myself. If death was going to visit me on ship, so be it.

The angel of death had spotted both Paulo da Gama and me. His arrows were on the bowstring as we Arabs would have said, his bombards were in the poops, as the Purtugali people would put it. The arrow left the bowstring, but not for my soul. Paulo da Gama died and I felt very sorry for him, especially because I thought he had substituted for me. He was a great man, brother of their Admiral. I was an ordinary pilot. We were on the same ship. I had many questions buzzing in my mind. Why was I spared? Actually, why was I afflicted in the first place? Why was Allah kind to me? Again, why was he annoyed in the first place? Was it because I had piloted these people to India? I had sailed on the African coast earlier, negotiated the Bahr al Zanj as we called the sea around Africa, and gone over to the Bahr al Hind. I never had a trace of scurvy. So I don't know why I was punished this time.

I will pass over our return to Lisbon. We had limped back. The Captain-Major had gone to bury his brother in the Azores, the name they gave to a string of islands. Nicolau Coelho arrived a month earlier and informed their King that India had been reached and 'discovered', they had found the sea route, crossed the Bilad al Islam ( a sea which they soon started calling the Indian Ocean rather than the ocean of Islam), which was not land-locked. There were many Christians there, though they had taken to idolatry and were half-apostates. They must have also informed their King that they had knelt and prayed at the 'churches' in Calicut—how Shakoor and others would have laughed had they heard this.

The Captain-Major followed in a caravel. He looked cheerful once again. The bad days seemed forgotten when we had just seven men per ship about the time when *Sao Raphael* was burnt. He must have forgotten Paolo for a while, while he awaited his titles and rewards. I couldn't help thinking though that for his houris, he would have to wait till he went to heaven, though I understand that houris are reserved for the followers of Islam only. Brothers one remembers in solitude, at night before sleep drowns you, or in dreams. At least that's the only time I remember my father. But now in Fartaqal, I'll remember him—I make a vow to this effect.

I have been picking up their language far too quickly. I was reluctant to learn it. Odd ideas haunted me—could language lead one to the Devil? Some of these Purtagalis would go through their forehead-navel-shoulders touching routine when they saw me. I would turn around and say in Arabic, don't do that, I am not dead as yet, though if I stay with you vermin, I could be dead as far as my soul is concerned. Others would smile and ask, 'And how are you, Moor?' Most of them would call me Moor and never by my name. Was it so difficult for their lips to twist and contort around something as simple as Taufiq. The women would eye me with curiosity but in the poorer quarters they would smile and beckon, 'Come Moor, come!' One evening there were two of them on a balcony, their lips red and their bosoms showing. 'Come, we won't eat you up,' said one. 'We'll only fondle you,' said the other, and laughed as if this was the greatest joke in the world, for the two of them fell over each other, laughing. They saw me blushing, and laughed some more. One of them actually came down the stairs perhaps with the idea of chasing me, but then seemed to have changed her mind. The lowest woman in the harem of the lowliest Amir in Cairo would not have behaved like this.

Yet I spent a restless night thinking of the two women, their pink faces, and their sumptuous breasts bursting out of whatever they were wearing. I walked past the street again next day but couldn't locate the balcony or the house. I was to learn more about their women. For a Cairene woman a half-smile and the deliberate parting, may it be ever so slight, of the veil was a good enough sign. Here they practically issued an invitation, what my benefactor Shakoor in Calicut would have called a *dawat-nama*. They smiled also in an odd way—their cheeks would pucker up but the lips would never really part. I was left with the feeling that there was no joy behind the smile. Sometimes the face was so scrunched up you didn't know if they were suppressing a smile or were about to howl. Their anger too was cold, it never blazed through the eyes. And they were cold in bed.

Their priests wore fine robes and looked more impressive than our muezzins. They were intent on converting me each time they set their eyes on me. I could always imagine someone wanting to accept Islam; it seemed so natural. But for a Muslim to be converted to any other cult or religion was unthinkable. I couldn't imagine this. Hence, my astonishment at the folly of these idiots as they cast their nets wide for me. My only answer was looking at them with contempt.

One comes across surprises even in captivity; because after a year or so I started considering this captivity. If you are amongst strange people, people not of your faith, and can't go home or eat your own food, can't hear the azaan, can't leave the shores—if that is not captivity, what is? It was just after nightfall that a man knocked at my door. That was a surprise. If anyone came to see me (and they were very few), it was in daylight. The man was dark. He had a slight stoop, was dressed in a ragged cloak and carried a bag over his shoulder. 'Moor?' he asked. One couldn't be ruder than that, but I kept my composure. 'Thanks to Allah, yes,' I muttered, forcing a false smile upon my lips.

'I have a few things to say to you,' he said and sat down, without being invited. 'Say them,' I replied rudely. But his was a long story and he had many things to say, as I was to learn shortly.

'I hope you have another bed,' he asked, looking around. 'Another bed! No, no!' I almost shouted back. What did the fellow want with a bed?

'Moor, what I have to tell you will take days. I don't want to risk being seen coming here too often—may land you in trouble.'

Was the fellow a criminal? Allah, what was I getting into? I showed him the door. 'Out! Out!' I cried. He was unperturbed. 'Don't,' he said, 'you'll benefit from what I have to tell you. I have taken risks in coming here.' I closed the door and we sat down.

'Do you have any wine?' was his next question. I was no longer surprised at the audacity; I was getting used to the man. (He hadn't given me his name yet.) He pulled out a bottle from his bag. We drank. Portuguese wines were even better than Syrian wines or the ones made by the Christians in Cairo, which Murad would get for us.

My guest's stories were long and spilled over the night and the next day and the next night. There would be other voyages, he told me. The Captain-Major was nowhere in the picture. 'You will of course be marked out for them. Why should they keep you here, otherwise?' There was logic in what he was saying. I merely nodded. Best to keep silent, with this kind of a visitor.

'You must be wondering why we went haring off to India? Costs a lot of money, fitting a fleet like that and sailing all the way there. But here King and country have been mad after voyages. Gold, pepper, and Christian kingdoms beyond the seas—these are our priorities. If you are interested in Christians, then you are equally interested in infidels, isn't it? Infidels like you have to be killed or baptized. Soul-salvaging is very near to the hearts of our Kings. We are also interested in slaves—we don't have many people, you know. Slaves have to be worked and their women bedded. Slaves too are baptized and only then can you bed their women. Fucking infidels can put your soul in jeopardy. The Holy Father may disapprove even if you confessed! The slaves are baptized in Africa itself, before they set sail for the Tagus. What if the ship sank! Then the black souls of the black slaves would be in trouble since their bodies had not embraced the true faith.' He laughed loudly, though frankly, I didn't see the joke.

Over the next three days he educated me. I got to know that like the differences between Shiite and Sunni, the Christians of Rome and Istanbul fought among themselves. But once the Muslims conquered Istanbul, the Christians of Europe started weeping as if their mothers had died! He kept mentioning a place called Byzantium and I still don't know where the place is. As it is I got confused between what the Christians call 'Rome', which is in Italy and what we call 'Rum', which is Istanbul.

He talked of Ceuta, a Muslim town in Africa, which the Portuguese had invaded. They lost just eight men in the assault and they killed thousands and enslaved an equal number. 'Our soldiers were astounded at what they saw in Ceuta—beautiful houses, silks from China, cloth embroidered in silver thread, carved furniture. Yet the King was bereaved. When he returned with his fleet of two hundred boats, they found the Queen dead. She was no ordinary person, Philippa of Lancaster, the daughter of John of Gaunt, who had egged the King on. Both her sons fought in Ceuta and were knighted by the father, the King. But she couldn't welcome them back. The plague got her.'

'Allah be praised.' I couldn't help exclaiming.

He didn't flinch. In fact the rogue smiled as he went on. 'Fifteen years earlier Spain had done much worse to a town, very near Ceuta on the North African coast. It was called Tetuan. Half the population they killed and the other half they enslaved. We Portuguese are saints in comparison. But we were the ones after the slaves. We didn't have enough men, you see.'

All this was just a preamble. He was more interested in telling me, over the next three days, how the Portuguese navigated the seas, how they came up to Cape Bojador, the one which projected over twenty miles from the mainland. 'I am told you Arabs called it "Bon Khatar", "Father of Danger". Many Portuguese ships vanished here, including Jaime Ferrer's, who had set out to find the 'River of Gold'. He belonged to Majorca and made maps, but they couldn't have been much use to him, when his boat sank. Fishing boats went down. The shoreline was desert here, and the coastal currents fierce. The only way was to sail deep into the sea and come to the coast only miles after passing the cape. There were other things, Moor, you would have no idea about. For a hundred years these people had been trying to ferret out the secrets of sea navigation. The Doge of Venice gave an important map to one of their princes. They got people from Italy to help them. They were terribly secretive. Nicolo de Conti, the great Italian traveller (who spoke both Arabic and Persian), had left his description of India with people in the Vatican. These got to Lisbon. Conti had described Calicut. Slowly the Portuguese, from the days of Prince Henry "the Navigator", collected information about the route to India. That became the greatest national secret.

'The trouble about secrets is they turn restive, and the people holding on to them turn equally restive, sometimes feverish. Well, after an African voyage, the pilot and two of his sailors fled to Castile. They had charts with them. They were followed and captured and the sailors were decapitated there itself. But the pilot was dragged with hooks in his mouth and quartered.'

I didn't know the meaning of quartered and he explained, how a man was hacked into four pieces. Thank Allah, I told him, that we are not as cruel. 'Well, you people are not bad at plucking out eyes,' he retorted. Then he suddenly started sobbing. His whole body was wracked with convulsions and tears streamed down his eyes.

'The man who was quartered was my father.'

~

But I must talk of what confronts me in my solitude every day, what sows the seeds of unrest in my dreams every night. I am talking of a fortnight (or was it three weeks?) at Calicut that was unforgettable. It was a time that has to come in everyone's life—be he man or woman. I could now imagine what Ehtesham had gone through in the days he first came in touch with Zainab. I must start where I left off, that point in my chronicle, just prior to things going awry between the

Admiral and the Samudri Raja. I was 'discovering' the people in Calicut, the way the Purtugali people had 'discovered' India. I had discovered their friendliness and informality . . .

There was a composure about her that was striking. I tried to avoid looking at her lest I be considered too brazen. Her father had my belongings removed from the inn and moved to a house adjacent to his. I protested meekly, half-heartedly, but he wouldn't listen. He wasn't meant to. There was just a door between the two houses, always bolted. Later I found it was bolted from my side. For the first day or two I felt uncomfortable, but then the man was as old as my father and if he wanted to be nice, why should I deprive him of the pleasure? I liked his attitude. Though he was rich and had many servants—a spice-grinder, cooks, a toddy-tapper, one to pound rice, another to draw water from the well, he seemed to treat them as equals. When I praised his house, he was dismissive, but in a pleasant way.

'What does a man want but a dry roof over his head and a bamboo screen to stave off the spray from the sea? That's all,' he said.

But Samina had made my nights restive, she couldn't have guessed that, could she? Her face stayed with me when she was no longer there and the bare smooth arms and the bare back just scantily covered by the diagonal stroke of cloth. Once through an error (such errors are often deliberate) our hands touched and she didn't draw back. The memory of the pliant hand troubled me. I was nervous in her presence and at some time she must have sensed it. Nervousness and hope go together, also nervousness and yearnings, at my age half one's yearnings are of the flesh, aren't they? Love and subterfuge get along well too, at least before the first opening into open love. The accidental brush—hand with the hand was to linger with me. Day dreams can be self defeating—the poor wish to become rich and find gold buried in their backyard. The lonely dream of the leap into love, the 'possession', if that's the word, of the other, her smile, voice and touch, not forgetting the waterfall of her black hair. And always you want her presence around you like incense-smeared haze.

All this troubled me. Memory is a tree and when you are alone you live under its shade. Memory is a tree that needs to be hacked sometimes, its branches lopped off.

# the spies

&

The Muhtasib was angry. Things were not well with the state. But then when are things well, he mused. Was there ever a time when everyone prayed, when tradesmen didn't cheat, there was no theft or murder, and people didn't misbehave with their women slaves? Was there ever a time when hypocrites, the munaffiqs, didn't go about paying lip service to the Holy Book, their fingers on the rosary, but actually lusting for boys and women, and thirsting to move into wrong apertures? He shook his head vigorously as if hornets had attacked him.

The elation of the past week had vanished. The new Sultan had praised him, and what he had done deserved praise. He had noticed the restiveness of the Mamluks, for they had not been paid. He came to know that they were planning to ride to the citadel, the *burj*, and demand their wages. That was the time-honoured practice. Whenever the Mamluks found their pay running into arrears, month after month, they would go to the burj, surround it and shout slogans. Often the treasury didn't have enough money and the troops would be palmed off with twenty percent of what was due to them. Slogans would be shouted and the parleys would become acrimonious, if not downright abusive. His information had prevented the afternoon from getting ugly. The treasury was ready with some money to cool tempers and the Mamluks had gone back, partly satisfied.

Perhaps he had cast his net too wide. His spies had, as always, been coming in from all sorts of places—Alexandria, Istanbul, Jeddah, Mecca, Madina, even Baghdad, not forgetting the desert. He was concerned only with Cairo, but after all, spies were men—they traded, sailed, and they tagged along with camel-caravans as they plodded their way for Haj. They kissed the black stone and swore to remain pious, though all that abstemiousness would vanish within a fortnight of their return. He had now learnt to talk to them, to offer them fenugreek tea or dates. One picked up more through gossip. A muleteer, a trader, a perfumer—how was the poor bugger to know what the state, which meant the Muhtasib, wanted? They looked around for petty things and missed the bigger scene. A rich trader who dealt in horses told him his story. He had fallen in with a Venetian and a Turk whom he already knew. At the inn they had all got a bit drunk and the Venetian told him it was good to be a nephew of the great! Why not a son of the great, asked the Egyptian and found the white man laughing at him. Because Popes have nephews, said the man giggling. That didn't make sense either. The Venetian clarified the matter as if talking to a child. Some of the Popes had spawned bastards, and they were known as nephews. And how they were favoured!

Then the Turk got into the act. What he told the Egyptian was even more startling. When a ruler among the Ottomans came to the throne it was his right to kill his brothers. Right? The Egyptian had looked bewildered. His friend in Istanbul, who sold him the horses, looked equally bewildered that the Egyptian didn't know something so elementary. Not only did the new ruler have the right to kill his brother, but also all the nephews. Any potential successor to the throne had to be done away with. It was sanctioned by custom. It was almost law! Though, if he harmed the nieces or the nephew's wife, there would be murmurs and the ruler's stock would go down.

Good to know your enemies, he thought, as he put on his robe. Otherwise, what was this piece of information worth? Nothing. But if a royal scion left Constantinople of a sudden and sought shelter in Cairo, he would know why the fellow fled. The Muhtasib was obeying a summons. He ordered just two of his staff to accompany him; and no *tablakhana*, the drummers who would precede him when he went on his tours to the market. Sheikh Abu Jibril had sent for him—he was respected, and had the ear of the new Sultan. Pomp was to be cast aside when you met such people. The trouble with this job was there were quite a few people who had the ear of the Sultan, and hence could summon him, the Muhtasib, with a snap of their fingers. There was that son of a pig, Abu al Khayr who had actually asked for a certain trader to be handed over to him. The court had consulted the Muhtasib. Handed over? Who in the name of Iblis was he that a trader could be 'handed over' to him? he had asked. What was worse, he knew the man, fellow by the name of Mahmud who traded on the Red Sea in all kinds of things from animal hides to saffron and spices. Moreover, his son Abdullah traded in horses and was the one to tell him the story about nephews. He told the court official that Abu al Khayr just wanted his hands on the trader to extract money. Well, that's what he has asked for, said the Sultan's confidant. The Muhtasib didn't let his astonishment show.

'How much does he expect?' he asked. Deadpan, not a flicker of an eyelid, not a hair on his thick eyebrows uplifted. The answer was 250,000 tomans.

'No, I would say no.' No gust of self-righteous passion, no talk of 'How could you do this to a Muslim'. That's all he had said and walked off.

There was that other self-righteous Sheikh, Abu al Sud. His records had nothing against him, though the Muhtasib knew he kept seven slave girls. That didn't even merit a furrow on his brow. But this Sheikh had his fits of piety and indignation—one often leads to the other—and he would go into paroxysms of rage all of a sudden. Sale of flesh, Muslim flesh! Corruption! Stealing from Muslims! He'd order someone to be beaten by shoes, another amputated, a third to be chained. While ordering hanging he would notify the Sultan, notifying as distinct from asking permission. The Sultan almost never interfered in al Sud's fiats, the Muhtasib knew.

A new Sultan had taken over—Qansawh al Ghauri. The dark cloud of the Ottomans, would he be aware of it? With these thoughts rattling in his mind the Muhtasib walked up to the house of Abu Jibril. After the greetings and the half-hug and the kiss on the cheek, the Amir asked him what news he had brought. That couldn't be the reason why he summoned me, thought the Muhtasib. On the surface things are fine, he told him.

'And beneath the surface?'

'It is Allah and his angels who know what transpires there. All we get to see is a flicker of shadows. Now and then we get a scent of things.'

'As you got of the Mamluks riding to the citadel. That was good work, al Maheeni.'

'But it was a sad day for the state,' said the Muhtasib with unfeigned modesty.

'All this should have been taken care of earlier,' said the Sheikh. 'Didn't the Prophet (peace be upon him) say, "pay the labourer his wage before the sweat dries on his brow?" Why should the court wait for the burj to be besieged?'

Both of them had closed their eyes and raised their arms at the mention of the Prophet. What is he trying to pump out of me, the Muhtasib wondered. But he was playing along. 'As the Sheikh would know, it was not as simple as that. Who am I to tell the Sheikh of the friction between the Mamluks of the river, the *Bahris*, and those of the citadel, the *Burjis*. There is also a wide gap between the veterans, the *Qaranisah*, and the upstart Mamluk, the newly imported *Julban*. It was the Julbans who had disturbed the peace and I don't have to tell the Sheikh who informed us.'

'You have good spies.' The Muhtasib acknowledged the compliment with due humility. 'What else is new, Muhtasib?'

'Difficult to say. The power of the Ottomans is rising. Their shadow is falling over the sands of Egypt.' It was the first time he had allowed himself this kind of pseudo-rhetoric.

'How do you say that, al Maheeni?'

He answered, 'Their soldiers are strong and disciplined and trained for war. They are called Jannisaris.'

'Are you suggesting that our Mamluks are not?'

'I am not suggesting that. They have firearms that can kill a person at a hundred yards. One can't throw a spear that far.'

'You should leave war to the warriors, Muhtasib.'

He didn't take the rebuke too well, but said nothing. The Sheikh was not content with this. 'Don't forget Muhtasib that we beat the Mongols at Ayn Jalut. No one else could do it, not Baghdad, not Istanbul. The Baghdad King was rolled into a carpet and smothered, remember? What a way to die, with all those woolen fibres clogging up your nose. Whenever you start losing confidence in our soldiery, remember Ayn Jalut. Not having faith in our soldiers is treachery. Your thinking is looped, your bearing diffident when you discuss war. I was testing the waters with you. If we hadn't beaten the Mongols, the hordes would have driven the Ottomans into the ground.'

There was a pause during which the Muhtasib noted that he hadn't been served sherbet or fenugreek tea or coffee. The Sheikh resumed, 'The Ottomans are not about to attack us today. I know you will say that we should think of tomorrow. Well, I did not call you to discuss the future. We will leave that to astrologers. I wish to talk about the present. (*So now we come to the point*, thought the Muhtasib.) Our morals are in the mud today. A gutter flowing under a butcher shop would be cleaner than the hearts of some of our Cairenes. In our own city, in our own country, Islam is being pushed like sheep being prodded by a goatherd. And you will ask, who are the goatherds?'

(*Has he been talking to Ali Hasan Zulm*? thought the Muhtasib) 'I will ask no such thing', said the Muhtasib out of cussedness. If the Sheikh was put off, he didn't show it. He went on. 'The goatherds I was referring to are the Christians, Copts, Mormons, Yahudis.' (*So he has been talking to Ali Hasan*, reflected the Muhtasib.) He kept quiet. Abu Jibril expected a response. 'Well?' he asked after a few moments. The Muhtasib just shook his head to indicate he had nothing to say. He wanted to know what was behind this tirade.

'Aren't you going to say something?'

Now the Muhtasib was forced to answer. 'What do you want me to say?' he asked.

'Aren't you going to say something in your defence?'

'My defence? I didn't know I was an accused.'

The fellow was getting cheeky, thought the Sheikh. Does he take me for a grocer or a baker?

'You soon will be if it comes to that.'

Al Maheeni wanted to divert the course of conversation. 'What have you got against the Christians, all of a sudden? They have lived here for centuries.'

'What have I against them? What have I not? Magic, they are indulging in magic! Don't you remember what happened in Shentena al Hagar? They conjure up Mariam and she starts hovering over the church! Have you ever heard anything like that? Don't you see the hand of Iblis here? Obviously, you do not.'

'I have not seen Iblis, so I wouldn't know how his hand looks like.' (What was one to do with the fellow, thought the Sheikh. Such audacity!) 'I'll have to speak to the Sultan,' he said.

'The Sultan knew everything that happened in Shentena,' replied the Muhtasib.

'You mean the old Sultan. Not al Ghauri.'

The Muhtasib knew he had slipped up. Others were supposed to have aberrations, not him. Abu Jibril was in no mood to stop. 'I called you to talk about that Muslim who is painting the figures of Mariam and Christ on church walls.'

This was a bad day, thought the Muhtasib, he had been caught off guard for the second time. Allah! this seemed to point to Ehtesham. He knew the fellow would come to no good. Too many thoughts were crowding his brain, far too many. He had no idea the fellow had been painting in a church. What made the idiot do it? If the Sheikh knew about it, half of Cairo would have known. How was it that he, the Muhtasib had no inkling? He had lost interest in Shentena once the crisis there was over and the Sultan, never mind if he was the old one, was off his back. No Christian slaughtered, no priest beaten (a little shove here or a slap there couldn't be taken into reckoning), no church brought down—that was enough for him. After all, the Muhtasib's responsibility was Cairo, not some hellhole in the scrub! His mind had been off the bloody place—that was the trouble. Anyway, how was he to know that this wretched Ehtesham would sneak into a church and start painting the walls? He had even warned the fool. The Muhtasib hoped he had masked his surprise well. Wouldn't do to let the Sheikh know he was caught flat-footed.

'I don't know why you are keeping quiet, al Maheeni. But it is not your words I am interested in. It is actions, and so far there has been nothing from your side. You have had people flogged for missing a prayer, or not fasting in Ramadan. But someone paints figures and faces—does all that is forbidden to Muslims and you ignore all this. He is rivalling the creator—worse, he is mimicking him. Even worse he is an apostate. To paint Mariam or Issa in a church! Does he want to convert? Why have you not had him dragged through the streets, got him stoned by the mob and hung what was left of him at the Zuwailya gate?'

He didn't think it necessary to answer. He got up and as he was departing, he said, 'I will have that church in Shentena looked up.'

'He has painted the church in Cairo!' bellowed Sheikh Abu Jibril.

# the exile

&

The Muhtasib came in with a big entourage this time, a dozen people including his two sons. He rode past Dar el Salam and what is today known as Zohara, past neat cobble-stoned alleys, houses white-stoned, high walls of brick, Roman arches. He was received with ceremony, one Christian holding his stirrup as he dismounted. (It was unusual for him to ride—only the Mamluks could, but he was going into Coptic country and had to do so with some minimum dignity.) They took him first to the Hanging Church known in the area as al Moallaka, the seat of the Coptic Patriarch, and then to the Church of St Sergius or Sergis or Abu Sarga as they called St George after whom the area is known as Mari Girgis today. The Muhtasib saw the nave divided by marble pillars and entered with some trepidation. He had heard about the miracle associated with the place, the Holy Virgin appearing in a vision to Anba Abraham, the sixty-second Patriarch who had spent three days in prayer and fasting. The Caliph heard of it, the appearance of Mariam. It was Caliph al Imam el Mouiz Lidin'illah. The year was 969 AD. If the Patriarch has seen the Virgin Mary, then surely he can intercede with her and move the Moqattam Hill, he says to the Patriarch. Doesn't your Bible say, 'If you have faith as a grain of mustard seed, you shall say to the mountain: remove from hence to yonder place, and it shall remove.' (Mathew 1720). An earthquake occurred and the mountain moved. Witnessing this, the Caliph even permitted the restoration of the church. The Patriarch and his flock were left in peace thereafter.

Yes, miracle territory was always slippery, but the Muhtasib kept an impassive face, as if it were made of wax. The Deputy Patriarch pointed out the ceiling, shaped like Noah's ark. He barely raised an eyelid to take in everything, light drifting through stained glass and Noah's inverted ark staring him in the face. They took him to the ebony-inlaid-with-ivory screen, and they brought a lighted candle behind the screen and the screen turned translucent. He smiled a grudging half-smile. He nodded when they showed him the pulpit with its marble pillars for Jesus and his twelve apostles. Only one pillar was of black marble in order to symbolize Judas. It was black and bare. The others were decorated beautifully. He had heard of Judas, but the other apostles were unknown to him. Nor did he wish to know more. Best to stay away from other faiths, their saints and mythologies. He was not even sure if the scriptures allowed him to hear about other faiths in such detail. He would keep a fast and absolve himself of any sin he may have inadvertently committed.

The circular bronze chandeliers in the centre of the nave, from each of which fifty candles spurted flame, caught his attention. He looked at the roof, expecting it to be smoke-blackened. But the ceiling was too high for it to be stained, he noticed. The screen was surmounted by thirteen icons—dark-robed and venerable figures on a background of gold. They moved the screen and he saw the splendour of the paintings on the canopy, four angels, painted in gold, holding Christ aloft. This wasn't the place where Ehtesham had done his mischief, he decided. The place was much too old and awesome.

*keki n. daruwalla*

'You have some pagan gods here also.'

He let that drop casually as if he was saying the most innocuous thing in the world. The Bishop thought that the fellow had done his homework.

'The Muhtasib is well informed, as always. But we have thrown away these images in the well down below to perish in the dust.'

'You did well,' said the Muhtasib. Thank God he didn't want to see the images, thought the Deputy Patriarch, or what would he have said. They were well preserved down below, a limestone niche which showed the goat-footed god Pan trying to seduce a dancer holding a sistrum; the bearded Dionysius with his right arm around a maiden's waist and the left holding a huge flagon of wine reaching from hip to shoulder.

Tight-lipped and grave, the Muhtasib came away. It was not what he said here in Mari Girgis that was of any consequence, he knew. What mattered were the rumour mills in the Muslim quarters, in Qasr al Shama and Khan al Khalili. The Muhtasib gave the Christians hell, they would say. He stormed at the Bishop, the Deputy Patriarch! The Copts trembled like leaves shaking in a high wind. Reality was dust—perception was reality.

~

The first word came from the Abbott. 'They are looking for you, Ehtesham.' His face was grim and he stared at the young man. Ehtesham knew from experience that whenever something serious was afoot, the Abbott's eyelids would forget to flutter. There was just one wrinkle that ran vertically down the Abbott's well-fleshed face, from his cheekbone to the corner of his mouth. That solitary wrinkle looked like a trench today.

'There is no mystery to it, Ehtesham. They obviously know what we have been up to. It is my fault that I allowed you to get into this. I'll have to live with my guilt for a lifetime. But you could die for this. A man of the church has to live with many guilts, some real, some self-imposed. We feel uncomfortable without being beset by guilt, for sin is an obsession. If you haven't sinned, how do you confess? Contrition is a major part of our faith.'

'This has been a happy year. I did what I feel I was born for. I painted. I have never had such a feeling of fulfillment before.'

But this was about life, the priest tried to tell him, something more important than a swatch of paint on a globe of glass or a slab of wood, or drawing a figure, even if it was of Virgin Mary, or Lazarus rising from the grave. This was about life, about seeing the sun or the face of his wife on a winter morning, inhaling the scent of spring, or seeing his son (he would surely have one in time) toddling towards him. While there was life there would be art, even worship. Without it there was only the grave and the maggots, unless of course one was fed to the jackals.

Murad came in with similar news. Something odd was afoot, he (Murad) was being eyed queerly by someone or the other on the street. No one had any reason to follow him. It was his connection with Ehtesham which had got him this honour, he thought. The two of them went over the prospects. Would the spies, the *bassasein*, dare to arrest the nephew-in-law of Abu Khalil, chronicler of the Mamluks and the crusades, erstwhile warrior of Islam? They would. The crusades didn't mean a damn thing now. If he had fought at Ayn Jalut against the Mongols, or at Ohod side by side with Ali, they wouldn't have cared. Once the Muhtasib's cohorts laid their hands on him, they were not going to spare him.

The torture would get them maybe that extra houri in heaven. No one has ever kept an account of the number of people 'martyred' in the quest of this mirage, the elusive after-life houri. Seventy-two of them, as promised in the Book, are evidently not enough for some of them.

They had to be quick. Seeking shelter with someone, or a decent disguise wouldn't do. Fleeing to Asyut was out of the question. They would be waiting there with knives and chains. He had to leave Egypt. He could try and disguise himself and proceed to Mecca. But that had its own hazards. Pilgrims were often attacked; in fact there were gangs which preyed only upon pilgrims. The previous Sultan, Qayt Bay (who ruled from 1468–1496) was pretty stingy when it came to the two great shrines, or the traffic wending its way there. When the big fire took place in Madina in 1481, he had been very slow in opening the purse strings to repair the sanctuary. Mecca was not a good idea, for the control of the Mamluk Sultan stretched till there. Alexandria was the answer.

Where would he put up in Alexandria? Here, the Abbott intervened. Why, with Lamego of course. There was hardly any time to send word to Zainab, Murad told him, but Ehtesham wouldn't listen. He went home and found no one around. He reasoned that they didn't expect him back so early. By evening, Zainab found a man lurking around the house and Ehtesham did not show himself in the courtyard or the balcony. He would not even peep through the mashrabbiya.

The Abbott tried to reason with them—Murad and Ehtesham should not go together. But the tension was too much now. When he saw their determination, he made the arrangements—a pair of mules and a guide to take them through the delta.

Exiting Cairo was the problem. If they moved out at the dead of night they were bound to be suspected. So they set forth at dusk, when the crowds were thick in the bazaars and they could proceed unnoticed. They met the guide at the outskirts, a tall thin Nubian who carried an iron-tipped stave. The mules were also there, shaggy and thick-legged, along with the muleteer, stocky and turbaned. The Nubian was not happy at all with the mules and cursed both the muleteer and the two fugitives. 'Can't you people of the city *walk*?' he snarled. The first thing he did was to take off their harness bells. A while later he asked them if they had brought any weapons with them. When they lied and said they hadn't any, he cursed. 'You stir out in the night on a caravan route without a sword!' he shook his head in bewilderment. The two fugitives didn't want to tell him they carried a dagger each. If it came to shedding blood, they would not hesitate.

The night was not as quiet as they thought. They heard the howl of the jackal packs, at times too near for comfort. The Nubian laughed. A lapwing seemed to follow them, its shrill cry mapping the wilderness for them. A fox scurried across their path, startling Murad's mule who darted off, and was reined in with some difficulty, amidst laughter from the party. The lapwing would disappear for a while and then suddenly re-emerge with her shrill cacophony. The Nubian had long smooth strides and easily kept up with the mules and their riders. The muleteer was talkative and had to be told off. 'Voices carry far in the night,' the guide told him, 'so shut up.' But after an hour or two the silence got to the Nubian also and he would mutter his little philosophical nuggets. The night is not black—it has many colours, tawn and black and silver. Night is not greedy, men are. The night does not rob, men do. Night does not copulate, men and women do. (He wasn't put off when the others laughed.) The

*keki n. daruwalla*

night had no chimeras, no sphinx, no half-man-half-lion. One was never alone at night. The stars were one's companions and they never betrayed you. The moon could. The moon was treacherous. But since neither of his two clients were interested in the treachery of the moon, he kept quiet. No use talking to these city folk.

They were lost in their own thoughts. Ehtesham was in the grip of that desolate loneliness that comes after love and parting, and the bitterness of approaching exile. It had been a tough day. It started with the quarrel with Murad who had insisted on accompanying him to Alexandria and beyond. More important was the simmering quarrel with Zainab—the reproaches firstly: why did he have to paint in that church? He had hidden the fact from her and yet she knew it or at least suspected something shady. There was also the emotional wallow: she would come with him. Zainab wept, Ehtesham wept, not forgetting Habiba who had been summoned from her mother's house. It had been quite exhausting. The argument ended only when he shut the door. Murad and Habiba were horrified—they thought, absurd as the thought seemed to them, that he was about to beat her. Instead they made love, hurriedly desperately, with an ardour that had not been evidenced in happier days.

By dawn they skirted the caravan route and much before noon the Nubian had housed them in a peasant's hut. They had walked through carob fields, past wells, zigzagging through hamlets, but heading towards Alexandria all the time. Here he asked them questions point blank. Were they thieves running away with someone's treasure? Had they committed a felony or a murder or something of the kind? In that case his charges would go up, and in that case these bloody mules were the last things they should have brought along with them. Murad and Ehtesham let him have his say and then laughed in his face. Did they look like criminals? He could have a look at their baggage. They had to reach Alexandria fast to catch a boat and didn't want to waste a night, and the sun was too strong in the day. Whether the Nubian swallowed all this, they never came to know.

But in Cairo it had been a bitter morning at Zainab's. An hour after dawn the *bassasein* were at the house, knocking on the door. Habiba, who had slept over during the night, asked what they wanted. 'Open up or we'll break the gate,' they threatened. 'What business have you in a respectable house,' shouted Habiba, 'and so early in the day?' After an exchange of threats from their side and abuses from Habiba's, they broke open the gate and entered.

Habiba raised the kind of din which would have woken up the dead. Entering a house with the husband away. How dare they? How do we know he is away, they asked. People gathered in the street. They entered the yard. They wouldn't let the men of the Mokhabarat and the Muhtasib go in. We won't let the sanctity of this house be violated, they said. Word was sent to Abu Khalil. He hurried in. But no one seemed to know him here. A higher class of people was needed to know the likes of Abu Khalil. There were long arguments, for the onlookers took sides, though most were for Zainab. Nothing could stop the hunt for Ehtesham and they finally broke into the house and searched every corner and possible hiding place, and overturned beds and tapped the floor for suspected cellars and underground chambers. Each side claimed a victory of sorts, when Ehtesham was not found. The fellow has run away, claimed the soldiers. Where would a decent man be at dawn? one of them asked rhetorically. In his bed, sleeping with his wife. Thieves however are out at night. What can a thief, a felon do, what would he be worth, if he slept every night at home? He would have to beg.

*keki n. daruwalla*

A friend dropped in at the house of Abu Jibril. He had a hard time getting past the street because of a big crowd that had clustered around a house. Soldiers and the informers were looking for some criminal. People said he was a pious man, who used to go to mosques and paint glass globes and chandeliers there. Painted glass globes? asked Abu Jibril horrified. Was the man arrested? No way, the bird had flown, the night had veiled his presence, or shall we say his absence, replied his friend, quite tickled with his enigmatic phraseology. Abu Jibril was not similarly amused. These blundering soldiers and that pathetically incompetent Muhtasib, what could one do with them? One apostate painter they were told to get, and they couldn't catch and crucify the bastard—actually, first chop his right hand off and then nail him high on some gate. But that posed a problem for Jibril. If his right hand was cut, how would he be nailed? Why, drive a nail through his shoulder of course. Nail the forearm and those infidel fingers that painted those idolatrous paintings as well! He would go to the Sultan in the evening itself and discuss the fate of this Ehtesham. Meanwhile. he would dash off a note to the Muhtasib.

Reports had obviously reached the Muhtasib, too, about what was happening, the search, the crowds and the fact that Ehtesham was missing. The crowd was already speculating how he had vanished into thin air—was he spirited away by his wife or that witch of a Habiba, or was this Ehtesham a necromancer or worse, a scion of the devil? People around the house were getting frightened, he was told. The painter could turn himself into mist, fog, night itself. The Muhtasib sent in Akhtar, the bruiser, the man who had brought Lamego to him. Akhtar always came in with his toughies. He took command, which meant slapping Habiba and throwing her out of the room and then cornering Zainab.

'Now tell me quietly where your husband has gone.'

'I don't know.'

'Try and remember.'

'I have no idea.'

'When did he go? No idea again?' She nodded. 'If you don't tell me, I'll tear your veil off. Do you understand, wife of an apostate?' He thought she hadn't understood or was incapable of understanding, or didn't want to understand. He told her that if she thought she couldn't be slapped around, she was mistaken. She could be taken to a dungeon. She could, or rather would, be thrown into an Amir's harem, did she realize? Or worse, be turned into a Mamluk's mistress, or sold as a slave, or given as a gift to desert Bedouins. Bedouins are rough in bed, he snickered, they'll treat you as they treat their horses, drive you to exhaustion.

Before he could do any physical violence to her, fortune smiled. The perfumer came in—he just couldn't resist coming to the house to see what was going on. The moment Habiba saw him she raised a fierce din. This was the man who had his eye on Zainab, who had insulted her and for which he was given a shoe-beating. The crowd reacted angrily now, for some of them knew the perfumer for what he was. The soldiers were shoved and pushed. The perfumer was beaten up. Zainab, too, was raising a din. She shouted and people rushed in and dragged Akhtar out of the room. Abu Khalil was ignored by both sides, old men often are. Akhtar, and the rest of the invading members of the state, left by the evening. The search in Cairo for the fugitive painter picked up. Riwaqs were raided. People were sent to Asturlabi's house and Murad's. Finding Murad gone, they were convinced that the twosome had fled Cairo. The next day even the Abbott was questioned, but with dignity. By noon, the Muhtasib came to the conclusion that Ehtesham had escaped to Alexandria.

# BEYOND THE
# RED SEA

# the red sea

❦

He had been on the Red Sea for over a week and the earlier restiveness had left him. It was bluer than what he had ever seen and the teeming coral underneath, white and sometimes tinged with red, puzzled him. He hadn't ever heard of it. It was the boat owner who told him that coral was the main danger in navigating the Red Sea, and that there were known channels running along the reef through which the pilots navigated. At night he couldn't take his eyes off the waters, for they gleamed with a lambency no one could explain. Who among the passengers would have known that they were sailing down a continental rift into which the Indian Ocean had poured its waters and its fish and molluscs and shells and other water creatures who gave off a soft radiance in the dark, a 'bio-luminescence' that almost lit up a distant ship at night? Nor would anyone have known that the Pharaohs sent their boats down these waters to get copper and turquoise from Sinai and that the great Empress Hathshepsut had sent her boats to the land of Punt for her incense trees. Giraffe tails made their way up the sea, if not the long-necked beasts themselves. Beybars, the strongest of the Mamluk rulers, sent a thousand giraffes as a gift to the Khan of the Golden Horde in 1260. The Queen of Sheba, who sailed the Red Sea on her way to Solomon, didn't ring any bells in Arab memory either. Romans were here with their triremes and before them the Phoenicians. If someone had told them that the Red Sea was another name for civilization, they would have laughed, boat owner and pilot and the look-out on the mast, Arab or Nubian or Malabari.

Porcelain and aromatic resins, ivory and silk from the Far East—all of it made their way to Jeddah and the ports on the Red Sea, and later to Cairo on camel back, once the Red Sea ended. Mamluk merchants brought goods from China. The holy Zamzam water was carried up for the devout. Now of course the spice trade had dwarfed all the rest. Ginger and pepper were the buzz words. Coral or no coral, whether you had harbours of white sand, or parched desert on both sides, whether there was or wasn't an island of birds as traveller's tales made out, commerce and catamarans were not bothered, and this waterway played its role as a life-giver to the lands around it.

The boat passed both desert and swamp on either side and the first week had been a bit of a torture. Just getting your thoughts together was painful. In a trice Ehtesham's life had changed. Mercifully, he thought, Murad had been successfully rebuffed. He was not taking the boat down the Red Sea—he had been persuaded to return to Cairo. The Muhtasib couldn't put a finger on him; Murad hadn't put a foot wrong, except that he had befriended the heretic painter. He also had contacts among the Copts, not a good testimonial. They must be thinking of me as an apostate, isn't it? he had asked Murad, as they had stood at the wharf. Murad had made the usual dismissive noises, but that hadn't consoled him. He wasn't accepting defeat either. Are we made of glass that we can get broken at a touch, thought Ehtesham. The sea could destroy him, as also the desert. A man can't fight against these without Allah's help. But he would not be broken by some long-bearded fatwa-frothing fanatic with the glint of murder in his hate-reddened eyes. He would survive on the Indian coast or wherever. If I can't make a living, I will burn under the sun and row a boat with flayed muscles. I may die of fatigue but not despair, he said to himself.

He willed himself to think of Zainab with love, rather than despair. A little lust—love's shadow, the monkey on its back—crept in, as it always does. He started contemplating the moods of the sea and watched swamp and desert slide by. The land was barren and brown on both sides but now and then finely formed ranges of inland mountains came into view. The sea was lined with tiny harbours and coves. As each boat reached anchorage it would be greeted with frenzied cheering. At night the boats huddled together as if looking for security. They anchored in one desolate haven after the other. In some places they got good fresh water, at others brackish. The Bedouins brought fresh water from oases and sold it. Now and then he saw tamarisk growing tall, and when he asked around he was told it was used for roofing houses. There was not much fruit to be had. Arabia, he concluded, was a land of dry watermelons and stone-hard figs. Jeddah distracted him with its bustle, and he swore he would do the Umrah, the Haj pilgrimage, one day. As he sailed day after day numbness wore him down, and a listlessness came over him. His fellow passengers, Arabs all, with a sprinkling of Mappilas, told him it was the sea which was doing this to him, taking away his appetite and making him vacant-eyed and speechless. He knew better. He was silent because he resisted words. What words could soothe or distract him, he wondered, he who had run from his city like a thief, from wife and home and the walls he was painting?

When he could move away from self-pity there were other things to worry about, that Jewess and the other half a dozen Jews Lamego had put on the boat, though he hadn't been asked to look after them or anything of that sort.

He thought of Taufiq, at times—had no idea where he was. Could he be the one who had brought the Portuguese to India? He had heard various rumours. He couldn't have had any idea that another fleet had come to the Indian shores, this time after discovering the land now known as Brazil. These Franks brought you trouble, he thought. Things would have been fine if he had not met the Abbott. He didn't even know where he wanted to go on the Malabar coast. But people on the boat talked of the Zamorin and Calicut, and that is where he decided to disembark.

# taufiq
## at lisbon

~~~

T he man came again—the son of the quartered father, and secret-stealer. Nothing of this kind ever took place in Cairo. No one from the Mokhabarat was known to have gone over to the Ottomans. None of the Muhtasib's informers had crossed over to the Mokhabarat. (Though if they had, I wouldn't have known.) They wouldn't have desisted out of fear alone—the Muhtasib would have had their balls severed or squeezed, depending on his mood—such treachery wouldn't have occurred to them.

It was bitterly cold, a few days after the birthday of Issa. He came after nightfall, he always did. I told him I wouldn't let him enter without his spelling out his name this time. Before he left—after a two-night stay—he told me who he was: Martim Dias. He added that he was not afraid of divulging his name now—for if I ever let out that I had been in touch with Martim Dias, I would be slaughtered, not by him but by the King's men. The Portuguese are good at killing, he said. So are we, I thought. The man had brought wine in abundance and also bread and he made himself comfortable, almost as if he owned the place. His talk revolved around rumours and the voyages that were being planned. He was surprised I had no inkling of them. But workers in the wharves on the Tagus know it, he said. Whores know it, those that have given favours on credit to sailors. I answered that I was not in very close touch with whores—a small lie, and hence pardonable.

To digress a little—restless as I was, I had roamed the streets and located the two girls who had laughed at me. They were on the balcony again though there was a cold breeze about as winter was setting in. I walked up the steps and got a rather friendly welcome. After chatting for about half an hour, the short one, fairer and more aggressive, asked if I was only going to talk. No, I said, walking in with the other, a shade darker and more reserved. She was smooth as well, and that always affects me. Samina too had affected me with the gloss on her face, on the back of her hand and her instep. The tall dark one treated me like a boy, though she was probably my age, caressed me and astonished me by kissing me on my mouth. She surprised me even more when she asked me to take off all my clothes. All? Yes all, she said. These white women! When our limbs were entwined she passed on a few tips, very gently, almost inaudibly. And when we had finished and I had got back into my clothes, she wouldn't let me open the door without first giving me a hug. They are good, Portuguese women.

Martim Dias continued, 'You know this much, don't you, Moor, that there are sailors who can't even pay a whore? But the gold from Africa will double, slaves and spices will bring in wealth, then the money will trickle down to the wharves and the orchards. We are preparing ourselves for the future, our next fleet almost ready and it is not your Captain-Major heading things this time. Cabral leads it, Pedro Alvares Cabral, Cavalier of the Order of Christ. You know what a cavalier means? No? An Amir. He is an aristocrat, descended from Aphonso I, the first King of Portugal. He will captain a much bigger fleet, mind you. Your Gama had just four ships and two hundred men.

This time there'll be four times their number both in men and in ships. There'll also be many more cannon with Cabral.'

'They're going for trade, aren't they? What do they want with so many cannon?'

'They will put the Red Sea on fire, friend.' He kept staring at me to observe my reaction. But in a foreign country you keep your expressions in check—surprise, anger, joy, hatred, all masked by an impassive face, lips moving into automatic half-smiles. I wasn't about to give anything away.

'There'll be a lot of gold on the ships.'

'This time there will be no dearth of gifts for the Zamorin. The King wishes to surprise his royal brother in Calicut, the black King reclining on that bed with toes encased in pearls.' I told him that was all nonsense; there were no pearls on his toes.

'They all say the King was fine—it was the Moors who poisoned his ears. That means your type. Of course we think he is Christian, though he never made the sign of the cross! Let's wait for the next meeting—this time with Cabral. But it's not going to be all gold and gifts. The ships' holds will be full of cannon shot. Cabral will conquer the sea in a way Gama didn't even dream of. Word has spread here that there is no gunpowder in the littoral. The admirals can do as they please.' He sank into silence for a few moments. 'I came here out of curiosity. What of you, Moor? Haven't they contacted you?'

I saw no point in lying. I had not been asked, I told him. Get ready all the same, he said. You never know when the summons will come. They may want to keep the news from you till the very last. It is the Portuguese obsession with secrecy. The King does not let the Queen know that he intends to have sex, till he actually jumps on her.

He reverted to the pilot business. 'Have you heard of Bartolomeu Dias, greatest of our navigators—it was he who went around the Cape a dozen years ago. He has been drafted. Nicolo Coelho, who commanded the *Berrio*, he is also on the fleet. There'll be more captains than sailors this time. That's not all, Moor. There will be our priests on the ship, Franciscan missionaries. They could be as deadly as cannon shot. They are being sent to bring the heretical Christians to the true path. And Islam is not going to be free from their clutches either—tough times ahead for heathen and heretic alike.'

I asked him once why he was so hell-bent on speaking ill of his own people. Silly question; his father had been executed. If your father has been cut up into four parts, you are not going to write *qasidas* on King and judge. After his father was killed he actually went into a Spanish monastery for two years, he told me. In his own words, he was trying to come to terms with himself and the times he was living in. A monastery was also the place where he himself could come to no harm. He didn't like what he read. The tracts he got to read were so bigoted, tracts from the Synod of Norbonne or the Fourth Lateran Council. (I couldn't fathom what he was talking of, the names sounded so outlandish. But he wrote the names down for me.) Jews and Muslims had to wear badges. There was a Pope called Gregory who asked half the countries in Europe to confiscate Jewish books on the first Saturday of Lent. (Lent, he explained, was something like our Ramadan, a month of fasting.)He went on about the Yahudis and it didn't interest me that much except that they were tying up the Muslims with the Yahudis. I couldn't think of a bigger insult to our faith.

Not everything Martim Dias said made sense to me. Their minds were outward bound. They were looking beyond the seas, he said. He kept repeating that these were momentous times. By their calendar it was 1500, he never tired of saying that, fifteen hundred years after Issa was born. Some of their priests expected great things to happen, a Messiah (that was what they called a Mehdi) to appear. Dias laughed, and said they expected another Jesus, that is Issa, to appear. 'The Hidden One', that was the name of this Messiah. I hurriedly read a qalima. It was blasphemy to even think of a prophet after Muhammad, peace be upon him.

'Why should he hide, this Mehdi of yours? Surely Allah would want him to show his face to the people. It was lepers, who didn't show their faces. I hope he is not Iblis in disguise!'

He didn't answer, but just looked intently at me and smiled. I don't know why, but I started trusting the fellow—developing a sort of liking for him. The Messiah would give the Purtugalis the right to rule the world. Some of them thought he had already appeared on earth in the shape of Prester John, the King they were searching for.

Others were thinking in terms of the wrath of God, he said. This was the time for the scourge—plague, famine, earthquakes. All this and more would fall on the wicked. It drove people to churches, more candles were lit there, more confessions were made of sins committed and sometimes not committed—what was a confession worth if there wasn't a crackling sin to disclose? He cackled as he said that. I don't know why I laughed uncontrollably, till tears ran down my eyes. Even he was surprised.

'Isn't it far too early to sail? It is bitter winter still. Where's the hurry?'

'That's your trouble, you can't understand. Castile and Portugal have, just a few years back, signed a treaty dividing the world among themselves—sorry, dividing the oceans between the two of them. The sea around India belongs to Portugal. The King doesn't want some Spanish fleet to usurp our seas. Do you understand?'

Who could understand these fools, I thought. Dividing the sea waters of the world! Or had they actually divided the world? Allah would punish such arrogance. Would it be plague? Would it be flood or fire?

Two nights later he slid into the dark and was gone. I don't know if I was glad or unhappy at his departure.

~

The summons came suddenly. Barely a week was left for the voyage and I was asked to join. Martim Dias was right—they didn't trust me. Did they trust themselves? We set out from the Tagus. The only one I thought I knew was Nicolo Coelho. As time went by I met some others who had been on the voyage with Captain-Major Gama. I was on the ship of Bartolomeu Dias. The men looked at him in worshipful awe and some of that got rubbed off on me. But he was friendly, talked to me throughout the voyage as one seaman to another. His queries on the way we Arabs navigated were perceptive and he had heard about my mentor, Ibn Majid (who had not?).

It was too cold for my taste. It was still winter as we set out. Cabral proceeded west as if he wanted to catch the sun before it set. As we moved further and further west, and sometimes south-west, the pilot of our ship started getting agitated. We were supposed to be going east, weren't we? Why in the name of Satan are we moving the other way? he growled. We are not going to India, he said. We are proceeding to the sunset instead of sunrise. Other sailors couldn't tell him either why we were drifting west—not really drifting, our sails were full and we were going more west than south. No cloud, no rain; hot blistering sun. I didn't want to argue and tell him that the Admiral was giving a wide berth to the coast and avoiding the dangers—rock and shoal and adverse current—that had

*keki n. daruwalla*

wrecked many ships. That was what Ibn Majid had told them in Milind—stop hugging the coast and head for India.

One thought that intrigued me during the journey was that oceans were not boundless—nor was space, for wasn't there a sky to cap space? Somewhere or the other the sea was bound to be ringed by land, by straw hut and sand and palm trees.

Men became very happy when they saw small birds. They believed that they were near land. But we saw small birds and no land. A man fell overboard—he was drunk—and no one could do anything about it. For two days the calm caught up with us and the Captain ordered stricter rationing of food and fresh water. The planks became so hot we blistered at a touch. Fortunately this didn't last long and we cheered the wind when after almost two days it hit our sails.

Then came the storm; first heavy cloud and no rain, then heavy cloud and heavy rain. It drove us further west and then Allah be praised, we saw land; rather, we saw a mountain. The Admiral named it Monte Pascoal. By their calendar it was 22 April. The next day we landed and another two days later the whole fleet sailed into the harbour. The people who lived here started coming to the shore to look at us. They were naked and brown. The Admiral called them to the ships, gave them food and tried to talk to them. But neither side could understand the other. The Franciscan priests put crucifix necklaces around their necks. In the next few days we sailed along the coast, went up a river, caught some fish, the sailors sang and we generally enjoyed ourselves. The parrots here were beautiful, with big curved beaks, and they screeched a lot. Cabral called the place Vera Cruz, and he sent one ship back with news of new lands discovered, to Lisbon. Of course, he declared that the land now belonged to Portugal. (I always thought that land belonged to the people who lived there.) Cabral also took me off Bartolomeu Dias's ship. Dias doesn't need any help, he said. He was the one who 'discovered' the Cape of Good Hope and went around it. So I was taken off and placed on another ship.

The winds favoured us as we turned eastwards. We made it quickly to the Cape and that is where the storms struck us again. This time the wind was just too strong and the waves too high. We couldn't save a man in the four ships that went down. Bartolomeu Dias couldn't be saved either. Allah, who had saved me from scurvy, had saved me again. Each time a big commander had paid with his life, while I was saved.

We were looking for Sofala and its gold. Word went around that men here ate human flesh, mainly of their enemies—nobody eats friends after all. It was a bad harbour—narrow mouth and the water shallow. My ship was ordered in, just the one from the whole fleet. Was Cabral testing me? He had lost too many ships to risk a few more. I steered carefully, wary of shoal and shallows. The sailors were worried about the man-eaters, what they call *adamkhor* in Hind. As always the people gazed at my white companions as if they were monkeys. The Captain of my ship thought the onlookers were ugly. I thought they were handsome. Hadn't he seen black men before? He didn't answer, but told me that the Purtugalis were supposed to have put up a factory here—a settlement for trade, that is what they meant by factory. But Bartolomeu was the one who would have governed the settlement, and he was on the ocean floor with his ship. I had no time to cluck in regret, was concentrating on keeping my ship safe. We didn't stay too long and sailed ahead to Mozambique where we stayed for a week, got fresh water and meat in our ships and sailed ahead.

It was at Kilwa my captain told me he may need my help. In translating, he added. Translating what? Well, Cabral had orders from King Manuel that the people of Kilwa had to give up their heathenish ways. I didn't understand what a 'heathen' meant. He consulted others and said, 'Kafir, Kafir.'

'These are not Kafirs! They are Muslims!' I was screaming. They smiled, 'That's what we mean.' I was breathing very hard and I could hear my heart beat like a hammer. I kept quiet. I didn't want a scene.

Sultan Ibrahim of Kilwa sent maize and vegetables and live goats—boatloads of them. The boatman also carried a letter inviting the Admiral for a meeting. Nothing happened for some days—my companions said that both the dignitaries suspected each other. Then the Sultan of Kilwa agreed to meet Cabral on the sea. Two boats were nailed and tied together, and planks of wood placed over them, and over the planks, carpets. The retinue was unarmed except for ceremonial daggers in silver scabbards. They blew on horns made of elephant tusks. The Purtugalis responded with trumpets. There was one snag. The Sultan was not the Sultan. That is what I thought as the Admiral and his entourage, of which I was also a part, approached the raft. I had seen him a number of times during my last voyage with Ibn Majid. When I climbed on to the raft I was certain it was not him. But I didn't say a word. In fact the impostor was the well-known Malik Lukman Ali. I was too small a person to scuttle the meeting. The proposals from the Portuguese side concerned setting up a trading post, purchase of gold and finally the abandonment of Islam, Allah and the Prophet, by the King and the entire population. King Manuel's letter was handed over both in Purtugali and Arabic and I was made to read the badly written and barely intelligible Arabic translation. The Malik, not known to Cabral as Malik, wanted time. These were serious matters, he said. I translated as best as I could. When we reached our boat I told the Captain that I was not sure if this was Sultan Ibrahim. He looked more like a noble, a Malik I knew. I was questioned the whole night. How did I know? Did I recognize the Sultan? Where and when had I seen him earlier? I should have only known the King of Milind, for that is where I had joined Gama's fleet. Fortunately they didn't torture me though there was no dearth of snarling and the mouthing of obscenities. I was asked to stay in the Admiral's ship.

The impostor Lukman Ali had said he would consult his advisers and only then give an answer. An air of expectancy and impatience pervaded the Admiral's ship. I knew there would be no answer. You want trade with a people and first ask them to renounce their God and their Prophet! No answer came. The Admiral asked for water for his ships. An entire boat with huge clay pots set out from the shore. Eight men were rowing the boat. They didn't come near, however, and stopped suddenly. We looked on as the oarsmen lifted their oars and one by one smashed all the pots. Then they jeered at us and rowed back. Most of my companions were livid. I was hard put to hide my smile. They have given the answer, I said to myself. The Admiral lifted anchor and we sailed on towards Milind.

The welcome was considerable here—song, dance and drum; fresh water, sheep, goats, fowl. The nutmeg and ginger and other things would be given on the voyage back, said the King. Cabral left two convicts—the *degredados* as they called them—under instructions to look for the land of Prester John. Things came full circle now. I was asked to lead the fleet to Calicut.

*keki n. daruwalla*

# cabral at calicut

This time the shore was lined with people and the Nair nobility as the fleet came in. The people of Calicut had no means of knowing that it was a depleted fleet, with five ships having gone down, one lost and another sent back to Lisbon with the news about the discovery of the Vera Cruz 'island', what turned out to be Brazil later on. The people of Calicut, especially Moor and Mappila, had no illusions about the Portuguese. Gama's voyage was not forgotten—the niggardly gifts, the abrasive manner, mistaking the Zamorin and the Hindus for Christians, thinking Kali was Virgin Mary—the gaffes were too numerous. The hostage-grabbing had also not been forgotten. Calicut was keeping its fingers crossed.

Cabral too had his misgivings. The Muslims wouldn't welcome him, he knew. Their trade and way of life would be affected. Dom Manuel's letter, though wrapped in purple silk this time, was too blunt, too demanding, and terribly arrogant. The parleys with the Zamorin would need a lot of skill. Christian doctrine would need the support of cannon shot in good measure. The first step had to be hostile—he sent Afoso Furtado to demand Nair hostages before Cabral would set foot on the shore. The Zamorin, a new one this time, surprisingly, gave in. The hostages were brought in, five of them, some of them Gujarati merchants, and Cabral stepped on shore.

This was a new Zamorin, Mana Vikrama, and he himself came to receive Cabral. At the Royal audience the Zamorin was not reclining languidly like the previous one. His throne was of silver, the arms of gold and he sat upright, his fingers smothered with rings and the pearls in his earrings as big as dove's eggs. Dom Manuel's gifts were displayed by the sea farers—jewelled sceptres, brocades, carpets. Then the never-ending convoluted letter from Dom Manuel was read out—it proclaimed his enmity with Islam, asked the 'Christian' King of Calicut (never mind if the guy was a 'heretic Christian') to throw those circumcised Muslims out from his kingdom. In every sentence Manuel hammered in 'the will of God' like a blacksmith straightening a warped sheet of metal. 'If', said the missive, 'due to the influence of evil minds we find in you the contrary of this . . . our unwavering objective is to follow the will of God rather than that of men . . .' He would not fail 'through any contrariness' on the part of the Zamorin to 'pursue trade and intercourse' in these lands, 'which the Lord God wishes to be served by our hands'.

How the Portuguese managed to know the wishes of 'Lord God' was never spelled out to the Zamorin. Six Brahmins, their torsos bare (except for the sacred thread sidling past the right shoulder and the left nipple), their scalps shaved except for a plume of hair dangling on to their necks, were scribbling away feverishly on palm leaves, taking down whatever they could make of the Portuguese fire-and-brimstone letter. Ganesha never scribbled faster as Vyasa dictated, even when the latter rattled off three chapters in three minutes, for he was suffering from dysentery and wanted to get to the loo before he soiled his langot. The Malabari king mumbled in Malayalam, trying all the while to control the anger that rumbled in

*keki n. daruwalla*

his belly. The faces of courtiers and the Moors fell. Yet an understanding between the two parties was hammered out on a sheet of silver—a friendship testament of sorts. Nothing untoward happened for the next two months. The Zamorin was cooperative and helped the Portuguese, promising them precedence over the Moors when it came to buying spices. Cabral's Factor, Ayres Correa, went ashore and set up his trading post, except that it took two months to get permission to start trading. Taufiq was sent with Correa. He knew the place and the lingo. Things were fine. So was the wind. There couldn't have been a better time for sailing to the Red Sea. A ship, owned by an Arab, had been fully stacked with spices and was about to embark for Jeddah. Ayres Correa thought this was in contravention of the agreement with the Zamorin. How could the Moors set off on a trading mission, when Cabral himself was still stranded here? Weren't they supposed to get precedence over all others, especially the Moors? Ayres worked on the Admiral. Cabral seized the ship.

All hell broke on land the next day. The Mappilas and the Moors had had enough of the Portuguese. They stormed the trading post with sword, sickle, spear, stave, anything to beat out the brains of these navigators. The fight was bitter and went on for hours. The Portuguese first fought, were outnumbered, then ran to the boats. They were slaughtered—Factor, Franciscan friars, degredados—the lot. Well, almost. Only seventeen out of the seventy escaped. Cabral saw red, as did all the Portuguese on board. He kept his patience. Perhaps the Zamorin would make amends of sorts; send some sarong-clad half-naked notables to apologize with a gold tray and jewels, pearls perhaps like those dove egg-sized ones the Zamorin wore on his ears. He would take the bastards hostage, the Nobles or the Nairs as they called them, once they came grovelling. It was sheer treachery, he thought. They allowed trade, gave safe passage, signed a treaty and then slaughtered his men. It never occurred to Cabral that this could have been an accident, a spur-of-the-moment reaction against the foreigners who wanted to change the time-honoured way of life of the people of Calicut.

No notables came. No apology, the script hammered on a silver or gold tray, no bloody notables, no Nairs. Next morning the cannons started roaring, pouring shot after shot into the city. So heavy was the bombardment that most of the town was vacated. People didn't know what had hit them and ran screaming. Gunpowder and shot had not come to Indian shores till then. There were people who had never heard of it. (Babur's matchlocks were to make their appearance twenty-five years later.) The Zamorin himself, with his women, left his palace and ran, possibly barefoot, possibly holding the folds of his waist cloth in one hand, like any other member of the populace.

Ten merchant ships were anchored in the harbour. The Portuguese caravels captured them one after the other. None of the ships offered any resistance. After the capture the slaughter started—cut, thrust and slash and blood ran over the planks, dribbled into gunny sack, dripped into the holds. Those who jumped from the ships were caught and put to the sword. In each ship, though, Cabral saw to it that some people were left untouched. Worse followed; after all, 'treachery' had to be avenged, the Arabs and other Muslims taught a lesson. The Zamorin also needed one. The ships were driven towards the strand and the people who had been spared were now tied up in full sight of the city. Then each of the ships was set on fire, and the victims writhed and howled, their screams reaching the strand and curdling the blood of their near ones.

# taufiq
# in calicut

〰

I was asked to go ashore with the Factor. They thought I could be of use perhaps, not just with language but also my acquaintance with the ways of the people. Even as I landed I said to myself I wasn't going back on ship, certainly not to Lisbon. Father and daughter had been constantly in my mind, but now, all of a sudden, the urge to meet Samina became irresistible. I would have jumped across a hundred-foot deep pit, crossed a desert on foot, put out to sea in a storm balancing myself on a plank over a giant wave, just to meet her. I sought out Shakoor and he gave me the tightest hug I have had in years—almost broke my ribs. He laughed, his eyes gleamed and he couldn't speak for a while.

'I knew you would come. Some day a boat would arrive, tall mast, unknown flag, big ship with brocades, silk, gold, and you'd be on it. Samina was pensive sometimes.'

'Why pensive?'

'She doesn't dream of gold and brocades. She would dream of boats being washed ashore. Dreams are also a part of destiny.'

'I am taking up quarters here—wish to get off the boat for good,' I said. His face fell because I wasn't staying with him. I felt unequal to the moment—wasn't prepared for too much happiness. I turned away from him abruptly—emotion leaves its calligraphy on the face. I took a thatched house for myself near where the Factor had been given a largish house for his entire retinue—about seventy. I didn't want to live with Shakoor this time—too much of hospitality can smother.

The next time I met Shakoor was after a week. We talked of this and that, feeling our way, till he came to the point. What did we intend? 'We' of course stood for the Portuguese. I was now permanently lumped with them. Was there an embargo on trade with Jeddah or Alexandria? A few ships come in with foreigners in strange dresses flaunting gunpowder and an unintelligible language and they think they can change the faith of a people and a way of life. They tell you which friends you can have, what gods you can worship. Have they also told you when to marry?

Me? I asked startled. Yes, you, he said. I laughed, a bit artificially, I must confess.

'Don't laugh. Answer me! Nothing is impossible with these people. Thank Allah they can't un-circumcise us, or they would try. In the last thirty years I don't remember slapping someone. But seeing these people I could pick up a rock and hurl it at them.'

His mood changed. From anger to despondency is not always a long walk. 'I will be ruined if they have their way,' he said. I reminded him of his palm groves and his lands. 'They aren't worth much,' he countered. 'You can't live on coconuts. My boats will be worth nothing. What can you do with boats if you can't put them out to sea—I mean the Red Sea. I believe they will not let us trade, not while their fleet is here. When they leave, the winds won't be blowing our way. They want favours, permission to trade, and the first thing they do is demand hostages. Ever heard of such a thing? I employ a hundred people—on boats, in the market, some even in other ports. How do I feed them? I have a daughter to marry off. There will be a thousand guests at the wedding.'

He was almost talking to himself. I tried to allay his anxieties: it was futile. One has to fight one's own fears, others can't still them for you. I came out of my shack with Shakoor to escort him till the road. It was the least I could do. All that I had offered him was coconut water. A burly man came by, square-faced and pocked. He greeted Shakoor with a respectful salaam. When we were introduced I found his name was Akram. He greeted me half respectfully and half patronizingly. In Hind if someone is older even by a month, he thinks he is entitled to play the uncle. After he left, Shakoor told me he was a butcher—he sold the best meat in town. He was said to be a 'namazi' fellow, saying his prayers five times a day. 'Hope he does his wuzu properly,' I said. He kept quiet. I couldn't help elaborating on it. I could almost see him bringing his cleaver down on a leg of meat when suddenly the call for prayer sounds. He washes wrist and elbow and ties his tahmat tighter (what if there is a bloodstain or two on it?), and spreads his prayer rug. I was laughing and Shakoor showed his uneasiness. 'Akram is quite close to the Qazi,' he told me. A Qadi is called Qazi in Malabar.

'Whatever his connections with the Qadi, I didn't like his face.'

'You don't live here, Taufiq. You can afford to dislike his face. We can't.'

Slowly, I started visiting Shakoor. You can't resist desire indefinitely. Will crumbles eventually. Samina looked just the same, perhaps a bit fuller in the breasts, the skin as glossy as ever, the smile spreading across her face like a ray of light when she saw me. I noticed that her hands trembled when she brought me coconut water. There can't be a clearer sign than that—the meeting excited her equally. One can't talk of every meeting, and one can't record things like hand touching hand through intentional 'chance', arm brushing against breast, shoulder against shoulder. I would become tense when I went to the house. Surely Shakoor could see through all this? If you have boats all over and trade with hundreds of different people, surely you have an eye for these signs that show on the face. He never raised an eyebrow though. He would sit with us sometimes and then leave us alone. Once, to my utter shame, I was rigid with desire as I entered the house. Samina noticed and laughed. It was uncontrollable, her laughter, gurgling like a spring of water.

There were times when I almost saw the violence of my feelings mirrored on her face—but that could be a mirage. You sometimes see what you want to see. Even at moments when I would have given anything to touch her hand or put my arm on her shoulder, the mind would wander and I would think it was just as well we didn't allow man and woman to meet like this in Egypt.

I once plucked up courage to ask her how it was she wasn't married till now. She just shrugged her shoulders. Shakoor came to know what I had asked her. He brought the matter up next day and slowly the conversation drifted towards Samina's marriage, with me as groom. He must have seen my eyes light up. We had many conversations on the subject. I could easily stay back, at least that's what he thought. So did I, and when I mentioned it to Ayres Correa, he seemed to have no particular objection. The route was now well-known and they could manage. What would I do here, I asked Shakoor. He replied there was no dearth of boats going up the Red Sea. I could have my pick. The same applied to the African coast, with which a thriving trade existed. Suppose I don't like it here after a year or two. Suppose Cairo pulls me back. What happens then, I asked. Then she follows you, he said. That is the law of life.

Shakoor went off to Cranganore to look after his business. A ship was being loaded with some of his cargo here too, but that didn't seem to keep him. I plucked up courage—I just wanted to hug her, hold her hard against my chest. She said no, not while father's away. I stopped going to the house. I'd visit them when he returned.

Things don't happen the way you plan. Shakoor returned a day before we, the Purtugalis (or Portuguese as they are also called) that is, took over a Muslim ship in the harbour. It was the beginning of the end. Cabral ordered the capture, but it was the Factor, Ayres Correa, who had insisted that it should be done. Next day, in the morning, things became tense. You can smell tension, see it mirrored in the faces of the crowd. No provocation, no hot words exchanged and a ship is taken over, with all its enormous goods! How did this happen? How could it be allowed? People started questioning: why, why, why? What right have you over the ship? Are you going to release the goods at least? The Factor was not the most diplomatic of negotiators. It never entered his head that there could be violence. That night the Moors and the Mappilas quietly surrounded our warehouse. Their numbers swelled. Many of us were asleep. We were just seventy in number including three Franciscan priests. They were in hundreds. Late at night I peeped out and saw that we were literally besieged. The Factor was asleep. I woke him up. He was in a bad mood. A small altercation and the trouble flared up.

I saw Shakoor and waved to him. He waved back, and shouted something but the words were drowned in the din. He kept gesturing, letting me know through sign talk to get out of the place—he was pointing to the door all the time.

But how could one get out of that mess? I remembered that
he too had some of his cargo on the ship which the Portuguese
had taken over. I saw Akram, his face dark as a thundercloud,
and I knew there could be big trouble. One doesn't know who
lighted the match. One never knows. But the riot broke like
a storm. First, they swarmed around us and grappled. It was
spontaneous, sudden—blows started raining on the Portuguese.
Behind them there were people with staves, behind them were
the swords and cleavers. We too drew our swords—even I did.
They could obviously make no distinction between me and the
Portuguese. The fighting went on for over two hours. We also
drew blood, but we were outnumbered. Akram was inciting
the mob and clearing a bloody path with his cleaver right
up to where the Factor was standing. Correa was so hemmed
in he couldn't even use his sword well. With one stroke of his
short, heavy cleaver Akram smashed his collar bone. Another
blow to the head saw the Factor falling and getting trampled
over by the crowd. Too late, but I caught hold of Akram's arm.
We wrestled for a while. He was stronger but I kicked him hard
in his stomach and he fell. I kicked him in his face. But then
the swarm of people swept me off my feet into the compound.
With great difficulty some of us extricated ourselves from the
arms of the rioters, who were turning more frenzied by the
minute. Once in the open we thought we could hold them off.
We couldn't. No aid could come to us from the fleet. Our men
started dying, people who had been with me for months. We
ran towards the sea and our ships.

Less than twenty of us escaped, more than fifty died. We
swam to the fleet. When the Portuguese saw us swimming,
they sent their caravels to pick us up. The silence on the ship
was ominous and the anger among the men was so red-hot
it could have set the fleet on fire. Within an hour of getting

on to the ship I was lamenting my fate. I had determined to leave Cabral and stay on in Calicut—get married. If, in your dreams, you are always holding someone in your arms, how do you keep away?

The next day the bombards opened up. Shell after shell crashed into the town. Houses crumbled, people ran, abandoning their homes. Who knows how many died? I saw puffs of dust rise as buildings went down. Now and then a tree would be severed in half like a man decapitated. I had never seen anything like it—found myself praying that Shakoor's house would be spared, or if the house had to go, Samina and Shakoor should be spared. There were ships in the harbour, ten of them, and they were captured. Then the slaughter began—those people were unarmed but they were put to the sword, most of them, and their goods looted. The most blood-smeared dream can't equal the horror unveiled to our eyes—the cries for mercy and the cruel sword thrusts that answered those cries. None of the people in the ships fought.

Care was taken to spare some people in each ship. We didn't know why. I was soon to be enlightened. The survivors were tied up and the ships were moved towards the shore and put to torch in the sight of all the relatives of the crewmen, who came running to the strand and wailed and wept and tore their hair.

We sailed to Cochin, got a good reception there, heard that a fleet of ships was sent by Calicut to give us battle, but Cabral had better things to do—take the huge cargo of spices back to Lisbon along with elephants. Yes, there were three small elephants in one of the boats. They were supposed to be presents for the Portuguese King. Then provisions ran short and the Portuguese cut up the elephants and ate them! In all my dreams

I could never have imagined a thing like that. I of course never touched that haram meat. And I feel sorry for the elephants.

What is there to tell now—the return to Lisbon with the kind of cargo they could not have imagined, the tremors in Europe especially in Venice. Then the rumours started percolating from the court. The King was unhappy with Cabral—that Dias fellow, the night bird, not the great Captain who was on the sea-floor, told me that again. Six ships had gone down, and he had broken all ties with the Zamorin, the same one whom the King had announced to be a Christian King in his letters to the high and mighty of Europe. Trade was all very fine but to lose six ships, turn a 'Christian' King into a heathen, and make an enemy of him—was something different.

Egypt would be in trouble, I realised. Dias told me that a Venetian merchant, based in Lisbon, had said that the spices that now cost just a ducat, would cost anywhere from fifty to a hundred ducats in Venice via the Red Sea. I chafed at the bit, like a camel tethered while fires rage nearby. I also was on fire—I wanted home, Cairo, my friends and Calicut and Samina. Sometimes I drowned my fires in that house with the tall girl and the short one. They laughed less now and caressed more. You have much fairer men here, I told them repeatedly. What makes you so fond of me? We don't want these pink faces, they said. We prefer tawny skin, and your dark eyes and your black hair. And we like your sturdiness and your virility. I blushed hearing this and they laughed some more. I sometimes went into the inner room with the shorter one; sometimes. She laughed more than the tall one and bounced more on the bed. But the one who soothed me was the tall one. I will never mention their names. Their honour must be kept intact.

~

By their calendar we in Cabral's fleet had reached Lisbon on 21 July 1501. After less than a year the Captain-Major Gama had me summoned and join his fleet of twenty-five ships. To me it appeared the ships were more stuffed with cannon and shot than goods for trade. I will skip the voyage this time, for it was a bit of a repetition—same landscape, same ports, same people; more or less.

# figueiro
## the *mirim*

After four years I was drafted again in the fleet through the Lord's will. The previous voyage with the Captain-Major had drained me. I was often sea-sick and must have been a sorry sight: head hanging over the railings, eyes watery, mouth stinking. Yet I never demurred when asked by the church to go to these lands and harvest lost souls. In all Christian humility, I can say that the desire to serve our lord Christ the Saviour has always been uppermost in my mind.

I had my misgivings. If previously we had set out for trade, this time it seemed vengeance. Bringing infidel lands into the folds of the Church was never the aim. It was either Mammon or Caesar. Christ always took third place despite the King's fervour.

Trade and gold seemed to be the driving force, the veritable wind in the fleet's sails. Half the fleet belonged to affluent merchants of Lisbon. The King couldn't equip such a large fleet. At each port, it was gold we were after. The degradadoes left behind by previous Captains to find out where the gold came from and get to the Kingdom of Prester John, had done nothing of note. They hadn't stirred a finger and remained stuck in the ports, sleeping with black women.

The Captain-Major commanded twenty-five ships this time. Ten of these carried the kind of cannon and shot the oceans had never witnessed. Moreover, he was Admiral of the fleet now and 'almirante amigo' of the monarch. We had only a sprinkling of the men who had been on our first voyage. I was delighted to see the pilot of our first venture, Taufiq, with us. Though a Moor, he was always pleasant and never devious. Moreover, he wouldn't change his faith in order to advance his career with us. Such men need to be respected, even if they are infidels and thus destined for hell fires.

We picked up interesting details about the previous voyagers though, of Da Nova's fleet which had followed upon Cabral's voyage. We learned he had captured a Moor's ship near Calicut, found over 1500 pearls among the passengers whom he then slaughtered, every one of them, except the pilot. We were still new to these seas, and a pilot was always precious. Pillage, pearls, slaughter—that was the sequence.

I made my disapproval known. Surely slaughter, even of heathens, could not be the purpose of our voyages. In another ship, Nova had found a Jewess from Seville. The Jews, the murderers of our Lord, had rightly been thrown out of Spain. Portugal had fortunately followed suit, though after much persuasion from Castile. (Why could we ourselves not think of expelling them?) The Jewess told the captors how the Moors had forced the Zamorin to become hostile to us, and then for no good reason, she had jumped into the sea and drowned. Was this her way to atone for the sin of being a Jew? I am at sea when confronted by such disturbing questions.

There was no change in Vasco's ways as we sidled along the African coast. The moment we approached a port he asked for hostages and a meeting with the sovereign. None of us could approach land till he had the hostages in hand and had fired one or two bombards to frighten the natives.

(Sound, I noticed, frightens animals and Africans alike.) If the black King didn't turn up for a meeting soon enough, he would send threatening messages and fire off more bombards. This happened at Kilwa, where two of our ships, which had gone astray, had joined us. It was a most impressive spectacle as we entered the harbour, enough to bring any local to his knees, we thought. So many ships, such a surfeit of cannon would scare these dark chieftains. The King shied away, not unexpectedly, if I may say so. The moment he at last appeared, jolted out of his somnolence by the Admiral's threats, Gama asked him to pay a tribute of ten pearls and 1500 miskals of gold a year to King John.

At Milind we would again have been received well. Friends remain friends. But horrible weather prevented the ships from moving into the harbour. The Admiral decided instead to traverse the sea to the Indian coast. Meanwhile, long before we reached Milind the Admiral had sent six of his ships to plug the Red Sea. The pepper and ginger traffic from Calicut to Mecca had to be stopped. The Moors had to be punished, not only for being Moors, but for having treacherously killed our men, fifty of them, including the three Franciscan priests in Calicut. The betrayal of Cabral by the Moors could not be pardoned. The Zamorin would suffer too, for he had obviously conspired in the treachery.

Then, of course, came the affair of the ship *Mirim*, which the locals called by some other name. A huge ship it was, with about seven hundred men, women and children returning from their annual Muslim pilgrimage, if the sacred word 'pilgrimage' can really be used for that black-stone mosque on the Red Sea. The owner, one Joa Fiquim, was reported to be richer than any Arab in Calicut. He had slaves, jewels, ships, possibly more ships than wives. We fired our bombards—they didn't respond. No shots were fired from their side though we could see they had guns. They tried to bribe the Admiral, or so I thought. This Joa Fiquim or Faquim or Faqih came on board and, we heard later, offered all the wealth he had—and he had a lot of it on the ship. Gama had the entire hold of the ship cleared and the goods transferred to the Admiral's own ship; so far so good. After that I didn't like what was happening. I had been watching Taufiq, the pilot, and his face was dark as thunder . . . after all they were his ilk. He looked emaciated and I am not sure if he was taking his meals at all. He didn't speak a word all those four days and I felt for him. His teeth were clenched and anger blazed from his eyes.

The Arab merchant offered himself as a hostage now. He would procure whatever wealth the Admiral needed from Calicut. The women started pleading for their lives. The Admiral wouldn't budge, and he didn't dissemble—didn't know how to. Four days went by with the Moors raising their offers. They would furnish the entire fleet with spices, and wouldn't charge a cruzado, if only the lives of the people on the ship were spared. They would give enough money to fetch a king's ransom. But our Captains seemed bent on revenge.

These people in the ship hadn't killed Cabral's men. Was vengeance justified? Is revenge in such cases ever fair? It was a metaphysical issue, I realized. Sometimes one feels that only the Lord has answers to such questions.

On the fifth day, the third of October, final orders were given. The *Mirim* was primed with explosives and was about to be set on fire. The women pointed towards their infants. There was no way you could miss what they were saying. This language can be understood the world over. It was here that I and my brothers in Christ, the other Franciscan priests, put our foot down. The infants must be saved and baptized. Against the wishes of the Captains and da Gama himself, we got the children into our ship, about twenty of them. No sooner had we secured the children than orders were given to burn the *Mirim* down. Now the Arabs turned desperate. With sticks and planks and swords they fought the sailors and put some of our not-too-willing soldiers to death. Many jumped into the sea rather than be burnt alive. Between fire and water, people choose water. Seeing this, the Admiral lowered our men, equipped with spears, in small boats to kill them. The soldiers went about it the way one spears big fish. The women, who in any case did not know how to float in water, and were floundering, were similarly speared. The sea turned the colour of wine.

I happened to glance at Taufiq. Horror, shame and anger were all scripted on his face. It had been a horrible day. I thank our Lord that in His mercy we were granted the lives of those twenty children.

# taufiq
## the *miri*

〰

I never meant to keep a chronicle of this voyage. What was the point? The same seas, same gulls, sun burning you to bronze, the damp of the cool nights. Not worth writing about. I was once again ordered into the fleet, Vasco da Gama's, whose volatile temper itself could ignite half the bombards in his ships. This time though I made the Portuguese promise that they would let me go once we reached the Indian coast. But who knows what Allah has in store for him? One can, at the most, bow to the west and pray, keep the fasts one can, and not sin. Some sins who can avoid—the sins which come with hot blood and utter loneliness? One can fast, pray, speak the truth and not spill blood unnecessarily, and hope for the best.

This time the Portuguese were much more confident. They knew the seas and the lands they passed by. They bullied the envoys and kings of Africa. They had donned the robes of masters, behaved like masters; and knew what they wanted—gold.

Who knows what destiny has in store for him? I was to witness Karbala enacted on the seas. Most, if not all the people on this ill-fated ship called *Miri*, were returning from Haj. They should have resisted right from the start, but they trusted the greed of the white man. The Portuguese could be bought off, they thought. There was all this jewellery the women were wearing; which Indian woman doesn't? That was enough to satisfy this Gama fellow. Then this al Faqih, the owner of *Miri*, wealthiest man in Calicut, and a very decent person by all accounts, was led before the Admiral. The Portuguese incidentally kept on calling him Joa Fiquim. He offered himself as hostage. His nephew would go on land and get whatever wealth the Portuguese wanted. That was the point. Money and gold were not on the chess board for once. The Admiral wanted blood.

Even during negotiations, the ship was being primed with gunpowder by Portuguese sailors. When did the pilgrims realize that this was not some crude blackmail? This was for real. Sentence had been passed. Only the axe was being put in place. I knew from the first day that this was for real. The Portuguese had decided that the attack on Aires Correia, the Factor in Calicut, had been the result of a conspiracy; that the Moors had planned it and the Samudri Raja was a part of it. In the scale of vengeance, ten thousand blacks or browns would hardly suffice for fifty Portuguese killed.

Put us in irons and take us to Calicut, said al Faqih. We'll load your ships with spices and won't charge anything. Even in war people who surrender are pardoned. Since we did not fight, the same rule should apply to us. Gama would not budge. If the heart is made of stone what can the suppliant do? The Portuguese set fire to the ship. Those who resisted were killed, but the pilgrims were now fighting. The ship was set aflame and the Portuguese ran—they didn't want to be a part of the burning ship. The pilgrims leapt on the flames, threw water and doused the fire. The Portuguese clambered on to *Miri* and kindled fires afresh. Now the fighting turned fierce. How did I restrain myself from joining the fray on behalf of the doomed? Even the women, who were till now pointing out their bracelets and necklaces, and tempting the Portuguese towards compassion (or greed), now threw their jewellery in the sea, so that the white men couldn't get to it, and started fighting. Only when the fires started burning them did they jump into the sea. Then the Admiral had the boats lowered and the spears lowered.

The Red Sea turned red.

The thought that I had brought these cruel barbarians to the Malabar coast started haunting me now. To imagine that they may never have reached Hind, that Gama may never have made a fool of himself by presenting those silly gifts, that he may not have made a bigger fool of himself by thinking that the goddess Kali was the mother of Issa, whom they call Christ; to think that all this would not have happened if I had not guided them across the ocean! It was a terrible, suicidal thought. The disaster of *Miri* would not have occurred. It is a heavy burden on the soul, to have spawned history, and such a terrible one at that.

On top of this there was nothing I could do, no death I could stave off, no infant I could save. How do I escape? Will Gama dare anchor off Calicut after what he had done to *Miri*? How do I slip out? Could I escape at night? There were look-outs on the mast constantly. At night they were doubly vigilant. If they anchored miles away, would I be able to swim to the coast? All these doubts swarmed around me like bees when the hive has been disturbed.

We sailed to Calicut and things did not seemed to have improved. The new Samudri Raja, now clearly alarmed, wrote to the Admiral and sent a leading Brahmin with the letter. You must have killed six times the men you unfortunately lost when your trading post was attacked; and you have, I am sure, taken more goods from various ships, than what Cabral lost that unfortunate night. Live in peace with us now and trade with us on your terms. Fill your holds with our spices, and we will not object. This was the kind of letter he wrote, much more dignified, of course, and dressed in language befitting royalty. Kings don't use coarse words. The Brahmin spoke almost like a suppliant. The Admiral somehow got further enraged. The Brahmin said the Zamorin was willing to hand over twelve Arab merchants to Gama as atonement for what had happened to Cabral. He could do with them as he liked. As for money, the Zamorin was ready to pay that too. The Brahmin was arrested. The bombardment began.

The difference between the Admiral now and the Captain-Major four years back was not just the newly found desire for revenge. He was no longer dealing with an unknown King, nor with Christians, but with Hindu heathen and hated Moor and he had more cannon on the seas than anyone else, from Milind to Mecca. He wanted the Samudri Raja to throw out all Muslim families from the city, over four thousand households, people whose ancestors had been here for a century, who now spoke the same language. Shot after shot sailed into the town. The fishermen's huts were turned to thatch and palm leaf, the houses of the rich to rubble. For three days the cannons roared. Calicut was empty, everyone ran away.

The fate of the ships anchored off the coast was worse. The Admiral let those belonging to Cannanore go their way—their King had been friendly. The other twenty ships were looted. (He had sent his smaller boats, which they called caravels, to capture the ships.) Looting always got first priority. Slaughter followed. All the men were rounded up and they came in hundreds. He ordered their hands, ears and noses to be hacked off. In his kindness he spared their tongues. Then he had their feet bound, lashed with coir rope. It was then he thought, or was it some adviser who told him, that they might untie the rope with their teeth. He ordered their teeth to be smashed. This was done with oar and hammer. The defaced men, the toothless, nose-less, ear-less, arms-less men were put in a ship which was set on fire. It drifted to the shore. The Brahmin was similarly deprived of his hands and nose and ears, his feet bound, and he was placed in a smaller boat which was not set aflame.

The families came to the strand crying and tried to douse the flames. They were driven off, the mutilated prisoners hung on the mast and the crossbowmen were ordered to shoot at them. Later, the Portuguese told me that in one boat sent ashore with that terrible cargo, Gama sent a message to the Raja saying he could make a curry of the mutilated men. The Mongols, when they sacked Baghdad, did they behave this way?

The Samudri Raja didn't seem to learn. He sent another Brahmin as an emissary. The man came with his small son and two nephews. The Brahmin was mutilated and sent back while the boys were hanged, all three of them.

There was no way I could have stolen out of the ship. Suddenly the fleet sailed for Cochin. Gama's uncle, Vincent Sodre, was left behind with six ships to see that not a leaf of a pepper vine, not a scrap of cinnamon bark, not a cardamom pod got out to the Red Sea. I was not on those six ships. I was on *Flor de la Mar*. The day we sailed for Cochin, it was exactly a month after the final burning of *Miri*.

~

Cochin could have also been bad for the Portuguese. The monk from Lanka was there once again. It was the monk who brokered peace when matters came to a head at

Cochin. The ruler, Unni Goda Varma, was incensed that the Portuguese had bought a cow and slaughtered it for dinner. Some butchers, Muslims who else, had sold them to the Portuguese. There was a lot of tension. The Portuguese understood that pork was anathema to the Muslims, and so had stuffed the prohibited meat into the mouths of tortured Moors. They did not understand how holy the cow was to the Hindu. If the butchers bring you another cow, hand them over to the Raja. That was the Monk's advice. Next time they came with a cow, the Portuguese handed them over to the Cochin authorities and they were at once impaled on wooden stakes.

The sojourn in Cochin was long. The year 1503 seemed to have dawned favourably for Gama, because another invitation came from Calicut. The Zamorin didn't seem to change his ways. Another Brahmin was dispatched to Cochin from Calicut, inviting the Admiral for trade again, and promising to make good the sum which they had lost when the trading post was attacked. This time, because a Brahmin had been sent, they took it as a token of regard—never mind if they had mutilated and killed previous Brahmin emissaries. The envoy was himself said to be carrying a lot of jewels. How could he be that rich, I thought. By now I had some idea of the really wealthy traders in Calicut—Moor, Mappila or Gujarati. Five days after their new year we set sail for Calicut. He also sent a boat asking Vincent Sodre, who was now in Cannanore, to return to Calicut.

I was seething. Was the Zamorin still bowing with folded hands before this cruel man? We will make reparations! The money you lost we will give back, just don't fire your bombards. At Calicut I hoped that a Portuguese party would go ashore. I could easily go with them and stay back. Instead, the Brahmin alone was sent ashore. He didn't come back.

Another came—neither Brahmin nor Nair. Traders have laid out the spices and Samudri Raja all the money. All yours, come and take it! Like fireworks, Gama's temper flared. He was not going anywhere and nor was any Portuguese going ashore.

It was a still night. All one could hear was the sea making the usual noise on the shingles. I was awake, looking for a chance to slip out. Deep into the night I heard the sound which oars make on water, half-swirl, half-splash. No boat owner in his senses would come anywhere near Gama, I thought. Was it a fishing boat, some ignorant desperate fool going for a nocturnal catch? But who could be fishing at this hour? Suddenly, I realized and so did the watch, that it was not just one solitary boat. They were many and they milled around the ship. Spears started sailing over the deck, some of them lethal. The alarm was sounded, the Admiral woken up. Some bombards were hastily fired from our ship, but they were of no use. The boats were too near and the shots splashed into the sea.

The fighting was close and fierce. The Portuguese were on the receiving end for once. The attackers, because of their colour, were like shadows, flitting from one kill to the other. Once the bombards were of no use, the playing field became level. Things turned very tense and the Admiral started shouting orders, but when the enemy is at your throat, and you can hardly see him, orders can't win battles. The fighting lasted well into the day. Man is selfish and I thought I would have to go back with the ship to Cochin, if not Portugal. But miracles happen. I spotted Shakoor's boat, *Bismillah* written in black Arabic letters across the bow. What was more surprising, the man was there himself, and he was urging his men on. You can be bold as Rustam or Khalid bin Walid, if you don't think. (Thought is a coward.) I jumped into the sea the moment our eyes met.

In a close hand-to-hand combat generalship may not win you the battle. Reinforcements can. Vincent Sodre with his ship suddenly returned from Cannanore. He fired off his bombards, for he was still at a distance and could target the Calicut vessels. The battle was over. The Calicut boats withdrew.

~

The first day in Calicut was miserable. The city was in commotion. Everyone admitted that the battle hadn't been won. If only that other ship, commanded by Vincent Sodre had not come up, things might well have been different. The town was still agog with rumours and fears. Would the Portuguese bombard them again? Did they have enough powder and shot? Had they come prepared for battle this time or just to take the non-existent loot promised them? Everyone had a view on the battle and tactics and strategy. I had left all my things behind. Fortunately my cruzados and the gold I had been able to collect were still with me. No eating house was open, but I refused to go to Shakoor's place the first day.

# samina

The walls of the courtyard had been blown away by the cannonade two months back and two of the rooms had been badly damaged, though Shakoor had patched them up perfunctorily. People were chary of rebuilding, not knowing when the Portuguese would arrive again and let go with powder and shot. Taufiq had taken his time coming here, a good three weeks. He had to steel himself to arrive at Samina's door. They sat out in the yard all the same, the evening quiet as leaf fall, the last light of the sun cradled on distant tree-tops. The house was far from the killing grounds of the beach. It had taken Taufiq some time to take on board the sensations and the atmosphere of Calicut now. The place had looked fevered and blotchy in a strange defeated way, dirty and uncared for, the people dour-faced and dejected.

Not that the Zamorin had not taken precautions. He had stockaded the sea front with palm trees, planks and the like. These too had been blown away. For the first time the impact of gunpowder was being felt in India, even if it was just on a sliver of a coast. The embankment was dusty this time. Calicut had, so to say, been disassembled. There was a general mood of depression in the city. Gama had escaped, despite the trap laid for him. Shakoor was surprised that Gama had swallowed the bait. A sagacious commander would not have. What was worse, he had threatened vengeance even as he left. As for the Zamorin and his court, they knew there was no way one could counter the Portuguese cannons, no way that a coastal city could be protected against them. The Samudri Raja was no longer the Lord of the Seas. He could not live up to his grandiloquent title. Moreover, his vassals had betrayed him, Cochin and Cranganore, by siding with the Portuguese, though this was only expected, because the two Rajas would rather be rivals than vassals, and the whole of the west coast knew this.

Shakoor appeared slovenly, shoulders drooping and black sacks under the eyes. He had the drifting faraway look of someone unfocussed, of one unsure what the next moment would bring, or whether the next moment would be there at all, waiting for him. Yet, he had fought. It was a shock for Taufiq to have seen him on the boat urging fellows to go for the Portuguese. He was essentially a trader, a peace-loving man. Taufiq wouldn't have associated Shakoor with battle. Was his little fleet intact—his six boats? He must have suffered, and badly at that, or he wouldn't have been there, spear in hand in a stealthy night attack. What can you tell them, he thought. Something was unravelling in his mind, and he didn't know what it was, the slide of a serpent rope devoid of the hiss, the unknotting of something tangled he was not consciously aware of.

'Calicut is now a lost dream.' Shakoor was speaking to no one in particular.

'Or a dream that has lost its way. Lost dreams can be found. Nothing remains in ruins for ever.' Taufiq was aware of the effort he was making in trying to console the older man.

'Their thirst is unquenchable.'

'Are you hinting at their greed or vengeance?'

'Both, Taufiq. We have heard horrible tales about the *Miri*.'

They are correct, Taufiq said. He was there, saw the drama unfold, flame by flame, sword-thrust by sword-thrust.

'Someone has to remind them about Qayamat, Taufiq. They will have to answer a lot on Judgment Day.'

'Who knows when Qayamat comes, or if it comes at all?'

'Never say that, Taufiq. Sins don't come free. We may not get paid for our good deeds, but sins we all have to pay for.'

She came in just then, Samina, looking more beautiful than when he had last seen her; hair braided and oiled, cheeks still glowing with the lustre of lacquer.

'The kitchen remained intact, with all my pots and pans. Even the stoneware jars containing jaggery, the pickle jars, and the grain bins were safe.' She laughed. 'The roof of this room was teetering on its pillars.' She pointed to the room where they received people, the one with a carpet and a leopard skin turning slightly mangy atop. 'The walls were knocked out. The green candle chandelier, do you remember it? That escaped. First thing Abba did was to have it taken off from the roof. We didn't want it crashing down.'

Shakoor spoke up. 'Lest the remnants of the walls holding the roof collapsed, we put strong wooden supports. We were better off than many others.' Shakoor told him that he should have seen the wreck that was Calicut, when the fleet left. The beach seemed littered with the charred hulks of boats, lying askew on the sand, smelling still of burnt wood and flesh. For days they lay around, the steerage turned to cinders, the sails turned to burnt paper. The masts were too thick to burn. There were bodies on the beach. An Ezhava, who helped in burying the dead, said he carried that burnt odour about him for days.

'My dreams carried that odour. I dreamt of white men dressed in leopard skins, of strange things floating slowly towards a giant red flower which was eating them up. They could be anything, bodies, driftwood—only, who would swallow driftwood?'

Nightmares must have flowed across her eyes, he thought. Taufiq didn't respond to what Samina had just said. They had been victims, faced fire and fury. He had just been an onlooker. There must be other bad dreams doing the rounds, haunting people by night. The city itself must have turned into a bad dream.

Shakoor got up, his joints creaking, went in, changed into a new shirt and shambled out of the house, leaving the two together. She kept looking at his receding figure. 'You can't imagine my relief when he returned from that night attack unharmed. I hadn't argued when he put two of his boats into the fight or when he went into the boat himself. If you have to fight you have to fight. If I had somehow prevented him, he would have felt a chunk missing from his life, till the end of his days. A man must do something he thinks he must do. One should not take that away from him.'

He reached tentatively for her hand, his wrist shaking a little, his mouth turning dry. There was no startled reaction from her side. All she said was, 'You are staying here now, aren't you? You are not going back again?'

No, he wouldn't go back, never, would remain here in her shadow. He didn't crave for any happiness apart from this. He had, after all, thought of her every night before he slept. 'When I came the last time under Commander Cabral, I thought I would meet a married woman. What has taken you so long?'

'You.'

She hadn't withdrawn her hand. How could women be so frank in Hind? Weren't they supposed to be shy and reserved, which really meant you cloak your feelings under a hijab, an unseen one of impassivity? You reach for her and she doesn't

*keki n. daruwalla*

draw back as if stung by a snake. You put your arm around her and she turns towards you and smiles. He had pictured another woman in his dreams. When he stared at her she looked right back into his eyes. He withdrew into his shell for a while, terribly afraid of being considered shameless, his wrist shook again and she stilled it by holding it in both her soft hands. 'I am frightened.' 'Don't be frightened,' she answered. 'Wanting is good.' They got up and he backed her into a corner and pushed against her body, his arms gently enveloping her neck. Four years, strung together by diffuse daydreams, were pressing against her body. His forehead got lost within the cleft between her breasts, till she caught it between her hands and adjusted his lips on one of her nipples.

# of cairo and the
# unravelling of mystics

ભ

Ehtesham's craft halted at port after port on the western
coast. It had picked up pilgrims, mostly Indian,
returning from Mecca and Madina. At every port, as a
sprinkling of the passengers got down, others boarded
while the owner looked for barter and trade. Ehtesham saw
people moving on bamboo rafts, on catamarans, on sailing
boats of different kinds. He saw life as it unravelled in
coastal India. The diversity staggered him—flower sellers,
bangle sellers, street musicians, half-naked drum beaters;
the *madari* with his monkey and his drum, shaped like an
hourglass. Leashed, ungainly bears danced to the delight
of the baiters. Cows with horns smeared with turmeric
wandered around unattended. Also unattended were the
women ranging from tribal dark to fair, their apparel
colourful, the tribals with a red sash around one breast, an
infant suckling on one pendulous breast open to the world;
women selling everything from collyrium to flowers to little
clay idols of elephant gods, cowries by the bushel, mother-
of-pearl bracelets. Their laughter and the way they carried
themselves was an eye-opener for him. He was glad to
be here.

Meanwhile, things had happened in Cairo he was unaware of. He didn't know that one of the Muhtasib's sons, Zakarya, was on the *Miri*. He had never heard of *Miri*.

From one of the most squalid quarters of Qahira, word had come to the Muhtasib that a dervish was addressing rallies daily after prayers. The fellow would not go to the mosque himself. No one seemed to know his name. His face was charred black though he sported a thick beard to hide it. The informers even said that near his shoulders his arms seemed light-skinned. It was obvious that he had been wandering around for years and had been burnt by the sun. He would attract crowds by lifting his stave which had a silver knob, and shouting 'Haq! Haq!' No one knew anything of his past and it was almost impossible to elicit anything from him in this regard. There were various rumours about: that he had gone on long pilgrimages and had returned changed and disoriented, the length of the pilgrimage accounted for the sun burn; that he had gone to a seminary in Qom or Ispahan and had been converted into a Shiite and infiltrated back into Qahira. Others said he had gone to Najaf and the Shiites had thrown acid on him and kicked him out. There was gossip too, that he had been scalded by boiling water thrown on him by a Turkish whore, whose amorous advances he had spurned; that he was a criminal fugitive from Baghdad who was masquerading as a mystic. The trouble was he spoke Arabic like an Egyptian and not like a Baghdadi, and as for the seminary in Qom, no one had heard him speak a single word of Persian.

He was used to giving very odd answers to questions put to him. When asked whether more merit accrued to one in an Umrah, a pilgrimage to Mecca at the ordained time, or during an ordinary pilgrimage, his answer was 'in neither'.

The listeners were bewildered. 'What do you mean?' they asked. 'Allah is everywhere,' he said 'and his love is spread over the entire cosmos. If that one-eyed beggar who is squatting in the front can't afford to go to Mecca or Madina, does it mean he is lesser in the eyes of God than some Amir with a dozen mistresses or one of the Sultan's judges who sends people to the gallows even if they are innocent?'

The man was making a big impression, said the informers. The crowd is greater each time he speaks. Where does he come from, asked the Muhtasib. We don't know, they answered. 'Find out!' No one knows, Muhtasib!

The people of the Mokhabarat were all around him when he made his next appearance, and he was heckled. 'Munafiq', 'apostate'—such were the imprecations hurled at him. He fenced with them and won his duels. In his next meeting there were other agents around—wouldn't do to get the same people to shower abuses on him. But before they could rail at him he had spotted them and pointed them out as 'mukhbirs' to the crowd. They were cornered by the people and beaten up. Their names were forced out of their unwilling throats, they were called 'dogs' and thrown half dead from the gathering. The Perfumer had his knee broken.

All this made the chief of the Mokhabarat and the Muhtasib sit up. The dervish had preached against the sword on two occasions. When the Muhtasib heard of this he was aghast. 'He is preaching against the state. The sword is in every sense the symbol of the Sultan.'

The mystic was taken before a judge who had just sentenced a woman first to fifty lashes and then to be hanged. The gendarmes saw to it that the dervish was present when the sentence was pronounced. He was, if one could put it that way, let off scot free—just ten lashes. That evening he showed his scarred back to the gathering, ten red stripes engirdling his spine. Each stripe had left two tears on the skin, secreting a thin thread of blood and ooze. The next evening he took off his shirt again and showed his back. It was completely healed, as if by magic. People held lighted candles near his back to see if this was illusion. It was not.

'It is Allah's will,' he shouted. 'Feel it, feel my back, as smooth as the back of the judge's concubine. They wanted to imprison me, but the bolts were so rusty and the hinges of the prison gate so stubborn that they wouldn't open! That's how I am here.' That was also the evening when he said that the days of the Mamluks were over. They will hang on the Zuwaylah Gate and the Ottomans will be here, if not by the fajr namaaz then surely by the Maghreb, if not today, tomorrow, if not now then in five years or ten or fifteen. The lines have already been written in the book of destiny. The fate of the Mamluks cannot be altered.'

The authorities were utterly shocked and utterly delighted at the same time. The man had signed his death warrant. He was led, hands bound and shackled, to the compassionate judge who had given him only ten lashes just a fortnight back, the one who had sentenced the adulterous, or was it just a plain lecherous woman, to fifty lashes and the gallows; the one who owned the smooth-skinned, velvet-buttocked concubine. The mask of compassion fell from the face of the judge this time for he had been informed in advance of the Sufi's comments on one of his sleeping partners. His face sardonic and grim, the judge asked the accused, 'Have you bowed to the west today?'

'I have not. Why do you ask?'

Judge: 'Because it may be the last time you may make your obeisance.'

Dervish: 'Since you have asked, I may tell you I haven't.'

Judge: 'And why not? Don't you bow towards the Qibleh?'

Dervish: 'This cosmos is Allah's and Allah is the cosmos. Whichever way I bow I bow to Allah.'

Judge: 'This is no laughing matter, traitor. Do you pray?'

Dervish: 'That is a matter between me and my Allah.'

Judge: 'And is your Allah different from ours?'

Dervish: 'My Allah wouldn't allow a judge to threaten me with death before even hearing the case.'

Among the witnesses hurriedly summoned, who called him a cheat, a criminal, an apostate was the Perfumer, who hobbled in dramatically and showed his broken knee. His aroma spread through the court and people were seen to take deep breaths in order to inhale the perfume. The Perfumer charged the accused with speaking against the Sultan. Worse was to follow. For, the fiery Ali Hasan 'Zulm' was also there. You have said that Mecca is not sacred, he charged. The accused denied this vehemently.

'Then what made you say that there is no difference between a loafing beggar who can't make the trip to the holy of holies, and a pious Haji who goes there, spending his life's savings? If Allah has created the cosmos, can you say He has created the dirt and the filth too, that He hasn't differentiated between the sacred and the evil? Is there no difference between a house of worship and a stable? If Mecca is not sacred, why did Allah see to it that the Prophet, peace be upon him, was born there? Why was the Prophet (peace be upon him) not born on the moon?'

'Because there are no inhabitants on the moon,' replied the dervish.

A subdued titter went round the court room, even though it was packed with informers and the detritus from the streets. The judge thought it was high time he intervened. He declared that he wasn't going to put too fine a point on whether the accused was mad or had lost his memory. He dubbed the dervish a traitor, a Kafir and an apostate, and pronounced the pre-ordained sentence. The Dervish was hung on the same gate that the Mamluk Sultan was to be hanged fifteen years later by the Ottomans.

Thus ended the days of Tahir bin Ilyas, swinging at the end of a rope.

# of bone and blood
# and marrow

Akram, feared as he was—butchers generally are—had become something of a hero. He had fought the Portuguese and felled Ayres Correa, their Trade Agent. There were a dozen people ready to say they had seen his cleaver descend on the Factor who had gone down, never to rise again. Surprisingly, he also seemed to have scored points for having got hurt; Taufiq, after all, had beaten him down to the ground. Needless to say that those who feared him, feared him even now, and those who hated the fellow, hated him still. Love and respect can vanish, but fear and hatred abide. Mostly.

Old grudges also have a habit of not dying easily; you could, if you were drunk, almost attribute a touch of immortality to them. People who hated the Qazi and his fiats, would always hold it against Akram for being close to him. The Qazi, though, had played it low. Don't attack the Portuguese, he had said. The Zamorin has asked them to come on land and live and trade. We are treaty-bound, they are guests and the angels themselves will frown if we kill any of them. He took the wrong line. At that moment people were not exactly obsessed with the angelic orders. The infuriated traders got their way, the ill-tempered usually do. Akram was one of them.

Taufiq's mouth was dry and his shoulders bunched and stooping as he walked towards the butcher's shanty. The shop, like most buildings, had been shattered, and Akram was plying his trade in a sort of a bamboo hut. (Rumour had it that when a cannon ball smashed through his shop, it scattered all the mince and the meat, and the poultry kept by a scavenger flocked to the ruins, salvaged the mutton shreds from under the rubble and had a hearty meal.) Akram looked the same as ever, his face bulging like a bloated aubergine. He wore a white kurta, which was not stained by even a drop of blood, Taufiq noticed, and swirling around his waist was a green *tahmat* or waist cloth, its lower hem trailing the floor. Taufiq also noticed the sheep carcasses hanging limply upside down from a beam, the trotters tied together. His eye took in the ivory-coloured fat and the pink flesh. He made an effort to straighten his spine and wet his lips before entering.

One eyelid of Akram rose for a micro-second. 'Yes?' he enquired, still looking down, sensing the other's presence. With a heavy knife Akram was beating a tattoo on a lamb's thighbone, just the wrist moving and yet the bone being cleanly cut and the pieces skittering away on the wooden board. Finally, he looked up and the shock of hair swirling on his forehead flopped back.

'What brings you here? I don't like you.'

'I know that. That's why I am here.'

The butcher was at his truculent worst. 'You fought for them, them!' He couldn't bring himself to pronounce their name. 'You fought for those who slaughtered Muslims; they killed us the way I cut up sheep. You fought for them and went with them to that other traitor, the Cochin Raja. We are told that it was you who introduced that Monk to the Purtugali people. He has done a lot of mischief with the Cochin Raja. Regrettably he will never come near my knife. But you are different. You have come running to me on your own, driven by what instinct I don't choose to know. You want to show Shakoor's daughter that you can brave me in my own house? Is that it? Or do you feel no harm will ever come to you, that you are one of Allah's favourites.'

Taufiq tried to express himself—difficult when you are speaking to a butcher whom you had beaten up two months (or was it three?) back. It was as close as you could get to a fight to death. Over the past few days he had been at the centre of a blizzard of thoughts. But he told Akram that he had fought to save his skin, who doesn't fight if his own life is threatened whether by kin or sworn enemy? He was repentant now, though the other laughed. The repentance was a bit too expedient.

'A butcher drives to the bone, the marrow. Words are not enough for him.'

Hearing this Taufiq went a step closer to the butcher, who in turn took a firmer grip on his knife. Even when Taufiq started whispering, he kept a firm hold on that thick, heavy blade of his. Why was this Egyptian whispering? The world knew he had brought the Portuguese from halfway around the world, through treacherous shoal and sterile unmoving calm; and Akram saw his shoulders stooping even though he stood erect, sensed something raging within him, saw the hesitant lines on the young pilot's face, tired lines that went ill with his young handsome looks.

'We will see,' he said, 'when the time comes. The place for atonement is Mecca. Or if Mecca is too far, you could think of going to the Qazi. He could forgive you, or prescribe what you should do, fast, or put *chaddars* on the tombs of Pirs or feed the poor at shrines.'

Taufiq was not buying any of that. The moment the name of the Qazi was uttered he thought of Ehtesham and the Muhtasib. His dislike for the latter welled up, and the poor

Qazi got confused with the Muhtasib in his addled brain. 'My *baazi* will be played differently, and it will have nothing to do with the Qazi.'

'Talk with respect about holy men. The Qazi is one such. Such men are useful when the times are hard.'

'We will see, when the time comes,' said Taufiq ruefully. 'Only, the time could come as early as tomorrow.'

As Taufiq walked off he hoped Akram didn't think he was seeking some sort of consolation. It was the last thing he was looking for. Akram eyed his receding figure, a little baffled, wondering the while about what was going on in the young man's head.

# of dreams and atonement

There were islands within him, he knew, but he had never got down to exploring them. Had thought of them in passing when depressed maybe, but never considered it worthwhile seeking them out. He had the time now, but it was too late fishing for them, that is if you ever fish for islands. Yet the hurt within him was deep-stained and he knew there was nothing he could do about it. There must be something to be said for these Hindus and their numerous lives, he thought. Seventy, maybe eighty—they were promised as many lives as Muslims were promised houris in paradise, provided, of course, you put a few Kafirs where they belong. On the Indian coast he had noticed, they were called hoors, just as Ramadan became Ramzan here and Qadi became Qazi. No hoors without slaughter. Logically, the bigger the boor, greater the number of hoors. Sad thought. Good for the Hindus that these eighty-odd lives ahead of you acted as props. Moreover, any mishap in this life you palmed off on sins in your previous birth. No comeuppance for what you did or had done here and now. Where was he to find props? This life at least had turned meaningless for him, he was convinced. He had voyaged across the oceans, with all those slave-driving, gold-gathering, pork-eating Portuguese trawling behind him, and look at what they had done. There had to be atonement somewhere. You couldn't slide into marriage or a job, become a big boat owner, and have a large house, wine from Syria, the best cooks, the best meats, after having done that. Wouldn't be just. It may not have been a crime, piloting them, but then look at the results, he thought.

But if a gazelle drags a whole lot of slavering predators behind her into the oasis and they drink up all the water and devour most of the food, do you blame the gazelle? He had no answers, there seldom are, when you are caught in the meshes.

He wanted to look outdoors, but the windowpanes were black and opaque.

~

He walked into her room quietly like light slithering in through haze, early light putting its delicate foot down on the sill through a half-opened window. He was surprised he had not noticed anything: the leaf-litter on the ground, the paved courtyard, the walls smooth, the green chandelier—wasn't all that in the past, before the cannonading from the ships? Wasn't that chandelier supposed to be on the floor? Why was there a haze here? He didn't know. Her smile was an open window. She was reclining on a bed, her back resting against a pillow that in turn rested against the wall. Her arms opened up like a window nudged open by a gust of breeze. Low sun entered the room, the light granuled through a film of moisture, through a heavy-breathing mist that stood outside and was not entering the room.

'I can't sit on the bed,' he said, shamefully aware of his hypocrisy.

'You can, if I ask you,' she smiled.

He sat down, he couldn't resist. Resist what? That doesn't

have to be answered. What you can't resist, you can't resist. His hands started brushing her arms, her shins, her calves. He didn't dare to reach upwards. Courage fails brave men when it comes to fondling women above the knees.

The haze was not just a matter for the eye but also for the ear. He thought he heard her say, 'You are very slow.' He didn't know what she meant, or pretended not to know. Even the words were not fully audible. Why were both sound and sight coming filtered through a haze, he wondered. He was aware his scrambled thoughts were confusing sound and vision. She caught his hand, putting her palm on the back of his hand. A slight spasm of fear shot through him. Did she think he was too bold? She seemed to notice that little flare of fear in his eyes and smiled gently and caressed his hand. Suddenly the empty spaces within him seemed to fill up.

The room grew melancholic as if soot had drifted down on blank spaces. Her hand was gone, the touch no longer palpable and he seemed to be caught in a morass of contrary feeling. The walls turned grey suddenly and he felt for the vacancy deep down in his insides. He couldn't recollect what had happened afterwards. Then he seemed to find himself in another room, but it was the same room, only it was better lit, amazing how the movement of light can change things. It played on her face. Shafts of light seemed to buzz in, as if an imperceptible layer of sound was riding on them. The bed was the same however, and so was Samina and the smile was as benevolent when his hand reached out to her breasts. After that there was no stopping him. The next thing he was aware of was the scoop and swell of the love act itself as she rose with the tide, both of them reaching a sort of a crest before the eventual ebb.

~

*keki n. daruwalla*

He woke up from the dream, shaken. He hadn't dreamt of her that way. He wasn't even sure that she had ever entered his dreams. When it came to her he had striven to put his carnal thoughts away. She had to be kept pure in thought and dream, he had told himself often.

He hadn't bolted his door, and it opened stealthily to enquire into the sudden quiet outside. He felt suffocated. He wanted breeze through the window. He got sunlight through the lattice.

He got up, had his bath, ate a leisurely meal and proceeded to the butcher. Now he made his intentions clear. The knife-and-cleaver man was stunned. Get a fatwa from a divine or a direction from the Samudri Raja, he said. The Zamorin unfortunately was in the process of abdicating—you didn't stay on as king if you got beaten so thoroughly. After the havoc wrought by Vasco da Gama, the Zamorin knew his fate was sealed. He was said to have already receded into a Mat, a religious retreat. Fiats can be hard to come by, when you need them . . . Get an edict from the court, he said. Taufiq replied he was doing this on his own. No one would blame Akram. You never can tell, the other said, here they impale you with wooden stakes through your heart for a serious crime.

The debate went on for an hour. On the quiet, Akram had sent word to the Qazi, who arrived promptly. 'Don't go ahead with this, my Son,' he said to Taufiq.

'Don't call me Son. But, with respect, I want to go ahead with this, and it is of my own free will. Akram is committing no crime.'

'So be it then. Take Allah's name and let what is to happen, happen.'

There was no further talk. After a while, Akram said 'Not both, only one, only the left.'

'Both', said Taufiq, 'and you start with the right.'

'No, the left, and you will have to be bound.'

'I am strong enough.'

'No one is strong enough,' said Akram, shaking his head. They bound him, trussed him up. Quite a crowd had collected by now. People were holding him. 'Ab bhi waqt hai, there's still time, withdraw,' said the Qazi. 'Allah is all-forgiving.' The crowd echoed him, 'Allah is all-forgiving. Desist.'

He shook his head and droplets of sweat trickled down his nose and his chin. Two men now held his left arm from the elbow in a vice. The cleaver came down but Akram only hit the board, didn't come anywhere near the target, and he watched as Taufiq, gripped by a spasm of panic, withdrew his hand in a flash.

'There's still time. Withdraw from your insane resolve.'

But Taufiq shook his head. This time the cleaver descended in a swift arc on the wrist and sliced his hand away. He fainted. So did Akram.

# EPILOGUE

# ninety days later

'Be careful with your stump,' said Samina, his wife of two months. 'It still hurts, doesn't it? Put your weight on your left elbow and don't worry. It is going to be all right. Don't get too excited, it will be all right.' He was tremulous with desire and fear. She tried to calm him, caressed his cheek, kissed him on his eyes and cheeks, rolled her thumb around his nipple and took him in for their first consummation.

# ninety days earlier

Ehtesham had been a day too late, Shakoor late by minutes, caught as he was in the rear of the crowd that had gathered at the butcher's. Ehtesham had arrived by boat the next day. He was to go back soon, too, for news came that the Muhtasib had been replaced by the Sultan Qansawh al Ghauri. Rumour had it that he had been replaced by a man who had started his career as a falconer, a bazdar, rose to become a bailiff and had now climbed on to this post. Al Maheeni was a broken man since losing his son in the *Miri* disaster.

Some four years later, in 1506, the Mamluk fleet which came down the Red Sea to take on the Portuguese, was routed.

---

*They would have come in here all the same, by sail ship or steam boat, via Madagascar and Milind or through the Suez. And the darkies would have gawked at them as they walked down the gangplanks, in doublet and hose or coat and tie, the Lat Sahibs and the Linlithgows. The natives would have gawked some more when the Anglo-Saxon tongue descended* on them, its sharp consonantal words sounding like the clicks of lizards, when they first heard them. Rail and telegraph would have followed willy-nilly, and indigo plantation and the abolition of suttee and child marriage. Liberalism, too, had to dock somewhere, on some run-down wharf. A certain Clive would have won a battle and yet been impeached, and Burke and Sheridan would have thundered against Hastings all the same, whether a Taufiq had guided one Vasco across the seas or no. There's something inexorable about history—also about gunpowder and gunboats.

*keki daruwalla*

# acknowledgements

I t is sad (and a bit of a shame) that debts to other books are written off with one liners. It is not possible to mention all the books I consulted on Portuguese history, seafaring, Cairo, Islamic art, the Mamluks et al. I owe a great deal to *A Journal of the First Voyage of Vasco Da Gama 1497–1499* by E.G. Ravenstein, F.R.G.S., 1898; *Empires of the Monsoons* by Richard Hall; *The Portuguese Seaborne Empire 1415–1825* by C.R. Boxer; *The Prester John of the Indies: A True Relation of the Lands of the Prester John, Being the Narrative of the Portuguese Embassy to Ethiopia in 1520* by Father Francisco Alvares (translated by Lord Stanley of Alderley, 1881); *Arab Seafaring in the Indian Ocean in Ancient and Early Medieval Times* by George F. Hourani; *The Frontiers of Europe*, ed. Malcolm Anderson and Eberhard Bort; *Cairo: 1001 Years of The City Victorious* by Janet L. Abu Lughod; *Voyages and Travels to India, Ceylon, The Red Sea, Abyssinia and Egypt in the Years 1802, 1803,1804,1805 and 1806* by George Viscount Valentia; *Asia in the Making of Europe* by Donald Lach and *The Career and Legend of Vasco Da Gama* by Sanjay Subrahmanyam.

A special word of thanks for the American University, Cairo where I worked in the library and, among other books, was lucky enough to chance upon a translation of Ibn

Majid's book: *Arab Navigation in the Indian Ocean Before the Coming of the Portuguese, being a translation of Kitab al-Fawa'id fi usul al-bahr wa'l-qawa'id of Ahmad b. Majid al-Najdi* by G.R. Tibbetts.

My thanks to Prabhat Shukla, now our ambassador in Moscow, who first gave me an inkling of what Vasco's pilot had done. That casual conversation sparked off the novel. Lastly, my thanks to my editors Ravi Singh and Paromita Mohanchandra for the trouble they took to publish it.

*keki daruwalla*